ALSO BY JUDITH A. BARRETT

Maggie Sloan Thriller Series

Grid Down Survival Series

Riley Malloy Thriller Series

Donut Lady Cozy Mystery Series

One Eye on the Killer

Maggie Sloan Thriller

Book 4

Judith A. Barrett

ONE EYE ON THE KILLER

MAGGIE SLOAN MYSTERY SERIES BOOK 4

Published in the United States of America by Wobbly Creek, LLC

2021 Georgia

wobblycreek.com

Cover by Wobbly Creek, LLC

ISBN 978-1-953-870-07-0

DEDICATION

One Eye on the Killer is dedicated to the color emerald-green and
to all those who have physical disabilities.

PREVIOUSLY...

MAGGIE

My name is Maggie Sloan Ewing; my tall, blue-eyed husband is Larry Ewing; his original name was Kevin, but he's become so accustomed to being called Larry that he claims Kevin is his undercover name.

Luckily, my imaginary men, Palace Guard and Spike, helped me with physical therapy. I didn't expect them to stick around, but they did. FBI Agent Kate Coyle became my best friend, and she and my imaginary men toughened me up and taught me some pretty cool shooting and fighting skills.

Did I mention all the murders? Evidently, a librarian with the soul of a spy is a murder magnet, and Police Officer Ewing must have felt the pull too. His name is Kevin, but I dubbed him Larry. I was surprised a simple nickname was such a sore point between us, so I lied about it. He adjusted to the nickname, but he still calls me out on any lies.

Larry is a dang good partner, especially when it comes to taking down bad guys. He disappeared for a while, and I thought he'd gone undercover again. No big deal until he told me he'd been offered a great new job with the Georgia Bureau of Investigation, about which I hadn't heard a peep. To top it off, he suddenly decided to turn down this fabulous opportunity unless I went with him. I got even with him for keeping secrets from me though. I married him.

LARRY

To set the record straight, I asked Maggie to marry me. She also forgot to mention that she became engrossed in the artsy world of her grandmother and investigated, in her very unofficial capacity, the puzzling clues that pointed to a long ago, unsolved heist of famous works of art.

Even though the attacks on her intensified, and I was driven to distraction as I worried about her while I was in training for my new job with the GBI, Maggie was determined to discover the truth hidden behind the art and the series of fires, and why a killer was so obsessed with his desire for her to die.

To give her credit, though, for a change, she didn't face the killer alone: she called me for backup.

CHAPTER ONE

"Your first day as a Georgia Bureau of Investigation Officer—very exciting. You look very official in your uniform." I smiled at my tall, blue-eyed husband with his cute brown curls then stood on my tiptoes and kissed his chin before he pulled me into a hug.

"Be safe," I mumbled as I buried my face in his chest.

Larry released me then lightly kissed my forehead. "Please don't shoot any killers today."

The imaginary men, Palace Guard and Spike, elbowed each other, and I glared. "I'd like to remind you all that I agreed to give being normal a chance."

After he started his truck, he lowered his window. "Not kidding. Be safe."

I smiled my best version of Spike's panda smile, and Palace Guard and Spike silently laughed as I waved.

When we went inside, Lucy, my brown, German shorthaired pointer, trotted to the back door. I poured a cup of coffee then headed to the porch while Spike followed Lucy to the grass.

Spike was five-eight and almost as broad as he was tall, but his mass was all muscle. He had thick brown hair, a broken nose, bushy eyebrows, and a leathery face from years of playing ball in the sandlots with kids; he had two smiles: his panda smile and his shark smile. The big kids said bad guys turned themselves in when Spike flashed his shark smile, and all us kids worked hard for his panda smile; but he was a softy when it came to Lucy, and she knew it. Lucy flopped down for him to rub her belly, and Spike obliged. After her belly rub, Lucy investigated the new backyard.

I stood on the porch and sipped my coffee while I watched Lucy and Spike. *We need rockers on the back porch. Time to start a list.*

After I drained my cup, I turned to go inside and almost ran into Palace Guard, who wore his running shoes, shorts, and blue Chelsea soccer shirt.

"Good idea. Spike, we're going for a run. Will you and Lucy be okay?"

When Spike waved good-by, I rushed inside and changed into my running clothes then Palace Guard and I raced out the front door.

When Larry and I drove around the neighborhood on our Columbus, Georgia, house-hunting trip after we had decided on our rental house, I mapped out two running routes through the neighborhood.

"Long or short?" I asked as we jogged to warm up for our run.

My tall, imaginary Buckingham Palace Guard spread apart his long arms, and I would have run face-first into his hand if he hadn't raised it like a railroad crossing bar.

I giggled. "Long it is."

When we returned to the house after our hard run of forty-five minutes, I collapsed on Larry's olive-green sofa. *Correction: our sofa.*

I stared at Larry's green and cream braided oval rug that covered most of the living room floor and furrowed my brow. *Maybe I understand Larry seeing the inheritance money from Olivia as mine instead of ours, after all.*

When Spike and Lucy came inside, Lucy flopped down on the cool, kitchen floor, and Spike held his nose.

"Oh, hush. I'll take a shower in a minute; after all, that's what normal people do." I tossed my hair as I headed to my bedroom with my nose in the air. *Our bedroom.*

After I showered and dressed, I mixed a batch of sweet tea then filled a glass with ice. As I poured the hot liquid into the glass, the ice crackled. I gave the tea a few minutes to cool down then took a big gulp as my phone rang. *Darren Martin.*

"Hello, Gray Lady. I heard you and Larry were married and moving to Columbus; I thought I'd check on you and welcome you to your new home."

I smiled. *No surprise that Mother called her artsy friends in Columbus. Wonder how many of them called my friend, Darren Martin, the art dealer.*

"Thank you, it's nice to hear from you. We moved this weekend."

Lucy moved to the braided rug from the kitchen floor after she had cooled down.

"Do you need any help unpacking or getting settled? I'd like to invite you to visit Mama with me then maybe lunch, if you're available; Mama's having a good day, and she's been asking about the Gray Lady," Darren said.

"Everything's unpacked except for a few boxes that we'll get to later, but thanks for the offer. I'd love to meet your mother, and lunch sounds nice."

"Good. Shall I come get you, or do you have a car?"

"I'll be there soon."

Palace Guard raised his eyebrows, and Spike crossed his arms.

"It was Darren Martin. He offered to help me unpack, and I thanked him. This normal stuff is hard. I'm going to visit his mother and have lunch. Is that okay with you two?" I glared then strode to the room that I decided to call the master bedroom to change my shirt for a blouse. After I opened the closet door, I pondered my choices.

Who am I kidding? Time for a consultation. I texted Jennifer. "Gray Lady going to visit a senior living place then lunch. What do I wear?"

"Your gray pin-striped blouse. You can wear your black slacks or your jeans."

I stared at my phone then rushed to the living room. "Do I have a gray pin-striped blouse?"

Palace Guard rolled his eyes then strode to my closet and pointed.

"Thank you," I said.

After I changed into my gray blouse and jeans and pulled my hair back with a red ribbon, I headed to the front door. Spike and Lucy were lounging on the sofa. "I take it you two are staying."

Spike nodded, and I hurried to my car. When I climbed in, Palace Guard was in the back seat with his seatbelt on, and I pretended not to notice.

As I followed the signs to visitor parking, a middle-aged, overweight man in a dark blue suit stood at the entrance. When he saw me, he waved. After I parked, Darren hurried to my car then walked me to the front door, and Palace Guard followed. "Thank you so much for coming. Mama wants to talk to you and has been after me for two days to call you. It's been months since she's been lucid for two days."

When we entered the senior center, the sharp odor of commercial cleaner made my eyes burn. A section of the lobby was cordoned off with bright orange cones, and a stout, middle-aged man with a florid face mopped the section. I coughed when he dipped his mop into his concentrated bleach solution and ran it through the small wringer attached to his bucket. The small, folding sandwich board next to the cones announced: CAUTION! WET FLOOR!

Darren hurried as he led the way down a bright hallway. "The housekeeping staff clean and sanitize the residents' rooms, but Gerald takes care of the common areas with a stronger cleaning solution. He usually mops the lobby and hallways after hours except on Mondays."

As we continued our walk, he pointed to the exit door at the end of the hall. "Some of the residents here are wanderers. The door is an emergency exit and has a silent alarm and a video camera. A fence surrounds the entire facility, but there are some remarkably spry old folks here who would climb the fence in a heartbeat." Darren chuckled. "Mama told me I needed to learn to climb over fences while I'm young."

When we entered Mrs. Martin's large, sunny room that had a privacy screen across one corner, a gray-haired woman who dozed in her wheelchair next to a window raised her head then grinned at us in recognition.

"Mama," Darren said, "the Gray Lady is here to visit you."

Mrs. Martin tittered. "You might be the Gray Lady, but with your red hair and green eyes, you are the spitting image of my dear friend, Margarite Flanagan. Pull up a chair, Maggie Flanagan, so I can get lost in my memories of the good old days."

I smiled as I scooted a chair with a padded seat and a carved wooden back close to her. Palace Guard took position near the doorway.

"There's a whole wing of folks here that are Gray Lady fans. Several of them were downright jealous when I told them you were visiting me."

"Mama, I invited Maggie to lunch," Darren said.

"Just give me five minutes' warning before you leave because sometimes I forget things. Are you making reservations?"

"I didn't, but that's a good idea. I won't be long." Darren kissed his mother on her forehead then left the room.

After he left, Mrs. Martin said in a quiet voice. "I asked Darren to invite you here because Faith, my healthcare girl, is in a little trouble." Mrs. Martin pressed the buzzer on the side of her wheelchair.

When a plump, middle-aged woman whose nametag on her blue smock read, FAITH, came into the room, I smiled. *Only someone Rebecca Martin's age would see a woman with salt-and-pepper hair as a girl.*

Faith pushed up her dark-framed glasses that had slipped down her nose. "Did you need something, Mrs. Martin?"

"Thank you for coming so quickly, Faith. This is the Gray Lady. I want you to talk to her."

Faith frowned as she stepped back to peer down the hallway. "Thank you, Mrs. Martin, but I need to be working."

I smiled. "Mr. Martin and I are going to lunch. Would you be able to join us?"

"I don't know. I get off at one today." Faith pursed her lips.

"We'll plan on it then."

Faith's eyes welled up. "Thank you, Gray Lady. I'll ask Mr. Martin where I should meet you." She cleared her throat. "I'll put in your order for your favorite lunch right away, Mrs. Martin."

After Faith left the room, Mrs. Martin said, "Faith has been helping me stay in touch for the past two days. I wanted you to help Faith, and I wanted to see Margarite Flanagan's great-granddaughter, who exposed the most hateful woman I have ever met." She sniffed. "Clara Hayden was a manipulative bully."

I raised my eyebrows. "Your medications have an amnesia side effect? Why don't you ask your doctor for a change?"

"I did, and she understood why I asked, but she explained there weren't any good alternatives for my conditions. Please don't tell my son I've cut back a little on my meds because he worries too much. It might not have been the best plan, but I'm old." Her eyes twinkled. "I need you to help Faith; thank you for coming today."

I glanced at Palace Guard, and he narrowed his eyes and pursed his lips.

Larry will be fine. What he doesn't know can't—

Palace Guard crossed his arms and glowered.

Fine. I'll tell him.

Mrs. Martin removed her glasses then squinted at the door. "Is your friend at the door real?"

My eyes widened. "He's real, but he's imaginary."

She nodded. "Thought so. Friends are nice, aren't they?"

She leaned back as she closed her eyes. "Excuse me. I wore myself out."

I stared as she slipped into a soft snore; when I turned my gaze to Palace Guard, his expression of disbelief made me laugh.

"Nice to hear your musical laughter again, Maggie Flanagan," Rebecca Martin mumbled.

When Darren came into the room, he said, "Faith told me she could meet with you at one after she got off work, so I've made our reservations for one thirty and invited her to join us. I hope you don't mind."

"Not at all. I think it's a great idea. Thank you for inviting me to meet your mama; she's a wonderful person."

Darren smiled. "I've always thought so. I'm sure Mama enjoyed the visit. Shall I give you a tour of the facility? It wouldn't hurt to let Mama rest before her lunch is delivered. Sometimes she goes to the dining room, but I suspect she's too tired today. Happy, but tired."

As we strolled through the halls, Darren said, "The facility is successful because of the volunteers, even though some of them are as old as or older than our residents." Darren chuckled. "Our volunteers aren't allowed to provide help with the physical tasks, but their patience and willingness to sit with the residents and listen is invaluable."

When we reached the administrative offices, Darren paused. "Our volunteer coordinator, Gracie Jane, is rarely in her office. She scoots around and fills in where she's needed. I'll introduce you if we run into her."

When Darren's cheeks pinked, my eyes twinkled.

Ah ha. Darren has a soft spot for the volunteer coordinator.

"Let's go outside; I'll show you the park for the residents. The only exits from the park are back into the facility."

Darren opened the door to their park. "The sidewalks are wide enough for two wheelchairs to pass with ease, and all the flowers and plants are edible."

I smiled. "I'm not sure I would have thought about that."

Palace Guard nodded.

When a dog barked at the other end of the park, Darren said, "Gracie Jane implemented a program for dog and cat volunteers. Volunteers who foster dogs or cats from the local animal shelter bring them here for more socialization. Many of the residents always had pets before they came here and enjoy the company of the animals."

Before we returned inside, a woman called out. "Hey, Darren. You two-timing me?"

Darren's blush rose from his neck to his face, and he grinned. "Gracie Jane, meet my friend, the Gray Lady."

A woman with brown skin and dark brown eyes who was in her mid-thirties zipped down the sidewalk in her wheelchair to join us. She had pulled away her long black hair from her face with a bright green bandana that she had folded into a wide headband and tied at the back of her neck. "Welcome, Gray Lady. Mrs. Martin has been looking forward to your visit."

"The facility is beautiful, and Darren has explained some of your programs to me. I love your dog and cat program."

Gracie Jane rolled alongside us as we strolled to the door. "Do you have a dog or cat, Gray Lady? Are you looking for a job in Columbus? We'd love for you to volunteer a few hours a week if you're available."

I smiled. "I'm not looking for a job because my husband is here on a temporary assignment; we have a big, brown, German short-haired pointer, Lucy."

"I love all cats and dogs, but I have a soft spot in my heart for big dogs," Gracie Jane said. "Stop by my office before you leave, and we'll talk about how Lucy can spend a little time with us."

I smiled as I glanced behind us, and Palace Guard winked.

She is good at recruiting, isn't she?

"I will see both of you later. Duty calls." Gracie Jane wheeled away toward a lone man with his head down as he sat on a park bench.

When the man noticed Gracie Jane, he glanced around then rose to leave, but she caught up with him, and he dropped down onto the bench.

"She's very aware, isn't she?" I asked as we strolled down the hallway.

"Yes, she is." Darren sighed, and Palace Guard raised his eyebrows.

A utility cart with shelves was in the hallway when we reached Mrs. Martin's room. The cafeteria worker smiled as she hurried to her cart. "Your mama woke for her lunch, Mr. Martin."

A wizened man arranged the tray in front of Mrs. Martin's wheelchair, and he and Mrs. Martin smiled when we entered the room.

"You must be the Gray Lady that Mrs. Martin mentioned. We're happy you could come visit us, and we hope to see you real regular," he said.

I smiled at the royal "we" that he used, and when Palace Guard saluted him, Mrs. Martin giggled.

I choked back my giggle then fake-sneezed into the crook of my elbow. "Excuse me."

Mrs. Martin winked, and I couldn't hold back my laugh.

"I do love your laugh, Maggie Flanagan—it's exactly like Margarite's."

"Mama, this is your five-minute warning that we're going to stop by Gracie Jane's office then go to lunch, except it's a five second warning." Darren grinned as he kissed her on the cheek. "Love you, Mama. See you this evening."

When I hugged Mrs. Martin, she whispered, "Thank you for helping Faith."

She cleared her throat as I stepped away. "I do hope you have a nice chat with Gracie Jane, and thank you again for visiting me. You and your friend are delightful."

"We enjoyed it. Thank you for inviting me."

As we strolled to Gracie Jane's office, Darren said, "I made reservations at my favorite café in Columbus, Sano Café. You and Faith live in Columbus, and I have work to do this afternoon. Here's the address."

Gracie Jane held a clipboard in her hand as she waited for us at the main exit.

"Come into my office." Darren followed us to Gracie Jane's office and hovered at the doorway as she handed me the clipboard. "This is our volunteer application; it includes a place for you to sign, so we can complete our standard background check. We'll be good to go by tomorrow. I'll call you, and you can bring in Lucy to see how she likes us."

After I completed and signed the form, Gracie Jane looked it over. "Well done, Gray Lady. You've passed the first test, which is completing our form." She glanced at Darren as she giggled. "Some of our volunteers claim our print is too small to read, so I read it to them."

"Sounds just like the library where I worked."

As we headed to our cars, Darren said, "The café is in downtown Columbus—easy to find but give me a call if you get turned around."

I found a parking place a block away from the downtown café. As I strolled to meet Faith and Darren, I slowed to gaze at the small shops and the customers inside them—locksmith, pottery, cards and gifts, bookstore, and wooden toys. *It's great to see a thriving downtown.*

When I reached the door, Darren was waiting inside. "We just heard one of the aides from Mama's center died in a car crash over the weekend. Faith was a little shaken and needed to sit. She's at our table," he said. "This way."

He led the way to the back of the eatery where Faith sat at a table for four.

After we sat, she said, "Thank you for being flexible. I'm not comfortable talking at work because there's so much to do."

Darren pointed to a section on the menu. "They have soup and half a sandwich for lunch, if that interests you."

"Sounds perfect." I examined the menu as Palace Guard slipped into the chair across from me.

A young man who wore a white apron brought three glasses of sweet tea to our table and grinned. "I guessed. Anybody want anything different?"

"They let the owner wait tables here, Rafael?" Darren asked. "Were you properly trained?"

The young man chortled. "I'm allowed to bring drinks, bus tables, and sweep the floors. That's about it. Oh, and tell the chef's secrets. She roasted chickens this morning before she made the chicken salad, but you didn't hear it from me."

We chuckled in appreciation. After our server arrived, Faith ordered a cheeseburger.

"Half a chicken salad sandwich, and a bowl of shrimp gumbo," I said.

"I think I'll have a pastrami sandwich and fries," Darren said.

While we waited for our lunch and sipped our tea, Darren said. "Mama has surprised me the last two days. She was her old self— not forgetful at all."

Faith nodded.

I smiled. "That's great. I'd read that happens sometimes. I did enjoy the tour too, Darren. It's a nice facility."

"I've been there for fifteen years. I can't imagine working anywhere else," Faith said.

When our server brought our food, we dug in. Before we finished eating, a large man came into the shop, and Faith glared at him. The man picked up his to go order and left with his sack.

"Hard-headed man," Faith mumbled.

When we had finished eating, Rafael bussed our table.

"This was a wonderful choice, Darren," I said. "My soup and sandwich were excellent."

"Glad you enjoyed it; I need to rush off to work."

As he rose, Rafael handed Darren the check, and he grinned when I tried to protest. "I made arrangements in advance. Stay as long as you like."

After he left, the server refilled our glasses, and I sipped my tea. "What's going on, Faith?"

"The thing is, I don't have any proof. I know jewelry because my dad was a jeweler, and I went to his shop every day after school from first grade until I graduated from high school."

She sipped her tea then giggled. "Guess I'm not a very good storyteller. I always start in the middle or at the beginning of time."

I chuckled. "You established the basis for your expertise in jewelry. Got it."

"Oh, good. So, I know real from paste. Many of our residents keep their favorite jewelry with them, even though it's against the rules, and most of the jewelry is extremely valuable. They love to show off their jewelry to people. They don't wear it, though, because they don't want to be caught and have their favorite jewelry sent home with family or have management put it in the safe where they can't see it. It's like their last thread to their lives as they once were. Does that make sense?"

I nodded. "A little sad, but I understand."

"One of the residents has been here since my first day, and she has shown me her baubles, as she calls them, at least once a week without fail. Two weeks ago, she was showing me her jewelry, and I noticed that two of her more expensive pieces were paste. I asked her if she ever loaned out her baubles to family or friends, and she was adamant that she'd never do anything like that, and I know her well. She wouldn't, but I had to ask."

"And you couldn't report it because she wasn't supposed to have any jewelry in the first place."

"Right, and speaking of reporting, I'm required to report any infractions of the rules to my supervisor, which I have not done in fifteen years." Faith stared at the table and frowned. "At first I thought someone in the family was exchanging the jewelry so that the very valuable pieces wouldn't be unsecured."

"That sounds logical, and I would think a fairly common thing to do. The real jewelry would be in a safe place, and the owner would still have her memories."

"Right," Faith said, "except another resident, who shows me her jewelry regularly, also had an extremely valuable piece replaced with a replica that was not as well-crafted as my father's work or even John Howard's, but not bad."

"A different person? Are the rooms close to each other?"

"Completely different wings, and the women don't know each other, so there aren't any common relatives."

"Ugh." I narrowed my eyes. "I don't like this story."

"I don't either. Last week, a third person had a valuable piece missing with a replacement of a well-done counterfeit."

"What can I do? How can I help?"

"I have absolutely no idea. I'm getting nervous for the residents because whoever is making the switch has access to examine their valuables then again to replace the original with the well-crafted fake."

"What about Mrs. Martin? Does she have any fakes?"

Faith's phone buzzed a text. "Is it okay with you if I peek? I've been expecting to hear from my boyfriend."

"Go right ahead; I understand completely."

She read her text and smiled. "His aunt lives in our facility—that's how I met him. He lives and works in Charleston, South Carolina, and he said he's coming to visit his aunt tomorrow. I'm not exactly positive what he does there, but I'm pretty sure he works online or something because he told me once the connections in Columbus weren't the best for him in his new job."

Faith replied to her boyfriend with a quick text.

"Thanks for understanding. Mrs. Martin showed me only a few pieces of her jewelry a while ago before she started having so many bad days, and I didn't see any fakes. She told me if she forgets their stories, I could remind her. My theory is that because Darren sleeps in her room, the thief doesn't have access to her jewelry."

"That's interesting—kind of indicates the switches are done at night. How can you be sure they are fakes? Is there anything I could read that could help me understand? Can you teach me?"

"Put your phone number in my phone, and I'll send you some links. They're pretty technical, but I'm sure the Gray Lady will catch on quick." Faith's smile was weak, but it at least was a smile.

"What about you? Could the thief know you're a jeweler's daughter?"

"I'd say no because any of Dad's customers most likely don't remember, but the jewelry trade would know; other than that, I'm just another one of the health aides."

"Perfectly normal health aide. There's something to say for blending in."

Faith chuckled. "I've been called normal my entire life—as in 'Why isn't a nice, normal girl like you married?' Normal comes up a lot—I'll take it. Ever since I was a little girl, people said I was a nice, normal girl."

"That actually sounds sweet. I'll study the links you send me. Can I contact you if I have any questions?"

"I'd be tickled to talk jewelry stuff with someone. Please do."

"Gracie Jane invited me to volunteer with my dog, Lucy. We'll be around sometime tomorrow for Lucy to check out the facility."

"Really? Well, I'll enjoy having you around. Just be careful what you say. It's best not to let anyone know what you've seen."

I nodded. "Can you tell me what you've seen?"

"Maybe some time but not at the center."

Before we rose, I slipped an extra tip onto the table.

"If you need me, text or call anytime," I said as we hugged at the door.

As I returned to my car, I saw a jewelry store that I had passed on the way to the café but hadn't noticed. The painted business name on the window with its faded lettering and peeling edges gave the shop an old-world charm. *Bustamante's Fine Jewelry & Repairs.*

On our way home, I glanced at the rearview mirror. "Studying jewelry is normal, right?"

Palace Guard rolled his eyes.

"It is," I grumbled as I pulled into the grocery store parking lot. "Tacos for supper. Let's pick up what I need for now then later I'll plan a week's worth of meals and stock up."

CHAPTER TWO

After we were home, I put my groceries away then poured a large glass of sweet tea to take to the porch while Lucy wandered. When she returned to the porch for me to rub her face, I said, "We're going to be volunteering at the Senior Care Center."

When Spike applauded, Lucy rolled over to her back for him to rub her belly, and I smiled.

"I guess if your hands are free enough to clap then they're free enough to give that girl her favorite belly rub."

Spike nodded and grinned.

I scanned the yard and the porch. "Does anyone remember what time Larry gets off work?"

Spike shrugged, and Palace Guard pointed to my phone. I sighed as I checked online for the Midland office hours.

"Five o'clock. I'll plan for six-ish for supper then we can relax or go to the hardware store. It'll be easier to bring home rocking chairs in the truck."

At five thirty, Larry barreled through the front door and waved to the imaginary men before he lifted me into a hug. I wrapped my arms around his neck then after he returned my passionate kiss, he set me down on my feet and raised his eyebrows at my gray pinstripe blouse. "Where's the cleavage?"

I giggled as I unbuttoned the top button, and he leered. I punched his arm, and he chuckled as he rubbed his arm. "Ow."

I snorted. "Nice delayed reaction. My plan for this evening is tacos for supper then if you're up to it, maybe we could go to the hardware store to buy rocking chairs."

"Tacos don't take long, and I'll help. Why don't I change then we can all go to pick out rocking chairs?"

"Even better. I want to hear all about your day."

I changed to a T-shirt then watched while Larry changed. "You certainly are Mr. Sexy Pants. You know that, right?"

He narrowed his eyes. "Are you trying to distract me? Did you shoot any killers today?"

"No. I was perfectly normal all day."

"Not believing that. I'd ask to check your pistol to see if it had been fired, but you'd have already cleaned it. Let's go."

Lucy trotted alongside me to the truck as Palace Guard and Spike waited in the back seat.

"We need a grill and rocking chairs; is there anything else?" Larry asked.

"Probably a lawn mower, but we can wait on that if we don't see what we want."

"I've got tools in my truck, but I'd like to have some tools for home repairs too, and penta flowers, if they have any."

"Really?" My eyes filled then overflowed onto my cheeks.

Larry glanced at me. "Yes. Penta flowers are part of you."

I brushed away the tears. "I used to think the flowers reminded me of Parker, but they mean *home* to me."

Larry nodded. "Wherever we are, as long as we're together, we're home."

Lucy's whimper sounded like a giggle, so Larry and I glanced at the back seat occupants. Spike held his finger near his mouth and mimed a gagging reflex.

"Cut it out, Spike—we're entitled. We've only been married five days," Larry said.

I rolled my eyes. "We can pick out rockers together. While I choose my grill and the lawnmower, you can collect the tools you want then I'll meet you at the garden center to check for flowers and gardening tools."

As we entered the store, Larry said, "I'll grab a flat for the rockers then check out while you take another flat for the grill and lawnmower."

I beelined to the rockers and sat in one to test it. When Larry joined me, I said, "This is perfect. See what you think."

Larry sat in the chair next to me, and we rocked. "Yep. I'll load these then take them to the truck." Palace Guard followed Larry, and I raised my eyebrows. *He's going to guard the chairs while we shop.*

Spike held his thumbs up.

"Good. You and Lucy with me?"

I grabbed a flat and rolled it to the grills. I frowned at the limited selection.

"Need help?" A tall, bearded man with thick glasses and a store apron crouched in a nearby aisle as he shelved grill cleaning supplies.

"I need a propane grill with a thermometer that's flexible enough to grill for two or twelve."

"We don't have a lot in stock right now, but there's one that sounds like it could work for you." He led the way to a propane grill.

After I checked it over, I said, "This is exactly what I want."

He loaded it onto my cart and slapped a sticker on its tag. "Floor model discount," he said. "You need tools? They're at the end of that aisle."

"Thanks." I left the cart where it was while I picked out barbeque tools. I placed them on top of the box then pushed the flat to the lawnmower section.

"Lawnmower? What kind—gas?" My new friend from the grill section sauntered toward me.

"Yes, gas. Maybe with a no-pull starter," I said.

"This one may work, and it would be easy to adjust from one level to the other. Small yard?"

I nodded. "This is perfect. I'll need two gas cans."

"Of course." He disappeared down an aisle then returned with two red gas cans. "Anything else?"

"That does it, at least for starters. Thanks." I smiled as he saluted with two fingers then sauntered away while I pushed the cart to the garden center.

Must be the wrong season for pentas. I wandered around the perennials section then stopped at the camellias and put two on my cart next to the garden hose and other gardening supplies.

Larry pushed his cart next to mine. "No pentas?" he asked.

"It's okay. I think I like any flowers. We always lived in an apartment, and I never knew how much I like digging in the dirt and fiddling with a yard."

"You have a gardener's soul. Let's check out."

Larry took over my cart, and I pushed his cart to the checkout stand.

"Use your credit card," I said while the clerk scanned our items.

"My new one?" He narrowed his eyes, and I glared at him.

When Larry pulled into the driveway, he said, "I'll unload if you want to start supper."

"It won't take long if we work together, but I'll let you carry the heavy items," I said.

Larry helped me carry the smaller items into the house then after the two rocking chairs, grill, and lawnmower were on the back porch, he came inside. I handed Larry a cold beer; while I cooked, I told him about Darren, Mrs. Martin, Faith, Gracie Jane, jewelry, the facility, and the delicious food at the café.

"All in one day," he mumbled. "What did you leave out?"

"Mrs. Martin's medicine." I explained how many of her drugs caused amnesia, so she cut back for two days, so she could talk to me.

"She must have been worried about Faith." Larry shook his head.

After we ate, I said, "What about your day?"

"Terribly mundane, compared to yours. I spent most of the time doing paperwork and reading procedure. Everybody has to start somewhere." He grinned. "Want to watch the sun go down on our back porch?"

Dang it. He said, "Our."

As we rocked, Larry said, "I'll grab two beers and turn up the TV real loud while you grab a pencil and some paper, so we can write notes just like the old days."

Double dang it. He's onto me.

I trudged into the house and returned with paper and a pencil. I scribbled: "Might be more."

He handed me a beer, and I handed him the note.

He glared at me before he scribbled back then held the paper up for me to read: "Listening."

When I reached for the paper, he held onto it and said, "Nobody can hear you except me, Palace Guard, Spike, Lucy, and whoever bugged the beer. Your turn."

"Ha, ha." I tried to glare, but he glowered.

"I told you about Gracie Jane, the facility, and how good Gracie Jane is at her job—"

Larry interrupted. "Volunteer coordinator. Yes, you told me that."

Spike stood next to Larry with his hands on his hips while he tapped his foot.

"Cut it out, Spike," I said.

"Spike is right. Waiting."

Can I tell him he's being a bully? Palace Guard shook his head.

"It's just a little thing. Lucy and I will be volunteering at the Senior Center a few hours a week."

Larry's mouth quivered then he burst into laughter.

My eyes widened as I stared at him; when I realized he knew all along, I rose and shouted, "You were playing me the entire time. Did you guys know?"

Palace Guard shrugged while Spike bent over with laughter. I stomped into the house and slammed the door behind me before I ran to the bathroom to grab a towel to stifle my laughter.

When I heard Larry's footsteps coming toward the bathroom, I faked a few sobs.

Larry tapped on the door. "Honey?"

About time. You bet you owe me an apology.

I cracked the door open, and he stood with his head bowed and his hands behind him. "Honey, you forgot your beer." He showed me my beer that he had held behind his back.

I totally lost it. I fell against him in laughter, and he pulled me into a one-arm hug.

"I'd love to tell you I'm sorry," he smirked, "but I'm not."

"I set myself up, didn't I? You knew before you walked into the house. How did you find out?"

Larry took a sip of his beer as we strolled to the back porch with our arms around each other. "Your background check. I got a courtesy call from the local gendarmes."

"Of course. I should have anticipated that; I need to step up my game."

As we rocked in unison, Larry asked, "What if this jewelry thing is wider than just our area?" He pulled out his phone. "Heather would know."

He sent her a text: "Any cases of $$ jewelry replaced by fake at nursing homes?"

Heather: "Asking for a friend? There too? I'm working that here. How did you hear about it?"

Larry scooted closer to me, so I could read the text, and Palace Guard and Spike crowded me as they read too. My eyes widened. "I never dreamed it would be widespread. You are really smart, Larry."

He reached over and kissed me before he replied to Heather. "Here too."

"GL found it, didn't she? Did she shoot a killer yet?"

"Dang it, Heather. I have other skills." I slammed my hand on the arm of the rocker.

Larry, Palace Guard, and Spike laughed much too hard before Larry replied: "Can't divulge my source who claims she has skills other than shooting killers. Talk to her yourself."

After he sent the text, I said, "That was slick. Sneaky, but slick."

Larry held up his hand, and Palace Guard and Spike smacked it.

Heather: "I'll call her tomorrow. I miss you two."

We watched the sun as it dipped down into the horizon then ran inside when the mosquito onslaught began.

Thanks to my experience as an early-riser and a short-order cook at two diners, I slipped out of bed, dressed, and mixed the cinnamon rolls before Larry woke. While the dough rose, I started a pot of coffee then worked on my list for my grand grocery shopping trip.

When Larry turned off the shower, I poured a cup of coffee and headed to the bedroom. "Here you go." I set his cup on his dresser and hugged him before I returned to the kitchen to bake cinnamon rolls and cook bacon and eggs.

Larry dressed then hurried to the kitchen. He refilled his cup and mine while I served our breakfast plates.

"You are very sharp in that uniform, Mr. Sexy Pants," I said as we ate. "Did you iron your shirt and pants?"

"Sure did—Jennifer washed them, and I ironed them at Jennifer's before our wedding. Guess we need an iron and an ironing board."

Larry cleared our plates. "Breakfast was great. I sure lucked out when I kissed the cook."

Lucy padded from the master bedroom and nosed the back door. After I opened the door for her, she trotted outside, and Spike followed her.

Larry glanced at my list. "Grocery shopping today?"

"Yep. I'm planning meals for the week, so I won't have to go to the store every day. Any special requests?"

"Maybe we could try out the grill tonight. You expecting any trouble?"

"Of course not. Was that a trick question?"

Larry hugged me. "Sure was. I think I need a remedial cross-examination course, though, because you saw right through it."

After he kissed me good-by, I clung onto him and stroked his cheek. "Be safe."

"Hey, that's my line," he frowned. "You be safe more."

I giggled. "Your competitive side is showing."

Ten minutes later, I finalized my list as my phone buzzed a text: "It's Faith. Here are three links to get you going."

Me: "Thanks! Enjoy your day."

Before I checked the links, Palace Guard and I read Jennifer's recipe for ice box lemon pie.

"This is interesting. The recipe calls for egg yolks instead of cream cheese, and it's baked." I shrugged. "I'll give it a try."

After I mixed the ingredients, I popped the pie into the oven.

While I sat at my computer, Palace Guard watched me enter the links then click on the first one. "This is not a quick read. Let's go to the store. I just realized I'm not the best one to pick out an ironing board or an iron. What do I do?"

Palace Guard put his hands on his hips and made a fierce face.

"Kate?"

Palace Guard shook his head then pointed up and made the same fierce face with his hands on his hips. "Oh, Mom Force— Jennifer."

Palace Guard nodded.

I sent Jennifer a text: "Need help. I need to buy an ironing board and an iron. What do I get?"

Jennifer: "Who's going to iron?"

Me: "Larry until I learn how."

Jennifer: "Don't learn. Ha. Will send links for a low-cost retail store in Columbus."

I clicked on the links from Jennifer then showed the results to Palace Guard. "This makes no sense at all to me. Do you understand what we're supposed to look for?"

Palace Guard nodded.

"Good, then we're set."

I removed the lemon pie from the oven then set it on the counter to cool before we left to go shopping.

Palace Guard scanned the store after we entered then led the way to the aisle marked *Housewares*. When he stopped at the ironing boards, my eyes widened. I peered at the ironing board results on my phone but didn't see anything that was remotely similar. Palace Guard pointed at one, and I lifted it off its rack to the shopping cart.

I stared at my phone. "Now, an iron."

Palace Guard shook his head then pointed at an ironing board pad and a cover. *Who knew?*

After I added them to the cart, he pointed to the irons across the aisle.

I checked my phone then pointed at an iron that was close to the same price as the one on my phone. "This one?"

Palace Guard smiled and pointed at a box three feet away from me, but it was on the top shelf. I strode to it then stared up over my head. *I'll have to climb onto that bottom shelf to reach it.*

Palace Guard lifted the box from the high shelf and handed it to me. As I turned with the box in my hands, a woman who stood at the end of the aisle stared at me. I set the iron into my cart then rolled away from the aisle in the opposite direction. After I was two aisles away, I snort-laughed, and Palace Guard grinned.

"Busted, we were." I giggled as we continued to the front and the checkout lane.

I loaded our purchases into the back of my car then continued to the grocery store. We shopped, loaded groceries then headed home.

"Next time we go to the retail store, I want to look for a chalkboard I can use to post our menus for the Ewing Café, or should it be the Ewing Bar and Grill?"

I glanced at Palace Guard as I held up my hand; he rolled his eyes before he smacked a high five and grinned.

I nodded. "We'll ask Larry; he gets a vote as co-proprietor."

After I unloaded the car and put away the groceries, I put the icebox pie into the refrigerator before I made a batch of sweet tea then poured a glass and carried it to the back porch to enjoy the breeze.

When my phone rang, I called out, "It's Heather."

Spike dashed to my side while I answered.

"Hey there, Gray Lady. Is now a good time to talk? I understand you may have stumbled across a jewelry scam."

Spike put his hand on his heart at the sound of Heather's voice. After I sat in my rocker, I put my phone on speaker, so Spike wouldn't continue to crowd me.

I gave Heather the background information about Darren, his mother, and Faith.

"Not very conclusive, is it? It's not uncommon for families to replace jewelry that has a potential to be stolen with very good replicas because what is most important to the seniors are their memories."

"That was what Faith and I thought too, but Larry said you might be interested."

"I'll certainly keep it in mind." When Heather giggled, Spike did his exaggerated swoon, and I snickered.

"Is Spike there?" she asked.

"Right here. How did you know?"

"You kind of told me with your snicker. What haven't you told me yet?"

My eyes widened. *Are all my friends detectives?*

Palace Guard raised his eyebrows and nodded.

"I guess you're right," I said. *Oops. That wasn't supposed to be out loud.*

"What am I right about? Were you talking to me?"

"No, I was agreeing with Palace Guard that I hadn't told you yet that Lucy and I will be volunteering at the senior center."

When Heather laughed, Spike collapsed on the porch, and Palace Guard shook his head.

"If it was anyone else," she said, "I'd say that's nice, but for you, keep in touch. There's a possibility I may find another connection and will need to hand off the coordination to someone on Kate's team. What's for dinner tonight?"

"Steak. Do I set places for you and Todd?"

"Slick way to ask whether Todd and I are still together, girlfriend. We are. Unfortunately, we can't make it this time. Nice to hear you got a new grill."

Spike moped the rest of the afternoon while I focused on laundry, and Lucy napped. When I glanced outside, my sentry, Palace Guard, was marching around the house.

My phone rang. *Glenn.*

"Kate told me I had to call you. My daughter's bossy sometimes. Are you in trouble? Any danger?"

"No, I'm fine, and so are Larry and Lucy."

"Good. Don't tell me anything else because I can't tell Jennifer and Ella what I don't know. What can I tell them?"

"I got a new grill. It was the last propane one they had, and I got a nice discount. We're having steaks tonight."

"That's awesome news. Spike and Palace Guard okay?"

"Yep, they are."

"Good. Call me if you need me, or text me. We need a special code that a wife who owns half a detective agency like Jennifer won't get."

Your favorite short daughter?"

Glenn guffawed. "Too long, but I like how you think. How about SD? Now I just have to remember it. You take care, my favorite short daughter."

I folded the laundry and hung Larry's uniform shirt and pants in the closet. After I scrubbed two potatoes, I put them into the oven and poured a glass of tea while I pulled up the first link from Faith.

"Well, this totally discounts all of the so-called internet wisdom." I chuckled as Spike peered at the screen over my shoulder.

"This next section is a list of resources that are the best for beginners. I'm at the level of a beginner wannabe."

I stretched my back then we woke Lucy and met Palace Guard outside.

"Run?" I asked then hurried inside to change. When I dashed out to the front porch, Lucy and Spike waited in the yard while Palace Guard bounced on his toes on the sidewalk.

Sure am glad we agreed to start slowly for a warm up.

We jogged for a block then increased our speed to a racing clip. We kept up the fast pace around the block and back to the house as Palace Guard stayed two steps ahead of me, as usual. When we reached the house, Spike and Lucy had abandoned the front porch. I ran inside and collapsed on the sofa. "That was hard."

Palace Guard dropped onto the braided rug in front of the sofa and grinned.

"Best part is nobody shot at us. That was kind of nice." I returned his grin then pushed myself to my feet. "I need a shower, so I'll be dainty when Larry gets home."

When Palace Guard lifted his eyebrows in disbelief, I said, "You're right. Dainty doesn't work for me. I'll be not stinky."

At five thirty, Larry dashed into the house, snatched me up into a hug, and whirled me around. "You smell amazing, Mrs. Ewing." He carried me to the bedroom then set me on my feet while he changed clothes, and I watched.

"I need an ironing board and iron." Larry frowned as he examined his clean uniform shirt and pants that looked only a teensy bit wrinkled to me.

"Got them. I saved the receipt, so we could take them back if they aren't right." I pulled the ironing board out of the closet then told Larry about Palace Guard helping me get the box with the iron from the top shelf, and Larry chuckled as he set up the ironing board.

"Pad and cover?" he asked.

I smiled as I pointed to the top of his dresser. "Right there."

After he put the pad and cover on the board, he asked, "So, where's the famous floating iron?"

I pointed to the closet shelves. "Bottom shelf."

"Of course, bottom shelf." Larry smirked as he pulled out the box.

"We didn't get distilled water because I read on a reliable product testing blog that using distilled water is an internet myth." I bit my lip.

"You're exactly right." Larry's eyes widened. "Do you research everything? Scratch that. I know you do." As Larry unboxed his iron, I hurried to pull out the steaks from the refrigerator then started the grill under the watchful eye of Palace Guard. When the flame whooshed, I said, "Nothing like firing up a new grill."

I closed the lid to give the grill a chance to heat up while I made our salad and set the table. The fresh scent of the hot, clean clothes as Larry ironed his uniform drifted from the bedroom. *What a calming smell. No wonder Larry loves to iron.*

When Larry joined me in the kitchen, I said, "I never smelled freshly ironed clothes before. I don't think Mother even had an iron."

"It is unique, isn't it?" Larry washed a tomato and cut it for our salads. "I've learned that ironing relaxes me because it can't be hurried, and the hot steam coming from the clothes is therapeutic."

While I carried the steaks to the grill, Larry followed me with two beers. "I brought a beer for the grill master. That's the rule, right?"

While I grilled, I told him about my conversation with Heather, my call from Glenn, and the links Faith sent to me.

Larry smiled. "Glenn's a smart man. Moe said their detective business has taken off. Paul's taken on most of the load, so Glenn can work at his preferred slower pace, and Ella is taking online classes to be licensed and working with Paul and Glenn as a trainee while Jennifer runs the office."

"That's great. Sounds perfect for all four of them."

After we cleared the dishes and arranged them in the dishwasher, Larry said, "We could sit on the porch for a bit and digest then I need to take a run."

While we rocked, Larry told me about his day. "It's more sitting than I'm used to, but I'll adjust; this is only my second day, and I want to understand how the regional offices operate. I'm getting excited about the crime scene specialist training because the guys at the office told me it's hard to get into that training. I didn't even think about that when I applied." He shook his head.

I smiled. "I'm proud of you. Let's run."

After we changed to our running clothes, Palace Guard, Spike, and Lucy waited for us in front of the house.

"Are we doing the bang bark?" I asked, and Spike grinned.

As we jogged our warmup, Larry asked, "What's the bang bark?"

"It's part of my training. When Spike gives Lucy the command for the bang bark, Palace Guard and I zig-zag to avoid being shot. Actually, another training exercise we did was when Palace Guard dove to the ground, so did I. Want to try it?"

"Doesn't sound all that hard—sure."

Palace Guard ran between us; as we turned a corner at an alley, Palace Guard dove to the ground before we reached a dumpster, and I dove next to him. Larry stopped then dropped to the ground.

"Can I take back the part where I said it didn't sound hard?" he mumbled.

As we ran, I smiled when I noticed Larry stayed a half step behind Palace Guard. Before we turned to the road, Palace Guard and I dove, and Larry dove a few seconds behind us.

"That was a huge improvement," I said as I scanned the area before I rose. "It took me a lot longer to get to where you are."

"I cheated." He grinned. "I copied you and stayed a few inches behind Palace Guard, so I could copy his moves."

Palace Guard took off, and I had to push to catch up with him; Larry stretched out his long legs and was in step with Palace Guard before I was.

When we turned the corner and Lucy barked, Palace Guard ran a zig-zag pattern, and I ran alongside him. Lucy barked a second time as Larry raced past us and continued straight ahead. After we joined him, he matched our steps.

"Dead man running, right?"

"Yep. You were shot."

He scowled. "Dang it."

After we reached the house, Larry asked, "Do we have any tea?"

"Sure do and dessert too."

"Perfect, but I need a shower first to soothe my bruised ego."

Spike's and Palace Guard's shoulders shook with laughter, and Lucy grinned.

After Larry finished his shower, I took one to clean my salty, sweaty body. While I cut the pie, Larry poured iced tea then we took our dessert to the porch.

"This is good." Larry cleaned the crumbs off his plate.

We rocked and enjoyed the breeze while we talked about all the places we'd like to visit someday.

Larry scanned the fence and porch. "I'm glad we got tools for my projects. Maybe you could help me with a list sometime. The guys at work talk about the lists their wives make for them." He narrowed his eyes. "I need to fix that bottom step. It's loose."

I rolled my eyes. "I'll put it on my list before I go back over my first lesson that Faith sent me."

I carried our plates and glasses inside and put them into the dishwasher then went to my computer room to start a list for Larry and to study my lesson.

I kept nodding off, so I ambled into the living room. Larry was asleep on the sofa with a book on the floor next to him. Spike and I took Lucy outside then I said, "Larry, time to go to bed."

He woke then grinned as he sat up. "You woke me up to tell me to go to sleep?"

* * *

The next morning, I popped our leftover cinnamon rolls into the oven after I started a pot of coffee. After Lucy and I went outside, Larry padded out of the bedroom and kissed the back of my neck as I poured two cups of coffee.

"Good morning, sweetie. I guess I was tired. Don't make lunch for me. We have a big meeting in Macon, and one of the guys is getting married, so we're taking him out to lunch to try to talk some sense into him." He chuckled then took a sip of his coffee while I stared at him.

Does he even know what he just said?

Palace Guard shook his head.

Larry drained his cup then refilled it before he swaggered to the bedroom.

When he was dressed and returned to the kitchen, I had breakfast ready and waiting on the table.

He peered at my face. "Is something wrong?"

"Just a little tired. Us old married folks get like that sometimes."

He nodded, and I picked up the cast iron skillet.

Palace Guard's eyes widened. When he shook his head and motioned for me to put down the skillet, I sighed and returned it to the stove.

"What's your plan for today?" Larry bit into his cinnamon roll.

"After Gracie Jane calls me, Lucy, the men, and I will go to the Senior Center, so Lucy can see if she'd like to visit there a few times a week. I'm looking forward to it. I never had the time or opportunity to volunteer before."

"It does seem perfect for you and Lucy." Larry polished off his breakfast and glanced at the clock. "Gotta go."

He gave me a peck on the cheek, and I pulled him close for a long, passionate kiss.

Take that, you old married man.

"Wow. I'm going to think about that kiss all day." He hugged me before he dashed out the door.

I put my hands on my hips and turned to Palace Guard. "I wasn't going to hurt him. I was just going to test his reflexes."

My phone buzzed a text.

Heather: "Everything ok there?"

Me: "Yes, why?"

Heather: "One of our suspects died suddenly. Keep your men close and your eyes open."

Me: "Will do."

Palace Guard read over my shoulder.

"I hate to hear that, but we don't even have a suspect, do we?"

Palace Guard shook his head.

After I swept and mopped the kitchen, I sat at the computer to finish reading my first lesson while Lucy napped, and Spike kept me company.

I jotted down a few notes while I read. "Makes more sense after reading it a second time."

My phone startled me when it rang. *Gracie Jane.*

"Your background check went right through, Gray Lady. Are you and Lucy available? I'll have your nametag ready for you. Is Gray Lady okay? Our usual Wednesday volunteer has a fever and sore throat, so it would be nice to have you and Lucy here."

"Gray Lady is perfect. We can do that," I said.

After I hung up, I stood in front of my closet. "I don't see anything else gray in my closet. I thought I had all my old clothes. Guess I was wrong."

I grabbed my keys. "I'm going shopping. Anyone interested in going with me?"

Palace Guard met me at the car. On my way to the retail store, I said, "I saw scrub tops there, and I think they had gray ones. They would be perfect for the Gray Lady to wear."

The store had four gray scrub tops in my size. I put all four in my cart then after we returned home, I tossed them into the washer to take out the sizing and added the few dirty clothes from my basket.

When they were dry, I put on one, and hung up the other three in the closet before I examined myself in the mirror. *Perfect.*

The four of us loaded into my car to go to the Senior Center. We parked at the far end of the lot to leave room for visitors close to the entrance then strolled to Gracie Jane's office.

"There you are, and here's sweet Lucy. Thanks for coming. Here's your name tag, and I have one for Lucy that goes on her collar, if she doesn't mind. I'll give you a proper orientation tomorrow, but for now, I call us *involved volunteers*. If you see something that doesn't seem right, let me know."

CHAPTER THREE

I put on my nametag then fastened Lucy's onto her collar before we headed to Mrs. Martin's room. Mrs. Martin had her back to the window when we entered the room. "I saw you coming up the walk, Maggie Flanagan. You have two men with you today."

"Sure do, and this is Lucy."

Mrs. Martin held out her hand, and Lucy strolled to the wheelchair and nuzzled Mrs. Martin's hand.

"What a sweet, old girl you are, Lucy." Mrs. Martin cooed then scanned the room. "Bring Margarite Flanagan's fairies next time if you can. I miss them."

"I don't know where the fairies are. Sorry."

"They'll find you. They always do."

Faith's eyes were red-rimmed when she came into Mrs. Martin's room. "Hello, Gray Lady and Lucy. It's nice to see you. Mrs. Martin, I have your morning medicine; there's a new pill today. It's a second heart medicine."

After Faith filled Mrs. Martin's drink cup with water, she handed the medicine cup to Mrs. Martin and held the drink cup for her.

Mrs. Martin took her medicine. "Thank you."

"If you'd like, Gray Lady, you and Lucy could follow me today, and I'll introduce you to people."

And give me some on the job training on real and phony jewelry.

"That sounds great. Is that okay with you if we come by later, Mrs. Martin?"

Mrs. Martin stroked Lucy's neck. "I'd like that." Mrs. Martin cooed. "Wouldn't we, Lucy?"

As we walked along the hallway to the next room, Faith said, "Some of our residents like to be called by their first names, and others, like Mrs. Martin, would be horrified if a younger person called them by their first name. The easiest way for me to determine what they prefer is to call them Mrs., Mr., or Miss then let them correct me. One of the other girls calls everyone by their first name then complains that some people here are difficult to work with. Want to bet which ones those are?" Faith's smile was weak, so my smile was soft.

When we entered the room, the resident's face lit up when she saw Lucy.

"How's my sweet puppy? Such a good girl." She cooed in baby-talk in the high voice people use to talk to babies and animals.

"Here's your medicine cup. There are four cups today. Four. This is number one. One."

The woman took the cup and examined the contents. "One," she said, and Faith nodded then handed the woman her glass with water. After she took the pill, she handed Faith the empty cup and the water. They went through the same process with cups two and three.

Faith held out the fourth cup.

The woman shook her head. "Three."

"Yes, you always have three. Four is new. You have new four."

"New four." The woman reached for the cup and glass of water.

"Thank you," Faith said after the woman handed her the empty cup and glass.

"Would you like to see my pretties, puppy?" The woman shifted to her cooing voice.

"Lucy would like that," Faith said.

"Aww. Sweet Loosie-Woosie."

I controlled my shudder. *Faith is so patient.*

The woman pulled out a small box from under her pillow and flipped open the lid. "See the pretties?"

"They are pretty," Faith said. "Look at this one." She pointed to a diamond broach. I examined the piece. Faith raised her eyebrows, and I shrugged.

"Time to put your pretties away," Faith said, and Lucy and Spike backed away from the woman.

"Yes, the puppy said to put my pretties away." The woman closed her box and slipped it under her pillow.

Faith stopped a few doors down the hallway and asked, "What did you think about the broach?"

"It looked perfect to me. I couldn't see anything wrong."

"Exactly." She grinned. "Fake."

"Oh, they were perfect. Real diamonds have flaws, right?"

"Correct. That was an easy one."

"You looked like you'd been crying when you came into Mrs. Martin's room." *Did I overstep? I bit my lip.*

Faith sighed. "I don't handle bad news well. Makes me a bad fit for this job, doesn't it?"

She peered at my face. "One of our aides was in a crash over the weekend. Nancy and I went to school together. Now they're saying it was a hit and run, but the worst part is it was deliberate."

"I am so sorry."

She hugged me. "Thanks. Let's go find some more phony jewelry."

I chuckled. "Is everyone getting that new pill? Is there a study going on?"

"Must be. Many of our residents are getting the new pill, and some of them get a second new pill in the evening, but all of them are on the same medications."

"Does Mrs. Martin have any jewelry?"

"She does, but she told me the fairies told her to quit showing it to people."

I smiled. "She's a remarkable woman."

I need to talk to Mrs. Martin.

Faith checked her list. "Our next resident is another one with jewelry."

When we entered the room, the elderly woman in the chair next to her bed smiled. "Good morning, Faith. Hello, Gray Lady and doggie."

"This is Lucy." Faith put the medicine into the cups and double-checked her list while Lucy padded to the woman, and Spike followed.

"Hello, Lucy. You are a fine lady. Thank you for visiting me."

Lucy leaned against the woman's chair while Spike rubbed Lucy's ears, and I smiled.

"You have a new medicine today," Faith said.

"I think I'll pass," the woman smiled.

"Are you sure?"

"Yes. Doc wants my afib heart thing to be stable before we make any more changes."

"I'll mark it down, and the nurse will call the doctor. Is that okay with you?"

"Absolutely. I think following procedure is important." She leaned down and snuggled Lucy. "Don't you agree, Lucy?"

After she took her medications minus the new one, she asked, "Is it okay if I show the Gray Lady my necklace?"

"Yes, ma'am, if you like." Faith recorded the medications and added the note about the patient's refusal.

The woman reached into her pocket and removed a pearl necklace. "My daddy gave me this when I was ten. He told me I would always be a lady if I had pearls. He died a year later."

"You must miss him."

"Yes, I still miss him, but I have my pearls."

"May I see them for a moment?" I asked, and she placed them into my open hands.

I examined them from the woman's viewpoint then shifted to my new beginner's analytical viewpoint as I wrapped one hand gently around the necklace, and the cool pearls warmed in my hand.

"I can feel the love he had for you." I smiled as I returned the necklace to her.

She nodded as she returned it to her pocket.

When we were in the hallway, I asked, "Do many people refuse the new medication?"

"No, but I respect her decision. The medication nurse will talk to the doctor, and they can battle it out behind the scenes. Meanwhile, I'm the good guy." Faith wiggled her eyebrows.

"I like it." I smiled. "So, the pearls warmed up in my hand. Fake, right?"

"Yes, but the interesting thing is that they were fake when she came here."

My eyes widened. "Wow. It was all he could afford."

Faith nodded as we continued her rounds, and I learned a new tip about real or imitation jewelry after we left each room.

After she completed her round, we headed back.

"Have I reached the beginner's level?"

"You passed the beginner's level yesterday when you asked me to teach you." Faith hugged me. "I'm going to do some quick shopping on my lunch break. My boyfriend, Eric, was supposed to go back today, but he texted me and asked if I was available to go to dinner tonight. He's never done that before. I'm hoping—well, you know." She giggled. "I'll see you tomorrow for your next lesson and maybe with some exciting news."

I smiled. "I can't wait."

After Faith left, I asked, "Shall we spend some time with Mrs. Martin?"

Lucy grinned as Palace Guard and Spike nodded.

When we stepped into her room, Mrs. Martin's eyes were closed. We turned to leave but she said, "I was resting my eyes. Come on in."

"We thought we'd visit for a while. I'd love to hear about the fairies. Mother told me stories about her grandmother's fairies, but I've never seen any."

Mrs. Martin frowned. "What's your mother's name? No, don't tell me. I remember now. Your grandmother's name was Devlin Grace, and your mother's name is Isolde. I'm not surprised you've heard about the fairies. Even as a young child, Isolde was hard of hearing, and the fairies were sometimes her only friends."

I blinked in surprise. "Mother never mentioned that she saw the fairies too."

"Sometimes people are a little uncomfortable about sharing their gifted side. What about you and your imaginary men?" While she sipped her water, I checked her pitcher.

"Good point. I've never told Mother about them." I squinted inside the pitcher. "Where can I get ice for your water pitcher?"

"There's a utility room with an ice machine at the end of the hall. I'll tell you a fairy tale when you get back." Mrs. Martin giggled. "I've always wanted to say that."

Lucy and Spike stayed with Mrs. Martin while Palace Guard and I strolled down the hallway in search of the utility room. I filled the pitcher with ice then headed back.

"Gray Lady?" a woman called from a room.

When we went into the room, I couldn't see anyone. As I turned to leave, Palace Guard pointed to the far corner when a woman was on the floor and was wedged near her window between the wall and her wheelchair.

"This is embarrassing." she said. "I thought I'd be sneaky and stand where I could see something in the parking lot that was none of my business; instead, I lost my balance and managed to get stuck between the wall and my chair. The only good news is that I didn't miss a thing."

I unlocked the wheelchair wheels then moved it, so I could get behind her. I helped her to a sitting position then wrapped my arms under her arms. Palace Guard placed a foot in front of hers to keep her from sliding, and his hand on her back, so he could help me lift. Palace Guard counted with nods as I counted silently. *One, two, three, lift.*

He helped her balance as I moved the wheelchair into place to sit then we eased her into her chair.

"Very slick," she said. "You have a wonderful talent for using leverage to your advantage." She smoothed her dress and fluffed her hair. "I'm Edna. What do I owe you?"

"You owe me the story of what you saw that was none of your business." I grinned.

"You won't tell on me, will you?" she asked, and I rolled my eyes as I pulled up a chair to sit in front of her.

"Fine. Do you know the new jeweler who bought Mr. Bustamante's business in town? His name escapes me at the moment." Edna furrowed her brow in thought then snapped her finger. "John Howard, that's it. He comes regularly and probably has a close relative here, but I've checked, and no one seems to know who that might be. Maybe he cleans people's jewelry or something. We're not supposed to have any in our rooms, but everybody does. Where was I? Oh, he had pulled into the parking lot as Faith was on her way to her car. I had heard there was bad blood between the two of them, so I decided to see if there were going to be any fireworks."

She shook her head. "Terrible of me, I know, but I'm not much into television or movies, so I get my entertainment where I can."

Edna peered at me. "Not a very good excuse, is it? I'll have to work on that. Anyway, when John saw Faith headed to her car, he hurried to cut her off. I know they had words because after he said something, Faith's face got red, and she was waving her arms. He reached out to touch her, but before he could, she blocked his arm with her forearm. I was impressed with her reflexes. He looked furious then he shook his fist at her and stormed to the entrance."

After Edna cleared her throat, she said, "That's when I fell. If you don't mind, I believe my binoculars may have slid under the bed."

I fake-coughed to keep from laughing then peered under her bed that was next to her wheelchair. The binoculars were a little out of my reach, so Palace Guard handed them to me.

After I gave her the binoculars, Edna said, "I need to remember not to let my nosy side take over my better judgement." She sighed. "I'm too old to give up that much fun. Forget I said that."

Too easy. Do I go for it?

I shrugged. "Said what?"

Edna snort-laughed, and I giggled.

When Palace Guard and I returned to Mrs. Martin's room, she was singing a soft lullaby in a language I didn't know. Lucy slept near her feet, and Spike dozed in the visitor's chair.

"That's a beautiful song," I said. "Look how relaxed Lucy is."

"She is, isn't she? I owe you a fairy tale."

I refreshed her glass of water with cold water and ice then sat on the floor next to Lucy and stroked her head.

"You're more comfortable sitting next to your Lucy, aren't you? It's very kind of you to let Lucy's protector sleep."

"I'm not used to other people seeing the imaginary men." I smiled.

"I understand. That's how I feel about Margarite's fairies. Your grandmother didn't see the fairies; maybe that's why Isolde never talked about them very much. My favorite story about Isolde and the fairies is that the fairies taught Isolde how to sign. When Isolde visited me, she'd always wander off to the dining room and sit under the table. I knew the fairies told her outrageous stories because of the sheer joy in Isolde's giggles. One time, Devlin Grace asked me what Isolde did under the dining table that was so funny, and I told her that Isolde was entertaining herself with a tea party and was pretending her guests told delightful stories. Devlin Grace looked me straight in the eye and said, 'Pretending is for children.'"

Mrs. Martin snort-laughed at the memory. "I couldn't help myself; I laughed until the tears ran down my face. What did she think Isolde was? Devlin Grace must have realized how ridiculous she sounded because her face became downright crimson, and she stomped out of the house. I heard the fairies burst into song, and when I peeked into the dining room, they were signing in fairy language as they sang to Isolde who giggled at the words that I couldn't understand. After that, I was determined to learn fairy language."

"What a wonderful story. I wonder if Mother remembers the fairy sign language."

"You know she does, whether she'd ever admit it might be another story if she has a streak of Devlin Grace in her."

"Was the song you were singing to Lucy in fairy language?"

"Most people think I'm rambling nonsense words to a tune." Mrs. Martin chuckled. "Yes, that's an old fairy lullaby. As I get older, I've discovered I'm more fluent in fairy than English. Must be a special bonus of becoming elderly. Another advantage of being old is that I can look back on my early larcenous years as charming escapades of a fanciful, wild girl."

"I'd love to hear your larceny stories."

Mrs. Martin smiled at her memories. "I was an accomplished jewel thief. Clara focused on art, but I found art too fragile and too bulky, and Clara was too greedy, so I cut ties with her. I was better off solo, anyway. If you ever have any questions about jewelry, you just ask me. Actually, our facility has a wealth of talented folks. Let me know if you need a signature forged or a lock picked."

"I'm interested in learning more about replica jewelry," I said. "Faith gave me some reading to do. I'm curious—does Darren know about your wild side?"

Her eyes twinkled. "He never asked. Margarite cautioned me never to talk about my extraordinary talents with anyone except her, so I didn't, but I know she'd approve of you, Maggie Flanagan. Bring me your questions. I speak larceny as fluently as fairy."

I snickered. "That would be fun."

"I would love a chance to share what I know. Believe it or not, my days of climbing up trellises and through windows are behind me." She tittered.

I chuckled then peered at her face. "Darren said you were very ill for quite a while; I have a personal question that you don't have to answer, but do you have good days and bad days?"

She shook her head. "Not anymore—it was my medicine, and I deteriorated from occasional bad days to permanent horrible days. My former doctor said I didn't have a choice because old people have memory problems. When the fairies laughed and said he was wrong, I wrote myself a note as a reminder to fire my doctor. Now,

I have a new doctor who listens and has common sense, which is why I'm surprised she prescribed a new medication. I called her office to ask about it, but I haven't heard back from her yet. What do you think about the new pill? Should I skip it tonight if I don't hear from her?"

Palace Guard and Spike nodded, and I shrugged. "I don't know what to say, except it might be prudent to wait until you hear from the doctor."

"The men say wait; I'll wait," Mrs. Martin said. "Besides, I think the new medicine made the fairies sick because I haven't seen them all day."

I nodded. *Good reason to stop taking it.*

"How about a quick jewelry lesson before you leave?" Mrs. Martin pointed to the closet. "Look in the bottom drawer and bring me the metal box."

When I handed the box to her, she unlocked it, and I sat next to her.

"Tell me what you know so far," she said.

"If it looks perfect, it's probably not real. Pearls that warm in my hand aren't real. That's about it."

"That's a really good start. What about gold?"

"I don't really know anything except I'm allergic to gold."

"That is absolutely priceless. You are definitely Maggie Flanagan. Margarite was allergic to gold too. She had a beautiful emerald stone in a gold ring, and she never wore it."

"Mother has it now and loves wearing it."

Mrs. Martin pulled out a necklace. The links in the delicate chain appeared to be gold, and the pendent was a large diamond surrounded by smaller diamonds and tiny pearls. "Real or fake?"

I wrapped the links around my finger while I examined the diamonds. "I see different colors in the large center diamond. Are those considered flaws that would mean it's real?"

"That's one indication of a real stone. Feel the diamond."

"It's very smooth with no rough edges at all."

"Stones can be polished, so they feel smooth. When diamonds are water-tumbled, they are smooth. So, what do you think? Real or fake?"

"Real."

"It's an excellent fake. Acrylic can be tinted to mimic a diamond, but our biggest hint is the size. This is too big for a pendant that isn't in a safe deposit box or around a movie star's neck. How's the gold?"

"My finger isn't itchy at all."

"Sometimes gold is coated like the links in this necklace. The chain is real. Crazy, isn't it? If you want to know whether something is real or fake, take it to a pawn shop. Those folks know their stuff. When I was stumped in the olden days, that's what I did. I learned a lot including there are lots of cheap chumps who buy fakes then pass them off as real, so I started a side business of verifying jewelry for suspicious wives and girlfriends. I was making so much money with that little venture that I almost gave up thievery. Almost. I would have except examining jewelry didn't have the thrill of lifting a piece or two. This is a piece one of my clients gave me as a memento in addition to a huge cash bonus before she divorced her husband."

I rose, and Lucy and the men followed me to the door. "I'm going to keep studying, but I think I'm going to have to rely on my experts. We'll see you tomorrow."

On our way home, I said, "I never thought I'd meet a real jewel thief, much less a successful, retired one. I just thought of something—if Mrs. Martin's fairies return, would you be able to see them?"

Spike scowled, and Palace Guard shrugged.

That's interesting. "You don't believe in fairies, Spike?"

Spike narrowed his eyes and shook his head.

He's lying. He's Irish; he believes in fairies.

Palace Guard smirked.

When we reached home, we all headed inside. Lucy and Spike went out back while I poured a glass of tea before Palace Guard and I sat at the computer for our next lesson in valuable and replica jewelry.

An hour later, we'd finished the lesson. As I listed my questions for Mrs. Martin, my stomach growled. "Time for a bite of lunch."

When we went into the living room, Lucy was across Spike's lap, and while she slept, I thought I heard Spike humming the fairies' tune. I peered at Palace Guard, and he nodded.

After Palace Guard and I slipped quietly to the kitchen, I made myself half a cheese sandwich. "I need help with menus. It was easy to cook at Reggie's because the breakfast menu was limited, and I cooked whatever the plan for the day was at Diane's."

Palace Guard made his fierce face then pointed up. "Good idea. I'll ask Jennifer."

I sent a text to Jennifer while I finished my lunch. "Need dinner menu suggestions."

I stared at the lawnmower box. "Larry might be interested in putting the lawnmower together—I'll ask him. I'm ready to go back to my jewelry training."

While Palace Guard and I read, my phone buzzed a text from Jennifer. "Will send list by email. For today, buy precooked ribs and make potato salad."

"What a good idea. Let's run to the grocery store."

After I read Jennifer's potato salad recipe and added ingredients to my shopping list, Palace Guard and I left Spike and Lucy sleeping as we slipped out.

Spike and Lucy were in the backyard when we returned. As I put the potato salad into the refrigerator, Spike and Lucy came inside. Lucy took a long drink, then picked up her leash.

"What a good idea. Let's go to the park."

Spike opened the front door, and Lucy beat us all to the car.

Spike carried Lucy's leash as she wandered from one side of the path to the other while we strolled through the park. The light breeze made our slow walk pleasant. When two minivans with four children in each van emptied near the playground equipment, Lucy tugged on the leash to slip it out of Spike's hand and eased closer to the playground equipment. She stopped at a bench in the shade outside the playground fence and flopped down in the dirt.

"This is a good spot to listen to the squeals, isn't it?"

After the children left, Lucy trotted to the car, and we headed home.

"Perfect timing." I parked in the driveway. "Larry will be home in a half hour. All I need to do with the ribs is put them in the oven long enough to warm up. Jennifer is brilliant."

Larry hurried into the house and grabbed me into a hug and passionate kiss.

"Happy to see you." He nuzzled my hair when I held onto him. "Be right back. I picked up some local beer. The guys told me about a local microbrewery, and I stopped to pick some up for us. We should go sometime."

He returned with the beer and placed it in the refrigerator.

"After you change, would you be interested in putting together the lawnmower? Or we could just sit on the porch and try out the local beer while our supper is in the oven."

"Beer and lawnmower." He dashed to the bedroom to change his clothes, and I smiled. *I love that guy.*

"Good thing I thought about a tool chest," he said when he returned.

I carried two beers to the porch while he brought out all his new tools and the tool chest. After I sat crisscrossed on the floorboards, I read the directions to myself while Larry put together the lawnmower.

Palace Guard sat beside me and elbowed me; I side-glanced him. *If I keep my head down and read then I won't stick in my nose and try to tell him how to do it.*

After Larry finished, he leaned back against the post and took a long gulp of beer. "Do we have gas?"

"I got two cans but haven't filled them up. I can do that tomorrow. Are you ready to eat?"

"Sounds great. I'll put my tools into the toolbox then be right in."

When Larry came inside, I had set the table, placed the ribs on a platter, and stuck a spoon into the potato salad. After he washed, we dug in.

Larry wiped his face with a napkin and licked his fingers. "Almost all of us that were at the meeting today will be going to Knoxville for the training at the same time. Most of the guys go deer hunting in the fall, and I've been invited to go, but I need to get a deer rifle after I do a little research. I'll need some gear too. How was your first day?"

I told him about Mrs. Martin's jewelry talents and her fairies, my mother and the fairies, Faith and her excitement about her boyfriend, and my jewelry training.

"Just a normal day." I grinned.

"A normal Maggie day, minus a killer." He snorted.

After the dishes were in the dishwasher, Larry said, "I'd like to organize my toolbox."

"I wouldn't mind spending some time on the last jewelry lesson. Do you know if there's a shooting range we could go to?"

"Glad you mentioned it. One of the guys lives out in the country on a farm with his folks, and we're all invited to lunch on Saturday. There's a shooting range down the road from their farm; we talked about the range but didn't decide if we're going to shoot. You and I can check it out without them if the guys decide not to go."

"That sounds great."

Larry whistled as he, Lucy, and Spike headed to the back porch, and I smiled.

When Palace Guard and I finished the lesson, and I had my notes, I stretched. Lucy had stretched out on the sofa, and Spike sat on the edge near her head as he scratched her ears. Larry sat on his chair with three open catalogs on the table next to him as he scrolled on his phone.

"The guys gave me some old catalogs to look through for what type of deer rifle I might like. I've been reading some stuff. Did you know today is our one-week anniversary?"

"And they said it wouldn't last." I bent to give him a kiss and smiled. "Shall we take Lucy outside for one last walk then go to bed?"

Larry yawned then stretched before he headed to the back door. "I didn't know I was tired, but I guess I am."

Lucy trotted along behind him, and we all went outside.

The bright moon cast eerie shadows and gave the bare tree limbs a skeletal look while the lonely call of a hooting owl added to the sinister atmosphere of the night.

When I shuddered, Larry asked, "Are you cold?"

"Not really—the spookiness of the night gave me a bad feeling. I think I'm just tired."

* * *

After Larry left for work the next morning, I read Jennifer's email and chuckled at her first hint: "Most recipes serve four. Don't cut back; instead, plan on leftovers."

I saved the list Jennifer sent me then read through her recipes before I jotted down our menus for the rest of the week, starting with leftovers tonight. I replied to her email and thanked her for the suggestion to pick a protein different from the day before then pick a recipe.

Spike leaned over my shoulder to read then poked me.

"What? You know I like lists. I'm sure this will all be automatic later."

Before we left the house, I remembered to stick the two empty gas cans in the back of the car. "I'll fill them on our way home."

As we approached the senior center, Lucy sat up straight on the back seat and scrambled over Spike to be close to the window.

"I'm not going to miss my turn, girl. We're almost there." I smiled. *We take our work seriously.* Palace Guard nodded.

After I parked, Lucy bounded across the grass to the entrance, and Spike raced to catch up with her.

I picked up her leash and carried it with me. "You forgot your leash, Lucy."

She sat while she waited at the entrance, and I handed it to her. When we went inside, the depth of sadness in Gracie Jane's face— her downturned mouth and furrowed brow—startled me. "Come into my office, please, Maggie."

She spun her wheelchair around. After we were inside her office, Gracie Jane said, "Please sit. This is really hard. I know you just started, but I understand you worked closely with Faith yesterday. I received a call early this morning—" her voice broke. She took a breath then continued, "Faith was found dead in her car this morning. The police are being very tight-lipped, but a reliable friend of mine told me Faith had been murdered. I wanted you to know."

I stared at her in disbelief. *Not Faith.*

I shook my head. "She was a friend. She'll be missed by so many people."

CHAPTER FOUR

Gracie Jane nodded. "I'm sure the news is all over the center. People will be asking you all kinds of questions. I needed to warn you in advance, so you won't be dragged down into the hysterical drama and speculation that will more than likely reach a fever pitch. I called our grief counselor and asked her to assemble a team as quickly as possible to help calm our staff and residents. I've already been approached by several volunteers. I've told them it's a tragedy, and that we will all miss Faith."

I rose. "I need to check with Mrs. Martin first. I did the rounds with Faith yesterday, so she introduced me to her patients."

"I know. That's a real bonus for us because you know who saw her yesterday. Let me know if anyone needs extra help." She shook her head. "Faith is a real loss. She was a wonderful person and always so patient with our residents. She will be missed."

I paused before I left. "It's going to be a hard day."

She nodded.

Before we reached the hallway, I inhaled then exhaled a long, slow breath. "Let's go see Mrs. Martin."

When I went into Mrs. Martin's room, tears flowed down her face. When she saw me, she wiped her eyes. "Maggie Flanagan, I'm an old woman, and most of my friends have passed away, but the sudden death of a young person is a tragedy."

"I agree." I sat next to her, and she took my hands and sighed.

"The chaplain invited some local pastors to the center, and they are making the rounds. Their words are comforting, and I appreciated the visit."

Her eyes narrowed, and her face was grim. "I want to hunt down the killer."

She shook her head then her mouth quivered into a weak smile. "The killer should be scared. Our entire senior center is ready to take him down. You let me know how we can help, Gray Lady."

My eyes widened. "Rebecca Martin, I expected sadness and grief, but I didn't expect a posse of vigilantes."

"Well, that's exactly what you have." Her jaw tightened.

"If I need help, I'm not afraid to ask."

"Good. Now, what are your plans?"

I frowned. "No plans yet, but what could the motive be to kill Faith? I wonder if the fake jewelry is involved."

"My specialty. I'm ready for my orders. I'm a ninety-five-year-old private in the Gray Lady's army of vigilantes."

I raised my eyebrows. "Careful. We work undercover. You don't need to be a target too."

"Gotcha." Mrs. Martin winked. "I've been undercover my entire life. You know, I think we might want to stop people from taking that new pill. No one will ever know it came from me."

When Spike strode to Mrs. Martin's side and offered up his hand, Mrs. Martin smacked a high five.

"What's my friend's name?" she asked.

"Spike."

"Is it okay with you if Spike spends the morning with me?" she asked. Spike grinned and nodded at the same moment that I said, "No."

I glared at Spike, and he narrowed his eyes and put his hands on his hips. Palace Guard stepped between us and held up his hands.

"Are you going to break the tie?" I asked.

"I will," Mrs. Martin said. "Let the other man spend the morning with me."

"Palace Guard?"

"Of course, he is. What's his name?"

All three of us stared at Mrs. Martin, but when Lucy barked, I narrowed my eyes at the laughing fairy who sat on Mrs. Martin's shoulder.

"Your fairy is a tease. His name is Palace Guard."

Mrs. Martin chuckled as her fairy pouted. "So, can Palace Guard spend part of the morning with me?"

"Yes, and I'm glad there isn't any more of whatever that medicine was in your system."

Lucy, Spike, and I headed down the hall to visit Edna. When we reached her room, I glanced back at Mrs. Martin's room. *I hope Palace Guard can keep Mrs. Martin out of trouble.*

Spike and Lucy grinned.

"Is this how Larry feels every day when he leaves?"

Spike did a jig, and I tossed my hair as I put my nose in the air.

Gracie Jane caught up with me before I went into Edna's room. She had an empty canvas tote on her lap. "May I speak to you a moment?" she whispered. "I have to pack Faith's things for her father and need a witness when I open her locker."

"I don't mind helping."

"Thank you. The staff room is near the cafeteria."

When we passed the cafeteria, I coughed at the strong odor of bleach. "Does bleach bother you?" Gracie Jane asked. "I've heard that people who were around pools or chlorine spills are especially sensitive, but I've grown kind of immune to it and don't even notice it anymore. Gerald's cleaning the cafeteria before lunch."

We entered the staff room that had a row of metal school-style lockers along one wall. Gracie Jane pulled out a key from her pocket.

After she handed the key to me, she said, "Open the third locker from the door."

I opened the locker and glanced at the contents: a set of scrubs and a sweater hung on a hook, and a box of energy bars, a box of ballpoint pens, a small notebook, and a hairbrush were on the lone shelf above the hook.

Gracie Jane tapped on the sheet of paper she had on a clipboard. "Put each item on the table, so I can record it on the inventory list."

After the locker was empty, she placed the items into the tote, and we signed the inventory sheet.

"I knew you'd help me," she said. "I'm not into listening to anyone quite yet."

As we headed back toward Edna's room, Gracie Jane said, "Two staff deaths in such a short time is a strain on everyone. I overheard a nurse say this morning that we're cursed. We don't need that type of negativity to take hold. I'm planning a staff meeting later in the morning. If you're available, I would like for you to attend." Gracie Jane zipped ahead of me in her wheelchair to go to her office.

When Palace Guard and I entered Edna's room, Edna was sitting in her wheelchair as she faced the window. Her binoculars were on her lap.

"Good morning, I brought another visitor; her name is Lucy."

"What a pretty girl you are, Lucy." Edna's eyes brightened as Lucy padded to her side.

"You've heard about Faith, right?" Edna rubbed Lucy's face and ears.

"Yes, I have, and my heart is breaking for her father."

"I need to tell the police what I saw, don't I? Could you arrange that for me?"

"I'll take care of it right now. Could Lucy stay with you?"

"If it's okay with her, I'd love the company."

On my way to talk to Gracie Jane, I slowed my steps then headed to the park and sent a text to Larry. "I'm okay. You available to talk?"

My phone rang. *Larry.*

"What's wrong?"

I smiled. *He didn't get to say are you okay.* "Faith was murdered last night, and one of the residents saw her argue with a man in the parking lot yesterday. I need to tell the Volunteer Coordinator, but should I call the police first?"

"You just did, sweetheart. What's the resident's name?"

"Edna Cross."

"You can tell the Volunteer Coordinator you contacted the police. Thanks for not shooting the man." Larry hung up.

Am I insulted? I shrugged as I continued to Gracie Jane's office.

Gracie Jane and I entered the reception area at the same time from different hallways.

"Were you on your way to see me?" she asked. "Let's go into my office."

"Edna Cross saw Faith with a man in the parking lot yesterday and thought they were arguing. I called the police, so she can tell them her story."

"You know she makes things up, right?" Gracie Jane narrowed her eyes. "It wasn't necessary to bring in the police."

Oh, really?

"They can worry about that. I'm sure they're smart enough to figure that out." I smiled as I turned to leave.

"Don't ever call the police again. We can't afford any bad publicity."

I cocked my head. "Why is that?"

She slammed her hand down on her desk. "You can leave anytime you aren't comfortable with our rules."

I nodded and strolled out of her office. *I hit a nerve.*

When I reached Edna's room, she was dozing in her chair while Lucy relaxed at her feet. Spike waved, and I said, "Lucy, ready to go?"

Edna woke and smiled. "Thanks for letting Lucy visit me. Did you find Gracie Jane?"

"I did, and the police will probably come talk to you."

As we entered Mrs. Martin's room, Palace Guard grinned, and Mrs. Martin beamed.

"Did you know the new pill is being recalled?" Mrs. Martin's eyes twinkled.

"No, I didn't. Where did you hear that?"

"One of the men who is an internet expert is telling everyone that he read it online last night. Nobody is taking the new medicine until they talk with their doctor."

"Sounds smart to me." I closed the door then sat next to her.

"How did you pull that off?" I asked.

"Palace Guard and I went to the park and ran into our guru who walks the path around the park every morning. I mentioned I'd read it on the internet, and he took ownership as the internet expert before anyone else did." She snickered.

"That was fortunate—just running into him." The corner of my mouth quivered. "How did you make that happen?"

"Since my dashing around days are behind me, I described him to Palace Guard who scoured the park then selected the perfect spot for me to sit in the sun."

I chuckled. "Excellent plan."

Palace Guard beamed, and Mrs. Martin blushed. "We came up with it together."

I opened her door as I spoke loudly enough for any passersby to overhear. "Can I get you anything before we leave for the day?"

"No, I'm fine. It was a wonderful visit. Darren and I completed the paperwork last night for you to be an approved visitor. Do you plan to be here tomorrow?"

"Sure do. If anything changes, I'll contact Darren."

"Good, thanks. I've worked up an appetite. I might go to the cafeteria for lunch today."

I stopped by Gracie Jane's office, but it was empty, and there was no note on her door. *Guess I wasn't required at the staff meeting after all.*

On our way home, Palace Guard poked me as I drove past the gas station, and I made a U-turn. "Thanks, I would have forgotten."

I filled the two cans and my tank while we were there. After we were home, Spike and I coaxed Lucy out back. While Lucy wandered, I texted Detective Heather in Harperville. "Call? I have a question about senior centers."

Heather called immediately. "Are you okay? What's going on?"

"I'm fine. Did you hear about the murder here?"

"Just did."

"I told you about Faith earlier. She was the aide who was murdered last night. One of our residents saw Faith and a man in an argument yesterday. I called Larry then when I told the volunteer coordinator that I'd called the police, she was very angry. In fact, she told me to never call the police again because it was against the rules."

"What?"

"Yep, and she said I didn't need to return if I couldn't follow the rules. She said it was bad publicity for the facility."

"Wow. I see red flags all over the place. Are you going back?"

"Of course. She'll have to revoke my volunteer status, but Mrs. Martin, Darren's mother, has already listed me as an approved visitor. So, what do you think? Is it bad publicity for the police to talk to a resident?"

"Absolutely not, but she certainly called attention to herself, didn't she? Unfortunately, there's nothing to investigate. Maybe she's just overly protective."

"True. What else can I do to provoke her into telling me what's going on with her?"

Heather laughed, and Spike rushed to my side and put his hand on his heart. I rolled my eyes and put her on speakerphone.

"If police make her nervous, I wonder how she'd feel about an audit. Someone may pay her a visit."

"You know, I just realized I've never met the administrator. I think I'll see what I can learn about their business model."

"You still wear your carry piece?"

"Of course."

"Of course. Sometimes Larry's nervousness is catching. Call me any old time." She hung up.

I stared at my phone. "Maybe I should call Glenn. He understands because people hang up on him too."

When Glenn answered, he said, "No, thank you. I already have all the insurance I need." When he hung up, I laughed.

"He'll call me back."

My phone rang. "You okay?"

"Yes, I'm fine. I just needed to talk to a normal person."

"Ah, but you couldn't think of anyone, so you called me for my suggestions. Can't help you there, before you ask."

Dad joke. I chuckled. "How busy are you?"

"I'd love to dig into a Maggie problem. Whatcha got?"

"I need to understand who manages the operations and finances for the senior center where I volunteer. I'll text you the name and address. I don't know anything else. Oh wait, I do. Could you also check the volunteer coordinator? I'll add her name to the text."

"Send it to me. Paul might be interested in a little diversion too."

After I hung up, I frowned. "Faith was supposed to meet her boyfriend last night."

I sent Glenn another text. "Thought of something else. SD."

When he called, I said, "Faith was scheduled to meet her boyfriend last night. He was supposed to have returned to work, but he stayed in Columbus to take her to dinner. She was excited and hopeful the surprise meeting meant a proposal. His name is Eric, and he lives in Charleston, South Carolina, but that's all I know. I don't know what he does."

"Piece of cake. Throw us something hard next time, and I'm kidding." Glenn chuckled.

I smiled. "Thanks, Glenn."

After we hung up, I sent Glenn a text with the information I knew then dropped onto my rocker.

"I think I've run out of brain cells. I need a bite of lunch."

My phone buzzed a text. *Darren.*

"Have you eaten? Need to talk."

Me: "I haven't."

Darren: "Meet me downtown at Sano Café?"

Me: "15 min?"

Darren: "Perfect."

"Who's going with me?" I hurried to the bedroom to change out of my scrub top and into a T-shirt and grabbed my purse.

Spike and Lucy were on the sofa, and Palace Guard waited at the door.

On the way to the sandwich shop, I said, "I wonder if Gracie Jane called Darren, and he's trying to run interference. I hope so because I was looking for an excuse to ask him about her. I'll have to think of some casual way to ask. Something subtle."

When I entered the shop, Rafael greeted me at the door.

"Could you make sure I get the check this time?"

"Will do." He smiled.

Our server brought my glass of sweet tea to the table then took our order.

"Sorry for the short notice. I just heard about Faith and realized you probably saw my mother this morning. How's she doing?"

"She was shocked like everyone else, but she's okay."

"That's good to know. I was worried, but I didn't want to burst in to try to fix something that wasn't broken. That bad spell she had for a while makes me overprotective sometimes."

I nodded and waited for Darren to say more when Palace Guard raised an eyebrow. *I agree. This isn't about Rebecca Martin's health.*

"What do you know about jewelry?" Darren asked.

"Absolutely nothing. I inherited some jewelry not long ago and turned it over to my lawyer and Mother to decide what to do. I guess it never interested me."

Darren sipped his tea. "I was always fascinated by art, even though I'm not an artist. Mother told me I had a gift to see the value of art. She has a gift to see the value of jewelry."

Rafael set our sandwiches on the table as he slipped the check under my plate and winked.

"Both of those talents are rare." I bit into my sandwich, and Darren nodded as he picked up his sandwich.

After I'd eaten half of my half sandwich and most of my soup, I asked, "So what did you need to talk about?"

So much for casual. Palace Guard grinned.

Darren frowned. "Gracie Jane called me. She was upset about some rule that I'd never heard of, and I'm still not clear what it was. She wanted me to talk to you, but I don't know what I'm supposed to talk to you about. Are you in trouble? Do you need me to get you a good lawyer?"

My eyes widened, and Palace Guard blinked. *Didn't expect Darren to decide to add me to his short list of people to protect.*

"I can't tell you what the rule is, but Gracie Jane was upset that I called the police to tell them one of the residents saw Faith and a man argue in the parking lot yesterday."

"I'll bet it was John Howard. He has had a crush on Faith for years, but he's never said anything to her. John did not like Faith's boyfriend at all. John told me Eric wasn't trustworthy, but he never said why. I know he's broken-hearted over Faith."

"The resident thought the man raised his hand while he and Faith argued. Did they fight a lot?"

"John's very expressive and talks with his hands. If he raised his hand, it wouldn't have been to harm Faith. I would assume he was trying to emphasize a point, and they did argue a lot over Eric. Faith thought he was interfering in her life, and he thought she was making a terrible mistake."

"Was John Howard the man who picked up his order when we had lunch Monday?"

"I don't remember John coming in, but I was a little distracted by work and Mother. Probably so. His shop is just a few doors down."

"Seemed like Faith was mad at him."

Darren shook his head, and his weak smile was wistful. "Faith was always mad at John about something."

"So, do I need to apologize to Gracie Jane or something?"

Darren chuckled. "No. Gracie Jane is a wonderful woman, but she sometimes goes overboard about something trivial when she's upset about something else. I'd expect her to apologize to you."

"That's a relief. I like Gracie Jane."

"So do I." Darren blushed as he glanced at our server. "I'll take care of the check on my way out; I need to get back to work."

I held up the check and waved it. "I beat you. It was my turn to buy."

"Thanks, Maggie. Pretty slick." He chuckled as he rushed out of the shop.

After we were home, I shooed everybody outside so I could dust without any critiques from Spike. I strolled to the porch to join them and closed my eyes to listen to the neighborhood birds while I rocked. When my head jerked, I realized I'd dozed off. After I stretched, I considered going inside, but the sunbeams held me captive until my phone rang.

I hurried inside to answer. *Gracie Jane?*

"Hello, Maggie. I'm sorry I overreacted this morning. I didn't mean to snap at you. I hope you'll forgive me."

I raised my eyebrows. *Whatever. Did Darren call Gracie Jane?*

"I'm fine. Everyone is under a lot of stress right now."

"I know, but I'm embarrassed by my unprofessional conduct." She cleared her throat. "Are you available to go with me to see Faith's father? I'd like to take him Faith's personal things and offer my condolences."

That's it. She needs a buffer.

"Of course. When would you like to go?"

"Could you meet me there in thirty minutes?"

"Sure. Text me the address, and I'll see you then."

When Palace Guard cocked his head, I said, "Gracie Jane called to apologize and asked me to meet her at Mr. Bustamante's house to take him Faith's personal things and to offer her condolences. Now I need to find something to wear. My gray striped blouse and black slacks?"

Palace Guard nodded

After I changed, I told Spike where we were going, and he waved.

I parked down the street from the address and strolled to the house. Gracie Jane waited in the driveway for me, and I glanced at her car when I passed it before I walked behind her as she wheeled herself to the door. *She has hand controls to drive her car. It's nice she isn't limited by her inability to walk.*

After Gracie Jane knocked, a large, middle-aged man with dark hair and the build of a former college linebacker opened the door.

"Hello, Eric," Gracie Jane said. "This is Maggie Ewing. She worked with Faith too."

Eric's face was lined with grief as he invited us in. "Mr. Bustamante is napping, but please come in. Thank you for coming, Gracie Jane. Pleasure to meet you, Maggie."

After Eric helped Gracie Jane maneuver the threshold, I extended my hand, and he covered it with his two beefy hands. The gentleness of his touch surprised me.

"I'm so sorry for your loss," I said. "Faith was the most patient person I've ever known."

"We don't mean to intrude, and we certainly don't want to wake Mr. Bustamante. I have Faith's things from her locker that you and Mr. Bustamante might like to have." She set the tote on the table to remove the clothing and the small notebook before she handed me the empty bag.

"Thank you. I know Mr. Bustamante will appreciate having Faith's things. I'll peek to see if he's awake," Eric said. "I'll leave him be if he's asleep."

While Eric was gone, Gracie Jane rolled to the window and gazed outside. I picked up the small notebook and flipped through a few pages. I frowned as I dropped it into the tote bag.

"He's still sleeping. The doctor gave him something to relax him." Eric shook his head. "This has been hard on him; he needs the rest."

Gracie Jane nodded. "I'll come by another time. I need to scoot. No reason for you to leave too, Maggie. Eric, I'm sure Mr. Bustamante is able to rest because you are here."

Eric helped Gracie Jane as she rolled onto the sidewalk then he returned to the house. "I'll be right back. I meant to close the blinds in Mr. Bustamante's room."

While I waited, I stood at the window as Gracie Jane wheeled to her car, folded up her wheelchair, and lifted it into the back seat before she jumped into the driver's seat and drove away.

I raised my eyebrows. *She's faking?* Palace Guard frowned.

"Sorry," Eric said. "I'm glad I checked; he'll be more comfortable in a cooler room. I wanted to tell you before you left that Faith told me she trusted the Gray Lady, and I could too." He peered at my face. "I think I can."

I pulled out my Coyle Detective business card. "This is my cell. Call or text anytime."

He accepted the card then nodded before I left.

On my stroll down the street, I folded the tote bag and slipped it under my arm. When I reached out to open my car door, Palace Guard stood in my way. His arms were crossed, and he scowled.

"I need to read the notebook. Faith mentioned discrepancies, and I need to understand what she was talking about. I've only borrowed it; I'll return it to Mr. Bustamante."

I climbed into my car, and Palace Guard sat in the passenger's seat as he continued to scowl. He held up his finger and blew on it— the imaginary men's sign for Larry.

"I'll tell him later. If it's nothing then I'll return it, and no one will be the wiser. In fact, I could make a copy and return it tomorrow. Would that make you happy?"

Palace Guard narrowed his eyes.

"Okay, then be mad."

When we arrived at home, I went inside alone.

After I removed my shirt and slacks, I hung them up then changed my mind and tossed them into the laundry.

I brewed a cup of hot tea then sat at the kitchen table with the notebook and my phone. After I snapped a picture of each page, I uploaded the files to my laptop then sat on the sofa to read.

When I was halfway through, I glanced at the clock. *Five o'clock. Larry will be home soon.*

I stuck the notebook into my backpack and sent Glenn a text: "Eric Stephens."

While I stared at my phone, Palace Guard sat on the sofa next to me.

"Am I forgiven?"

He rolled his eyes.

"Oh, good. Did you realize we have only nice people involved? The murder victims are nice, and our three potential suspects— Gracie Jane, Eric Stephens, and John Howard are all nice people."

Palace Guard pointed at me and shook his head, and I burst into laughter.

"You're right. I stole the notebook and lied to practically everybody—I must be the killer."

Palace Guard held up his hand, and I smacked it for a high five as Larry came inside the house.

"What are you two high-fiving about?" he asked as he strode to me and grabbed me up in a passionate kiss.

Sorry can't talk; I'm busy right now.

"Leftovers for supper? Any shopping we need to do?" he asked after he released me.

"I meant to pull together a shopping list, but it's not quite complete. I can't think of anything unless you'd like to look at deer rifles."

Larry hugged me. "You're the best wife in the world."

Palace Guard shook his head while Spike fake-gagged.

"Something's up. What aren't you telling me?"

I followed him to the bedroom while he changed and told him about Gracie Jane, Heather, Darren, John Howard, and Eric Stephens. When I continued as we returned to the living room, Palace Guard and Spike went outside with Lucy.

"I'm not all that surprised at Gracie Jane's reaction. That's typical behavior, at least early in the case when people are still trying to adjust to the shocking news. I'm torn between going to look at deer rifles and relaxing on the back porch with a beer. One of the guys brought me a magazine with an article he said I'd like. Relaxing with a beer, a magazine, and my sweetie wins.

"Jennifer has a recipe for a lemon pound cake. Why don't I pop that into the oven while you relax?"

After I mixed the pound cake and put it into the oven, Glenn called. "I've got a bunch of info and more questions. Jennifer is typing it into an email for me. Let's talk tomorrow. Text or call me when you're free. Is Larry home?"

"He's sitting out back on the porch with a beer and a magazine about deer rifles."

"Good idea. I think I'll take out a beer to the patio. Jennifer invited Ella and Moe to supper tonight. I need to rest up."

"I miss you all, even Moe. Thanks for not hanging up on me. Talk to you tomorrow."

After we hung up, I loaded laundry into the washer then grabbed a glass of sweet tea on my way to the back porch.

"Can I interrupt your reading? How was your day?" I asked.

"It was busy, but I'm starting to get the hang of the office routine. The GBI has a task force assigned to the murders here. I heard Heather might be assigned to the GBI as part of the team, but she'll be undercover, so she can't hang out with us if she comes here."

"I don't like that at all."

"Knew you wouldn't, but if her assignment is at the senior center maybe you could be her new friend, like Rosa in Galveston." Larry finished his beer. "Let's go for a walk. I feel like fresh air and not sitting."

"Ten more minutes, then I can pull out the pound cake to cool."

After I put the pound cake on a cooling rack, Lucy led the four of us to the park on a leisurely stroll. Lucy chased squirrels until she lost sight of them in the trees then flopped down near a bench.

"Let's do a fast walk around the park then we can head back," Larry said.

"Only if you let me set the pace," I said. "Your fast pace is a jog for me, and I'm wearing my boots not my running shoes."

"It's the only way I can beat you. You still run faster than I do."

CHAPTER FIVE

"Why don't you and Palace Guard fast walk, and I'll stay with Lucy and Spike."

Larry and Palace Guard stretched out their long legs and took off.

"I need to remember we're going to run tomorrow," I grumbled.

When sweaty Larry and Palace Guard returned, we all strolled home. While I fed Lucy, Larry took a shower, and even Palace Guard reappeared with his wet hair slicked down and in fresh clothes.

I placed the ribs in the oven to warm up and made a big salad for Larry and a small one for me. After we ate, I sliced the pound cake.

"This is really good, sweetie. You're an awesome cook," Larry said.

Thanks to Jennifer's recipes.

* * *

After Larry left for work, I read the email from Glenn and took notes before I sent him a text. "Call you after lunch. SD"

"Perfect."

"Ready to go?"

Lucy and Spike dashed to the car while I grabbed my backpack before I locked the front door.

When we reached the senior center, Gracie Jane was in her office. I signed in before we all went to Mrs. Martin's room.

Mrs. Martin sat in her wheelchair outside of her doorway, and her face brightened when she saw us. "I was worried you might have a problem this morning. I guess Gracie Jane is over her little snit. Come on in. I have something to show you."

After we were inside, she pulled out a small envelope from her wheelchair pouch. "I agreed, with reluctance, to take the new pill last evening. Did I ever tell you how sleight of hand should be a required skill? I need to teach you sometime." She smiled as she handed me the envelope.

When I opened it, a shiny red capsule was nestled in cotton on the bottom of the envelope. "What is it?"

"Dan Shen also known as Red Sage. You can look it up for more details, but it's an herb that increases the action of prescription drugs that decrease the heart rate to treat irregular heartbeats, act as blood thinners, or treat high blood pressure. It also increases the side effects of those three types of drugs."

I frowned. "That doesn't sound good. Why not just increase the dosage of the original medication?"

"Exactly. So, what would be the impact of doubling to tripling the dosage of a heart medication on the elderly, weaker heart?"

"That's awful. What's going on here? What kind of study is this? Who's running it, and how do we stop it?" I asked.

A fairy danced on Mrs. Martin's left shoulder, and Lucy pranced while Spike did his jig. Mrs. Martin tittered, and I snickered as I rolled my eyes. "I know. That part's mine. So, give me my first sleight of hand lesson."

"There are two major points to master: misdirection and smooth motion. Any jerky motion draws attention. I'll show you in slow motion then you copy me."

After a half hour, we had to stop because we were laughing so hard.

I wiped my eyes. "I'm afraid to walk down the hall because I'll be so focused on smooth motion that I'll fall down."

"Now you know why I use a wheelchair."

Lucy grinned.

One of the older volunteers tapped on Mrs. Martin's door jamb. "Gray Lady, Gracie Jane asked me to tell you to come by her office when you're available."

Lucy flopped down next to Mrs. Martin, and I said, "I'll be right there. Thank you."

I grabbed my backpack before Palace Guard and I strolled to the office.

"There you are," Gracie Jane said. "Close the door, and have a seat."

Sounds serious.

Palace Guard nodded.

Gracie Jane cleared her throat. "Your background check was excellent, but one point I need to discuss with you is that you have a concealed carry permit. Is that correct?"

I narrowed my eyes. "Is that relevant to the volunteer position?"

"In a way. We don't allow firearms or knives on the premises. You are not permitted to bring a firearm with you when you volunteer. I understand your husband is a police officer and would be entitled to have his weapon on his person, but you have no official capacity to bring a weapon into the facility."

"Really?" She flinched when I reached into my backpack, and I rolled my eyes as I pulled out my business card then handed it to her.

"Coyle Detective Agency. Maggie Sloan, Licensed Private Investigator." Her eyes widened as she read. "You're a licensed investigator?"

"Yes. The Coyle Detective Agency hasn't sent me my new card with my married name. They're waiting for my updated license."

"Well, can I keep the card?"

"Why don't I get you the updated one, so you know my license has been updated too."

"Very good idea—I like it. Why didn't you ever mention this before?"

"I work undercover."

"You are perfect for undercover. I love that you're here. Thank you for clearing that up for me."

While Gracie Jane smiled, Palace Guard rolled his eyes then blew on his finger.

I ignored him.

On our way back to Mrs. Martin's room, my phone buzzed a text. *Heather.*

"Call me ASAP."

I hurried to the park and sat on a bench where I could see anyone coming up on me before I called her.

"Maggie, I'm here with Glenn and have you on speaker phone. This jewelry thing is heating up. So far, we know of four senior living facilities with at least two nursing aides murdered in the past month and with whispers of stolen jewelry. We're worried about you."

Glenn added, "The volunteer coordinator called the office and asked Ella if you were an employee of the agency because you claimed to be a licensed investigator. Ella told her to contact her local sheriff's department or her Georgia Bureau of Investigation regional office to initiate a formal query because she didn't reply to cold calls. What's going on?"

I snickered. "I love Ella. Gracie Jane told me my concealed permit wasn't valid at their facility, so I showed her my Coyle Detective Agency business card. She assumed I'm undercover, which would now be common knowledge at the senior center."

Palace Guard raised his eyebrows, and I waved him away as I turned my back. *So, fine. I told her I was undercover. Nosy Palace Guard.*

I continued, "That is interesting that Gracie Jane decided to follow up on it."

"Glenn has a contract from the FBI to provide two people. One will be undercover, and the second is the cover for the undercover. That's you. What do you think?"

"I like it. What does a cover for the undercover do?"

"Larry doesn't like this, and I'm not sure I do either," Glenn said. "You basically keep doing Maggie things to keep the bad guys and everyone else trying to guess what you're going to do next."

"So, I just keep investigating the fake jewelry and the murders?"

"Exactly," Heather said. "You have a knack for making bad guys nervous."

"Will the undercover person be here?"

"We think Columbus is the key, so yes, he'll be there as a volunteer. You know him, so you won't have to wonder who the undercover man might be."

"You said that Larry doesn't like this, so he already knows?"

Palace Guard grinned, and I wrinkled my nose at him.

"Of course, Kate wouldn't have it any other way."

"Must be multi-state if the FBI is involved, and sneaky Kate's the best."

"We think so too," Heather said.

A slender gray-haired man in a black suit and tie nodded as he strode past me with his hands behind his back. "Ms. Gray Lady."

I nodded and smiled. "Good morning."

After the man went inside the building, I asked, "Glenn, am I a licensed investigator?"

"You'll have to go through proper channels." Glenn guffawed, and Heather giggled.

"That's a dad joke, isn't it? You've been waiting this whole conversation to say that, haven't you? I'll call you after lunch."

Palace Guard waved from the door, and I rose. "Palace Guard is calling me, but I have a quick question. Who's the undercover man?"

I waited, but when no one answered, I furrowed my brow and narrowed my eyes. "It's Gary, isn't it?"

"Kate said you'd guess," Heather said.

I hung up. *Dang it. I don't trust Gary Sloan, even if he is my father.*

When I reached Palace Guard, I asked, "Everything okay?"

Palace Guard shrugged as he led the ways to Edna Cross's room. His pace was so fast, I had to trot to keep up with him.

When I reached her room, she said, "I asked a volunteer to find you. Glad he did because this is an emergency. My daughter is nervous about the murders and wants me to move in with her and her family. I love them all, but my daughter drives me crazy. She's already called a decorator to set up my living space in a corner of her living room. She told me her husband had a few misgivings, but she told me not to worry. Can you imagine how miserable I'd be?"

An out-of-breath elderly man leaned against Edna's door jamb. "Oh, good. You're here, Gray Lady. Edna said it was urgent. Do I need to call nine-one-one or pull the fire alarm?"

"No, Edna needed some advice. Everything's okay."

"Good." After he got his breath, he straightened his shoulders and sauntered down the hall.

I furrowed my brow. "Back to your daughter—did you ever live with her?"

"No. When I wasn't able to take care of my activities of daily living, or whatever they're called, at my own home, the social worker and I decided I'd enjoy having my own space while I was around people. We decided I'd be comfortable here."

I raised my eyebrows. "Maybe your daughter needs a little hands-on training. Why don't you suggest she spends the weekend with you? I'm sure the facility can find her a bed like Darren Martin's."

"That's perfect. I'll send her a text. Where's my Lucy?"

"I'll be right back." Palace rushed out ahead of me.

As I reached Mrs. Martin's room, Spike and Lucy met me in the doorway. When we returned, Edna's eyes lit up as Lucy trotted to her.

"Is it okay if I leave Lucy with you for a while?" I asked.

"That would be wonderful. We'll be fine, won't we, Lucy girl?" Edna pulled out a medium-sized dog treat from her pocket and held it in her open hand while Lucy, who had dropped into her best sit, gently helped herself to the treat; Edna giggled when Lucy's soft muzzle tickled her hand.

"My daughter called me right back and said this weekend isn't good for her. I told her that was fine because we could plan on next weekend. She's going to get back to me." Edna chuckled. "I think she's having second thoughts. Did you hear the new experimental pill everyone was taking was recalled? I heard they found metal shavings in the product at the processing plant. Everyone's called their doctor to complain, and the doctors are denying any knowledge. It was all the talk this morning at breakfast. I couldn't imagine missing out on all this juicy gossip."

I smiled. "Would you like for Lucy to spend the morning with you while I visit the rest of the hallway?"

"We'd love it, wouldn't we, Lucy?" Edna rubbed under Lucy's chin; when Lucy lifted her face, Edna gave her a kiss before she hugged her. "Sweet girl," Edna cooed as Lucy leaned against her wheelchair.

Spike sat in the visitor's chair when Palace Guard and I left for the next resident's room. We spent a few minutes in each room while the residents bemoaned how sad it was that Faith died and how awful it was that their new pill was tainted with metal and plastic. *That poor pill is getting worse and worse.*

After we left the sixth room, I said, "Maybe only two more. This is exhausting."

As we passed the next room, the blinds were closed, and no lights were on. Gerald, the janitor, stood in front of a small cabinet next to the wall in the middle of the room. *That's strange. What's he doing in there?*

I moved closer in silence and peered at the necklace he pulled out of the cabinet's top drawer. After he dropped the necklace into a sack that hung from his belt and replaced it with an identical necklace, he closed the drawer and turned to his cleaning cart in a smooth, almost lazy motion. I realized too late that the bright lights from the hallway had cast my shadow over the bed and dresser.

I cleared my throat. "Hi, Gerald. It was dark, so I thought Mary had dropped her call button. I guess she's already left to visit her family."

He pushed his cleaning cart closer to the door. "I wondered about that—guess you're right."

He nodded as he reached for a bottle on his cart, and in one swift motion, sprayed me with a strong solution of commercial cleaner. I threw up my arm against the flood of choking chlorine fumes as he concentrated the fiery stream on my eyes before he knocked me down with his cart.

I screamed as I fell and fought to open my burning eyes. I felt Palace Guard lift me to my feet and half-drag, half-carry me to the room's bathroom. He turned on the shower and placed me under the spray, and as I turned my face to the water, he gently pried my eyes open then left me. I held onto the shower grab bar and willed my eyes to stay open. As I shivered from the cold water, Palace Guard returned, and the water warmed.

My pistol's getting soaked.

When I began to tire, Palace Guard helped me stay on my feet while I continued to flood my eyes.

I smiled in relief at the sound of familiar running footsteps.

"I got you," Larry growled as he joined me in the shower and wrapped his arms around me.

"Hi, honey." I gargled the words as I relaxed at his touch.

When more footsteps rushed toward the room, Larry turned off the water. "I'll help you step out of the shower; the ambulance is here." He wrapped his arms around me. "I'll lead you to the cot."

After I was on the cot, a paramedic flushed my eyes, and I tasted the saltiness of the solution.

"You riding with us?" the paramedic asked.

"Damn straight."

On the way to the ambulance, I pulled on Larry's hand and whispered, "My pistol got wet."

"It's okay, Crazy Lady. I'll take care of it."

"What about Lucy?"

"Got Lucy covered."

I tilted my head back, and the paramedic kept flooding my eyes with water as salty as the ocean. I tried to relax with the calming sea breezes and the rhythmic waves, but the burning sun on the beach scorched my eyes.

As the sea water washed over my eyes and face, I clung to Larry's large, gentle hands.

"Gerald was taking jewelry and leaving duplicates," I said. "I didn't think he noticed me, but he saw my shadow. He sprayed me with commercial cleaner. Palace Guard got me to the shower right away."

"I know, sweetie."

"How did you get there so quickly?"

"Mrs. Martin called nine-one-one; when I heard the location, I knew it was you. Rest your voice. We're at the hospital."

After several hours, I was in a hospital room. When I stirred, Larry kissed me lightly. "Hi, sweetie. Before you ask, Glenn and

Jennifer picked up Lucy, and Spike went home with them. Palace Guard is here. He stayed with you when they kicked me out."

My throat was scratchy, and my voice was raspy. "Thanks." I reached out to touch him, and his sleeve was dry. "Your shirt is dry."

He chuckled. "The emergency department nurse made me go home and change. Why don't I talk, and you rest?"

I smiled while Larry told me about Palace Guard racing to Mrs. Martin's room and telling her to call nine-one-one by holding up nine fingers then one finger twice.

I held up a thumb for Palace Guard then when I tried to feel my eyes and face, something blocked me.

"You have an oxygen mask, and the emergency department doctor bandaged your eyes to let them rest. Palace Guard's fast action of getting you into the shower, and your toughness that kept you under the water saved you from any burns on your face or arm. You have a small cut on your chin from your fall, but it's minor. The plan is to check your vision tomorrow." Larry brushed my hair away from my face and adjusted my oxygen mask. He kissed my ear and whispered, "Thank you for being my tough sweetheart."

He climbed into bed with me and wrapped me in his arms, and I slept.

* * *

When I woke the next morning, I was disoriented by the sounds and smells until I remembered. *I'm in the hospital.* I held out my hand. "Who's there?"

Palace Guard gave my hand a light pat, and I smiled. "Thanks."

"Good morning. I'm your nurse, Mrs. Ewing. Do you feel strong enough to go to the bathroom if I help you?"

I coughed when I tried to reply, so I nodded instead.

"I'll keep my questions to yes and no answers. We definitely don't want you to cough."

I nodded.

She raised the head of my bed to a sitting position before she helped me swing my feet over the edge then ease to a standing position. After we returned to my bed, she said, "Well done. Do you think you could eat? Your breakfast will be here in a few minutes."

I nodded.

As she covered me with a fresh blanket, she said, "Mrs. Ewing, I understand you're the Gray Lady. Did you know you're a legend in the medical community?"

I shrugged and felt my face warm.

"I'm so sorry. I didn't mean to embarrass you. Is it okay if I call you Gray Lady?"

I nodded.

After the nurse left, I heard my favorite voice in the entire world.

"Good morning, sweetheart. Nice to see you sitting up."

I reached out for him and hugged him as he leaned close and kissed my ear.

"Love you," I whispered.

He sighed. "I know." He snuggled my neck then nibbled my ear. "And I'm so glad you do because I love you more."

When I shook my head, he laughed. "I intend to take full advantage of doing all the talking. Let's start with shooting bad guys. You officially have my sincere request that you go ahead and shoot any bad guy you like."

I smiled.

As a squeaky cart rolled toward my room, he said, "Breakfast is on the way. Do you think you can eat? Shall I feed you, or do you want to give it a try?"

I nodded and pointed to myself.

"Gotcha."

After the cafeteria worker placed the tray on my table, Larry said, "We'll be fine. Thanks."

I felt the table then found my plate. "Clock."

"Scrambled eggs are at five; a small bowl of grits is at eleven; dry toast cut in half is on a small plate at two. Definitely not set up for an unsighted person. While I rearrange your plate, you can sip your coffee. It isn't too hot and has a lid on it. I'll hand it to you."

After I held out my hands, Larry tapped my right hand with the cup, and I wrapped my hands around it.

I sipped my coffee and listened while my sweet husband rearranged my food.

"Your toast is buttered and cut into quarters at twelve through two on your plate. Scrambled eggs at six with grits at seven. You have an open napkin left of the plate and a fork and a spoon on the right with the spoon closer to your plate. One second and I'll put your head higher and put a small towel over your chest. After you pick up your napkin, there is plenty of room for you to put your coffee cup next to your plate on the left."

When he placed the towel, he said, "I'll hover and stay out of your way, but if you want me to interfere, hold up a hand."

I smiled and nodded.

After I finished eating, I touched my towel and snickered. *There's as much food on my towel as went into my mouth.*

"You made good use of your napkin—your chin is clean." Larry chuckled. "Are you still hungry?"

I shook my head. *Maybe a taco.*

As Larry removed my protective towel, he said, "What you really need is a breakfast taco, right?"

I nodded. *He knows me so well.*

"Thought so. I know my regulars."

I smiled and nodded again.

When I leaned back to relax, Larry lowered the head of the bed, and I sighed.

"The doctor told me your voice would be near normal in a few days. Meanwhile, I get to talk. Sarge called to tell me your mother wanted to come see you, but they are in the western part of Texas. He asked if they should turn around, and I said no because you tire so easily. They'll be back in four weeks. You should be much stronger by then. The doctor said you've got a couple of milestones to get past, but she suspects you'll be out of the hospital in three weeks."

I held up one finger.

"Are you saying one week, Maggie?"

I nodded.

"I'll help however I can. What can I do?"

I pointed to myself and made a walking motion with my fingers.

"Good idea. I'll check at the nurse's station to see if we can go for a short walk today. Be right back."

I felt Palace Guard pat my shoulder, and I smiled. *Old times, right?*

Larry rushed into my room, and I could hear the excitement in his steps. "You are definitely allowed to walk with assistance. Your nurse told me your doctor wants you to be able to walk to the nurse's station by the end of next week, but she told me she expected the

Gray Lady to push herself and everyone else around her, and she's in."

"Go," I said.

"I bought you a pair of slippers this morning," Larry said. "The nurse said I could take off your oxygen for your walk, but we'll need to put it back on when we get back to your room. One more thing— I brought a pair of your sweatpants and a T-shirt. Ready for me to dress you?"

I smiled as Larry raised the head, so I could sit up. After he removed the oxygen mask and dressed me, I stepped into my slippers and hung onto his arm. As I walked with hesitation to the door, Palace Guard patted my back. *Thanks.*

Larry whispered, "Palace Guard has your back."

I nodded.

"The nurse's station is to the right."

I turned left, and he chuckled.

After we had walked to the far end of the hallway and to the nurses' station, we headed back to my room.

"You have a choice," Larry said. "You can climb back into bed or sit by the window if you'd like the warmth of the sun."

I pointed in the direction of where I thought the window might be, and Larry snickered. "You pointed to the door, but I think I get the idea. Not the bed."

I nodded.

"Okay. I brought a book, so you can relax. Your chair is a recliner, so we can put your feet up, and you can nap if you like."

After Larry helped me sit in the chair, I raised my feet as he raised the footrest, and I leaned back and listened to the noises in the hallway until Larry woke me.

"Lunch is here, and they brought me lunch too. Want to eat in your chair?"

I nodded, and he lowered my feet before he scooted the table to my chair. "Four quarters of a ham and swiss cheese sandwich on whole wheat bread at five o'clock on your plate, tortilla chips at nine o'clock, and apple slices at eleven. Your napkin on your left. Give me a second to grab another small towel. I've asked them to bring you a large cup of ice water with a lid and straw. They'll learn. I have the same thing to eat, and it actually looks good. I put mayonnaise and mustard on both our sandwiches before I cut yours."

He placed the towel across my chest then scooted the visitor's chair close to me. While we ate, my large cup of water arrived, and Larry helped me sip on the straw.

After I ate, I patted my towel, and Larry said, "Much better than breakfast. You have a dab of mustard on the left side of your mouth."

I wiped my mouth twice with my napkin. "Perfect," he said.

Not long after our trays were picked up, a man asked, "Ready for your visual acuity test, Mrs. Ewing?"

I nodded, and Larry helped me into the transport wheelchair. "I'm coming along."

"Yes, sir," the man said.

When we reached our destination, a woman said, "You'll have to wait out here, Mr. Ewing. There isn't enough room for a third person in the examination room."

After I was in the exam room, Palace Guard patted my arm, and I smiled.

"I'm taking off your bandages. Ready?"

I nodded.

As she unwrapped the bandages, I felt freed. *I want to brush my hair.*

When she uncovered my eyes, I tried to blink. "The lights are low. If you can't open your eyes, it's okay. They are probably a little goopy. If you'll tilt back your head, I'll drop in a little saline."

After she added the drops, she said, "Blink for me then I'd like to examine your eyes."

I blinked and managed to open my eyes a little more than halfway. She held my right eye open, and I could feel her warm breath as she moved in close to my face.

"What do you see?" she asked

"Maybe a little light."

She held open my left eye and moved in close.

"What do you see now?"

"Nothing, just maybe dark."

She moved away. "I'll give you a paddle, so we can check each eye separately."

I held out my hand and felt the handle of the paddle touch my palm.

"Cover your left eye. What do you see?"

"A little light."

"Good. Now, cover your right eye."

"Nothing. Maybe dark."

"Okay. After I put more drops in your eyes, I have a temporary blindfold for you. A nurse will come to your room to bandage your eyes; you can ask to have your hair brushed, shampooed, or whatever you like before the bandages go on. We'll check you again in two days."

She applied the drops before she slipped on a paper cover for my eyes that felt like a surgical mask, and a tear slipped from my right eye down my cheek. *Why can't I see any light with my left eye?*

After she rolled me out of the exam room, she asked, "Mr. Ewing, do you have any questions?"

Larry went into her office, and the door closed.

I don't like this. Palace Guard squeezed my shoulder.

You're right. I trust Larry.

When Larry came out of the office, he rolled me back to my room in silence.

After Larry helped me into bed, I said, "Tell."

"The doctor expects your right eye to regain some sight. You protected it when you tried to cover your face with your arm. A commercial cleaning solution is highly alkaline and very dangerous because the injuries from alkali are more severe than acid. Acid burns then it's done. Alkali damage is irreversible because it penetrates deep into tissues and rapidly disrupts cell membranes. More of the solution may have made its way into your left eye."

"Doesn't sound good," I rasped.

"True, but the doctor said you may have protected both of your eyes from the full force. She wants to check you again before she writes up her findings, so your left eye has a little time to allow any of the swelling to go down that might keep you from seeing."

I shrugged. "Sounds better."

"Yes."

I made a brushing motion near my head with my hand.

"I'll grab your hairbrush."

Larry gently brushed the tangles out of my hair.

"Nice," I said.

He chuckled. "I grew up grooming horses. Anyone who was rough brushing out a mane was kicked. I was kicked only once."

I giggled, and Larry kissed me then stroked my hair.

When the nurse came into the room, she said, "We'll check your oxygen levels to see if you've graduated to a nasal cannula. Your hair looks nice."

She placed something on my finger. "Oh good. Much better. After I turn on the oxygen, I'll put in your drops and bandage your eyes with a little softer material to protect your eyes and keep them closed, so they can heal."

After she finished, she asked, "How does it feel?"

I rasped, "Better."

"Good. Time for you to rest. Do you need anything to help you relax?"

I shook my head and leaned back as she lowered the head of the bed.

Larry woke me as he brushed my hair away from my forehead. "Supper in thirty minutes. Walk after we eat?"

I nodded. *I can rest because I feel safe.*

"I have news. Because you caught Gerald switching out jewelry, the GBI obtained a warrant to check all of the jewelry on the premises. You'll never guess what they found."

I think I do.

"They found nothing. Not a necklace, earring, broach, or ring anywhere in the entire facility." Larry chuckled. "You told me their internal communication was phenomenal, and you were right."

Gray Lady's vigilantes banded together. Wonder where they hid them?

After we ate, Larry asked, "Ready for a walk?"

I nodded then sat up before I swung my feet to stand. Larry lowered the bed and waited while I fished for my slippers on the floor.

"Arm," he said, and I reached out until I found his arm and pulled myself to my feet.

"Go." *My voice is less raspy.*

As we walked down the hallway, he asked, "Did you rest with your nap?"

I nodded.

"I made a quick trip home and picked up more clothes for you, and I have your cell phone. Should I take your backpack home with me?"

I nodded.

"I have to go to work on Monday. I'll see about getting the time off to go with you when you have your next vision assessment."

I nodded.

"I'll leave early so you can get some rest. If they offer you something to help you sleep, it would be okay if you take it. Palace

Guard is staying with you, and we've worked out a method for him to contact me if you need me."

It's okay for them to share a secret. I'll hear later.

I held up two fingers.

"Two more times for our walk?"

I nodded; as we walked, he told me about the calls from his mother, Glenn, Jennifer, Ella, and Heather.

After we returned to my room, he kissed me good night before he left. While I waited for the nurse and my bedtime routine, I thought about Gerald and the jewelry. *He was taking orders. I'm sure of it.*

When the nurse brought my bedtime medications, she explained what each one was, but I was too tired to understand. Palace Guard patted my arm, and I took them all.

The nurse helped me get ready for bed. Our biggest laugh of the night was when I brushed my teeth and missed putting the toothpaste on my toothbrush the first time. She helped me undress and tied my hospital gown for me then offered me her arm to lead me back to bed.

After I crawled into the clean, crisp sheets, I thought about Larry as I drifted off into a sweet dream about Larry and fishing on a riverbank while birds sang, and bats circled overhead as they caught mosquitos. I caught a light whiff of chlorine and choked.

Wake up.

Palace Guard raised me to a sitting position and patted my back, and I realized I'd been dreaming. He scooted my recliner close to the bed before he helped me into the chair and tucked the blanket around me, and I slept.

CHAPTER SIX

"Good morning, sweetheart."

I smiled and waved. *I wish I could see Larry.*

"You slept in your chair? Were you restless?"

I nodded. *You could call it that.*

"Really bad dream. Palace Guard helped me," I said.

"Your voice doesn't sound so rough. Did you know that's an indication that you probably don't have any pulmonary issues?"

"Next up, eyes, right?"

"Sounds good to me. Here's your breakfast."

After I ate my bacon, scrambled eggs, and a tiny bite of a disgusting, commercially-baked cinnamon roll, Larry helped me dress then we went for a walk.

As we walked, I said, "I'm ready to go home. What do I need to do?"

"Ditch the oxygen, and you're probably close to that. Keep walking. You've got that nailed. Next is the ophthalmologist, but I don't know what she needs to see before she'll agree to release you from the hospital. I'll make that a question for her tomorrow. I'll also find out if having Lucy would make a difference. She's already a therapy dog at the senior center. That may help. I'll ask."

When we returned to my room, Larry said, "I do have news about Gerald. Want to sit in your chair?"

I nodded before I remembered I could speak.

After I sat, Larry flipped up the footrest and placed a lightweight blanket over my legs. "A wildlife officer who was investigating a report of the sound of a gunshot near a Christmas tree farm found Gerald's body on the side of a county road. Gerald's hands were bound behind him with tape and rope, and duct tape was across his eyes. He had a single gunshot entry wound on the back of his head. He was barefooted, and the bottoms of his feet were dirty, raw, and had been bleeding."

I shivered as a chill ran down my spine. "That's gruesome."

"You're right. I think it was a message to any other Geralds not to get caught like he did. The media is already having a field day."

"Do you think it could also be a message to anyone else that might have seen something?" I was still cold from the chill and pulled up the blanket for warmth and protection.

"I was concerned that his eyes had been covered with tape too. You might be right."

"I feel vulnerable here. Being in the hospital makes me nervous anyway, but this is too disturbing to ignore. If you and Palace Guard weren't with me, I'd walk out right now. Of course, it would take me forever to find the right elevator button to press to go down and even longer to make my way down the stairs." I snickered, and Larry chuckled as he put the footrest down then wrapped me in his arms.

"I'll come get you any time you say." He snuggled me as I leaned my head on his chest and inhaled his comforting man-odor.

"Speaking of seeing, I'll ask Heather what the best text to speech software is. I have some documents I'd like to read, or hear, as soon as I get out of the hospital."

"Wait a minute. Palace Guard said Kate is here." Larry released me. "Yep, I see her now. She's on her way in. How can I help?"

He knows me so well.

"Put me behind the door and put the pillows and my blanket on my bed then flip a sheet over them."

Larry put his arm around me and walked me to a spot behind the door. "Put your right hand out. The door is partially closed. Feel it?" he asked.

"Got it. Go out then throw the door open."

When the door burst open, I shifted to my left to keep from being hit.

"Thanks, I'm ready now."

I listened as Larry rolled my blanket and fluffed the two pillows before he threw the sheet over them. He stayed next to my bed as the elevator dinged and stopped at our floor. I held my breath.

When she burst into my room, Larry said, "Kate! What are you doing here?"

I heard her step into the room as she strode toward the bed. "Not much of an ambush, Crazy Lady. I can see you breathing under your sheet." She laughed.

I rushed toward her voice. Before she could react, I grabbed her arm, twisted then tossed her over my back. She laughed as she hit the floor, and Larry swooped in to grab me from behind and pin my arms before he lifted me off the ground and away from Kate.

"Truce," he called out.

Kate and I laughed even harder.

"You totally caught me off guard," she said, "and I'll deny it forever. Agent Ewing, you did not see a blind, crazy girl take me down."

"You two drive me crazy," he said as I wiggled to get loose. "Truce? Or do I call Jennifer?"

"Lordy, Larry. You sure know how to hit below the belt. Okay, truce," Kate said.

"Truce," I snort-laughed as Larry carried me across the room then set me on my chair. "Stay right there," he said. "Palace Guard?"

I felt Palace Guard's hand on my shoulder and tried to lean forward, but he held me down. *Dang. They double-teamed me.*

"We called a truce, and I can't see her if you stand in front of her like that, Larry," Kate said, and I smirked.

I heard him move to the side.

"That's better. Plans changed courtesy of Gerald's killer. Do you think you can spring her, Larry? I know Palace Guard is here, but too many people have free access to this room."

"She sees her ophthalmologist tomorrow for a vision assessment. I'll know better after we know more about her sight."

"Do they know I'm sitting right here?" I turned my head to the side as I asked Palace Guard.

He patted my shoulder.

"So, what's the new plan, Kate?" I asked.

When I heard her shift to my left, Larry shifted in the same direction.

"Your sister will stay with you," Kate said. "Dad said you had some documents you wanted to analyze. She'll be perfect to help you."

"You're the closest thing I have to a sister; does that mean you are going to stay with me?"

"It would be like the good old days at the cabin, wouldn't it?" Kate paused, and I knew she was remembering when her brother was still alive and visited us at the cabin. "But no. We'll take pity on Larry—I think he'd have Mom on speed dial. It's your other sister."

"Heather?" Larry asked.

"Seems logical to me," I said.

Kate sighed. "You two killed the suspense; I had this whole, big buildup planned. Heather can stay with you or at a hotel—the choice is yours."

"We'll talk about it, but she should get a hotel for tomorrow, at least," I said.

"We'll let Heather know when we decide," Larry added.

"The undercover guy will still be in place at the senior center. Consider him another resource."

"No, thank you," I said, and Larry snickered while Kate sighed again.

She should be careful around a pulmonologist with all that sighing. Palace Guard's hand shook a little on my shoulder, and I could tell he was chuckling.

My mouth quivered, and Larry cleared his throat. *He knows I'm laughing too.*

"You've got my number. Text me if you need me." Kate stormed out, and her footsteps passed the elevator then I heard the stairway door creak open.

"We have the second bedroom Heather could use," I said, "but we'd have to move my computer desk."

"It wouldn't hurt to have a place for guests to stay, but we'll need Ella to help us pack when we move to Tennessee," Larry said. "It would ease my mind when I leave for work if Heather was with you, but I'm sure we could coordinate the timing with her."

"Why don't we wait then? She can stay at a nearby hotel until we have a better understanding of when I'll be released."

"Palace Guard and I agree. We'll wait."

After Larry left, the nurse helped me get ready for bed; after I was settled and warm, she left. As I relaxed, I remembered Larry's sweet good night kiss and smiled.

* * *

When I woke, Larry kissed my yawning mouth. "Good morning, nice person, whoever you are." I giggled.

"Good morning, yourself, Crazy Lady. Heather called late last night. She'll be here later this morning, and your doctor will be here before breakfast for your vision assessment. Jennifer sent me a text asking if she needed to be here. Evidently, Kate told her she visited you last night." Larry chuckled. "Your nurse will be here in a minute to help you dress, and I'm going to see if I can find you a huge cup of real coffee."

"Wow. Real coffee sounds great. Lace it with a little carrot juice, would you?"

"Now, that's an idea. Be back soon."

After he left, my nurse's aide came into my room to help me prepare for my exciting morning. I selected my clothes by feel then she helped me dress.

Before she left, I asked, "How'd I do?"

"You picked out your clothes by the feel of the fabric, didn't you? I love the hot pink T-shirt you chose, and it goes amazingly well with your olive-green sweatpants. It's not what I would have selected, but it looks great. Well done."

I didn't even know I had a hot pink T-shirt.

Larry burst into the room. "Here's your coffee, sweetie. You can sip it on the way to your assessment. The transport guy is on his way."

I held out my hands and Larry tapped my right palm with the cup, and I wrapped my hands around it before I searched for the opening in the lid.

I took a big sip of the hot liquid. "Ahh. Thank you, this is wonderful."

After we reached a testing room, Larry came in with me. "I'll stay out of the way."

"Okay, but pull a chair into that corner to sit. We might be a while, and the lights will be very dim. Are you ready, Mrs. Ewing?" the doctor asked as she began unwrapping my eyes.

She left the covering on my eyes for a few minutes then removed the protective bandage from my right eye.

"What do you see?"

"Light."

"What about now?" she asked.

"Still light, but a shadow?"

After she tested my right eye, she placed a fresh covering over it.

"Now, your left eye." She removed the bandage. "What do you see?"

"Kind of nothing; kind of dark, maybe. Do I need more drops or something?"

"I'll put on a fresh bandage then we'll talk."

After she rebandaged my eye, she wrapped my eyes to hold the bandage in place.

"Let's go into my office. Mr. Ewing, you can help Mrs. Ewing if you like, or we can help her to the wheelchair."

"My arm's in front of you, honey."

I found Larry's arm then pulled myself to my feet. I held onto his elbow as we walked together to the nearby office.

"The chair is on your right," Larry said.

I found the seat and the back of the chair before I sat.

"You two are quite a team," the doctor said. "I'm actually very encouraged by your progress, Mrs. Ewing. The shadow you saw with your right eye was my hand that I put in front of you. I expect at least partial sight will return to your right eye before long. I was worried about your left eye because the initial exam indicated severe damage to the optic nerve, and the indications still point to damage, but all we can do now is wait to see if there's any improvement."

"You don't think I'll ever see normally with my left eye, do you?" I asked.

"Probably not, but I haven't ruled out that you may regain some sight in it. I'll check you again in two days. I've also contacted a specialist in Miami and will send him my findings so far for his review and opinion; I'll have more information next time I see you."

"Can I be released from the hospital now?"

"Ordinarily, I'd suggest several more days, but if we have a home health care aide change your bandages, manage the eye drops and ointment, and take your temperature every day, there's no reason for you to stay in the hospital with the progress you've made in adapting and self-care."

"My husband's a paramedic. Is that something he could do?"

"I don't see why not, and it would be less disruptive to your daily routine. Mr. Ewing, I'll sign the release while the nurse brings you the medications and explains to you the bandaging material you'll need. My office will contact you for the appointment on Wednesday. Call me immediately if she has any pain, no longer sees any light, or if there are any changes in her vision."

After we were in the elevator, Larry said, "I haven't been a paramedic since the last time you wanted to get out of the hospital when we were in Galveston. I'd almost forgotten about it."

"Your skills know no bounds." I snickered.

He snorted. "Certainly does come in handy when your hospital allergy kicks in, doesn't it?"

"I'm really bummed about my left eye," I said.

"I know, sweetie. I'm really sorry about that."

"If it's cloudy on Saturday, would you take me to the range?"

"I like how you think. Yes, we'll go to a range on Saturday. I'll get you some dark goggles for eye protection in case it's sunny."

On our way home, Larry said, "After you're inside and comfortable, I'll call the office and get the rest of the day off."

"No, go to work. I need to rest, and Palace Guard will hover. I'll have my cell phone; I can call you if anything comes up."

"If you promise you'll relax and won't touch the stove, knives, hot water, or anything else that would make me mad then I'll go to work."

"That's simple. I promise."

"I don't know about that. You have a knack for turning simple things into shooting a killer. Now I made myself nervous."

I waited to give Larry time to think.

"Okay, Palace Guard told me to settle down. I'll make you a sandwich for lunch before I leave."

After Larry left, I relaxed on the sofa for ten minutes before I was restless. "I have an idea. Is there something around I could pretend was a cane like a blind person would use?"

I didn't have to see Palace Guard to feel the cloud of disapproval that exploded in the room.

"Don't be so negative, and you haven't even heard my idea yet. It won't make Larry mad either."

Palace Guard put an object in my hand. "A curtain rod? Am I right? It's a little short. Oh wait, I can extend it. This is perfect."

I held the extended rod in front of me as I tap-tapped and took a tentative step forward. "I think I can figure this out, but this is the best part: if I use my left hand to tap, could you guide me by touching my right arm? We'll have to practice so I can understand which way to go. I could tell you where I wanted to go, like mumble or something. Let's try."

"Bedroom," I mumbled as I tapped and moved forward. Palace Guard touched the back of my arm on the left, and I adjusted to the left and continued.

After I felt competent with maneuvering around the house, I circled the dining table and chairs. "Let's go out back. We need to figure out the signal for step down or step up."

"Back door," I mumbled and attempted to step forward, but Palace Guard had a tight grip on my arm, and I couldn't move.

"It will be fine. This is to make sure I won't get hurt, and that would make Larry happy, right?"

Palace Guard touched the middle of my arm, and I moved forward and made a slight left turn before I continued straight and stopped. I put out my hand, found the doorknob, and opened the door. Palace Guard tapped my elbow once.

"One step down." I felt with my curtain rod then stepped down to the porch. "That was perfect. Take me to the second rocking chair."

After we turned, I tapped then found the chair and sat down as sweat dribbled down my back. "This is harder than I thought."

I rocked for a while and listened to the birds and the neighborhood dogs that barked at each other across the fences. I breathed in the sweet aroma of grass as the neighbor mowed and the not-so-sweet, stinky garbage odor from the cans with ill-fitting lids.

"Let's go to the backyard." I rose, turned, and tapped, and Palace Guard signaled for me to continue going straight. We stopped, and I turned left then stopped again. Palace Guard tapped my elbow three times. "Three steps. Do I use the railing?" Palace Guard tapped on the right side of my arm, and I stepped sideways to the right then found the railing. I tapped then stepped down each step one by one as I clung to the railing.

"I'm ready to go back into the house and have lunch." I turned around, but Palace Guard had me turn a bit more then he tapped on my shoulder three times. I found the railing, tapped, stepped, and hung onto the railing until I reached the porch.

After I was inside, I went to the refrigerator with Palace Guard's help and pulled out the plate with my sandwich before I sat at the table to eat.

I felt my sandwich then sniffed it. "It's ham and swiss with mustard and cut into four triangles. Yum."

Before I rose from the table, I swept crumbs onto my plate. I searched for the sink then placed my plate in it.

"I'm ready for a nap. Would you guide me to my bed?" *Too tired to correct myself.*

After Palace Guard helped me find the bed, I pulled down the covers. I kicked off my shoes and wiggled out of my sweatpants before I climbed between the sheets and settled down in our comfortable, non-hospital bed.

When I woke, I listened for hospital noises then I remembered. *I'm home. This is our bed.*

"Where are my sweatpants?" When I heard them drop onto the bed, I patted around until I found them. After I put on my pants, I stood on the floor and searched for my shoes with my foot.

Everything takes forever, but I'm learning, and I'm going to be ready for the killer.

I tapped to the living room while Palace Guard hovered at my elbow. When my cell phone that I had left on the table rang, I tapped to find it and was proud that I answered it before it rang around to voicemail.

"Hello?"

"Hey there, Maggie. It's Heather. I've checked into my room. Are you at home? Please say yes because I'll win the pool."

I snickered. "Of course, I'm home. Larry brought me home from the hospital before lunch."

"Before lunch? That's awesome—I get the bonus pool too. I knew I could count on you. Is there anything you want me to bring?"

"I need good text-to-speech software. I knew you'd know the best."

"I know exactly what would work for you. I'll check your computer to see if you already have it or download it when I get there. There are other apps with more features but starting with the simple text-to-speech makes sense to me. Anything else?"

"I probably could use a good headset. I have earbuds, but a headset might be more comfortable."

"That's easy too. I'm ordering takeout for supper. Do you have any dietary restrictions?"

"Nope. I'm not supposed to sneeze, cough, throw up, fall down, or make Larry mad. Those are the only restrictions so far."

"Ah ha. So, you talked Larry into going to work. Wish I'd had sense enough to start that pool too. I'll text Larry so he can pick up supper for us on his way home. Are you ready for company? Do you need to rest?"

"I've had my afternoon nap, and I'm raring to go."

After we hung up, I said, "I want to brush my hair. It feels like my ponytail came out."

Palace Guard nudged me to the bathroom, but I couldn't find my hairbrush. "I'll bet it's still in my backpack. Maybe Heather can help me with my hair this time."

I sat near the front window and listened. When a car parked in front of the house, I asked, "Heather?" I listened to the footsteps. "Yep, it's Heather."

Palace Guard helped me find the doorknob, and I opened the door as Heather stepped onto the porch.

"That was fast. Did you have help?"

"Palace Guard is here. Come in, and I'll show you what we were working on."

After Heather closed the door, I said, "Back door."

I tapped with my curtain rod while Palace Guard guided me to the back door. I opened the door then stepped down to the porch, and Heather gasped as I headed to the steps. I found the railing then stepped down to the grass.

When I turned around, I grinned, and Heather said, "That was awesome. You looked like a pro with your curtain rod-cane. So, Palace Guard was guiding you? How?"

"We worked out some signals, and he taps on my elbow."

"That was great. We need to get you an actual cane with a white tip. After I set up your text-to-speech, I'll find a medical supply or something where I can get you the right cane. Except you'll want it to double as a weapon too, won't you? Maybe I'll check a pawn shop or martial arts supply store to find you the right stick. We can always paint the tip white, so you can see it if your sight is limited. This is awesome. I was afraid you might be a little down, but you are attacking this sight thing the way you attack everything—head on. Has Kate visited you? What does she think?"

"She visited me last night, but I don't think I'm allowed to tell you that I ambushed her." I snickered.

Heather was quiet for a split second before she burst out laughing. "I am so glad you didn't tell me that. I do have a message for you from Kate. Gary Sloan was diverted to a different case. She told me it was the best get well present she could give you. Is that right?"

"Sure is, but don't tell her I said so."

"You'll explain sometime, right? Where's your computer? I'll check it then load and configure the software."

"It's in the bedroom, but we were thinking about moving it out."

"Where would you put it?"

"I don't really know. Is there enough room in the living room, or if we move the dining table, could it fit in the corner?"

"I'll look at your computer desk." After Heather returned, she shifted the dining table and chairs to make room in the corner. "This is perfect. I'll pull your desk in here then set up your computer."

I relaxed on the sofa and listened while Heather hummed as she moved furniture and set up my computer.

"All set. Come find your desk." She giggled.

I walked straight to the computer with the assistance of my curtain rod and Palace Guard. When I sat at the desk, Heather said, "Impressive. Here's your headset, and it includes a microphone. I installed the new software because it's much better than the basic text-to-speech that came with your computer. I'm starting you with the tutorial first. I expect to be back before you finish the entire tutorial because it has exercises for you. Can I get you anything else before I leave?"

"I may have a cup with a lid and straw somewhere. I wouldn't mind some sweet tea."

I listened while Heather moved around the kitchen then opened the refrigerator and poured my tea.

"Here you go," she said. "It's on the computer desk on your left. I'll wait to leave until after you've started the tutorial."

When the tutorial started, I adjusted the sound and shook off my momentary annoyance that I couldn't see the screen.

After I listened to the introductions and the brief instructions, I said, "I might actually enjoy this after all."

Palace Guard patted my shoulder.

"Thanks for the encouragement."

At the end of the first lesson, I said, "Pause."

I kept on my headset as I finished my tea before I rose and stretched. "My headset is wireless. Heather thinks of everything."

After I sat, I said, "Resume. Skip." I snickered. *Heather knew I'd skip the exercises. We're racing.*

As I finished the last lesson, Palace Guard tapped my shoulder, so I could wait at the door for Heather. When I opened the door, she laughed. "You've finished the tutorials, haven't you? Here's your new cane. Try it out then I'll paint the end white."

I handed her my curtain rod, and she gave me my new cane. "Oh, this feels nice. Is it a walking stick?" I ran my hand down the stick. "It's wood. Is this a small carved section?"

"It's a martial arts staff, except it's a little shorter version and has a ring of tiny flowers. I'll teach you some defensive and offensive moves later. Test it out."

I held the staff with my palm towards my body as I tapped on the floor. "Nice sound. Solid."

"Bedroom." I sauntered to the bedroom with my new cane while Palace Guard guided me with taps on my elbow then we strolled to the living room, front yard, down the sidewalk, and back to the house.

"Awesome," Heather said. "Is it okay if I copy the files you're reading?"

"That would be perfect," I said.

"I've got my laptop. After I've copied them, tell me where we're going to start."

Heather and I spent the rest of the afternoon on Faith's notebook. At four thirty, Heather tapped my shoulder. "I sent Larry a text. He'll pick up supper for us. I know it's cheating in a way, but I took notes and have some questions. Why don't we stop for now and pick up in the morning?"

"A break is a good idea." I removed my headset. "Do you suppose you could find my hairbrush? It might be in my backpack, but I'm not sure where that is."

While Heather searched for my backpack, I rose and strolled to the sofa then back to the dining table with the help of my new cane and Palace Guard.

"Found it. What about the gauze wrap?"

"Forgot about that. Larry's supposed to unwrap it then rewrap it. I'll ask him to unwrap it after we eat then I can brush my hair."

"Sounds good, and if you like, I'll brush your hair. Would you like a single braid?"

"I'd love it."

Larry's truck tires crunched on the driveway before he bounded into the house.

"Hi honey, I'm home." He chuckled as I heard him set sacks on the dining room table. "Who moved the computer desk?"

"Heather did," I said.

"Good. I was worried you'd moved it. Did Heather tell you she heard about food trucks going through town? We're having tacos and beer for supper."

"Really, Heather?" I squealed. "Tacos? That's wonderful."

"The people at the hotel told me about the food trucks that would be here today to test their latest creations before they continue to the food truck competition in Atlanta, and I texted Larry to pick up tacos."

"I also stopped to pick up cookies for dessert," Larry said. "Your cane is wicked. Does it shoot?"

Heather and I laughed then I thought about it. *Hmm. Not a bad idea.*

After we sat at the table, I clutched my beer with two hands then took a sip. "Best medicine ever."

"I heard they're famous for their soft tacos, so they won't fall apart when we pick one up to eat," Heather said.

"You're a genius," I said before I took a bite. "Wow, guacamole inside the taco."

After we ate, I asked, "Can we have our dessert on the porch?"

"Good idea," Larry said. "How can I help?"

I snorted. "Hold my beer."

I rose and strode to the back door with my cane as Palace Guard guided me. I opened the door, sauntered to my rocking chair, and sat.

"Here's your beer. Right hand." Larry said. "You two are great. Did she look like a pro to you, Heather?"

"Sure did. Maggie, you move with no hesitation. You are the picture of complete confidence."

"Good."

After we'd eaten our cookies, Heather said, "Maggie and I made plans for after supper, Larry. If you'll unwrap her eyes, I can brush her hair and braid it."

"Let's go inside. The doctor said the light needs to be dim when her bandages come off."

When we were inside, I sat at the table while Larry removed the gauze wrapping and the bandages.

"I'll close the blinds," Heather said.

After he removed the bandage on my right eye, I blinked. "I can still see light and maybe a shadow moving around."

"Good news," Larry said. "Heather walked in front of you."

He removed the bandage from my left eye. "Any change?"

"Not really. Still kind of nothing."

While Heather brushed my hair, I relaxed. "That feels so good. The bandages and gauze aren't tight at all, but I've been looking forward to them being off."

Heather braided my hair. "Looks good."

"Sure does," Larry said.

"I'm going back to my hotel," Heather said. "If you're called into work, Larry, or need me here for any reason, give me a call, and I'll return right away. Kate said you'd consider having me stay with you, but I'll enjoy the time alone in the evenings. You two were just married, in case you forgot. You need a little time alone too."

After Heather left, Larry instilled my drops and rebandaged my eyes.

I asked, "Can we go to the park? I'd like to walk and hear about your day."

"We sure can. You know, I keep looking around for Lucy to ask her if she wants to go along. Should I ask Glenn and Jennifer to return her? Or maybe we could go pick her up this weekend."

"I like both ideas."

Larry sent a text. "I asked Glenn if it would be convenient for him to bring Lucy back and offered to go pick her up this weekend if he can't get away."

"Perfect."

As we strolled along the path at the park, Larry said, "I went on a body recovery case today. An investigator found a body in an abandoned well. I didn't get any details about the case, which was fine, but there were several people on the scene that had never been around a decomposing body."

"How did you handle it?"

CHAPTER SEVEN

"Parker told me to always carry a small tin of mentholated salve, and I have. This was the first time I've had a chance to smear a little under my nose, and it worked. I've got a reputation now with the guys of being hardcore."

"That's brilliant."

"It is, isn't it? I've had the good fortune to have had excellent coaches. What about you? Catch me up on all that you did."

I told him about the curtain rod, the steps, and the new software.

"Sounds like the software is exactly what you need. You would not be happy if all you could do was to go up and down the three steps. Where did Heather find your cane? Do you know?"

"A martial arts supply store. Why?"

"That makes sense. It's a jo staff—a shorter version of the bo staff, an ancient Japanese weapon that takes advanced martial arts students years to master. It could be deadly in very skilled hands, but it's an excellent defensive tool to incapacitate an attacker. I think one of the guys is an expert. He'd know where you could go for training."

"That sounds interesting. Heather is going to teach me some moves. I'll ask her if I'll need any additional training after she's done."

"Wait a minute. Palace Guard pointed to himself. You're familiar with the techniques of the bo staff?" Larry stopped and hugged me. "This is great news. Palace Guard can watch Heather then work with you tomorrow evening after I get home, so I can interpret and maybe learn too."

A tear dampened my right bandage. "That's great. I can't stand the feeling of being helpless."

"You'll never be helpless, my warrior sweetheart."

I'm a warrior and a sweetheart. I like that.

I lightly explored his face with my fingertips. "Oh good. You look the same." I giggled. "Do you have any idea how awesome you are?" He gave me an extra squeeze before we continued our walk.

"When Lucy gets back, we'll need to go to the senior center. Do you think Heather will mind being our taxi driver?"

"Can we wait until after you see the doctor on Wednesday? Your appointment is at seven thirty, so I won't miss that much work."

"Okay. Let's head back to your truck. The bats are out, so the mosquitos will be biting me soon."

As we hurried to the truck, Larry asked, "How did you know the bats were out?"

"I felt one as it flew close, but I've been listening to their little squeaks."

"Wow. Your hearing has become remarkably acute."

"I don't understand what you mean. I've always had good hearing. Well, except for when I lost my hearing after the library explosion."

After we were home, Larry's phone buzzed a text. "Glenn wants me to call him."

We sat on the sofa together. When Palace Guard sat next to me, I was squished against Larry, and he snickered. "Palace Guard joined us. You have enough room?"

"I'm fine. Call Glenn."

"I have you on speakerphone. Is that okay?" Larry asked when Glenn answered.

"Just fine. So, I 've got a complication. Jennifer wants to come, and so does Ella. Moe wants to come if Ella comes, and Officer Perry doesn't want to be left out. Todd found out that the gang here might come to see you, and he wants to come see Heather. Sierra wants to come if Officer Perry does. If Sarge and Isolde hear the whole crowd is going, Sarge will be a speed demon to get there too. Isolde has already talked to Larry's parents, and I think they're planning a big RV race to beat them."

"That's terrible," I said. "What are you going to do? I know you have another plan."

"I thought about running away from home, but I'd want to take Jennifer, and you know where that would go, so I called Kate. She took pity on her old dad and will pick up Lucy and Spike tomorrow and drop them off at your place on her way to Atlanta. Jennifer already told Kate no ambushes, and I'm supposed to tell you the same."

I snickered. "That was the best version of a dad story that I've ever heard."

"Knew you'd like it. Remember, no ambushes."

"Got it."

After Glenn hung up, Larry chuckled. "He did tell a great story. Are you worn out yet?"

"Close. I'd love a shower before I go to bed though."

"I'll take off your bandages, so you can take your shower." Larry took off the bandages and ran the shower a few minutes to get the water to the almost-hot temperature that I liked before I stepped in and replaced the hospital odor with the sweet fragrance of my body gel then rinsed. After Larry wrapped me in a towel, and I dried off, he helped me to get ready for bed.

"How are you doing?" he asked as he bandaged and rewrapped my eyes.

"Shower was soothing, and I could fall asleep right here."

"Let's get you to bed. I might read a little, but I'll be right next to you."

I yawned as he helped me to our bedroom. "That sounds nice."

After I climbed into bed, I melted into my pillow and listened to a sweet song with words that I didn't understand. *Fairies are singing; I'm officially tired.*

* * *

Whistling and coffee pot gurgles woke me; I smiled as I swung my feet to the floor. After I found my cane near the head of the bed, I headed in the direction of the cheery kitchen sounds.

Before I reached the doorway, a wave of sadness swept over me. *I may never see again.* I leaned over and grabbed my roiling stomach as I panted in shallow, rapid breaths. *Slow down. Breathe in then out. Slow.*

When I calmed my breathing, I felt a light tap on the left side of the back of my arm and turned slightly left.

"Good morning, Palace Guard." He patted my back as I continued down the short hallway.

"Good morning, sweetie. Coffee's ready, and I've planned scrambled eggs this morning. Toast and eggs okay with you? I thought I'd put a little green chile and cheese in our eggs. If you don't like it, I won't do it again. Would you like to get dressed first?"

"Eggs sound good to me. If you'll pick out the clothes for me, I'd like to try to dress myself."

Palace Guard and I followed Larry to the bedroom. "I put your shirt, pants, socks, and a sweatshirt on the bed. Call me if you need help."

"I'll be okay." *A little positive self-talk is good.* "It'll be just like getting dressed in the dark."

I dressed quickly before I tapped my way to the dining table with Palace Guard's help.

"I'll unwrap your eyes to give you a break before I leave for work," Larry said. "Heather will be here soon. Coffee's in front of you."

I captured my lidded cup with two hands then took a big gulp before he removed the wrap and bandages.

"Your coffee is excellent," I said.

After the bandages were off, I cupped my left eye with my left hand as I tried to focus on the table and my surroundings. "The table looks darker than everything else, unless I'm fooling myself."

I pointed to where I thought I saw a shadow more. "Are you right there?" I asked.

"No, but Palace Guard is." I nodded, and as I turned my head to the left, I caught another shadow in my periphery on the right. I glanced to my right and the shadow had a little more form, like a blob. "Are you there?" I pointed to the darkish form.

"Yes. I'm next to the refrigerator. What do you see?"

"Move away from the refrigerator."

I watched as the shadowy blob moved to my left and toward the light before it stopped and blocked the light.

"Are you standing in front of a window or a light?"

"I'm standing in front of the back window."

"I see a shadowy form that moves." I smiled.

"Wow. That's great." The shadowy blob rushed toward me in a blur then Larry lifted me off my chair into a hug and kissed me. After he released me, he moved away, and I sat at the table.

"Best day ever. Well, except for Wednesday before last when we were married." He chuckled as he broke eggs into a bowl then whipped them.

I listened to the sizzle when he poured the egg mixture into the skillet and to the car that pulled up in front of the house.

"Heather's here," I said. "I'll answer the door."

After I rose, Palace Guard tapped my right arm, and we hurried to open the door for Heather.

"Aren't you fancy?" she said as she came inside. "No bandages this morning?"

"Larry will rebandage my eyes after breakfast. I can see shadowy forms." I peered at the smaller blob in front of me.

"What do I look like?"

"A Heather blob." I snickered.

She hugged me. "That's the nicest thing I've ever been called. Kind of pitiful, don't you think?" She laughed and hugged me again.

"Have you had breakfast?" Larry asked. "I assumed you wouldn't eat before you came here and cooked enough eggs for all of us."

"You assumed correctly, sir. Thanks. Coffee refill, my favorite Blind Chica?" she asked.

"Oh yes. Right here in my sippy cup."

Larry laughed. "I'd forgotten how well you two get along."

"You know, I always wanted to work for the police department and be Heather's understudy," I said, "but Kate said I could never pass the psychological test."

"That's true, Crazy Lady. Here's your breakfast. Scrambled egg at six o'clock, and buttered toast triangles at one and eleven. Your fork is on your right. There's strawberry jam on the table, if you're interested."

"I can take care of that for you," Heather said.

"Sounds good," I said.

"Jam's on board. Enjoy."

After we ate, Larry handed me a damp washcloth, and I scrubbed my face and sticky fingers.

"Show me how to rebandage Maggie's eyes, Larry, in case she wants to shower," Heather said.

"It's actually easy." Larry bandaged my eyes and rewrapped them.

"You're right. I got it," Heather said.

"Good. See you later. Don't shoot any bad guys, sweetie. Your aim might be off." Larry chuckled before he kissed me then left.

"I'll plug in my computer and take notes while you get comfortable." Heather loaded the dishes into the dishwasher and washed the skillet.

"Right here at the table works for me," I said.

"Okay. I'm ready. Whatcha got?"

"A little background on Faith: she knew about the fake jewelry and was teaching me to recognize real versus fake. Her father is a retired jeweler, and she spent most of her childhood in his jewelry store. After I read her pages that mentioned discrepancies, I first thought of jewelry, but then I also thought of medicine and money. I don't think she realized at first how serious the fake jewelry was. If she had known that the new pill was Dan Shen and its impact on those who were taking similar heart medications, she never would have dispensed it. She may have stumbled onto something about money that we don't know yet. I'm very curious about the application process for a person to be accepted as a resident, and I wonder if it's common for all residents to have valuable jewelry."

"I've started a list of our items to research. This is a good one to hand off to the team researchers. I'll make sure they understand the question."

"To tie in the Dan Shen with money, I'd be interested in knowing who benefits from the deaths of the residents. Sometimes people leave the bulk of their money to a favorite foundation or charity, and their valuable jewelry, which they love, to their family. Is there a common foundation or charity named as a major beneficiary in the residents' wills?"

"Wow. That one's definitely harder—over the fence it goes to the research team."

"The purely money part—is there any escrow held by the senior center?"

"That's easier. I'll give it to the research team, so they don't think we hate them." Heather chuckled. "Okay, those three are off to the research team. What's next?"

"What did you see?"

"From everything I read in her notebook, Faith was a nice person. I think she treated her notebook as a diary, at least at first. She seemed to be wary of Gracie Jane. I can almost see Faith's hackles raise when she mentions Gracie Jane. Did you ever see the two of them together?" Heather asked.

"I don't think I ever did, but that might not mean anything because the facility itself is spread out."

"She certainly didn't like John Howard, the man who bought her father's business," Heather said.

"According to Darren Martin, John Howard had a crush on Faith and didn't like Eric Stephens. Faith thought John Howard was interfering in her personal business. Darren didn't know why John didn't like Eric. Kind of sounded like jealousy to me. If Kate hasn't left yet, I wonder if she could get a few pieces of my jewelry that I could take to Mr. Howard for assessment."

"I'll text her before I add meet with John Howard to our notes," Heather said. "It's nice to have something concrete to do."

"You'll need to go along with me because I won't be able to see any facial clues."

"Perfect. On your question about who manages the senior center: the business is incorporated. The officers are all out of state; the management is a professional management company that manages a large number of senior centers. In other words, I couldn't find anyone that I could call in charge."

"Isn't that odd?"

"It is to me, but I'm just a cop." Heather snickered. "Glenn is still digging."

"I've got two other loose ends I'd like to pursue at the center. The first is that Mrs. Martin was worried about Faith. I'd like to know why. The second is that Gracie Jane told me Edna Cross makes things up. I never saw any evidence of that. I'm curious about why Gracie Jane said that, and I wonder if Edna could tell me."

"That's interesting; I've added the questions for Mrs. Martin and Edna Cross to our notes, and they certainly are good reasons for you to go to the center. Your real imaginary men go with you, don't they?"

"Of course."

"Good." Heather glanced at her phone. "I got a text from Kate. She contacted your lawyer's office; the admin, Shantelle, will have several pieces for her to pick up at their office."

"I'd forgotten about Shantelle and her jewelry expertise. Could you ask her for hints?"

"I can do that." After she sent the email, she said, "I feel like we've made more progress in an hour than the entire team was able to do with days of work. Nothing like boots on the ground."

"Sounds like grunt work to me." I snickered.

"Dang, you're good. You took my infantry reference and spun it into combat troops."

I patted my hair. "It's what we do. So, what do we do now?"

I listened while Heather drummed her fingers on the table. "Any way we could visit the senior center? Or would Larry disapprove?" she asked.

Palace Guard poked my shoulder.

"I don't see why we couldn't visit. Mrs. Martin listed me as an approved visitor, and I'd need someone with me."

Palace Guard poked my shoulder harder.

"Ow. Palace Guard doesn't approve."

Heather sighed. "Please, Palace Guard? We need you to go along too."

I thought I heard Palace Guard sigh then he tapped my right shoulder twice.

"Let's go," I said. "Am I dressed appropriately to go out in public?"

"You're wearing a red T-shirt, a charcoal gray sweatshirt, and black stretchy-waist pants. Pull on your boots, and you'll be the perfect Gray Lady in disguise."

As Heather drove to the senior center, I said, "I need my right eye to hurry up and heal. I feel underdressed without my carry piece."

"I understand what you're saying. Some of my work clothes when I was undercover were too skimpy to carry a decent weapon. Once I stuck a tiny pocket pistol into my bra, but it was danged uncomfortable and would have been awkward to pull it out. Can you imagine me saying 'Excuse me, Mr. Scum Bag, but I need to pull out a hanky or some other girly item from my brassiere, so I can shoot you before you kill me'?"

We laughed, and Palace Guard poked me.

Sorry. Didn't mean to say something that would embarrass you.

As Heather parked, she said, "Kate told me I'm your sister. I think she's your sister. Can I be Larry's sister?"

"Sounds good to me: My sister-in-law, Heather."

"Larry was originally your cousin when he was undercover after the library explosion, right? So, am I your cousin-in-law?" Heather snort-laughed.

"You are always thinking." I snickered. "Follow me." I led the way with Palace Guard at my elbow.

"Always have, girlfriend."

When we came to the receptionist's desk, I said, "Sis, would you sign us in? We're going to Mrs. Martin's room."

"There was no one at the desk. Is that unusual?" Heather asked as we headed down the hall to Mrs. Martin's room.

"Not really, but I never thought about it before. Does indicate a security issue, doesn't it?"

I slowed then turned at Mrs. Martin's room, thanks to Palace Guard's guidance. When I walked into the room, I asked, "Mrs. Martin?"

"Why, Maggie Flanagan. What are you doing out of the hospital? Do they know you escaped? Do we need to hide you?"

I snickered. "Mrs. Martin, this is my sister-in-law, Heather. Thanks to her and Palace Guard, I can get around a little."

"Nice to meet you, Heather. And I'm plumb tickled to see you again, Palace Guard. Have a seat, Maggie Flanagan. I know this is not a casual, social visit. Do we need to close the door?"

"You know me so well," I giggled. "Good idea."

"I'll get the door," Heather said.

"Get to your questions. I don't want you to wear out on idle chit-chat," Mrs. Martin said.

I nodded. "Why were you worried about Faith before she was murdered?"

"Good question. Faith wasn't herself. I knew she was troubled about something. When I asked her, she told me she was tired. When I called her a liar, she laughed and told me I was right, but I'd be safe if I didn't know. I understood more than she thought and knew she needed someone she could trust. So, when you showed up, I told her she could trust Maggie Flanagan."

"What do you think she was worried about?"

"I'm not sure, but I think it has something to do with jewelry. Her father was our local jeweler for years. He was a remarkably talented craftsman; he designed and made most of the jewelry I own. Faith began working with her father before she could see over the top of the worktable. She had a wooden box that she'd pull up to the table while she worked. I asked her once why she didn't pursue a more artsy career, and she reminded me that medicine was in her blood too. I'd forgotten that her mother was a nurse, and her grandmother was the first woman doctor in town. That was a big to-do, but that's a story for another time."

"I have another question. Gracie Jane told me that Edna Cross makes things up. Is that true?"

Mrs. Martin snorted. "Everyone in this facility makes things up. It's what we do to entertain each other. We have a weekly session in the cafeteria that we call our fireside stories. We used to have it outside, but the bugs drove us inside. But back to your question, Edna Cross isn't a master storyteller, but she's not bad. She does not make things up; she embellishes for effect. Gracie Jane was confused and thought she was talking about herself. Now, she makes things up. She's much more mobile than she lets on."

I nodded. *I can confirm that.*

"Why do you suppose she's pretending to need a wheelchair?"

"We discussed that at one of our storytelling sessions. Did I tell you the storytelling includes gossip?" She tittered. "We think she's hiding from a shady past. One of our storytellers who usually based her stories on facts claimed that Gracie Jane studied law. We tossed around all kinds of theories, but a whole roomful of liars can spin some fanciful tales when each one tries to outdo the other."

And Heather's taking notes. I snickered. "It actually sounds like it would be very entertaining."

"It is. The fairies and I never miss a session if we can help it. I really hated being on the bad medicine."

"Do many of the residents include the center in their wills? Or a foundation or something that the center set up?"

"Almost everyone does when they first come here, but then one of our residents who was a retired lawyer warned us that it wasn't safe to do that. At first, we ignored him because of his dementia, but almost all of us contacted our own lawyers and quietly redid our wills with no fanfare. After we had our brief discussion, we never talked about it again. It isn't safe to talk about some things around here. Most of the residents were afraid they'd be kicked out if they were caught; almost everyone has their assets tied up by the center. I don't because my son is fierce when it comes to me. He said don't sign the paper, so I didn't."

Wonder if Heather's hand is cramping yet.

"Have you thought about leaving the center?"

"No. All my friends are here, and we all understand each other. If I went somewhere new, somebody might think I'd enjoy socializing and group chair exercises and games. Ugh. One thing about Gracie Jane, she has sense enough to leave people alone who can't survive in a cheesy, happy group."

Is Heather writing that down?

Palace Guard patted my back.

Good.

"Palace Guard thinks you need to rest, you know," Mrs. Martin said.

"He's probably right, but I'd like to visit Edna Cross too, except I have one more personal question."

"Go right ahead, Maggie Flanagan. You're allowed."

"What on earth did the vigilantes do with the jewelry?"

"You may have to take it up with them, but I may have heard that dear Faith's locker was available." She cackled, and I snickered.

"Thanks, I should have known. I'll drop in on Edna Cross for a quick visit then we'll go."

"It was nice to meet you, Heather. Palace Guard, you are as sharp as ever."

On the way to Edna's room, Heather asked, "Are you doing okay?"

"I am running on fumes, but I'd like to visit with Edna at least for a minute or two."

I stepped into Edna's room. "Edna?"

Her wheelchair tires squeaked as she turned away from the window. "Gray Lady! You look amazing. Is the eye covering to let your eyes rest?"

"Exactly. I need a little healing time before I try to exercise them. This is my sister-in-law, Heather. We can't stay long, but I wanted to come by to visit you. How are you doing?"

"I'm fine. I signed up for a bird identification class because I got word some certain person was planning to take away my binoculars."

"Who?"

"Gracie Jane, of course. She told my daughter that I'm breaking the rules by having binoculars. My sweet daughter told her I was taking a bird identification class. My choice was to take a class or have my binoculars confiscated."

"I vote take the class," I said as Heather cleared her throat.

"We need to go. Hopefully, I'll be stronger on my next visit."

"It was wonderful to see you. Stay alert, sweet girl. There's a trap ahead of you."

"Who is setting the trap?"

"I'd tell you if I knew; I have the feeling you'll be ready."

"I plan to," I smiled.

As we headed home, Heather said, "We got a lot of information today. I'll write it all up for you and me to review. Too bad we didn't run into Gracie Jane. I would have liked to have met her."

"I don't think that was an accident. Gracie Jane was avoiding me for some reason, but I don't know why."

"You have a wealth of untapped resources at that senior center. Why does Mrs. Martin call you Maggie Flanagan?"

"She told me I remind her of her old friend, Margarite Flanagan, my great-grandmother."

"Who are the vigilantes?"

"Mrs. Martin told me she was a private in the Gray Lady's vigilantes. Sounds like she recruited the entire senior center, doesn't it?"

"Mrs. Martin is absolutely amazing. I could listen to her stories all day—true or not. I understand Faith better now. As soon as I get home, I'm going to quit my job and become a health care aide, or better yet, let's frame Gracie Jane, and I'll take her job."

I laughed so hard, I snorted. When I caught my breath, I said, "Gracie Jane needs a good publicist because, right now, her ratings as a good guy are at an all-time low."

"Let's grab something for lunch. What do you suggest?"

"Darren Martin introduced me to a café that's near Mr. Bustamante's shop. We could go there. The food is awesome."

"My stomach rumbled when you said awesome. Where is it?"

"Downtown. Park wherever you find a spot because the shops along the way are part of the downtown charm."

"Won't that be sad for you?" Heather asked.

"Of course not. I'll enjoy hearing what you saw."

When we went into the café, Rafael said, "Gray Lady! How great to see you again. We heard about the attack on you, and we all think you are amazing. Would you like to sit in the back or closer to the door?"

"In the back," I said.

After we were seated, I asked, "What do I want today for lunch?"

"Chef came in early to make tamales. How about a soft taco and tamales?"

"That sounds like heaven."

"Your server will be right here."

Rafael brought me sweet tea in a large cup with a lid and straw. "You are a celebrity around here. I've got an in with the Big Guy and put in a word for you. You can expect a fast recovery."

My weeping right eye soaked my bandage. I choked as I said, "Thank you. I need all the help I can get."

After he left our table, Heather leaned close and whispered, "I had a little overflow there myself."

The front door opened, and from the sound of the footsteps, a large man entered the café.

Our server brought Heather her large glass of iced tea. "Taco and tamales, right?" she asked. "How about a side of guacamole and some chips?"

"Sounds perfect," I said.

After our server left, Heather mumbled, "Large, middle-aged man with brown hair and dimples coming our way."

"Mrs. Ewing," a man said, "I'm John Howard. I bought Mr. Bustamante's jewelry business, and Faith was an old friend of mine." He cleared his throat. "Excuse me for interrupting your lunch, but I heard about your attack, and I'm sure it was related to the attack on Faith. I'd be honored to help you anyway I can."

He stopped at the cash register then left the café.

"Wow," Heather said. "For the record, our most likely suspects are you and Mrs. Martin. How am I doing?"

I snickered. "Not bad. Isn't it always the ones you least suspect?"

"I can't believe how fast all this is unfolding," Heather said.

The server brought our food to our table. "Ms. Gray Lady, your silverware and napkin are on your right; tamales are on the right side of your plate; chef cut them into one-inch bites for you. Your soft taco is on the left. Guacamole is on your plate, not in a bowl, and the chips are in a basket next to your plate close to the guacamole. Let me know if you need anything."

"That was very thoughtful," Heather said.

I nodded and stabbed where I thought a section of tamale might be. "Success." I stabbed and ate several bites of my tamale then scooped up some guacamole with my fork before I picked up my taco and took a bite.

"This is my new favorite place to eat," Heather said after we'd finished eating.

"I can buy if you'll pull out my credit card. It's in my wallet in my backpack."

"You can be responsible for dinner," Heather said. "Does that make you feel better?"

"Yes, as long as you don't come up with some way to finagle me out of it."

"I have an idea…did I see a new grill in your backyard?"

"Yes, but I'm the grill master when Glenn's not around," I growled.

"Perfect. You test the doneness by feel, right? That's how my dad always grilled."

"Of course, and Palace Guard can help me, so I'm checking steaks, not the hot grill."

"I'll stop at the grocery store and pick out steaks and accompaniments. Do we plan on Kate to eat with us?"

"It would be great if she would, but I suspect she'll need to get back onto the road fairly quickly. I'm not sure how much sandwich fixings we have. Maybe we should have extra on hand. As an alternative, I could grill an extra steak for a steak sandwich for Larry and a steak salad for you."

"Good idea—four steaks it is. While you grill steaks, I'll prepare the rest of the meal. How's that?"

"That'll work. I'm about due for some good grill smoke therapy. Add mesquite chips to your grocery list."

Palace Guard and I waited for Heather while she shopped. "She can move a lot faster if she doesn't have to keep an eye on me," I said, and Palace Guard patted my back.

After Heather returned to the car, she unloaded her cart. "Hang on. We're in a hurry because I bought ice cream for dessert."

On the way, she asked, "What's on our agenda for the rest of the afternoon? Do you need some rest time?"

CHAPTER EIGHT

"I do need a quick nap before Kate shows up with Lucy and Spike because I don't think I could last very long without one. I'd like to take a shower and shampoo my hair, but that's a lower priority than discussing your notes from today. I'll let you plan our schedule."

"If you'll nap when we get to your house," Heather said, "I can put away the groceries and type up my notes. After you're rested, I'll remove your bandages so you can shower. We'll just work around Kate's arrival. We'll have plenty of time for me to braid or style your hair while we discuss our notes."

When I was in my bedroom, I kicked off my boots before I grabbed my pillows. *I'll just rest a few minutes while the fairies sing.*

Palace Guard tapped my shoulder, and I rose from the bed and stretched. After I found my jo, I tapped to the kitchen with Palace Guard making only minor adjustments in my direction.

"Glad you're awake, Maggie. Kate stopped for a break for Lucy and will be here in forty-five minutes. Ready for a shower? If you'll sit, I'll unwrap your bandages. Want some tea?"

"I would love some cold tea, thank you." I made my way to my chair at the dining table and sat. After Heather tapped my right hand with my large cup with the lid and straw, I sipped, and she unwrapped.

"Ahh," I said after she'd unwrapped the gauze that held my eye bandages in place. When she removed the covering from my right eye, I blinked as I tried to focus on the blob in front of me. "Is that you in front of me, Heather?"

"Yes. Have I changed?"

"No, you're still the Heather blob you've always been."

"Ha, ha," she said. "I guess it's better than a lump."

You're too tall to be a lump.

Palace Guard poked my arm.

Sorry.

I crossed my fingers as she removed the bandage over my left eye; I blinked then sighed. "Still the nothing dark, whatever that is."

"Sorry. After you finish your tea, you can take a shower then I'll brush your hair. Any special request for your clean clothes?"

Something I can see. I shrugged. "Whatever you pick out is fine."

"I got a text from your friend Taylor while you were sleeping. She wanted me to paint your fingernails bright pink and neon green as a surprise from her, but I wasn't supposed to tell you. Why is that?"

Leave it to Taylor to burst my personal pity bubble.

I giggled. "When I was in the hospital after the explosion, Taylor painted my toenails all kinds of bright, non-spy colors but wouldn't tell me what color they were. I couldn't see my toes because I was pretty much immobile with all my broken bones. Drove me crazy."

Heather snickered. "So, what color clothes shall I pick out for you?"

Dang, she's good.

"Navy would be lovely," I mumbled.

Heather laughed. "You're going to have to sound grumpier than that if I'm supposed to feel sorry for you."

"I'll work on it. Lead me to the bathroom, and I'll jump into the shower."

Heather fiddled with the water while I undressed. I held onto her forearm for balance as I stepped into the shower. After I scrubbed with the peach fragrance shower gel, I shampooed then rinsed my hair.

"Ready to get out." I turned off the water before I reached for my bath towel and wrapped it around me. After Heather towel-dried my hair, I padded to the bedroom and dressed.

I tapped my way to my dining room chair.

"Will the hair dryer bother you? I just remembered your hearing."

"I didn't think about that. Can we try it?"

Heather turned on the hair dryer; when I covered my ears and cringed, she turned it off.

"I'll towel-dry as well as I can then comb out your curly tangles and pull up your hair into a ponytail."

While she combed, I asked, "What's the first item on our list to discuss?"

"You asked Mrs. Martin why she was worried about Faith. Just an observation, but it seemed to me that Mrs. Martin never answered any of your questions; instead, she directed the conversation in a different direction before she told you something she wanted you to know."

"Right. She mentioned that Faith knew jewelry, and her father was a craftsman. Faith could have very easily learned the craft of jewelry-making from him which is why she was so extremely skilled at spotting the phony jewelry."

"Yes. Also, I wonder if Mr. Bustamante created the look-alike fakes," Heather said.

"I don't think so because Faith told me that the replica jewelry wasn't as good as her dad's work. Of course, maybe she recognized the work as his, and he made the replicas thinking they were for the families, but that's a pretty far-fetched theory, even for me."

"The next question you asked her was why Gracie Jane might have said that Edna Cross made things up, and Mrs. Martin turned the conversation completely around to Gracie Jane not being as immobile as she appears."

"I can actually vouch for that. I met her at Mr. Bustamante's house to return Faith's things from her locker. Gracie Jane left before I did, and I happened to watch her from the window."

"Purely accidental." Heather snickered.

"Always." I smiled. "She rose and folded up her wheelchair before she lifted it into the back seat of her car then hopped into the driver's seat and drove away. I had glanced inside her car when I first arrived at Mr. Bustamante's house, and the accelerator and brake were operated by hand. It wasn't a cheap knock-off conversion like a good-natured local mechanic would have done for a low cost. It looked factory-installed, and certainly would not have been cheap or fast."

"One explanation is that Gracie Jane is able to stand and walk a few feet, but that's the full extent of her capabilities."

"Could be," I said. "On the next topic, is it usual for a senior center to take over a resident's assets? Completely tie them up?"

"I don't know. We'll have the team check that, but it actually seems logical to me. The resident is guaranteed they can't be thrown out or the price raised higher than they can pay. I don't think including the center or one of its charities in the will is usual though. More for the team to check."

"Maybe I should have been worried when Edna Cross said there was a trap ahead of me, but I was actually comforted because she told me I could handle it. I am curious as to who told her that though." I rose from my chair. "Feel like training me with my stick?"

"I'd like that. We could go out back, and I've been thinking about the best way to train you. You can't tell anyone this was my idea, but I think after I talk you through a few moves then I can point in a direction of an attacker, and Palace Guard can signal which way you should swing. Would that work?"

"That's brilliant. Let's go."

After Palace Guard corrected the direction I was facing, I headed for the back door. I stepped down to the grass, and Heather explained how to hold my stick and swing and swerve so that no one could take away my jo.

I stabbed, shifted, and swerved. When Heather said, "Again," I smirked. Spike's favorite word.

"Ready for an attacker?" Heather asked.

"Let's go."

Palace Guard smacked my right arm, and I ducked, swung, and swerved. When he tugged back on the neck of my shirt then smacked my left arm two times, I stepped back and swung then swerved to the left and swung twice in rapid succession.

"Wow," Heather said, "you two are awesome. Good work, Palace Guard."

We worked until I was panting from the exertion.

"That's enough for now," Heather said. "Let's go inside. Water or tea?"

"Tea." I stepped up to the porch then found the doorknob and let myself into the house.

"If you'd like to sit in the living room and put up your feet, I'll bring you a large glass of tea."

I kicked off my boots before I stretched out on the sofa. Heather handed me my large, lidded cup, and I took a big drink through my straw. "Thanks. Hits the spot."

After I'd finished my tea and slurped the last few drops, I paused to listen. "A car's headed this way. I'm excited—I'll bet it's Kate. Sweet Lucy's almost here. Palace Guard, I want to wait out front for her."

I stepped into my boots and grabbed my stick. Palace Guard guided me as I hurried to the front door, and we went outside. I heard a car coming down the road then Palace Guard pushed my back. *Down.* I dove for the dirt and flattened myself as much as I could as a bullet thunked into the side of the house. *Stay down.*

Three rapid-fire shots rang out from the front porch as the car sped away.

I started to rise, but Palace Guard's hand on my back held me down.

I listened as Heather raced to the end of the driveway. "Come inside," she shouted as she ran back to the house.

Palace Guard helped me up then we dashed to the house. When we were inside, Heather said, "On the phone."

Her voice changed to cop-speak. "Yes, a drive by shooting. I'm a detective with the Harperville Police Department. I shot the passenger. May have been a fatal shot."

After she hung up, she asked, "Are you okay? I thought I saw something push you to the ground. Was that Palace Guard? That car shot at you before I reached the door."

"Yes, Palace Guard is amazing."

"First time I've actually almost seen him in action. Well done, sir. Maggie, we'll have visitors soon."

"Larry will be the first one here," I said.

"No doubt." Heather snickered. "You're shaking. Excitement?"

"You got it."

"Sit on the sofa. You're making me nervous."

A car roared toward the house from down the road then skidded to a stop in front of the house. When the front door slammed against the wall as it swung open, I said, "Hi, honey."

Larry grabbed me up and held me tight. "You scare me to death. What were you doing?"

I guess I can't say I was waiting for a killer. He's probably not in the mood for a joke.

I mumbled into his chest. "I heard the car and thought it was Kate."

"You saved her, didn't you, Palace Guard?" Larry asked.

"He did," Heather said. "I glanced out the window and thought I saw a shadow push Maggie down. She flattened herself on the ground right before the shot hit the house behind her. Palace Guard is amazing."

"There's a cruiser. I'll be back in a minute." He set me down on the sofa before he left.

"I'm going out too," Heather said.

"I'd feel abandoned, but at least nobody's yelling at me, right?" I held up my hand; when Palace Guard smacked it with a high five, I snickered.

"What are you doing?" Larry asked.

Busted.

"We're celebrating the unsuccessful drive-by shooting."

"I don't believe you," Larry grumbled.

Fair enough.

"Heather was right about her shot," he continued. "A local police officer found a man on the side of the road two blocks away with a fatal gunshot wound. Guess his buddy dumped him."

"She fired three shots," I said.

"The officer also found a trail of blood from the road to the body then back to the road. Sounds like the driver was hit too; we've alerted all the nearby hospitals. You must have looked like an easy target. I hate that. My boss wants to know if you'd be safer with your folks. What do you think?"

"I belong here with you," I growled.

"That's my sweetie."

I smiled at the pride I heard in his voice.

"I need to go back to the office. Will you be okay?"

"I'll be fine. I've got Palace Guard and Heather."

He slowly brushed the front of my shirt.

"I'm leering," he whispered, and I giggled until he kissed me with more passion than his usual good-bye peck, and I melted.

"See you after work," I said after he released me.

"Be safe."

As Larry left, Heather came inside then clicked the lock. "I'm getting an even better idea of what life with the Gray Lady is like. You want some tea?"

"Sure do." I tapped my way to the sofa.

"I'll get busy with my part of the meal prep before Kate gets here."

While she worked in the kitchen, she said, "I didn't get a good look at the driver, but I'm sure he was a hired thug. Are you worn out?"

"It's really annoying, but I am."

"Just relax. We'll have more excitement when Kate, Lucy, and Spike show up."

"Sure will." When I leaned back, I was surprised how tense my shoulder and back muscles were.

When I heard footsteps then scratching at the front door, I jumped up and collided with Heather, who caught me before I fell. "Hang on, Gray Lady. I'll get the door. Why don't you sit back down, so Lucy won't mow you down?"

Heather opened the door, and I grinned as Lucy scrambled across the floor then leapt next to me on the sofa. I hugged her and cooed. "Sweet Lucy. Missed you, pretty girl."

"Missed you too," Kate said. "What's been going on here? Quit swooning, Spike."

I laughed as I imagined Spike as he hovered around Heather.

"Just a little drive-by shooting," Heather said. "No injuries except for the shooter and probably the driver."

"That's nice," Kate said. "How's your sight, Gray Lady?"

"According to the doctor, I may regain some sight in my right eye, but my left eye isn't doing as well."

"Cruds. Sure hate to hear that. How are you feeling?"

"Actually, pretty good. Can you stay for supper? I'm grilling steaks, and Heather's taking care of everything else."

"Can't. I need to hit the road. Mom packed me a picnic, so I won't starve, and she sent you a few things. I'll get the cooler."

When she returned, she carried the cooler to the kitchen. "Shantelle sent you some jewelry. She said to call her if you had any questions about it. Mom sent some sausage that I made, her cherry pie, cookies, cinnamon rolls, and a pan of lasagna. The sausage and lasagna are frozen. Here's something else, Heather. Do you have ice cream?"

"Sure do," Heather said. "I'll make room in the freezer for the lasagna and sausage."

"What was the something else?" I asked.

"Oh. The cherry pie," Kate said.

I'm sure I lie much better than Kate does.

Kate sat next to me on the sofa. "I've got all kinds of messages for you from Mom, Dad, and Ella—you know, the usual tell-Maggie-this and tell-Maggie-that. They're worried about you, and they want you there where they said you'd be safe. I told them that they were safer with you here." Kate chortled, and I snickered. "Heather, call me if Maggie needs anything. Maggie, you got this."

When Kate hugged me, tears welled up in my right eye. She strode to the kitchen and snatched up the cooler then she was gone.

"Are you crying?" Heather asked.

"That was so sweet." I sniffed.

"It was downright mushy for Kate," Heather giggled, and I'm sure Spike fainted because Lucy jumped off the sofa, trotted to the kitchen, and whined.

"Get up, Spike. You scared Lucy," I said.

Lucy scrambled to the back door then went outside.

"The door opened itself, but it didn't, did it? Spike opened it?" Heather asked.

"Yep. Would you call Shantelle for me? I'd like to talk to her."

Heather handed me her phone. "It's ringing."

When Shantelle answered, I said, "Hi, Shantelle. It's Maggie. Thanks for sending me some jewelry. Are you certain it's all genuine?"

"It sure is. I verified it myself then took it to a jeweler. I wanted everything to be certified so we could insure it."

"That's great."

"Now, you have to tell me why."

"There's some authentic jewelry at the senior center that is being replaced with replicas. I needed some pieces that I knew were authentic."

"Oh, good. A trap. Let me know if I can help. Just call me, and I'll head that way."

"Thanks. I'll remember that."

After we hung up, Heather asked, "Where do we start? John Howard?"

"I think so. After my doctor's appointment tomorrow, I'd like to go to the senior center then visit John Howard after that."

"Why don't I take the jewelry to John Howard? I'm not as well-known as you are."

"Hadn't thought of that. You could visit him while I'm at the senior center then come pick me up."

I rose. "I have trouble keeping track of time. Is it almost time for Larry to be home?"

"He gets off work in thirty minutes unless he's tied up with something."

"I'd like to sit outside. I need fresh air and nobody shooting at me."

"We've got fresh air, but after today, I can't guarantee no shooting. Would you like your bandages off now, or wait until after we eat?"

"Both, but I'll wait. I wouldn't mind a shower later after my dirt dive."

When I sat on my rocker, Lucy trotted to me and laid her head on my knee. I stroked her head. "I missed you, and I'm glad you're back. We'll go visit all our friends at the senior center tomorrow. They'll be happy to see you."

I heard the front door open, and Heather said, "She's on the back porch."

The back door opened then Larry kissed me, and Lucy whimpered.

"Okay, Lucy. You're a good girl, and I missed you too. How you doing, Spike?" Larry chuckled. "I missed your jig. Glad you're back."

"We have steaks, and I'm grilling," I said.

"You're the grill master. Okay if I light the grill for you?"

"I'd appreciate it." After I rose, I found his face and kissed his chin. "I was aiming for your mouth," I grumbled, and Larry kissed my mouth.

"Thanks. I'll pull out the steaks while you get the fire going." I headed inside with Palace Guard at my elbow.

"What can I do to help you?" Heather asked.

"I need the steaks on a plate for now."

While the grill heated, I hummed as I waited in the kitchen for the steaks to come to room temperature; Heather continued her preparations for dinner.

"That's a really haunting melody," Heather said. "I've never heard anything like it."

"It's a tune Mother used to hum when she was in the kitchen. I'd almost forgotten about it. I don't think she remembered that I could hear her."

After I threw the steaks on the grill, my stomach growled at the sound of the sizzle and the smell of singed meat on the hot metal grid. *I didn't realize how much I missed my grill.*

When I touched the steaks, each one had the perfect feel of medium-rare. "Steaks are ready to come off the grill."

Palace Guard guided me as I lifted each one from the grill and placed them one by one on a platter to rest. *Resting has become very high on my list of priorities these days.*

I smiled. "You can breathe now, honey."

Larry snorted. "You knew I was hovering the entire time."

"Of course. That's what you do."

After our food was on the table, Larry asked, "Okay if I cut your steak for you, sweetie?".

"I'd appreciate it. I know I'll learn how to cut my own food eventually, but maybe I'll have more sight later and will be less likely to cut off a finger." I popped a piece into my mouth. *Tender and succulent. Ahh.*

After I ate what I could, I said, "I left room for pie and ice cream."

Heather snickered. "Why am I not surprised? I'll pull out the pie from the oven after I clear the table."

"I'll clear the table," Larry said. "Pie is always a priority."

Heather placed a bowl in front of me. "Your spoon is on the right. I cut your pie into Maggie bites, Larry put your ice cream on top, and it's melting. Go, girl."

I can win this race. I dug in, and savored each bite of the crunchy crust, the sweet, warm cherries, and the softened, oozing, vanilla coldness.

I searched my bowl with my spoon until Larry put his hand over mine. "There's nothing left sweetheart. You've eaten it all."

"I didn't want to miss any," I said.

Heather removed my bowl and spoon. "I'll load the dishwasher. Are you ready for Larry to unwrap your eyes?"

"Yes, please."

Larry gently unwrapped the gauze then removed the right bandage, and I blinked. *Still a little light with blobs.*

"Same," I said.

"We knew it would be a slow process," Larry said.

Not a hint of sadness. Maybe he's right.

Palace Guard poked me.

"What?" Larry asked.

Oops.

"You're right," I said.

"Did you just fist-bump a shadow?" Heather asked, and I snorted.

"I'm ready for my shower," I said.

After my shower, I dressed in soft pants and a T-shirt. Heather towel-dried my hair with enthusiasm then attacked my tangled curls.

"Shall we just leave your hair down then I'll put it into a braid or ponytail tomorrow?"

"I like that. Thank you. Did you just invite yourself here for breakfast?"

"I can cook or stay out of the way. I'm multi-talented that way," Heather said. "And if that's all I can do for you, I'll see you early in the morning."

After Heather left, Larry and I sat on the sofa together. I leaned against him, and he held me. "Spike's pouting," he whispered.

"Let's go outside. Lucy wants to explore the yard," I said.

I carried my cane like a staff while I held onto Larry's arm.

"Is the moon out?" I asked.

"It's a half moon, but there are clouds drifting in. We might have rain tomorrow."

I listened to the crickets and tree frogs and sniffed the air. "You're right about the rain. It'll roll in tonight." I positioned my right elbow on the arm of the chair and supported my head as I leaned on my fist.

"Are you tired, Maggie? You're fading."

"I feel like such a lightweight."

Larry scooped me up and carried me inside. "I'll rebandage your eyes then you can pretend like you're awake, or you can snuggle down into our bed. I'll take a shower and join you in that snuggle."

I hung onto his neck and kissed his chin. "Best offer I've had all day."

"I love this bed." I hugged my pillow while Larry tucked the covers around me.

* * *

When I woke, I felt the bed next to me. *No Larry. Must be time to get up.* I bumped into a wall but didn't fall. *Take your time.* I moved more slowly and swept in front of me with my jo as I padded down the hall to find Larry, and Lucy clicked along behind me.

I stopped when I didn't smell any coffee. "Larry?" I asked.

"What are you doing up, sweetie? It's three o'clock in the morning."

"You weren't there, so I thought it was time to get up."

"I couldn't sleep. Too much to think about."

"Are you on the sofa? Let's snuggle."

Larry met me in the hall and wrapped his arm around my shoulder as we walked together. He threw the afghan over us when we stretched out together on the sofa.

"Hang onto me, so I don't fall," I said.

"Always." Larry breathed the word into my hair, and I relaxed.

I woke to the smell of coffee. "Coffee time?" I asked, and Larry chuckled.

"Heather will be here in ten minutes. She's going to scramble eggs. I pulled out some sausages to thaw, and the cinnamon rolls are on a pan to go into the oven to warm."

"You're awesome. What do I wear to the doctor's office?"

"That's Heather's department. Can I help you with anything else?"

"Fill my sippy cup with coffee is my first priority for the day."

"You got it, sweetie."

He tapped my right hand then held the cup for me until I wrapped both hands around it. As I sipped my coffee, I listened to the patter of raindrops on the windows.

I asked, "When did it start raining? How did you sleep?"

"I didn't hear the rain at all until I woke up. After we came out here, I slept very well in that tiny space on the sofa with you."

I snickered. "It seemed like plenty of room to me. Told you I belonged with you."

"And you were right. Refill?"

I tipped my cup to finish my coffee, but it was empty. "Yes, please."

Larry refilled my cup then replaced the lid. "Here you are. Spike said Heather's almost here."

"He would know. I'm excited to hear what the doctor has to say. I'd love it if the wrapping and bandages were no longer necessary. Do you think that's possible?" I asked.

"I wouldn't even try to guess. We can hope, though." When Larry strode to the front door and opened it, I listened to the rain and inhaled the clean smell of the wet grass.

Heather hurried to the porch and shook an umbrella before she came inside. "I think it rained all night. Ready for breakfast? Here, Larry. This is from Jennifer."

"What is it?" I asked.

"A sack," Heather laughed. "No big secret—Jennifer sent you more clothes. She told me to give them to Larry because you'd want the sizing washed out."

I smiled. "She knows me so well."

After we ate, Larry said, "As soon as you're dressed, we can leave for the doctor's office."

"Ponytail or braid?" Heather asked.

"Let's go with the ponytail. It's the fastest," I said, "and I'll need you to pick out clothes for me, so I can dress."

"I've got an idea for your clothes, but we'll talk about that later."

Heather combed my hair then pulled it back into a ponytail before she hurried with me to the bedroom and picked out my clothes.

I dressed and sauntered into the living room with my jo. "Let's go."

"Lucy and Spike could ride with me," Heather said. "We could meet you at the doctor's office. Larry, I'll take care of the dishes if you'll text me when I can pick up Maggie."

On our way to the doctor's office, I said, "I'm nervous. I don't know what to expect."

"I understand, sweetie." Larry parked in front of the doctor's office. "Ready to go in?"

"Yes and no." I inhaled a big breath then blew it out. "Okay, ready."

The doctor was waiting for us. "Good to see you. Let's go to an exam room first then we'll go to my office to talk."

She unwrapped my eyes then moved close as she peered into my right eye. She put the paddle in my hand.

"Cover your left eye. What do you see?"

"Light and blobs."

"Tell me about the blobs," she said.

"Blobs are kind of grayish-dark pillars or towers that move. They're not very well-defined though. They're blobs."

"Do you think the blobs are people?"

"Yes. I see two blobs. One close and one far."

"Good. Now let's see what's going on with your left eye."

She moved close again and held my left eye open. I felt her breath as she shifted positions.

"Put the paddle over your right eye."

I tried to will my eye to focus and see. *Just see anything.*

"Same. Dark." *I bit my lip to keep from feeling sorry for myself.*

"I'm going to apply a temporary patch over your right eye then let's go into my office," the doctor said.

As we walked together, Larry whispered, "Will you be okay?"

"No," I said.

"That's what I thought too." He gave me an extra squeeze before he said, "The chair is on your left."

After I sat, Larry stayed next to me with his hand on my shoulder.

"I heard back from my colleague, and your progress is what we anticipated. Your right eye will continue to improve, but your left eye may not. You don't need to have your eyes wrapped anymore, but you should wear dark sunglasses or goggles to protect your right eye, and an eyepatch over your left eye. Don't try to read or do fine work and wear a sleep mask at least two hours in the morning and again in the afternoon to rest your right eye. I'd like to see you again in a week but let me know immediately if there are any changes."

"Not what we wanted to hear," Larry said.

I nodded. *He said what I was thinking.*

"I know," she said. "I have temporary sunglasses if you need them."

I rose, and Larry turned me toward the door. "No, we're fine."

After we left her office, Larry said, "I have a pair of dark sunglasses in the truck for you. I'll text Heather then run grab your sunglasses. Palace Guard is mopey too." He hugged me. "I'm so sorry, sweetheart. I'll be right back."

I'll just stand here and be mopey-er than Palace Guard.

Palace Guard poked me, and I smirked.

What? Not a competition?

CHAPTER NINE

"Heather's on her way. Here, sweetie, try these on." Larry placed the sunglasses on my open hand.

I slipped on the sunglasses. "I can see why Doc recommended the sleep mask to rest my eyes. The light is very bright; I don't see any blobs." I blinked. "It might take a little time to adjust, but I can always close my eye when I want to rest."

"I have an idea. I'll be right back."

When Larry returned, he said, "I have a single thickness of gauze. I'll tape it over your right eye. Close your eye and take off your sunglasses."

He taped on the gauze above my eyebrow. "Put your sunglasses back on before you open your eye."

"I can still see light, but it's not as bright. Are you in front of me? I think I see a blob."

"Yes, right in front of you. You can pull off the gauze anytime you like. Heather's here. I'll walk you to her car."

"Let's go."

After Larry opened Heather's car door, he helped me inside then kissed me. "See you later. If you come across any killers, knock 'em dead." Larry chuckled as he closed the car door.

I snickered. "Was that cop humor, Heather?"

"I think it was closer to husband humor. You know, corny." Heather giggled.

Lucy leaned over the back of the seat and gave me a kiss on my ear.

"Thanks, Lucy. Ready to go to work?"

When we reached the senior center, Heather said, "I've pulled into the drop off. Shall I go in with you?"

"No, we'll be fine."

After she drove away, I said, "You can wait for me in the lobby, Spike, or you and Lucy can go to Mrs. Martin's room. I'll find you there."

Lucy yipped as we headed into the center. "Go see Mrs. Martin, Lucy."

As Palace Guard and I headed to Gracie Jane's office, she said, "Gray Lady, what a surprise. You're getting around much better than we expected."

"How are you?" I asked.

"Fine. I visited Mr. Bustamante yesterday. He misses Faith, of course. It's all very tragic, isn't it? Did you want to sit? Do you have any sight at all? I'm sorry. I didn't mean to pry."

"That's okay. I do have some sight, but I'm still adjusting to the light. I didn't get a chance to tell you that I was impressed by your car when we went to see Mr. Bustamante. Does it have all hand controls?"

"It does. I thought it was an extravagance, but my sister insisted. I think she got tired of chauffeuring me around." Gracie Jane chuckled. *Wish I could see her eyes.*

"It's a bit of a hassle to get my wheelchair in and out, but I've developed a system and have a bar to hang onto while I'm lifting it. My sister calls it my chin-up bar." Her giggle struck me as blatantly phony. "There are more gadgets every day to help those of us who are differently abled, as they say."

Liar.

"That's awesome. My sister-in-law dropped off Lucy and me at the entrance. She'll be back in a few minutes and will probably wait for us in the parking lot until we're ready to leave. Family support is really helpful, isn't it? It was nice to chat with you. I'll go find Lucy. She's probably visiting Edna Cross or another one of her fans."

As I shifted to turn, I asked, "Remember you said Edna Cross made things up? Does she have dementia?"

"I don't remember saying that. I guess my memory's not so great either." Gracie Jane's chuckle sounded forced. "Edna does have a little dementia, but so do most of our other residents. Really, nothing outside of the ordinary around here."

Nothing to see here?

As I tapped down the hallway, I walked with tentative steps. *I know you're watching, Gracie Jane.*

When we neared Mrs. Martin's room, I mumbled, "Thought I heard Lucy."

Palace Guard directed me farther down the hall, and when we reached Edna's room, Lucy yipped.

"There you are, Lucy. I didn't know you'd come see Mrs. Cross first. How are you, Edna?"

"It's great to see you, Gray Lady. Lucy and I are having a wonderful visit."

"I thought more about the trap you said I'd be ready for. Who told you about the trap?" I asked.

"I don't remember saying that. My memory's failing, they tell me," she said before she whispered. "Come close."

I stepped closer; when I felt her wheelchair, I put my hand on its arm and knelt next to her. Her rose cologne was a swirling, protective fog as she pulled me closer and breathed the words. "Internet guru heard the cafeteria lady tell Faith that Gerald had a thing for her, but we all knew that wasn't true. Ask Gracie Jane about the internet guru."

I nodded as I asked almost in a sigh, "Name?"

"Owen."

"You're awesome, Edna. Thank you."

She patted my hand as I held onto the arm of her wheelchair for balance; I pulled myself to my feet with the help of my staff, "Time for us to go, Lucy. Edna, we'll be sure to stop by again."

Lucy, Spike, Palace Guard, and I headed to Mrs. Martin's room. Lucy trotted ahead; I knew when she reached Mrs. Martin's room when I heard the squeal, "Lucy, girl."

"Hello, Maggie Flanagan. It's great to see you and your team. Come sit by me and tell me your Maggie Flanagan lies so we can laugh together."

"I need a chair." I felt around; when a chair slid into my reach, Mrs. Martin giggled. "Well done, Palace Guard."

"I love that you see the guys, Mrs. Martin."

"Have you remembered the fairy songs?"

"How did you know? I have."

"The fairies told me—they're tickled about it."

I cleared my throat. "I have a question for you."

Her room door closed. "Thanks, Palace Guard," I said. "Edna told me a very round about story about a trap being set for me. When I asked where she'd heard about it—"

"You got an even longer story, didn't you?" Mrs. Martin chortled.

"I did, and there's no way I could repeat half of it." I snickered with Mrs. Martin. "I think the ending of the story was what she wanted me to hear. She told me to ask Gracie Jane about Owen."

"She told you that? Flip it around. Ask Owen because he must know who is setting the trap. I don't know how Gracie Jane fits in, but she—"

Mrs. Martin was interrupted by a fire alarm.

"Again? We just had a fire drill last week," she said.

A cold chill of dread ran down my spine. When the fairies sang a song of warning, I said "It's not a drill."

I made my way to the door, but when I touched it, the door was warm, almost hot, to the touch. "Door's hot. We can't go down the hallway."

"Smoke's seeping under the door and through the air vents," Mrs. Martin said.

"What do you see outside?" I asked.

"Lots of black smoke billowing from the main lobby. The emergency exit on the other side of our building looks clear. People are starting to go out. Not many yet."

"We must be too close to the fire. Maybe we could—"

The building was rocked by an explosion.

"Oh no! No!" Mrs. Martin screamed.

"What is it? What happened?"

Explosion at the emergency exit.

"You said that, right, Palace Guard? Thanks for telling me." He patted my back.

Lucy howled then I heard glass breaking.

"Spike broke the window," Mrs. Martin shouted. "He's taking Lucy out. Go, Gray Lady, go!"

"Get Mrs. Martin out, Palace Guard. I'll dive out behind you."

"You are one strong young man," Mrs. Martin said.

I headed toward Mrs. Martin's voice when a second explosion rocked the building again, and large ceiling tiles fell to the floor. When I tapped the wall, I swung my jo and found the open window before a tile slammed me on my left shoulder and knocked me down.

I felt around to find my jo then used it to pull myself to my feet. I could feel the panic in my stomach rise to my throat, but my anger pushed away the fear and panic.

"Dang it all to pieces. I don't know which way the window is."

I felt a pat on my back. "I'm so glad you're here. Which way out?"

He tapped the left side of the back of my arm, and I stumbled in the direction that he guided me. Before I reached the window, the choking smoke filled my lungs, and I coughed so hard that I dropped to my knees as I clung to my staff.

I was suddenly airborne as Palace Guard handed me out the window to Spike's sturdy arms.

"Maggie," Larry shouted before he snatched me away from Spike.

I tried to speak, but when I inhaled, my spasms of coughing shook me so hard I was afraid I'd break a rib.

As Larry lowered me to the soft grass, Heather slapped an oxygen mask on my face. "Here you go, girlfriend. Slow down your breathing. Good air in. Bad air out."

"Lucy?"

Lucy licked my face, and I hugged her.

"Mrs. Martin?" I asked.

"She's fine, but the medics whisked her off to the hospital. I think they were nervous because of her age," Heather said. "You scared me because I was afraid you were trapped. I thought Larry was going to dive through that open window then you hovered midair before you floated outside. Palace Guard, right? Did he hand you off to Spike?"

I nodded as I removed the oxygen. "No hospital."

"I'm sorry, sweetie, but I don't agree." Larry still had his arms around me as he nuzzled my hair. "Your lungs haven't had enough time to recover from the chemical fumes, and you've breathed in a lot of smoke."

"I'll be safer at home. Call the doctor's office for an appointment. Please?"

"Put the oxygen back on, and I'll do it," Larry said.

"I'll run interference here while you call," Heather said.

"You have a transport?" A man strode to Heather and me as we sat together on the grass.

"No, my patient's fine," Heather said. "A little oxygen for her panic attack."

"Yes, ma'am. You just let me know if there's any way I can help you."

Spike growled.

What's wrong with you, Spike?

After the man walked away, Heather chuckled. "That young medic winked at me. Todd would be all huffy if he saw that."

I giggled. *Now, I get it.*

"What's going on here? Are you two telling secrets?" Larry asked. "I talked to your doctor, Maggie. She'll see you at ten tomorrow."

"Good." I removed the mask. "Can we leave now?"

"Okay with you, Larry?" Heather asked.

"No, but you'll be safer at home."

"Oh? I was right?" I smirked.

"Don't push it," Heather whispered.

"No." Larry helped me to my feet and handed me my jo. "I'll think of a reason later why you should have gone to the hospital."

"I'm parked across the street," Heather said. I tapped as I walked alongside her with Palace Guard's help, and Spike and Lucy stayed close behind us.

On the way home, I asked, "You didn't have time to see John Howard, did you?"

"No. When I heard the sirens, I turned around and sped back to the senior center. I didn't know what was going on, but I was certain you were in the middle of it."

"Let's change our plan. We can drop off Lucy and Spike at the house then we can go see John Howard. Do I need to change clothes first?"

"Yes, and maybe you could sit for a few minutes and have a glass of tea while you explain your new plan to me."

"It's really simple. We'll show him the jewelry. I can chat with him, and you can watch his facial expressions."

"I love how your plans start off with 'it's really simple.'" Heather snickered. "Why do I have the urge to call for reinforcements when we're about to embark on one of your simple plans, but we'll have Palace Guard along, right? Will Spike stay with Lucy?"

"You're asking about the plans for the imaginary men?" I asked.

"Oh, hush. They might hear you."

After we were inside the house, Heather said, "Sit somewhere, and I'll bring you a glass of tea. I'm going to organize your clothes; I'll put a pair of pants and a shirt together in a sack. All you'll have to do is pick a sack and dress."

"Great idea—thanks. Do I need a shower?"

"Yes." Heather strode to the bedroom.

"Guess I'll do that first then."

I waited. *She didn't hear me. Dang it. I wanted to sound cranky.*

I turned on the shower and undressed.

I let the steamy water massage my back before I soaped up then rinsed. *Didn't know I was achy. Hot water feels good.*

I stepped out of the shower and dried before I wrapped a towel around me and tapped to the bedroom.

"Pick a sack," Heather said from the kitchen. "The sacks are on a shelf in the closet."

I grabbed the top sack and dressed before I went to the kitchen.

"What do I do with the sack?"

"I'll put it next to the washer and dryer, so Larry or I can match up your outfits as they come out of the dryer. Ready for your tea?"

"We may have timed this just right to go to the Sano Café for lunch. Let's skip the tea and go."

"Talked me into it," Heather said. "I've got one more thing before we grab jewelry and go. I have the surprise from Jennifer. She made you seven patches in different colors. Your outfit is mostly green. Want to wear your green eyepatch over your left eye?"

"That would be awesome."

After Heather helped me position the eyepatch, we headed to the car.

"Arrr," I said as she backed out of the driveway.

Heather snorted. "That didn't take you long, pirate girl."

On the way to downtown, Heather handed me the soft jewelry sack. "Shantelle gave Kate three pieces. An emerald and diamond necklace. A small emerald serves as the centerpiece for the large emerald drop pendent, and both emeralds are surrounded by diamonds. The emeralds are a clear green, very similar to your eyes. The slender gold chain necklace has a heart pendant with a small gold fairy inside the heart, and the gold ring looks like twisted rope. I'll bet it would fit you. There's an inscription on the inside that I can't decipher."

I reached into the sack and felt each piece. "Sure sounds like Margarite Flanagan jewelry. I expected Shantelle to give us a few of Olivia's pieces."

I tried on the ring. "You're right. It fits me." I returned it to the sack. "It felt funny though. It's not Margarite's. The necklaces are. I wonder if the ring is Mrs. Martin's."

"I've parked about a block away. I didn't think you'd mind walking."

When we entered the jewelry store, a bell jingled over the door.

"Mrs. Ewing," John Howard said. "What a nice surprise. I heard your sister was staying with you."

"This is Heather, and we have three pieces of jewelry that we think may have belonged to our great-grandmother. Would you mind looking at them? I was told they may be fakes by another jeweler, and I'd like your thoughts."

"Of course. I'll be right back. I have my tools in the back."

Heather leaned close to me and whispered. "Good sign that he's not planning a switch."

I nodded.

"Let's see what we've got here. I'll unroll this felt on the glass case, so we don't scratch the jewelry. I'll start with the ring."

"Well, the ring is a work of art. Did you see the pieces before your injury?"

"It's been a while since I've seen any of them. My lawyer has been holding them for us."

"Wise move. The ring is gold, and the braiding is unusual, especially with the small diamonds that appear to be interwoven in the twists. It would be hard to price it because it is so unique, but it is very valuable. If you're interested in selling it, I'd recommend taking it to an appraiser first. Now, the inscription is very interesting Do you know what language it might be?"

"We don't," I said. "I always thought it was a secret message."

John laughed. "You might be right about that. I must tell you it was an honor to inspect such a fine piece. Ms. Heather, would you please put the ring back into the jewelry bag?"

Palace Guard patted my back, and I nodded.

"Now, the angel necklace…mmm…I was wrong. This is a fairy inside the heart, isn't it?"

"We think so," I said.

"This necklace would be a little easier to price. The chain, heart, and fairy are all gold. The small diamonds are diamonds, not synthetics. Another valuable piece."

"Shall I put it into the sack?" Heather asked.

"Thank you, yes. This emerald necklace is stunning. The pendant emerald is larger than we see on rings, of course, so most jewelers might call it a replica and leave it at that. It is definitely not a replica. Even the smaller emerald would make an impressive ring, and again, it is a valuable stone. You can put it away, Ms. Heather, even though I could admire the handiwork of these three pieces the rest of the day. Mr. Bustamante was a remarkably talented craftsman. The emerald necklace and the rest of the pieces remind me of the type of work that he used to produce. May I treat you to lunch? I'd love to hear more about your great-grandmother."

"I don't know," I said. "How do you feel about fairies?"

Heather snorted, and John chuckled. "I would love to hear about fairies."

We strolled together to the café, and before our food arrived, I repeated one of the stories Mother told me.

"Enjoy your sandwich," John said. "I have a story my grandmother told me about fairies."

It was hard to eat while we laughed at John's story. When he finished with a surprise ending, Heather said, "John, that was a wonderful story. I need to know if you ever saw the fairies."

"No one ever asked me that before. I always knew when I was a kid that the fairies guarded me and kept me safe, but I never remember seeing them."

Heather sighed. "I need fairies or imaginary people in my life. I can't deal with the thought that I might be normal."

John laughed, and I giggled when Palace Guard patted my back.

John sighed. "I hate to say it, but I have to head back to the store."

"We'll walk with you," I said. "It's on the way back to Heather's car."

After we were outside, I said, "John, I was with Faith at the café when you came in to pick up your lunch. She seemed really angry at you."

I held my breath, and Heather took my hand.

When he reached his store, John said, "Come inside for a moment. I'd like to tell you about Faith and me."

After we were inside, he closed the door. "Faith and I were high school sweethearts and were absolutely inseparable. We even went to the same college, so we could study together. We graduated, and Faith was planning our wedding, but I had big dreams and pushed Faith away because I thought she was holding me back. I was stupid."

He sighed. "After graduation, I left Faith and went to Las Vegas where I expected to become a famous jeweler to the rich and famous. I ended up working in a pawn shop. The people were nice, and I made good money, but I realized I'd thrown away the best thing that had ever been in my life—Faith. I was too ashamed to return and tell her, so I stayed in Las Vegas and drank. My intent was to drink myself to death, but Mr. Bustamante contacted me and asked me to take over his business because he was ill. So, for one time in my life, I did the right thing."

"But Faith was still angry," I said.

"Yes, and I don't blame her at all. She had every right to be, but I was sorry about how bitter she had become. I can't tell you how happy I was that she found Eric, except I hated him because he did what I should have done: give sweet, kind Faith the happiness she deserved."

"Thank you for explaining about Faith," I said.

Heather said, "I'm really sorry, but we need to leave. My sister is fading, but she'd never admit it."

I shrugged.

"We'll have to get together over fairy stories again sometime," John said, and I heard a breath of joy in his voice.

On our way home, Heather said, "How did I get promoted from sister-in-law to sister?"

I snickered. "I didn't see any reason to correct John."

"So, what do you think?"

"He's a good jeweler."

"Very Georgia answer," Heather said. "What do you really think about his story about Faith?"

"He left a few parts out, but isn't preservation of dignity a human trait? He dumped Faith and ran off to Las Vegas with a babe."

"A babe?"

"Yes, like a bimbo."

"A bimbo? Where did you pick up that language?" Heather laughed.

"I read. Tell me what you saw when he examined the jewelry."

"He was completely thorough in his examination. I was impressed that after he confirmed it was real, he didn't make a pitch to assess its value. Also, I was trained by the best pickpocket in the world, and he didn't try to pull a switch either."

"Darren Martin told me that John didn't like Eric, but he didn't have any details. John's story sounded plausible," I said.

"Is he off our suspect list?" Heather asked.

"Not necessarily. He might come off as a jerk who has learned his lesson, but I'll never forget Lillian. She was a sweet, old woman, a trusted friend, and a heartless murderer. Any good criminal can slip into a nice guy persona."

"She was definitely a surprise. Point taken."

After we arrived at the house, I removed my sunglasses before I collapsed on the sofa and put up my feet.

"How about some tea?" Heather asked.

After she handed me the lidded cup with a straw, her phone rang.

"The boss. I'll take it outside; I'm sure he heard about the senior center and wants a full report. I'll just step out back, so you don't have to listen to his yelling."

I put my cup down on the floor and lay back on the sofa.

Heather came back into the house. "Maggie, it's not good. Larry's going to call in just a few minutes. Scoot over."

After I sat up and made room for her, I said, "Heather, tell me so I can be prepared."

"Can't. I promised Larry."

When Heather's phone rang, I jumped because of the rising tension in the room.

You two feel it too, don't you?

After Heather answered, she said, "Here's the phone."

"What's going on, Larry? Heather wouldn't tell me."

"Heather has to return to Harperville tomorrow. They need her to lead an undercover team. I don't know any details, which is fine and probably safer for Heather, but Moe called me and gave me a heads up."

"Can't we adopt her or something?"

Heather snickered. "Best plan ever."

Larry chuckled. "I agree with Heather. It's not like she would be bored if she stayed, but she's the best, and they need her. I don't know how tired you are, but you might want to think about what you need Heather to do before she leaves this evening."

After he hung up, I handed the phone to Heather. "Well, this certainly calls for a change in plans."

"I'm absolutely sick about the thought of leaving you. I can't help but worry about how you'll get around."

"It might not be all bad for me to take some time to stay home and heal. I still have the software you installed so I can focus on the documents I have, and would you help me set up my cell phone to work by voice commands? I'm not convincing myself at all. How can I get you fired?"

Heather laughed. "If anybody could, it would be you."

"I know what we need to do this afternoon. I need more training with my jo."

"Change into sweatpants and a T-shirt. Let's give you a good workout. I'll show you where your sweatpants and T-shirts are. They aren't included in your sets."

After I changed, Palace Guard and I followed Heather outside. I knew Spike would come too, and when Lucy trotted out to the yard, I had my full complement of critics.

"Let's start you off again without your staff." Heather directed me in stretches, low squats, and turns. "That's a good warm up. Do those a couple of times a day to stay limber. Do you think you could run with Palace Guard's help?"

Palace Guard and I ran the perimeter of the yard; after our third time around, Heather called out, "Reverse."

I whipped around to reverse and lost my balance as I crashed face first to the ground.

I sat up and sputtered out grass. "That was tricky."

"I was thinking it might be hard. Let's take it slower. Walk at a normal pace."

When Heather called, "Reverse," Palace Guard tapped my right arm to signal the reverse. Before I stepped in the new direction, Palace Guard tapped my arm to indicate a correction. When I finally completed a successful turn, Heather said, "Break. Come sit on the porch. You need to cool down."

After I flopped down onto my rocking chair, I said, "I didn't realize I needed to relearn how to shift and change direction before I worked with my jo."

"You're really coming along. How do you feel?"

"Like I'm getting the hang of it."

"You and Palace Guard have worked out new signals, haven't you?"

"Thanks to you. Where do you come up with this stuff?"

"The fairies told me."

"For real?"

"Maybe. I'm not saying. Let's get back to work."

After I stepped off the porch, Heather said, "Now, let's go through the drill except this time, carry your jo."

I ran the perimeter, and on my second pass, my jo flew out of my hand. "What did you do?" I shouted.

Heather giggled. "Guess you should have had a better hold on her."

"You could have just told me," I grumbled in my best fuming voice.

"We'll have to include those instructions for any bad guys."

"I'd roll my eye, except it would kind of lose the full impact of disdain I'd like to convey." I crossed my arms.

"Here's your jo."

I tried to grab it, but she snatched it away.

Heather snorted. "You'll have to be a little faster than that."

I dived toward her voice and barreled into her. When she went down, I scrambled to find my jo then rolled away before Heather could grab me. After I jumped up, I hung onto my staff and ran as Palace Guard guided me in a zigzag while Heather's maniacal cackle followed me.

I rushed to the porch and sat in my rocking chair. When Heather stepped up on the porch, I said, "I truly regret that I couldn't see your face. Are you speaking to me?"

"You knocked me off my high horse. As well as I know your sneaky side and amazing skills, you caught me off guard. You have to promise me that you won't tell anyone, or I'll mix up your clothes. Deal?"

When I snickered, Heather sighed, "You don't care, do you?"

"Nope. What's our next drill?"

"Let's put you through the paces with jo. Swing, dive, roll, swerve, swing, and run. I'll stay here out of the way, and I'll be right back. I want to tell Spike to keep Lucy inside."

When Heather returned, she said, "That was fun. I think I was talking to a shadow. Now remember, you're surrounded by bad guys. What's your best skill besides your instincts?"

"My hearing."

"That's right. Think you can do it?"

"Yes."

After I eased to the yard, I stepped as quietly as I could. When I heard a slight sound to my left, I swung the jo, dived, rolled then jumped up. I stepped to my right then whirled around and swung at the slight crackle of the dry leaves behind me. As I made my way across the yard, I heard different sounds around me and used my jo to clear my way as I headed to safety with Palace Guard's guidance.

When I reached the porch, Heather applauded. "Well done."

"How did you step all around me without being hit?"

"I was happy that you didn't pull any punches. I had some gravel from the driveway that I tossed around you. You didn't miss one of those bad guys. I'm proud of the progress you've made so quickly. Let's talk about somebody with a gun. What would you and Palace Guard do?"

"If I was close enough, I could use my staff to knock the attacker down then run. Palace Guard will help me get away or dive a bullet, but there's a real possibility that I'd be shot."

"Yes, and most likely dead, which is not acceptable—just ask Larry. You have a carry permit. Nobody would expect a blind woman to shoot. Even after your sight returns in your right eye, you may not want anyone to know that your sight has improved. All you'd need to do is to continue to wear your sunglasses and your patch. Right now, you could shoot a blob, especially if Palace Guard told you the blob was a bad guy, correct?"

"Yes, and Larry will take me to a range where I can hone my aim to shoot blobs."

"Good. I want to check your pistol. Where is it?"

"Larry told me he put it on the top shelf in our bedroom closet."

When Heather returned, she said, "It's nice and clean. I've put it in your holster. Put it on for me. If you aren't comfortable, I'll put it back where I found it."

I stuck the holster inside my waistband. "Ahh. I didn't realize how undressed I felt."

"Perfect. Before I leave, I'll help you set up your phone."

After we finished with my phone, Heather hugged me. "I hate leaving you, but I know you'll be fine, and I'll bet Palace Guard and Spike agree with me."

Palace Guard patted my back.

"They do agree with you, but I know Spike is sad that you're leaving."

"Not my choice either." Heather sighed. "I pulled the lasagna from the freezer and put it in the refrigerator. Larry can put it in the oven when he gets home. I'm going to leave now, so I can travel while it's daylight. Call me if you need me."

After Heather left, Lucy and I sat on the sofa together, and I stroked her back while she leaned against me. "I could read some documents, go over Faith's notebook, or call Glenn to ask him what he's found so far, but I think I'll just relax until Larry gets home."

I stretched out on the sofa, and Lucy hopped down. After I removed the gauze covering from my right eye, I closed my eye while I listened to Lucy's soft snore.

I miss Heather. It's not fair that she had to leave.

My phone rang and interrupted my foray into self-pity.

CHAPTER TEN

When I answered, Darren Martin said, "Hello, Ms. Gray Lady. This is Darren Martin. Mama wanted me to call you to see how you were. She'll be released from the hospital in the morning. Mama's house hasn't sold, and I found a good home health care worker to come to the house every morning for her personal care and medications. Mama's happy about moving back home. Are you in the hospital?"

"No. My doctor checked me then cleared me to come home. I think your mama will love being back in her home."

"We're glad you're okay. You might not have heard about Edna Cross. She was making her way toward the emergency exit, but when the first explosion hit, she changed her direction and headed to the senior center's park. Did you meet Owen? He's a skinny guy and always wears a black suit and tie; he's our resident internet expert. Owen found her slumped in her wheelchair in the park and pushed her wheelchair to an ambulance through another wing. Edna Cross is in the hospital for smoke inhalation and minor burns on her hands. I understand she'll be okay, but she may be there a few more days."

"That is awesome news about Edna Cross, and I'm really glad your mama is doing so well. Have you heard anything about Gracie Jane?"

"We haven't heard anything." His voice cracked. "Some people were flown to the burn center in Atlanta; I just hope she's okay. I tried to check to see if her car was in the parking lot, but everything was still blocked off."

"I'm sorry to hear that. Hopefully, someone will hear soon."

Darren cleared his throat. "Mama wanted me to invite you to our home for brunch on Sunday, if you feel up to it. I'll check back with you after Mama's released to see if that works for you."

"Thank you, Darren, and please give your mama a hug from me and the guys."

When we hung up, I smiled. *Darren didn't even ask who the guys were. He'll give the message as is to his mother who sees and hears fairies.*

After I stuck my phone in my pocket, I tapped to the back door to sit on the porch. Lucy joined me, and I was certain Palace Guard and Spike did too.

"Did you notice I made my way out to my rocking chair without any help? I need to call Glenn."

Palace Guard patted my shoulder.

"Dial Glenn," I said.

Glenn answered on the second ring. "Maggie! We heard Heather had to leave, and I've been wanting to call you but didn't know if it was okay. Jennifer wants you to come here, but I don't agree because I know you and Larry are inseparable. Help me out."

"Heather left me with some new skills and ideas, and I've still got the guys and Lucy, and Larry is a phone call away. I'm fine. What other ammunition do you need?"

Glenn chuckled. "I'll give it a shot. So, what's up?"

"Did you have a chance to check out the senior center management and finances, Gracie Jane, or Eric Stephens?"

"I did. The senior center facility is owned by a group of doctors, and a senior health care management corporation that is based in New York has a long-term lease on the building. The main office in New York handles all of the accounting, human resources, purchasing, and sales for all their centers. It all looks very hands-off. All the staff is hired through contracting services companies. If there is something going on at the senior center, I have a strong feeling that the management corporation is completely unaware."

"What about the jewelry fakes in Harperville and the suspect that was killed?"

"The official findings were that it isn't related to what you're seeing there because the case here was determined to be family-related," Glenn said. "Two cousins squabbled over the jewelry that belonged to their recently deceased grandmother. When one piece was found to be fake, the younger cousin blamed the older one and murdered him. Turned out none of the grandmother's jewelry had been anything but well-made replicas. Pretty tragic, really."

"So, whatever's going on here is either local or maybe regional?"

"Maybe."

I frowned. "You don't sound convinced."

"It seemed too neat for my taste—not a stray thread anywhere. I'm going to keep digging. Let me know if there's anything I can do at this end because I don't have a clue," he said.

"What else?" I asked.

"Next is Gracie Jane. She finished law school ten years ago but was involved in a crash with a semi-truck and was badly injured. She sued the trucking company because she claimed to be permanently disabled. She got a sizeable lump sum with no strings which means she could have a complete recovery with no legal obligation to repay."

"Seems like there would be no reason for her to continue with a faked injury," I said.

"Certainly seems like it, doesn't it? Nice and neat," Glenn said.

"There's your neat word again. What are you thinking?"

"She's faking the severity of her immobility for a reason; we don't know why, but someone would. Who?" Glenn asked.

"Someone at the senior center knows. Mrs. Martin may not know, but she would know who does. I almost forgot to tell you that no one has seen Gracie Jane since the fire and explosions; Darren Martin was very upset when I talked to him earlier."

"We should still move forward with Gracie Jane's fake injury. You talk to Mrs. Martin, and I'll check with my contacts to see where Gracie Jane is. Are you wearing out, Maggie? Do we need to take a break?"

"Not at all. I'm encouraged that we're making progress. We don't have any answers yet, but I felt stuck until we took time to discuss."

"I agree. So, Eric Stephens. We've got another nice guy. He got in trouble as a kid but straightened out after he joined a youth group. He attended two years of college in New York City but didn't complete enough classes for an associate degree. He's a financial analyst in Atlanta and volunteered his time on home builds for veterans for a while. He was married, but his wife died while he was in the Army. They didn't have any children."

"How did he and Faith meet?"

"More nice guy. According to Faith's friends at her church, when the group went to a weekend retreat, Eric was one of the instructors, and Faith and Eric stayed in touch. Faith visited Eric on some of the build weekends to work with him. After Mr. Bustamante became ill, Eric took care of Mr. Bustamante on several Saturdays, so Faith could meet with her small group at church. Her church friends like Eric."

"No wonder John Howard doesn't like him," I said.

Glenn snorted. "I don't think I'd be an Eric fan either. What about you? What did you think?"

"He was genuinely concerned about Mr. Bustamante. I liked him enough to give him my card."

"You think he'll need it?"

"Yes, but I don't know why."

"Be careful. I wonder if there's more to Eric than he lets on."

"Depending on what's on Larry's schedule, maybe he and I could visit Mr. Bustamante on Saturday."

"Good idea. If Larry doesn't like Eric, I'll send Jennifer and Ella to follow Eric or run him out of town—your choice."

I snickered. "It would be tempting to see them in action, but I guess I have to pass."

"Speaking of Jennifer, she wants to know how you are getting along and if you need anything."

"I can't think of anything that I need, but I didn't even know I needed soft eyepatches. I absolutely love the softness. The sleep masks are a great reminder for me to rest my eyes, well, eye, like I'm supposed to."

"That's good news. I'll tell Jennifer, even though I know you haven't used a sleep mask yet, but you didn't tell me that, so I'm in the clear." Glenn chuckled. "I know you're supposed to rest. We'll talk again whenever you like."

After we hung up, I said, "Palace Guard, I need to put on a sleep mask. Can you help me find them?"

Palace Guard led me to the bedroom and to the closet. I found the masks on the shelf with the eyepatches. After I put on a sleep mask, we returned to the living room, and I stretched out on the sofa.

When I heard the scratch of a key in the front door, I realized I'd been asleep. I struggled to sit up as Larry came into the house.

"Hi, honey. Hi, guys. Good girl, Lucy."

When Lucy whined, I knew Larry was rubbing her face.

"This is a surprise." He strode to the sofa and sat with me. "I didn't think you'd actually rest. You must have been really tired." He hugged me. "Missed you, sweetie. Heather told me there's a pan of lasagna in the refrigerator. I'll pop it into the oven then I want to hear what you've been doing."

After Larry rejoined me on the sofa, I leaned against him while I told him about lunch with John, Heather's training, Darren's invitation, and Glenn's call.

"Hearing about your day makes me want to take a nap."

"Do you have any plans for the weekend?" I asked.

"The weekends are yours. What do you want to do?"

"I'd like to visit Mr. Bustamante on Saturday and go to the Martins' for brunch on Sunday. Is there somewhere we could go maybe on Saturday that I could work with my pistol? Heather told me my jo skills were great, but after she asked me what I would do if my attacker had a gun, she suggested I talk to you about carrying my pistol."

"You'd shoot an attacker blob, right?"

"Yep, because Palace Guard could tell me if the blob was a good guy or a bad guy."

"You're right, and it would be important for you and Palace Guard to train together. We can work on that. Sounds like a fun Saturday. I can sight in the scope on my deer rifle, but first, I'll have to get one. Maybe we could go to a pawn shop tomorrow or Friday to see what they have, if you feel up to it."

"I'd like that. We could even go this evening after supper if you'd like."

"I've got another idea. You mentioned Heather trained you with the stick? Let's develop some muscle memory for you to shoot the bad blobs."

"Okay, but I don't understand," I said.

"I'll show you after supper. I'll make my famous salad then pull out the lasagna."

While Larry chopped vegetables for the salad, I said, "Palace Guard, could you point me to the silverware?"

Palace Guard tapped the left side of the back of my right arm. "Thanks."

As I set the table, I asked, "When can I cook?"

"That's the doctor's call, but I think you'd need to be able to see the burner and oven controls," Larry said. "I'm not doing a bad job, am I?"

"Not at all, but I feel guilty because you work all day then have to cook when you get home."

"Sometimes you take care of me; sometimes I take care of you. This is my turn. Lasagna's hot. Let's eat."

I sighed as I sat. "You are so practical."

After we ate, Larry said, "I'll put away our leftovers and load the dishwasher then meet you on the porch."

As I headed outside, Lucy followed me, which meant Spike went along too.

When Larry joined us, he said, "Ready for your training? Pick a spot in the yard to take your stand."

I walked to a point I estimated to be the middle of the yard. "Do I hang onto my jo?"

"You'll need to drop your staff, so it won't impede your movement. Get ready to shoot."

I dropped my jo and assumed my standing shooter stance.

"Remember not every bad blob will come straight at you. Palace Guard will direct you where and when to shoot. You two will need to work out your signals. Want to practice a bit first?"

"Yes, we need a point signal, which probably wouldn't be the same as my walk directions signals. What do you think, Palace Guard? Point signals same as what we decided on for an attack with jo?"

Larry said, "Palace Guard agrees."

"We've got our ready and aim; what do we do for a signal for me to fire?"

Palace Guard touched the top of my head with his fingertips.

I nodded. "We'll try it."

After I resumed my stance, Palace Guard shifted me to the right and thumped my head, and I fired my imaginary pistol. He immediately shifted me to a ninety degree turn to my left and thumped. I fired; he shifted me one hundred eighty degrees and smacked my head. I shot. He gave me the signal to crouch and thumped. I shot. He signaled for me to shift to my right forty-five degrees but didn't thump. I shifted but maintained my stance until he flicked my head, and I shot. After I had turned and shot repeatedly, Larry said, "Break. Come sit on the porch, and I'll grab a couple of beers."

Sweat ran down my back while I searched for then found my jo. On my way to the porch, I brushed away my damp curls that were stuck onto my forehead. When I sat in my rocker, Larry handed me a cold beer.

"That was a workout." I rocked and sipped my beer. "You directed the scenarios, didn't you, Larry?"

"What gave us away?" He chuckled.

"You and Palace Guard stayed in the house after I came outside. Palace Guard lets me know when he's close, and what else would you two be doing besides coming up with a devious plan?"

Larry snorted. "I'll find us a range where you can shoot without an audience on Saturday. We won't do any of our maneuvers that we did tonight, but Palace Guard can help your aim. Rest your eyes between now and then, so you can shoot the bad blobs."

I sighed. "The cicadas have their chorus going, and the crickets have joined in. What does the sky look like?"

"There are a few thin clouds in the west. The sun's not quite below the horizon, and the sky is blaze-orange."

"My favorite sky. Can I wear my holster with my pistol now?"

"If I say no, will you do it anyway? Don't answer," Larry said.

I listened to the crickets and gave Larry time to think.

"Palace Guard won't let you shoot a good blob," he said, "and you're pretty good about following his instructions, so it should be all right. Please don't go looking for a bad blob to shoot, okay?"

When I laughed, Larry kissed my open mouth, and I returned the favor.

"Nice. Beer kiss." He chuckled.

After I tossed down the rest of my beer then belched, he laughed. I was ready for him; I pounced and plopped into his lap and kissed his open mouth. While we snuggled and kissed, Lucy trotted past us, and we were left alone on the porch, except for the crickets.

When I smacked a mosquito, Larry said, "Time to go in."

He wrapped his arm around my shoulder, and I put my arm around his waist as we walked together to the door.

* * *

The next morning, I patted the bed next to me, and it was empty. *I hate that I don't know what time it is, but if it's too early, I get to snuggle.* I tapped my way with care down the hall before I neared the kitchen and smelled coffee.

"Good morning, sweetheart." Larry kissed me on my forehead, and I tipped back my head and pointed to my mouth. Larry hugged me and gave me a much better good morning kiss. "Do you want your coffee at the table or on the porch?" he asked.

"At the table. I need to supervise your cooking."

Larry snorted. "We had two cinnamon rolls left, so they're in the oven. How do you want your scrambled egg, or do you want to splurge and have two eggs?"

I sipped my coffee. "I want one Thursday scrambled egg."

"Coming up," he said. "Before I leave for work, Heather told me I needed to brush your hair. You have a choice: ponytail or no ponytail."

"I think I'll try brushing my hair myself today. You can critique when you get home."

"As long as you don't tell on me, I'm okay with whatever you'd like to do." Larry refilled my cup and set a plate in front of me. "Fork on your right."

Larry set his plate on the table then sat with me. "Mmm. These cinnamon rolls are great. I need to find a bakery or get another shipment from Jennifer."

"I'm a master at making cinnamon rolls. We could make them this evening after we visit the pawn shops."

"We won't have time, will we?"

"Sure, we will. We'll pull everything together and let them rise in the refrigerator overnight. I'll give you baking instructions for tomorrow morning."

"Wow. We can do that? The guys who complain about being married must be idiots."

I spewed my coffee. "You are so eloquent in the morning."

While I tore my cinnamon roll into bites, he said, "I'll make my lunch while you finish your breakfast. What's your plan for today?"

"I thought I'd call the senior center to see if the other wings are in operation, and I might give Darren a call to see how Mrs. Martin is doing."

"And resting your eyes."

"Of course."

Larry kissed the top of my head. "I've loaded the dishwasher. Gotta go."

When I was sure he was gone, I sat at my desk and called the senior center, but it rolled around to a recording that told me my call was very important, and the office didn't open until nine o'clock.

I called Darren; when his voice mail answered, I left a message. "It's the Gray Lady, Darren. I was checking up on how your mama is doing. Call me when it's convenient."

I drummed my fingers on the desk. "I'm stuck. I'll listen to Faith's notebook. Let me know if I have a bad guy creeping around or a phone call."

Palace Guard patted me on the back.

After an hour or so, I took off my headset. "I listened to the section about discrepancies; I don't know how I missed it before. Faith said it was Nancy who told her about the discrepancies. Larry would be very interested in that information, wouldn't he?"

Palace Guard flicked my phone that was on my desk.

I picked up the phone and said, "Text Larry. Call when you have a break. No emergency. I'm okay."

My phone rang.

"So, what happened that you're okay now?" he asked.

"Nothing. I listened again to a section of Faith's notebook that I didn't understand earlier. Her friend, Nancy, was an aide at the senior center. She died in a crash that Faith told me was a deliberate hit and run."

"Right. I know about that."

"Faith's notebook mentioned discrepancies, but I missed what kind the first time I read it, but this time, I understood what Faith meant. Faith wrote that an aide who worked in wing two noticed a new medication that was prescribed for everyone seemed to be having an adverse interaction with other medicines. The aide was suspicious about four deaths in wing two because of discrepancies in the patients' records; however, there was no proof because all the records of the new medication being prescribed or dispensed had disappeared. Then on the last page in her notebook, Faith wrote, 'Nancy's dead because of the new med.'"

"Where's the notebook?" Larry asked. "Never mind. You have it. We'll be right there. Don't go anywhere."

Before he hung up, he whispered, "Good work, sweetie."

I made my way to the bedroom, found my backpack in the closet, and carried it to the kitchen table. "Larry was interested. He'll be right here to pick up the notebook. I need to brush my hair before he gets here. Come with me and tell me if I do okay."

After I brushed my hair, Palace Guard patted the back of my head, and I brushed it more carefully.

"How's that?"

He patted my back.

I returned to the kitchen table and felt in my backpack for the notebook. After I found it, I heard a car pull into our driveway then Larry's footsteps as he bounded to the front door.

He unlocked the door, rushed inside and hugged me. "Thank you for being okay." He kissed my forehead, and when I pouted, he chuckled then kissed my lips.

"Nice," he said. "Now, where's the notebook?"

"On the kitchen table. I took photos of the pages and converted them to text then gave copies to Glenn and Heather."

"But no one else has put the pieces together? Why?"

"I don't know. It's hard to read as a source of information because the style is like a personal diary. Maybe no one else has read all the way through."

"How are you doing, sweetie?"

"I'm bored, but you'd tell me that's good, right?"

Larry chuckled. "Sure would. I have to go back to work." He kissed me and dashed out the door. After he was gone, my phone rang.

"Good morning, Ms. Gray Lady. This is Darren Martin. I got your message. Mama is doing very well. She'll be released before lunchtime, and she's excited. Would you and your sister like to go to lunch with us?"

"I'd love it, but Heather left for home last night."

"We can come pick you up. Mama's looking forward to a nice lunch away from the senior center."

"That would be great, if it isn't too much trouble."

"Not at all, and I know Mama would enjoy seeing you. Is there anything I can do for you?"

"I have been wondering about Gracie Jane. Did you ever hear anything?"

"I heard from the burn unit in Atlanta just before I got your text. She had listed me as next of kin. I was surprised, but I knew she had no living relatives, and we are friends. The doctor who called assured me that she'd be okay, but she has a long convalescence ahead of her. Her office was not far from the original fire, and she was badly burned when she rolled through the flames to escape."

"Wow. Sounds like she was lucky to survive the fire."

"That's what the doctor said. I'll call you when Mama and I are ready to leave the hospital, or is that too short of a notice?"

"That's just fine. I'm looking forward to seeing both of you. Or at least, having lunch with you." I chuckled.

After I hung up, I said, "We're going to lunch with Darren and Mrs. Martin."

Palace Guard elbowed me. "Larry won't mind."

He elbowed me again.

"Fine." I picked up my phone. "Send a text to Larry: Going to lunch with Darren and Mrs. Martin. Darren will pick me up."

My phone buzzed then said, "Larry replied, 'Grumble.'"

I snickered. "Another reason he's my favorite person in the whole world."

I went to our bedroom and slipped my holstered pistol inside my waistband then hurried to the living room when my phone rang.

"Hi, Gray Lady, it's Heather. I've heard about the breakthrough with the dan shen. I know it was you. Well done, girlfriend. What's your plan for today?"

"I'm going to lunch with Darren and Mrs. Martin. She's being released from the hospital."

"Are you going to wear your pistol?"

"You know I am."

Heather giggled. "Good girl. Text me if you need me. I may or may not be undercover for the next week or two, but Moe's going to monitor my phone for me."

After we hung up, I said, "I need to tell Glenn where Gracie Jane is."

I picked up my phone. "Call Glenn."

"You okay, Maggie?" Glenn asked.

"I'm fine. I have a little information for you."

After I told him what Faith meant about discrepancies and about Gracie Jane, he said, "I'll redeem myself. I think the key to all the murders is to find out who benefited from the senior center deaths, and I just had a thought. I'll need to run it past Paul—he knows more than I do about corporations and such."

"Let me know what I can do," I said.

"Hey, Maggie, that's my line."

"Let us know what time to come get you." Jennifer called out from the background.

"She's not kidding. She has the car loaded and claims we'll be sleeping in the car. I'm going to claim my leg injury has flared up." Glenn chuckled as he hung up.

I took off my sleep mask and put on my eyepatch and my sunglasses before I poured a half a glass of tea. I carried my phone and glass to the back porch and rocked while I listened to the crows' raucous calls. *Warning the neighborhood about a soaring hawk?*

As Lucy investigated her yard, I knew where she was by her snuffle. I squinted with my right eye, but I still couldn't see her until I saw a shadow blob with the shape of a refrigerator. *Spike.* Next to Spike was a shadow that resembled a children's wagon that moved along with him.

"I can see Spike's and Lucy's blob shadows a little clearer."

Palace Guard held up a shadowy thumb in front of my face.

"Awesome! I see your thumb." I held up my hand, and Palace Guard smacked a high-five.

I smiled and rocked until my phone rang.

"Hello, Ms. Gray Lady, It's Darren Martin. We have a slight change in plans. Mama isn't as strong as we'd hoped and won't be released today after all. She'd still like to see you. Do you suppose we could pick up lunch from the Sano Café and eat with Mama at the hospital?"

"What a good idea. I'd love it."

"Thank you. I'll call in our order and come by your house then we can stop at the café on our way to the hospital."

"Perfect loop. I'll be ready."

After I told Palace Guard about the new plan, we waited on the front porch. As a car drove down our street, Palace Guard patted my back, and when Darren Martin pulled into our driveway, Palace Guard rested his hand on my shoulder, and I relaxed.

When Darren stepped to the porch, I examined his blob. *Yep, it's Darren.*

"Can I help you to the car, Ms. Gray Lady?"

"Thank you. If you'll open the passenger's door, I can make it to the driveway." I tapped my way down the porch to the familiar driveway.

On our way to the café, Darren asked, "How are you doing?"

"I'm adjusting. My sister-in-law set up voice activation on my phone and installed software on my computer to read documents to me."

"Mama's looking forward to seeing you. She doesn't trust many people, but she told me she trusts you. I hope you know how grateful I am that you saved Mama. You'll always be my hero."

I felt my face warm. "She's a strong woman and very special to me. I know you understand."

I cleared my throat. "Faith told me that Eric's aunt was a resident at the senior center and that's how she met him. Do you know who she is?"

"I heard he claimed that Edna Cross is his great aunt."

Interesting choice of words and there's a distinct tone of suspicion in his voice.

I continued, "I've been having trouble with what Faith told me because her church friends said Faith and Eric met at a weekend retreat."

"I don't know how long Mrs. Cross has been at the senior center; maybe they initially met before Mrs. Cross came to the facility."

"Did Eric visit Edna Cross very often?"

"He did for a while but not in the past few months. I ran into him in the reception area not long ago and asked him if he was there to visit Mrs. Cross. He told me it was hard to see her because she didn't recognize him anymore."

"That is odd," I said. "She takes a while to tell a story, but she always knows who I am. In fact, I was thinking since we would be at the hospital for lunch that I would drop in on Edna Cross, if you have a few minutes that you could spare before we leave."

"That would be fine with me. I have a meeting at two."

After Darren parked in front of the café, he said, "Rafael told me someone would run out our lunch when we pulled up." He lowered his window as he said, "Thanks, this is perfect."

After he raised his window, Darren said, "Our sandwiches are in a sack that I can set on the console, but our drinks are in a cardboard holder, Ms. Gray Lady. Do you mind holding them?"

"Not at all."

As he pulled away, I asked, "Why are they keeping your mama in longer than you hoped? Is she doing okay?"

"She's doing great. Her new primary doctor was worried about the impact of any smoke inhalation on her heart, but the cardiologist told me she'll outlive us all. Mama told me her new doctor is knowledgeable but overly cautious and a royal pain in the tush."

I chuckled. "I can hear her say that. Your mama does not mince words."

When Darren slowed then turned, he said, "I'll drop you off at the visitors' entrance then park. I'll bring the sandwiches and drinks. Do you want me to walk with you to the lobby first?"

"No, I would enjoy the fresh air. I'll wait outside for you."

CHAPTER ELEVEN

As I stood outside the entrance, Palace Guard stayed close. Two figures hurried past me into the hospital. "A man and a woman?" I whispered.

I thought Palace Guard was shaking his head.

"A teenager?"

He pointed to me.

"Oh, a teenaged girl."

Palace Guard patted me on the back as another figure approached.

Darren?

Palace Guard patted my back again.

When Darren approached me, he said, "I'm here. Ready to go in? Do you want to take my arm?"

Palace Guard stepped away to make room for Darren.

"Thank you."

While we waited at the elevator, Darren said, "If I hover too much, feel free to tell me. I've been well-trained to back off by Mama."

I giggled. "You've been trained by the best. I appreciate knowing that you wouldn't be offended if I try something solo."

When we reached Mrs. Martin's room she squealed, "It's my Maggie Flanagan. You are a sight for sore eyes. Mine, not yours." She laughed, and I laughed with her.

"I like your look, Maggie Flanagan. The dark sunglasses and the eyepatch give you a mysterious look. Where did you get that gorgeous, emerald-green eyepatch?"

"My best friend's mom made me a slew of patches and sleep masks. I didn't know I had an emerald-green eyepatch. That's awesome."

"It's an exact match of your eyes. Beautiful. She must be a wonderful person."

"She is."

"I'm going to interrupt," Darren said. "Mama, we have lunch. I can pull up one of the visitor's chairs to your table, so Ms. Gray Lady can eat with you. I'll sit close in the other chair."

After Darren set out lunches on the table, he told me, "I unwrapped your sandwich for you. It's a Cuban sandwich, and Rafael had the cook cut it into six pieces. You also have two fried sweet plantains, and your sweet tea with a lid and straw and your napkin are on your left. Y'all enjoy."

I picked up one of my sandwich pieces and took a bite. "This is really good."

"My turkey sandwich is good too," Mrs. Martin said. "I love the Sano Café's food; it's always delicious."

A few minutes later, Darren crumpled his sandwich paper. "I need to make a couple of calls if no one minds. I won't be long."

After he left, I said, "I think I'm only halfway through my sandwich. Have you noticed that men eat fast?"

Mrs. Martin chuckled. "I don't know why they do, but I like to take my time too."

"Do you know who runs the senior center? The owner is a corporation in New York; surely they hired someone for the day-to-day management."

"I've never really thought there might be an overall manager. The nurse director manages the nurses and aides, the nutritionist runs the cafeteria, and Gracie Jane manages the volunteers. Security and the cleaning staff are contractors, as far as I know."

I sipped my sweet tea. "Did you know I have a few pieces of Margarite's jewelry? I tried on a ring that I thought was Margarite's, but it didn't feel like it was Margarite's."

"I understand," Mrs. Martin said. "Not everyone would have noticed the difference, but you would have."

"It is a gold ring that is twisted or braided like a rope. It has tiny diamonds and an indecipherable inscription on the inside."

"It fit you, didn't it? So, whose did you think it was?"

"Yes, it did. It slipped right on, but I knew immediately it was yours."

"It was. It wouldn't have fit you if it wasn't yours now."

"Really? What does it say inside?"

"It's fairy writing. It says, 'You have the sight.' It means that you will always see with more than your eyes."

A tear slipped from my right eye onto my cheek. "That's very comforting."

"It is, isn't it? The fairies want you to have it. You know, not everyone believes in imaginary men or fairies. It's nice to see you again, Palace Guard. Thank you for pulling me out of the senior center."

Mrs. Martin tittered. "Palace Guard is very gallant; his bow is very stately."

I smiled. "Did you ever meet Eric, Faith's boyfriend?"

"Piece of work. All smiles on a snake. Did you know he claimed to be Edna Cross's nephew? He wasn't. When Edna Cross tried to tell Gracie Jane that he was not a relative, Gracie Jane laughed and told Edna that she was confused."

"When did he start visiting Edna?"

"After Faith said her boyfriend had an aunt at the senior center. He visited Edna two or three times. She was very agitated for days after his visit. Are you going to visit Edna while you're here? You should. Ask her about Eric. You'll get a story and an earful, eventually." Mrs. Martin snickered.

I smiled. "You're right about Edna Cross and her stories. I have another question about Gracie Jane and her disability. Why is she faking it?"

"It's become very lucrative for her. The residents at the senior center are very fond of Gracie Jane because of her youth and her perceived bravery and strength to work despite her disability. She's been in more than one will. Many of the residents have no relatives and were more than willing to designate poor, spunky Gracie Jane as a beneficiary."

"Did she ask them to name her in their wills?"

"Not directly—she's good. She has her monthly chats, as she calls them, with each wing in the cafeteria. She thanks those who have named her in their wills and gives them their monthly medals that she calls thank you tokens. People display their medals and brag about having more medals than anyone else in their wing. Gracie Jane gives bonus medals when she's named sole beneficiary. Now, this is gossip, so I don't know if it's true, but I heard a woman in another wing changed her will, and Gracie Jane took back all her medals. The resident was very distraught; I don't know if she changed it back, but someone said she had her medals again, so she must have."

"Isn't that illegal or something?"

"Who's going to report her? Would you want to lose all your status symbols?"

"You don't have any, do you?" I snickered.

Mrs. Martin snorted. "I seriously considered redistributing medals, but my son has forbidden me to touch them. Sometimes it cramps my style when he anticipates my every move."

"I know what you're talking about. My husband is the same."

"It definitely adds to the excitement to get around them, doesn't it?"

I flipped my hair. "I'm sure I don't know of what you speak."

Mrs. Martin cackled. "You even said that in your best Maggie Flanagan voice. Love it."

I giggled. "He doesn't buy it either."

Darren stepped into the room. "Why do I get nervous when I hear the two of you laughing?"

"It's okay, son. No thievery planned," Mrs. Martin said.

"I'd like to go visit Edna Cross before we leave. Do you have enough time, Darren?"

"Sure, she's on this floor. I'll walk you there."

When we reached her room, I said, "This was easy. I can find my way back."

"Call me if you get lost. I'll be with Mama."

"Hello, Ms. Gray Lady. It's wonderful to see you. Did you hear that the computer guru saved me?"

"I heard that you saved yourself by getting to the park. That was heroic."

"I wished I had my gardening gloves with me; I burned my hands. I know you can't see, but they're all bandaged. I always thought I might like to learn to play the mandolin. This put my entire musical career on hold. Did I ever tell you I sang opera at the Met? I hope not because it isn't true." She cackled.

"Tell me about Eric Stephens pretending to be your nephew."

"Eric Stephens' father was an old classmate of mine in high school. Philip wasn't much for studying, but his artwork was beautiful. He was especially talented at forging signatures."

She sighed. "I always envied him for that. Philip sat next to me in science and copied my tests. When I realized what he was doing, I transposed the numbers on my paper to all wrong answers then waited until he turned in his test before I corrected mine. When he got a zero on his test, and I got the highest grade in the class, he knew I'd caught him, but he didn't take it well. Philip claimed he was distracted and couldn't focus on the test because he was so disturbed that I cheated. Both of us had to take a new test, except the teachers administered our tests in different rooms. That was not his plan. Philip spent the rest of his life trying to get even with me, but he was too slow. I was always at least two steps ahead of him. He never learned. Can you imagine having the progeny of a tiny-brained sneak claim to be my nephew? He obviously inherited his father's brains because he either had forgotten or never knew about his father's puny efforts at revenge. The only good thing about Eric's visits is that my aim improved. After I beaned him with a lunch plate, he never came back again. The cafeteria manager spoke quite sternly to me about the broken dishes and threatened to serve my meals on paper plates before she gave me a small box of wooden blocks. I kept practicing in case he returned, but sadly, he hasn't; I continue to work with my blocks just in case."

By the time Edna finished her story, I couldn't contain my glee and laughed, and she laughed along with me.

After I calmed down, I asked, "How much of that is true?"

"Every part that you believed is true," she said.

"That's terrible because I believed the whole thing," I said.

"Must all be true then," she said, and I thought I heard Palace Guard snort.

"I did have one more question. You told me there was a trap ahead of me, but I could handle it. Who told you there was a trap, and that it was for me?"

"Why, my nephew, of course. Right before I nailed him with a lunch plate."

"Is that true?"

Edna whispered, "He's not my nephew. Be careful."

She cleared her throat. "Why would you doubt a dotty, old lady?" She turned away and hummed a familiar tune that I couldn't quite place.

"I've enjoyed our time together, but it's time for me to leave," I said. "Thank you for the maybe true story."

I tapped toward Mrs. Martin's room, and Palace Guard corrected me at only one turn. "Thanks."

When I reached Mrs. Martin's room, she said, "You're dragging, Maggie Flanagan. Did you have a productive visit with Edna Cross?"

"Yes, I appreciated the chance to talk to Edna, and you're right—I'm a little tired."

"Give an old woman a hug before you leave."

As I hugged her, she whispered, "The fairies are worried. Keep your men close."

"Will do."

"Ready to go?" Darren asked.

I sighed. "I'm ready."

After Darren pulled into my driveway, he rushed around his car and opened the passenger's door.

"Thank you so much, Darren, for lunch and for giving me time to visit with your mama and Edna Cross."

"You're welcome. You've been a breath of fresh air for Mama. She enjoys your visits. I'll let you know about Sunday."

After I was inside the house, I stumbled to the sofa, removed my sunglasses, and collapsed. "It might be more comfortable in my bed, but the sofa was closer."

Palace Guard flipped the afghan on me as I turned onto my side. "I'm just going to rest my eyes."

I woke when Palace Guard tapped on my arm. I stretched as I sat up. "Thanks. I need a large glass of cold tea."

After I poured sweet tea into my tall, lidded cup, I took my phone and tea out back where Spike and Lucy were already enjoying the fresh air.

Lucy barked and set off responding barks and howls from the other nearby dogs while I sipped on my tea. After Lucy became bored with stirring up the neighborhood, she flopped down next to me. When I picked up my phone, Palace Guard placed his hand over mine.

"I rested. Now, I'm working."

When Glenn answered, I said, "I'm fine. I spent most of the afternoon at the hospital. That doesn't sound right. I was visiting. I'll take a breath, so you can talk."

"As long as you're fine, I can relax and listen. You sound very excited. What's going on?"

"Remember you told me it was important to find out who benefited from the deaths? I don't have the documentation, but I think you can get it." I told him about the wills and Gracie Jane.

"Wow. You're right. We can dig into that. Deaths at a facility for elderly folks aren't typical red flags, but if there's a pattern of one person being the beneficiary to the wills, that changes the picture. I have information for you about Gracie Jane. Turns out her burns weren't as bad as the first responders thought. She was released from the burn unit yesterday and has disappeared."

"What? No idea of where she is?"

"Not at all. No one seems to be excited about that except you and me, by the way. The consensus is she was transferred to another facility to convalesce. We're still looking."

"Eric Stephens claimed to be Edna Cross's nephew. He isn't. As a relative to one of the residents, no one would have questioned his presence. Another tidbit that Edna shared is Eric's father, Philip, was a talented forger, and signatures were his specialty."

"Could his son have picked it up? That seems like a valuable skill. Eric could sign prescriptions and wills, for example."

"That's what I was thinking. Is there any evidence of forged signatures on any of the wills? Do you suppose the fire may have also destroyed any forged documents that were kept in the office at the senior center? But that wouldn't explain the explosions at the fire exit."

"I'll pursue the forgery angle to see if it leads me anywhere. What else do you have that will give me more work?"

I snorted. "I can't think of anything else."

"Let me know. Paul said to tell you to keep 'em coming. He's back in the groove of investigating and loving it. Be safe."

After Glenn hung up, I rose. "I'm really restless. I wish I could go for a run."

Palace Guard grabbed my arm before I could head to the door.

I sighed, and he removed his hand. "Fine. It was a wishful whine—that's all. Maybe I'll see well enough next week for a short run."

When Lucy yipped, I heard the crunch of the tires on the driveway. "Larry's home already? Time sure flies when you can't see a clock."

Larry strode inside and grabbed me for a welcome home hug and kiss.

"I'll scrub two potatoes then put them into the oven. Are you okay with going shopping? There are two pawn shops that I'd like to check. When we get back, I can warm up the ham steak and make a salad."

"Sounds great. I'll get my backpack and my sunglasses then I'll be ready."

On the way to the first pawnshop, Larry asked, "How is Mrs. Martin doing?"

"She's doing very well. The doctor wanted to keep her an additional day because of her age, but I don't think the doctor's going to be able to keep her in beyond tomorrow. I saw Edna Cross too. She burned her hands in the fire, but the burns must not be severe because she's not in a special unit."

Larry pulled into the parking lot. "Here we are—Bud's Pawnshop."

I asked, "Is it okay if I stick close to you? I'm feeling a little self-conscious about being around strangers, but I don't want to slow you down."

"I need you close to me because your gun knowledge is invaluable. You are a remarkably skilled fighter and gun expert who currently happens to be partially sighted. Got it?"

"Yes. I just forgot for a minute."

When Larry opened my door, he leaned down and kissed me. "One more thing, you are also my gorgeous sweetheart."

"You are the best medicine I could have; let's find my Mr. Sexy Pants a deer rifle."

While Larry and the pawn shop owner did the man talk thing that I never understand, I listened to two women nearby as they discussed the jewelry in a display case, and I frowned. *Sound like replicas to me.*

After they asked the clerk the cost of a necklace, I relaxed. *Excellent price for a replica. Good to know this is a reputable shop.*

When Larry and Bud got down to the serious business of deer rifles, I shifted my focus from jewelry to long guns.

After we narrowed Larry's choices to two rifles, he asked, "Which one, Maggie?"

"You wouldn't go wrong with either one," I said. "Hold each one and aim through the scope again to see which one is more comfortable."

I listened while Larry held and sighted through the scope of each rifle.

"That was a good idea, sweetie. The heavier rifle was more comfortable."

"Never thought of that before," Bud said, "but it makes sense. Most people would have chosen the lighter rifle, but the heavier one must be the better balanced of the two. I learn something every day. You must be a sharpshooter, Maggie."

I felt my face warm. *Stop blushing.*

"She is," Larry said. "One of the best."

"If you don't mind me asking, have you had the opportunity to practice your shooting since your injury?"

"No, but we're hoping to shoot on Saturday," I said.

"We're looking for somewhere she can shoot without gawkers," Larry added.

"I hear that. I've got a small range you can use. It's closed Saturday mornings, if you'd like to meet me there. You can lock up after you're finished."

I nodded, and Larry said, "That would be great."

"Here's the address. Is nine thirty okay? That gives me plenty of time to get here to open at ten."

Larry bought his deer rifle and two boxes of ammunition before we left the shop.

On the way home, he said, "That worked out, didn't it, sweetie? His dad was with GBI, but you probably heard all that. You ready for a gourmet meal?"

I smiled. "My favorite kind."

Palace Guard poked me.

I know, I'll pay attention to man talk next time.

I sat at the table while Larry pulled together our supper and told him about my conversations with Mrs. Martin, Edna Cross, and Glenn.

"I'm really grateful that Glenn is doing all the research. I can listen to documents, but my research skills are currently on hold," I said.

"I suspect Glenn is enjoying it. You are good at collaboration, most of the time." Larry set our salads on the table.

"I'd argue with you, but you'd probably just drag out old, one-off examples, wouldn't you?"

"One-off?" Larry chuckled. "Don't get me started."

"Have you heard of a good taco place yet?"

"Excellent diversion. I'm always willing to talk about tacos. I haven't, but that's a good reminder. I'll start asking around. Ready to eat? Want mustard for your ham?"

"Yes, please. On the side for dipping."

"Here you go. Baked potato with butter is at nine o'clock. Your ham is in the middle of your plate, and the mustard is at three o'clock. Your salad is in a bowl on your left, and your fork is on your right. Your sweet tea is next to your plate at one o'clock."

I speared a piece of ham and dipped it into the mustard.

Larry continued, "I stopped at a bakery on my way home and picked up chocolate chip cookies for dessert."

"Yum. Are we having cookies and beer on the back porch?"

"Sounds good to me."

After we ate, Larry loaded the dishwasher then carried our beer while I led the way with the sack of cookies.

While we nibbled, drank, and rocked, Larry said, "A couple of guys heard today that their training has been rescheduled to begin next year. What if we're told we'll be in Columbus for another year? How would you feel about that?"

"I wouldn't care as long as we're together."

"When I first applied, I was obsessed with going to the training, but it's all different now. I don't care where they send us if we're together. Pretty convenient, right?"

After I drank half my beer, I said, "I'm full, and the mosquitos are feasting."

"Good time to go inside," Larry said.

* * *

After Larry left the next morning, I put on the headset to listen to the rest of Faith's notebook then pulled off the headset. "I'm burned out. I need to take a walk to the park with Lucy."

Palace Guard pointed to my phone.

"I can't call Larry. He's busy. Did you know I can see you more clearly? Why don't we just go for a walk around the block?"

Palace Guard put his face close to mine and rolled his eyes, and I snickered.

"Point taken. Let's go."

Spike and Lucy headed to the door, and Palace Guard shrugged. I put on my eyepatch and sunglasses and stuck my pistol inside my waistband before I grabbed a ball cap and jammed it onto my head. As we headed out the door, I grabbed the keys then locked the house.

The morning breeze from the west kept the bright sunshine from being too warm but didn't do much for the humidity. My shirt was sticking to me before we'd gone half a block. A mockingbird ran through its repertoire, and dogs inside the houses we passed barked. Lucy didn't bark in return because she was above all that. She was free to wander and to investigate lawns and bushes. I smiled as I tapped along the sidewalk with Palace Guard holding my elbow in case I tripped.

When we returned to the house, my spirits had lifted. "That was a good morale boost for me; thank you, everyone."

After we went inside, I poured myself a tall cup of tea and sat on the sofa. As I sipped my tea, my phone rang.

"Hello, Gray Lady," Heather said. "What's on the agenda for today?"

"I think we're going to hide from the humidity."

"I have an inside scoop for you. Gracie Jane was denied entry to Canada at the Buffalo border, and evidently a pistol dropped out of the pouch on the side of her wheelchair when she wheeled away from the border checkpoint. Isn't that dumb? The press already has it, but it isn't likely to make the news anywhere, must less in south Georgia. I heard she claimed she was crossing for humanitarian reasons, and the gun was not hers. So, she'll be easy to find because she's under arrest, and I think they're sending her back to Georgia."

"Wow. Thanks for the clarification."

"Don't thank me because I didn't tell you anything." Heather cracked up before she disconnected.

"Another morale booster." I told Palace Guard and Spike what Heather told me.

I tapped to the bedroom and picked up a sleep mask. "I'm going to rest my eyes like I'm supposed to." I sat at my computer to listen to Faith's notebook again.

I was halfway through her notebook when Palace Guard broke my concentration as he poked my arm and pointed to my phone. After I answered, Darren said, "Ms. Gray Lady, Edna Cross took a turn for the worst last night. I think the amount of smoke that she inhaled hurt her lungs more than the doctors expected. If I come get you, could you come to the hospital? She's been asking for you."

"Absolutely. When will you be here?"

"Fifteen minutes."

"I'll be ready."

After I hung up, I told Palace Guard and Spike about Edna Cross then hurried to the bathroom and took a fast three-minute shower before I brushed my hair then rushed to the bedroom to dress.

Could have just changed my shirt, but I have to keep the color combinations together.

When Darren pulled into the driveway, I was ready to go. Spike stayed with Lucy, and Palace Guard accompanied me. When I reached Darren's car, I realized I'd automatically grabbed my jo on the way out. *Excellent. I'd be worried if I went anywhere without my staff.*

On the way to the hospital, Darren said, "Mrs. Cross was doing so well. It was a real shock that she went downhill so fast. She's been very agitated and insisted that she has to see you."

When we reached the hospital, Darren said, "If you want to go on in, tell the information desk you need to go to the ICU. They'll probably have someone accompany you; or if you wait, I'll take you to the ICU floor."

While Darren parked, Palace Guard and I waited near the door. After Darren joined us, he said, "We go left to the elevators."

Palace Guard slowed me as we neared the elevators. "Third floor," Darren said.

When we arrived at a desk outside a set of double doors, Darren said, "Mrs. Maggie Ewing to see Mrs. Edna Cross."

"Mrs. Cross has been asking for you, Mrs. Ewing. She calls you 'Gray Lady,' right?"

I nodded.

"Are you partially sighted, Mrs. Ewing?" she asked.

"Not quite." I smiled.

"Can you sign in?"

I held up my hand, and she put a pen in it then guided my hand to a paper. I did my neatest scrawl.

"If you'll take my elbow, I'll lead you to Mrs. Cross's room."

Before we entered the room, she said, "I'll take you past her bed to the side next to the window where there is less equipment. I'll move a chair next to her head so you can sit. Is that okay?"

"Thank you, I appreciate it."

"She may not acknowledge or speak to you, but we're confident she will hear you. Just talk to her like you normally would."

After I was seated in the chair, my escort left the room.

I scooted the chair closer to Edna and squinted to examine her face; when she opened one eye, I jumped.

"What are you up to, Edna?" I asked in a quiet voice.

"Glad you're here, Gray Lady. You won't believe what happened, but first let me show you something."

After she held her breath for almost a minute, a machine blasted its warning. When she started breathing again, the machine quieted.

"I know that trick," I said. "I did it myself in the hospital, but I did it accidently because I was trying to hear something."

"Did you hear something?"

"Sure did. What are you up to?"

"You're repeating yourself. I was dozing last night when someone tiptoed into my room. I didn't think anything about it because if you were in the hospital, you know that a patient's room is an airport runway at night with all kinds of people flying in and out. I rolled over to take my pill, but when the person slammed a pillow over my face, I held my breath and went limp. The only monitor I had was a heart machine—whatever it's called—and it eventually blared out a warning exactly like this one did. The person who was trying to smother me pushed down on the pillow one more time then dashed out of the room. I took a breath then held it again, and the machine went off again. I tried to tell the person who rushed into my room that someone tried to smother me, but they kept telling me to take a breath. I ask you, wasn't yelling at them that someone tried to kill me direct evidence that I was breathing? Rhetorical question. I've spent most of the day holding my breath at odd times and asking for Gray Lady. I knew you'd listen to me."

"Do me a favor. Keep breathing while I'm here. They'll think I'm a calming presence or something."

"I'll do that for you. I can't quit completely though because they might decide I'm fine and kick me out of ICU where I'm safe because they limit visitors."

"What was the other reason you wanted to see me, besides the obvious—I'll report that someone tried to kill you. Too bad the killer didn't speak." *Here's your opening, Edna.*

"Oh, but he did. I was going to get around to that. He said, 'I fixed your will for good, old woman.' I was deeply offended. I am quite spry even though I'm wheelchair bound and am definitely not an old woman. I almost told him so too, except then I remembered I wasn't supposed to be breathing because he killed me."

"You did an outstanding job. What else do you need me to do?"

"I need to see my lawyer. If I give you his name and number, would you call him for me? I need to be sure that if the killer ever succeeds that my will is solid and uncontestable. My biggest worry is that my killer will benefit from my death, and I got the distinct feeling when he killed me that he had a newer will that I never approved or signed."

"I'll do it. Tell me the lawyer's name, and I'll call him today."

After I left Edna's room, the woman who had escorted me said, "I'll walk you to the double door. Mr. Martin is waiting for you. Thank you for visiting; it was amazing how much you relaxed Mrs. Cross."

On our way to the elevator, Darren said, "Mama was napping when I left. Is it okay if we leave now? Mama wants you to visit again next week if she can't get released, and I told her I'd ask you."

"I think she'll be out of the hospital by tomorrow, but if not, it depends on your schedule."

"She'll enjoy hearing that we didn't plan on another hospital visit because you think she'll be home."

"Good."

When Darren parked in my driveway, I said, "I'm good from here. Thank you again for taking me to see your mama."

After Palace Guard and I were inside, I said, "Text to Larry: I'm okay. Call please. Send."

CHAPTER TWELVE

My phone repeated the message and ended with "Sent."

Three. Two. One.

My phone rang.

"I really am okay, but I—"

"Where are you? Is Palace Guard there? I'm almost to my car."

"Honey, stop," I said. "May I please speak to Agent Ewing?"

"What?"

"I have something I need to tell my favorite cop, Agent Ewing."

"Okay, Mrs. Ewing. I've stopped in the middle of the parking lot."

"Would you please return to the sidewalk? Edna Cross told me that someone tried to smother her at the hospital last night. She held her breath and her cardiac alarm went off and scared away her assailant. When she tried to tell the medical staff, they thought she was hysterical."

"Where is she now?"

"She's in the intensive care unit. She told me the man who was smothering her said something about forging her signature on a will."

"Why is she in the intensive care unit?" Larry growled.

"Because her cardiac alarm goes off when she holds her breath. It was actually a brilliant idea when you think about it because access to her is restricted."

Larry chuckled. "I remember when you held your breath in the hospital. You terrified an entire wing of nurses. Did you teach Edna your trick?"

"Of course not, and besides, I only held my breath to hear the beep. Completely different."

He snorted. "If you think so. Someone will follow up with Mrs. Cross. Talk to you later, sweetie."

After he hung up, I said, "Dial" then repeated the lawyer's phone number.

An administrative person took my message and told me the lawyer would call me back in a few minutes. I poured tea into my lidded cup and relaxed on the sofa while Lucy continued her ladylike snore on the rug near my feet.

My phone rang before I finished my tea.

After the polite niceties were out of the way, I said, "Edna Cross asked me to call you because she's in the hospital and is concerned that someone may have a will with her forged signature."

"I'll visit with her to ease her mind. Not everyone appreciates her unique storytelling style; my paralegal calls it rambling, but I enjoy the crumbs of information she drops along the way. Sometimes I think the birds may have carried away a few of the tidbits, but that just adds to the intrigue, doesn't it?" He chuckled. "Her will is untouchable because I filed it with the county probate judge when Mrs. Cross revised it not long ago. Not everyone wants their original will locked in a judge's vault, but Mrs. Cross was worried the original might get lost at the senior center. It doesn't matter how many phony wills there are with forged signatures. The only one that is valid is the one in the judge's vault."

"She'll be happy to hear it. She's very agitated."

He chuckled. "I've known Mrs. Cross for years. She is easily agitated, that's for sure, and can spin a tale, but what she says always has a grain of truth for those of us who are willing to appreciate her style and listen."

After he disconnected, I said, "I hope I always have someone who is willing to appreciate my style too."

As I sipped my tea and glanced up, Spike danced his wacky dance in front of me, and I applauded while a tear ran down my cheek. "You're kind of blurry, but I can see your dance, Spike."

When Palace Guard put his hand in front of me, I giggled and smacked a high five.

"I'd send Larry a text to tell him my vision is improving, but I don't want him to get hit in the parking lot. That man scares me sometimes."

After lunch, I slipped on my sleeping mask and relaxed on the sofa. While I thought of all the things I'd like to do but couldn't because of my limited sight, I drifted off. When I awoke, I didn't know how long I'd been sleeping.

This is maddening.

I wondered if Edna Cross was okay and thought about how wonderful it was that Mrs. Martin saw the men. *Why can't I see the fairies?*

Am I supposed to be doing something about supper? *Larry owes me tacos.*

I wonder if I should send Larry a text about tacos.

Bad idea.

I lifted the right side of my sleep mask, and Palace Guard grinned.

"Fine, I don't do well with bored, do I? Want to hear my list of things I can't do? Never mind, it's boring." I chuckled at my own joke and knew without looking that Palace Guard rolled his eyes.

When Lucy clicked to the back door, I went outside with her and Spike.

After Palace Guard joined me on the porch, I said, "I don't like the discrepancy between what Faith told me and what her church group said about how she and Eric met. I have two people I could ask—Mr. Bustamante and Eric. Or better yet, I could spend a little time with Mr. Bustamante tomorrow while Larry did his one-of-the-guys thing he does so well."

I stretched and picked up my jo. "I feel better with a plan. Let's practice."

After I moved to the middle of the yard, I tried to twirl the staff, but I was too short. "Okay, no twirling. I'm ready."

Palace Guard put me through the paces of lunge, turn, and swing. When Spike stepped in front of me, I lunged, and when he ducked, I swung. He tried to grab the staff, but I whipped it away from him and wielded my jo with all the momentum of my best baseball bat swing at his head. When I connected, his neck snapped, and he went down. I threw down my jo and as I hurried to kneel next to him, Lucy yipped her bang bark.

"Dang it, Spike. That's cheating. I thought I hurt you." I stopped to pick up my jo and stomped to the house. I slammed the door as hard as I could then leaned against my jo while I took a breath.

After I calmed down, I returned outside, and Spike was sitting in my chair. I walked out to the yard and collapsed on the ground.

"Dead is dead," I mumbled into the grass. When I rose to a sitting position, I brushed away the dirt and leaves on my face and shirt while Spike entertained me with his best jig.

"You made your point, Spike. Time to toughen up. I need to gather up all that pity party stuff and toss it."

I hummed a fairy tune as I sauntered into the house then poured myself more tea. My phone rang.

"Hi, sweetie," Larry said, "I'm okay."

I snickered. "Well done, Agent Ewing. I'm ready to hear why you have to tell me you're okay."

"I heard from the training center, and I'm in the class that begins at the end of this month unless we decide to pass and wait for the following class. I'm guaranteed a spot either way. We can talk about it later."

"That's awesome news, and I'm ready when you are. We can make it work."

"I knew you'd say that, sweetheart. I have more news. The guys told me about a café downtown that is open on Friday and Saturday nights, and their specialty is tacos, enchiladas, and tamales. Get dressed in your favorite clothes, and we'll leave after I get home. One of the guys is trying to get reservations."

"That's exciting. I'll take a shower and put on my favorite clothes—the clean ones."

Larry chuckled before he hung up, and I smiled. *Should be a rule. Marry a man who laughs at your bad jokes.*

"I need a shower. I've got a hot date."

When I pulled off my shirt, I held my breath then exhaled. "You belong in the washer, stinky shirt."

When I climbed out of the shower, I towel-dried my hair and combed out the tangles before I padded to our bedroom. After I dropped my dirty clothes and my eyepatch into the laundry basket, I opened the top sack of matched clothing and squinted at the contents.

All gray?

I dressed and put on my clean eyepatch then made my way to the living room.

"Are my clothes gray?" I peered at Palace Guard who shook his head.

"I think I can't see colors yet." Before I went to the bathroom to brush my hair into a ponytail, I said, "Just a data point. Not a complaint. I actually have very fond memories of gray."

When Larry bounded into the house, he swept me up into a hug. "Sweetie, you are as gorgeous as ever. I spent all day thinking about you."

I buried my face in his chest and inhaled. "You smell like my handsome husband. Did I guess right?"

He laughed. "How's your sight going?"

"The blobs are blurry people now, but I don't see colors; everything is blurry gray. Palace Guard told me I'm not wearing gray."

"Your eyepatch is red, and your shirt is red with tiny silver sparkles. It's a perfect undercover Maggie outfit."

I giggled as I followed Larry to the bedroom. "Undercover Gray Lady in red with my red boots? Déjà vu?"

After he changed out of his uniform, Larry jammed on his Texas Tech cap. "I needed a little red to match with my sweetie," he said. "The perfect match." He kissed me and patted my bottom. "Ready to go?"

When we reached the door, he said, "I'm glad you're going too, Palace Guard."

Before he locked the door, Larry said, "Maggie, Palace Guard is wearing a Texas Tech ballcap, a pearl snap shirt, jeans, and cowboy boots. He wins the best undercover award, which is only fitting for an imaginary Palace Guard."

As I made my way to the passenger's door, I watched my feet so I wouldn't fall down laughing at the sight of the two blurry men that I was sure were swaggering to the truck.

After we were in the truck, I asked, "So, where are we going?"

"It's called the Sano Café. They serve lunch Monday through Friday and are open in the evenings Friday and Saturday nights."

Do I tell him?

Palace Guard poked my shoulder.

"What?" Larry asked.

"I've had lunch at the Sano Café. The chef is superb, and the owner, Rafael, is awesome."

Larry chuckled. "You've been in town a week, and you're already on a first name basis with the owner of the best place to eat in town, and I'm not surprised. I think you'd be working there if you hadn't been injured."

"What a good idea," I said.

"I was joking, Maggie. Just joking," Larry said.

I covered my mouth to hide my smirk.

When Larry opened the café door, I cringed at the level of noise and the mass of blurry figures.

"Will you be okay?" Larry asked. "Is this too much?"

"Gray Lady," a man called out over the roar. *Rafael.* "I saved you a special seat in the kitchen—chef's table."

Larry leaned to whisper, "You just made my stock rise, Gray Lady."

When Rafael reached us, Larry said, "Hi, I'm Mr. Gray Lady, also known as Agent Larry Ewing in the daytime."

Rafael chuckled. "I know the feeling well, Agent Ewing. I'm smart enough not to interfere with my wife, the chef."

After I sat on a stool at a work-height table, Rafael said, "Gray Lady, this is my wife and the café's chef, Marissa."

"It's wonderful to meet you, Gray Lady." Her melodic voice reminded me of wind chimes in a light breeze.

A roar of laughter came from the dining area.

"If you'd like to check in with the guys, Larry, I'll be fine here," I said.

"You sure?"

"Of course; maybe I'll pick up some cooking hints."

After Larry left, Marissa asked, "You studied with Chef Daryl in Louisiana, didn't you?"

"You know Chef Daryl? He told me the best way for me to learn was to watch him. While Chef cooked, he weaved in cooking hints through his gossipy stories about other chefs."

Marissa laughed. "Word gets around in the culinary world. He's a legend, that's for sure, sha. I met him once at a conference and was in total awe."

"I'd almost forgotten about Chef. He gave me a notebook of his recipes, and I gave it to my best friend's mother."

"If you have any recipes, I'd love to try my hand if you'll be my taster."

"That sounds great. I'll have to follow up with Jennifer, and we'd need to include Larry as a taster, if you don't mind."

"I don't mind at all. I assumed you two were a set."

Marissa hummed a tune that sounded the same as one the fairies sang. I glanced at Palace Guard, and when he nodded, I smiled. *Fairies are everywhere.*

"I was really sorry when I heard about your attack," Marissa said. "Are you doing okay?"

"Most of the time. I'm still hoping to regain at least partial sight in my right eye, but my left eye was too severely damaged. I had a lovely pity party this afternoon, but it was boring."

"We all fall into that once in a while, don't we? I was in a car crash when I was ten years old. The car rolled down an embankment, and my right arm was crushed. The trauma center saved my life but not my arm. I might be a one-armed woman, but I'm a force in the kitchen. I was only seventeen when I enrolled in culinary school, but I could outcook every single one of them. When my instructor heard some of the trash talk going around, she required that the entire class cook for a week with their dominant arm behind their backs."

I giggled. "I would have loved to have seen that."

While Marissa chopped and stirred, I inhaled the aroma of a chef's kitchen while the booming men's voices from the main room all but drowned out the sounds of cooking.

"Rafael is more social than I am," Marissa said. "I'm perfectly happy hiding away in my kitchen."

"Larry's the same. I don't do as well with crowds and noise. I love hearing how much fun they're having, but I don't want to be in the middle of it."

Larry burst into the kitchen. "Are you doing okay, sweetie? I feel like I've abandoned you."

"I am having a wonderful time, and the kitchen is much quieter than the dining area. Marissa knew Chef Daryl, and we're swapping chef stories. Enjoy yourself."

After Larry left, Marissa said, "He's a keeper, isn't he? I love how he hovers but leaves you the space you want. Rafael is the same. He comes from a big family, and when we all get together, I hang out with his mama. She won't tolerate anyone else in her kitchen, so it's my refuge. She tells the best stories; I know all the family dirt. It's the same here and probably was everywhere you've worked too. No one thinks about the chef in the kitchen. I hear everything."

"What about Faith Bustamante? I've heard such conflicting information about her and Eric Stephens. Did they ever come here?"

"I'm not the best judge of Eric Stephens because I have a soft spot in my heart for John Howard. I've seen John's temper, but he genuinely cared for Faith. I wanted to shake Faith and tell her to open her eyes." Marissa clucked her tongue. "Such a shame. Eric Stephens seemed like a nice enough guy, but the week before Faith died, Eric told her his company had transferred him to an office up north. They spoke very quietly before he left the café."

Marissa opened the oven door, and the heady aroma of herbs and roasted meat swirled through the kitchen. "I noticed he didn't ask Faith to go with him, and she was crying when she left. I wanted to tell her that I thought she was better off, but I have barely enough social awareness to know that she would not have listened."

I nodded. *This is new.*

When the server rushed into the kitchen, Marissa said, "Perfect timing, as usual. The platters of tacos and tamales are ready."

After the server left, Marissa said, "Why don't you join Larry and his rowdy bunch? They'll quiet down in two seconds after they start eating."

"Thank you, that's a great idea. I enjoyed my time in the kitchen with you; now, I'll pretend that I'm partially social." I snickered as I left.

When I stepped into the dining room, Larry appeared at my side. "Ready to eat the best tacos in town? We're at the big table near the front."

I took his arm, and he led to me to a table and held my chair while I was seated. He leaned over and whispered, "My seat is on your right. Will you be okay?"

I smiled and nodded.

Larry introduced me to everyone at the large table, but I didn't catch anyone's name in the clamor. After a man shouted, "Dig in," the clinking sounds of a meal replaced the deafening roar of the crowd. *Marissa called it.*

"One soft taco is on the plate in front of you," Larry said in a quiet voice. "Napkin and silverware on your right, a small bowl of pinto beans is at one o'clock, and your lidded sweet tea with a straw is on your left. Let me know if you need anything."

I was self-conscious about crumbs on my face and brushed my cheeks and chin with my napkin between bites until Palace Guard patted my back.

I'm doing okay?

He nodded, and I relaxed.

I smiled in the direction of people who spoke to me, and Larry replied for me. *Definitely a keeper.*

On our way home, Larry asked, "Are you okay, sweetie?"

"I'm tired, but I wouldn't have missed it for the world. The food was great, everyone was nice, and Marissa is awesome."

Larry exhaled. "I was really worried. I didn't want you to be uncomfortable; I forgot that you make friends everywhere you go."

After we were inside the house, Larry asked, "Care for a beer, or are you ready to call it a night?"

"I'm too wired to go straight to bed. A beer sounds good."

We went out back with Palace Guard, Spike, and Lucy with our beers.

"What's our plan for tomorrow?" Larry asked.

"We're shooting at nine thirty. I'd like to visit Mr. Bustamante, and if Eric's there, you could do the man talk thing with him."

Larry sprayed his mouthful of beer then wiped his face with his shirttail and chuckled. "Warn me next time, would you? So, what do you mean man talk thing?"

"You know. Chat about man stuff and use your undercover investigator tactics to see what you think about him. I'm interested in his version of how he and Faith met."

"Sounds easy to me," Larry said.

"That's because you're so good at it, and that's also why you're such an awesome investigator."

"I'm awesome? You think so? Thank you."

I squinted at him. *Did he blush?*

Palace Guard nodded, and I smiled.

* * *

Coffee beckoned to me from the kitchen when I woke the next morning. I grabbed my jo and tapped to the kitchen. *I'm getting better at maneuvering with my jo.*

"Good morning, sweetie. I've poured your coffee."

I sat at the table, and Larry placed my cup in front of me.

I caressed my cup with two hands. "I'm used to being the first one up. I've turned into a slacker."

"You're definitely not a slacker. You must need the rest."

"What time is it? Are we leaving soon?"

"It's only six thirty. We have plenty of time. Do you want your usual breakfast?"

"Yes. How is our supply of cinnamon rolls?" I asked.

"We may want to make a batch tomorrow to make it through next week."

"That sounds great. I need to call Jennifer sometime to ask her about the recipes that Chef Daryl gave me. Marissa told me she'd like to try some of his recipes, and we could be her tasters."

"I'm part of the we, right?"

"Always." I finished my coffee, and Larry refilled my cup.

After we ate, I dressed and called Jennifer.

"I'm fine," I said as soon as she answered.

Jennifer chuckled. "You sound like Kate. I always assume she's in trouble too when she calls. How are you doing? Other than fine, of course. And how are Lucy, Larry, and your men?"

I snickered. "Lucy and Spike enjoy the backyard. Larry loves his job, and Palace Guard hovers while Larry is at work. I have an ophthalmologist appointment next week to check the sight in my right eye. My left eye was too badly damaged, but I may regain partial sight in my right eye."

"I'm sorry to hear about your left eye, but according to what we've heard, your quick reaction to cover your eyes saved your right eye. Let me know if you need any additional hover persons. We have spares."

I smiled. "Larry and I went out to dinner last night with his work crowd and their spouses. I talked with the chef who knows Chef

Daryl. Can you send me some of his recipes? She'd like to try them out."

"You haven't unpacked all the boxes yet, have you?"

"There are a couple of boxes in the spare bedroom closet that we didn't get to yet."

"One of the boxes has your notebook. I copied the recipes that I wanted before Ella and I packed Larry's things, and she added your notebook to one of Larry's boxes."

"That's awesome. We'll look for it. How's everybody doing there?"

"Everyone is well, and we are working hard and having fun. That's how it's supposed to be, isn't it?"

After we hung up, Larry asked, "What are we looking for?"

"Chef Daryl's notebook is in one of your boxes that we haven't unpacked yet. Ella put it there for me."

"That's easy. We can do that later, right? It's about time for us to leave."

On our way to the range, Larry said, "Our priority is for you to shoot your pistol at least once, so we can see how your feel for a target might be. After you decide you're ready for a rest, I'll sight in my deer rifle."

After we pulled into the range parking lot, Bud pulled in next to us.

"The goggles you asked me to order came in, Larry, and I brought you something extra, Maggie. The manufacturer sent me the latest in-ear hearing protection for women. Why don't you try it out and let me know how it works. If I send them feedback, they'll send me another free set and a good discount for any that I order. They don't even care if I tell them their ear protection is lousy as long as I tell them why, so they can fix it." Bud chuckled.

After I placed the hearing protection in my ears, I said, "It's comfortable. I've never been able to use in-ear before because they're too big to fit inside my ears. I'll send you a write up. Do we have an email address?"

"Good idea. Here's my card, Larry. Let me know how they work out, Maggie."

Bud unlocked the range, and after we went inside, he showed Larry how to turn on and off the security system and lights. He gave Larry a tour of the facility before he left. Larry locked the door, and we set up.

"Do you want to wear the goggles?" Larry asked.

"I'd like to see how I do without them. If I have too much trouble with the glare, I'll use them."

"Makes sense. Do you want Palace Guard to guide you?" Larry asked.

"Yes. I'd like to start out the way we'll be operating. Do you agree?"

"Yep," Larry said.

Palace Guard guided me until he was satisfied with my position.

"The target is ten yards from you, and you're in a good position to shoot at the center of the bull's eye. Fire when ready."

I relaxed my jaw as I breathed out then squeezed the trigger with a smooth, firm pressure. When I fired the shot, I lowered my pistol and asked, "How did I do?"

"Maggie, you hit right in the center—you're a pro. As long as you're pointed in the right direction, the bad guy is down. Do you want to shoot again?"

"One more time." I stepped to my left. "Point me at the target without moving me."

Palace Guard tapped on my right shoulder blade, and I made small adjustments to the right. When he patted the middle of my back, I relaxed and fired.

After I lowered my pistol, Larry said, "Perfect again."

"That's all I want to do for now. Is that okay?"

"Yes," Larry said. "The table is one foot in front of you. Put on the safety then lay down your pistol."

After I set my pistol on the table, I said, "I need to work with light weights. Just holding the pistol wore me out."

Larry held me. "Oh, sweetie. We're moving too fast. You need more time to heal."

"I'm not sure I can convince the bad guy to give me a little extra time."

"I know, sweetheart," Larry mumbled in my hair. "I hate it, but I'm worried too."

"I'll rest while you sight in your deer rifle. I'm ready for venison next fall."

Larry helped me to the observer's bench, and Palace Guard joined me. Larry shot his rifle until he was satisfied. I watched his blurry figure's body language as he fired and knew he was pleased with his purchase.

"I'm ready." Larry packed his rifle into its case. "You want to put your pistol back into its holster?"

I rose from the bench. "Yes, thanks."

On our way home, Larry said, "I'll clean our weapons this evening. I know I won't do it as well as you do."

"Let me give it a try. Kate used to tell me I cleaned by feel not sight. We're not in a rush, right? You can clean after me if you like."

"Not likely that I'll be doing that, but I don't mind examining your work. Shall we go home or to Mr. Bustamante's next?" Larry asked.

"Let's go to Mr. Bustamante's. If he's resting, we can return after lunch."

After Larry parked in front of Mr. Bustamante's house, I waited for him to come around to the passenger's door to help me out of the truck. When we walked up the driveway to the porch, I breathed in the calming fragrance of the neighbor's roses and gazed straight ahead while Larry was very solicitous. He whispered, "Doing great, sweetheart."

Larry helped me up the steps before he knocked on the door. When Eric opened the door, Larry said, "Mr. Stephens? I'm Maggie's husband, Larry Ewing. Maggie wanted to visit with Mr. Bustamante. Is he awake and up to receiving company?"

"Certainly, Mr. Ewing."

"Larry." Larry broke in.

"I'm Eric." The two men shook hands while I stared at nothing.

"How are you doing, Gray Lady?" Eric asked in a loud voice, carefully enunciating each word.

I'm blind not hard of hearing, goofball.

Palace Guard poked me.

"Not too bad, Eric. Thank you for asking."

"Come on in. Mr. Bustamante is sitting on the back patio. He loves being outside on a beautiful day like today."

Eric led us to the back patio and spoke to Mr. Bustamante in the same voice he used when he addressed me. "Mr. Bustamante, you have company. The Gray Lady is here to see you."

"Gray Lady," Mr. Bustamante's voice was clear and strong. "How nice of you to visit me. Please sit. Faith told me you were a wonderful person."

Larry led me to a chair and stayed at my side.

Mr. Bustamante said, "Go, go, you two. Let us reminisce in peace."

Eric's chuckle sounded strained to me. "Fine, fine. You're the boss. We'll go relax inside."

As Larry left, I heard the sliding glass door close.

"Why did you come see me, Gray Lady? Not that I don't appreciate seeing you. You're a hero to many of us who know Mrs. Martin and Edna Cross."

I gazed above his head at nothing. "They've become close friends of mine, but you're right—I'd like to ask you a question because I'm hearing conflicting stories. How did Faith and Eric meet?"

"It's not complicated. Eric was a financial planner in Atlanta and contacted me about managing my retirement. He came to visit me, and while his ideas were interesting, I told him I needed to run it past my lawyer. He seemed to lose interest and was preparing to leave then Faith—" Mr. Bustamante cleared his throat. "I don't know why he stayed in town after Faith's funeral. He must have business here to wrap up."

"That's so interesting. It is peculiar that he's stayed on."

"I've gotten several calls from some of the women in Faith's church group, and they said the same thing."

I nodded. "Faith told me how much she enjoyed her small group at church."

"They're a mixed group, that's for sure. Did you meet Owen at the senior center? He was the only man in the group. Faith always laughed and said Owen didn't care if any of the men made fun of him because he had a date once a week with seven women, and they didn't."

I snickered. "I'd heard he was a resourceful man. Speaking of which, are you well enough to take care of yourself?"

"That's the same question my sister asks every time she calls me," Mr. Bustamante said.

I'll bet he rolled his eyes.

Palace Guard patted my shoulder.

He continued, "My home health care nurse visits once a week, and Faith and I arranged ages ago for my evening meals to be delivered. As far as Eric is concerned, my lawyer invited Eric to a meeting on Tuesday to talk about my finances, but Eric told me yesterday that he wasn't sure he'd make the meeting."

"Do you feel safe with him here?"

I stared at nothing and waited.

"I don't know him all that well, but it's been nice to have another person around. My sister called me early this morning to tell me that she and my nephew will be here in a half hour or so to visit. She lives just a couple of hours away in Dothan, Alabama."

"Does Eric know your sister and nephew are coming?"

"He does. He talked about finding a hotel, but I haven't heard if he did."

"Shouldn't be hard to find something close, or maybe he'll return home. He may have stayed to make sure you were okay." I maintained my stare over his head. "You don't have any jewelry, cash, or valuables here, do you?"

CHAPTER THIRTEEN

"No, Faith and my sister ganged up on me a while ago, and we moved all the jewelry to my sister's safe at her house and deposited the cash in the bank. My lawyer has all my important papers."

"Sorry about all the nosy questions. My volunteer time at the senior center brought out my caregiver side. Why don't I just stick around until they show up?"

Mr. Bustamante chuckled. "I would love it, and you've just helped me prepare for my sister's visit. She'll enjoy meeting you. Now, tell me how my friends Rebecca Martin and Edna Cross are doing."

"When Mrs. Martin is released from the hospital, she and her son plan to move back into her house. Darren's found someone to stay with her during the day while he works. Mrs. Cross is in the hospital and took a turn for the worse, but she's receiving excellent care and recovering. I think she'll be well soon."

Mr. Bustamante said, "I have stories about the three of us that you might enjoy. We were all quite out of control in our younger years."

He is at least twenty years younger than Mrs. Martin. How's he going to spin that?

After a long, involved story, he concluded, "So, that's how I got involved with jewelry. It was to keep my friend the jewel thief, Rebecca Martin, supplied with well-crafted costume jewelry of my own design."

I smiled. "I loved your stories. How much is true?"

"As Edna Cross always said, every part that you believed is true."

I giggled. "That's so funny. I've heard Edna say that."

The sliding glass door slid open, and Larry joined us on the patio. "Mr. Bustamante, your sister and nephew are here."

Larry stepped to my side as a woman bustled out to the patio.

Mr. Bustamante said, "Alba, this is the Gray Lady, Maggie Ewing."

"Hello, Ms. Gray Lady. I've heard such wonderful stories about you. I thought you were a legend or a fairy." She tittered, and Mr. Bustamante guffawed.

"That's a story I'd like to hear," Larry said.

"Don't get him started, Larry," Alba said. "You're going home with us, Hugo. I'm going to your room to pack your things after I straighten up Faith's bedroom then we can leave."

After she went back inside, Mr. Bustamante said, "I thought she planned to stay for the weekend, but I should have realized she was here on a mission. I could argue with her all afternoon, but she'd win, or I could save my breath and go with her. Where's my nephew?"

"Chatting with Eric," Larry said. "Eric suggested he'd stay here and housesit. Ms. Alba said no."

Mr. Bustamante chuckled. "My nephew is a talented college football player but a haphazard packer. I'd advise Eric to pull his things together and leave."

This is all somehow very entertaining.

Palace Guard patted my shoulder in agreement.

"Is there anything we can do before we go?" I asked.

"I suspect Alba has everything under control. Thank you for coming to see me, Gray Lady."

Before I rose from my seat, Eric stepped to the open doorway and cleared his throat. "I'll be leaving now, Mr. Bustamante. Thank you for the hospitality. Bye, all."

"Have a safe trip," Larry said, and I waved as I maintained my straight-ahead stare.

Larry helped me up then gave me his arm. When we reached the threshold, he said, "One step up into the house."

Alba met us in the living room. "Thank you, Gray Lady, for visiting my brother."

"My pleasure." I smiled. "He has my number. Please call if there's anything I can do here for either of you."

When Alba hugged me, I was surprised by her embrace. "Your visit was good for him. He's been so sad, which is understandable, but you perked him up."

After we were in the truck, Larry asked, "What did I miss?"

"Mr. Bustamante told me that Eric was a financial planner from Atlanta who came to Columbus to discuss managing Mr. Bustamante's finances. When Faith died, Eric stayed for Faith's funeral. I'm even more confused because of the gap between the time that Eric came to town and Faith's death, so now I have another version of how Eric and Faith met. What you really missed was an intricate story about Mr. Bustamante, Mrs. Martin, and Edna Cross that was charming and mostly fabricated. What did you learn?"

"I've got another version for you that might support some of Mr. Bustamante's version. Eric told me Faith was interviewing for a job in Atlanta, and they sat next to each other at a coffee shop near his financial planning office. She invited him to speak to her dad."

"Faith never mentioned interviewing for a job in Atlanta. I'm not sure she would have left her father. I thought about asking Glenn if it was possible to ask someone else in Faith's church group how Faith and Eric met, but Mr. Bustamante told me that Owen from the senior center was in the church group. I'd like to talk to him."

"Do you know how to find him? Do you have a last name?"

"Of course not. That would be too easy." I snickered, and Larry snorted.

On our way home, my phone rang.

"This is Darren Martin, Ms. Gray Lady. Mama is being released from the hospital. She said to tell you she's being kicked out. Mama likes to make jokes. We'd still like to invite you and Mr. Larry to our home for brunch tomorrow. Does eleven work for you? Mama gave me a long list of people to invite then decided to ask only a few people."

"Sounds wonderful. Eleven tomorrow?" I raised my eyebrows at blurry blob Larry, and he pressed a thumb into my palm. "That's perfect. We'll be there. Is there anything you'd like me to bring? My cinnamon rolls are famous in two counties."

"Don't turn down the cinnamon rolls," Larry said in a loud voice.

Darren chuckled. "If it isn't too much trouble, we'd welcome your cinnamon rolls."

"Good. We'll see you at eleven."

After Darren disconnected, I said, "Thank you for the endorsement."

"I was being selfish. I get cinnamon rolls tomorrow. Can we make a double batch, so I'll have cinnamon rolls the rest of the week too?"

"Sure can."

"Besides cinnamon rolls, which are a definite priority, do you have any other plans for this afternoon?"

"I probably should rest, but I think that's it."

"Good. I've got a few projects around the house I'd like to tackle."

After we were home and had lunch, I slipped off my sunglasses and boots before I lay down on our bed for a nap. Lucy padded into the room and flopped down on the floor, and I relaxed. When Larry tiptoed into the bedroom and picked up the laundry basket, I smiled.

When Lucy nudged my elbow, I woke and yawned. "I was just resting my eyes, girl." I snickered, and she sniffed my face.

"You win; I'm getting up." I swung my feet to the floor and reached for my jo. A wave of melancholy swept over me. *It would all be easier if I could see.*

I tapped to the living room. *I don't even know where Larry is because I can't see.* I held onto my jo while I slid to my knees then slammed my fists on the floor.

"Sweetheart! Are you okay?" Larry rushed to my side and lifted me so high that my feet dangled.

"I hate that I can't see," I grumbled through my clenched teeth.

"I know, honey, and I'm so sorry." Larry held me tighter, and his fierceness dissolved my anguish.

I wrapped my arms around his neck. "You make me better. We can do this."

"Are you sure?" he asked.

"Sometimes it really gets me down, but I'm positive we can do this."

"Are you up to grilling a couple of hamburgers tonight?"

"Absolutely."

"Good. I was going to mow. Shall we do something else?"

"No, Heather signed me up for some podcasts on self-defense that she said might give me some ideas. There's one this afternoon I'd like to listen to. If it's boring, I'll come outside and smell the freshly cut grass and weeds."

"Mostly weeds," Larry chuckled. "When we're semi-settled somewhere I'd like to take a class on soil management."

"After you mow, we can make the double batch of cinnamon rolls."

"Will we have enough time? Cinnamon rolls come before mowing in priority, as far as I'm concerned."

"We'll be fine. Go mow."

After Larry went outside and started the lawnmower, I listened to the hominess of my husband mowing the backyard on a Saturday and smiled.

Before I turned on my computer, my phone rang, and I answered.

"Margaret, how are you doing? I didn't want to bother you, and Big D told me you would need your rest, but I thought you must be rested enough by now to talk on the phone. I've been worried about you, but I know your Larry is taking good care of you. Isn't it funny that Big D calls Larry Kevin sometimes? I think he gets confused." Mother giggled.

I smiled as I listened to her familiar, loud voice.

"We're heading back home. Big D has a doctor's appointment in two weeks for a checkup, and he said it was about time for us to catch up with our old friends in Harperville. I think the driving is wearing him out a bit. I know it would wear me out. How are you doing?"

I waited to be sure she wanted an answer before I spoke. "I'm doing fine. I'm starting to build up a little strength, and we see the ophthalmologist next week. She doesn't think I'll ever have any sight in my left eye, but she's hopeful that I regain some sight in my right eye."

"Big D and I want you to know that if there is anything we can do to help you, we will. The reason I called is that I want to come see you. I don't want to exhaust you though. Is it okay if we visit? Could we spend the afternoon with you then maybe go out to dinner or maybe there's a good takeout place. Big D says my cooking skills shriveled from disuse. I don't cook hardly at all anymore because we're so busy."

"I would love to see you and Sarge, Mother." *I'm actually surprised, but that's true.* "I think there's a campground not too far from us. I'm not cooking very much yet, but maybe we could pick up something, and we could eat at the campground. When do you think you can be here?"

"Larry's folks said they'd like to come too, so eating at the campground would be an excellent idea. We're talking about next week. Do you know when your eye appointment is?"

"Larry does; I think it's on Wednesday, but I'll have to check. Can you hold on? Larry's mowing the backyard. I'll ask him."

"Why don't you call me back?"

Mother hung up, as she always did, without saying good-bye, and I snorted. *It would have been weird if she'd said good-bye.*

I sat on the porch and rocked while Larry mowed. *It's loud, but it's a nice loud.*

He turned off the mower and joined me. "The yard's mowed. I'll put away the mower after the motor cools down."

"Mother called. She and Sarge would like to visit next week. Mother said they'd find a campground, and it sounds like your parents will join them. I suggested we could go to the campground for dinner."

"Would it be too much for you?"

"I'd enjoy seeing all of them, and we could leave if I get overwhelmed or too tired. It would be hard to do that if they came here."

Larry snorted. "Did she mention a day?"

"She was kind of leaving it up to us, but it sounded like they were interested in coming during the week. I guess that would mean we'd go after you were home from work. I have my eye appointment on Wednesday, right?"

"Your eye appointment is early on Wednesday, so there's no conflict. You can tell your mother we can join them on whatever day works for them, if you like."

"That sounds good. She asked me to call her back after we talked."

"I'll mix a little Worcestershire sauce into the hamburger and make our patties before I slice a tomato and an onion for our burgers. Do you want lettuce, pickle, or cheese?" he asked.

"Yes."

"What about toasting the buns on the grill? Do you want to do that too?"

"I might need you to do that because I'm pretty sure by the time I figured out they were toasted they'd be blackened."

Larry rose. "Do you want me to start the fire for you?"

"That would be great then I could cook after I talk to Mother."

I returned Mother's call.

"Margaret, I didn't expect to hear back from you so quickly, but Big D said that you and Larry think alike and would come to a decision without a lot of discussion. Of course, I told him he was wrong because it's important to consider all points from all sides before making a decision. He said I sometimes make things too complicated. I'm not sure what he was thinking because it's more complicated to rush into a decision without careful deliberation."

I'd forgotten how Mother considered her tendency to overthink as being analytical.

"Larry said my appointment is very early on Wednesday morning, so we would have no conflicts next week with coming to the campground for dinner. Whatever you and the Ewings work out is fine with us. Just let us know."

"Well, then. I guess I could call Lauren Ewing. Maybe they have a preference. Big D wants to come on Tuesday, but that's because he's ready to go home."

"Tuesday sounds good to me, but whatever you all come up with will be great," I said.

Mother hung up, and I tapped into the house with Palace Guard's help at the threshold. "Larry?"

"What did your mother say?"

"Big D wanted to be here on Tuesday; Mother's going to call your mother. I'm glad I don't have to be in the middle."

Larry hugged me. "Ready for me to carry out the burgers for you?"

"Oh, yes. I'm looking forward to trying to figure out the timing for the burgers. By the way, next time I'm moaning my fate, I need to remember that I've lost my sense of time too. I didn't realize how much I depended on my sight to tell time or even the passage of time."

As Larry carried the burgers, he asked, "Do you need some rant time?"

"Not really. My heart wouldn't be in it."

When Larry dropped the burgers on the grill, I grinned at the sizzle. "Sounds like the grill is at the perfect temperature."

Larry handed me my spatula, and I hovered over the grill. "It's tempting to mash on the burgers to see how they feel, but I'd squeeze out the juices, and we'd end up with dry burgers. I'll just listen to when they stop sizzling and get that greasy spoon burger bouquet."

Larry snorted, "Bouquet?"

"Of course, that's how us diner cooks talk. Fancy."

"I sure am glad you're back to your sassy self."

"You're slipping."

"What? Oh, no, I am slipping. My grill master is standing in front of her grill with no beer. Be right back."

When he returned, we clinked bottles.

"The sizzle has slowed. Time to flip 'em. If they land on the ground, we're going for the ten-second rule, agreed?"

"Agreed. I'll blow away the germs then put them back on the grill before the ten seconds are up."

I flipped the first burger, and it sizzled. "I can't be overly confident, now." I flipped the second one, and it sizzled too.

"Success," Larry said.

"Do you have a plate to put these on?" I asked.

"Sure do."

"I think my best bet is to hold the plate myself.

Larry handed me the plate.

"Here goes nothing." I cringed as I flipped both burgers onto the plate.

"Perfect. I'll carry in the plate for you," Larry said.

When we sat at the table, Larry said, "I put the pickles, cheese, and onion on your burger, but made a side salad with your tomato and lettuce because they'd slip out of the bun."

"Are you implying that I'm a sloppy eater?"

"Yes, dear," he chuckled. "I've been waiting for the perfect time to say that."

"Ha, ha."

After we ate, Larry loaded the dishwasher. "Are you ready to mix the cinnamon rolls?"

While I quoted the recipe from memory, and Larry mixed, I said, "I just remembered that brunch is fancy. I can't go because I don't have anything fancy to wear."

"What do you mean by fancy?" Larry patted out the dough to rise.

"You know, like a shirt that Mother would call a blouse and pants that she'd call slacks. I can't wear my black pants or my jeans, and I need a new blouse."

"In that case, I can remind you that Jennifer sent you fancy clothes along with a note to me on her suggestions of what to put together. You're set."

"I'm really lucky to have you and such a wonderful support system."

My phone rang, and Larry's mother said, "Maggie, I'm the designated spokesperson for the parents. I think Sarge nominated me." She giggled. "We'll be at the campground on Tuesday. I'll text Kevin with the details. We love you two very much."

She hung up, and I laughed.

"What's so funny?" Larry asked.

I waved my hand in front of my face to settle myself down. "Your mother was the designated parent to tell us that they'll be at the campground on Tuesday, and you'll get a text with details. Then, are you ready for it? She hung up." I giggled, and Larry laughed.

* * *

I woke and patted the bed and felt Larry's warm body. He sighed in his sleep before he rolled over and wrapped his arms around me to pull me closer.

I snuggled against him and drifted into the quiet cocoon of sleep.

Later, when Lucy sniffed my toes that were outside the covers, I giggled.

"Lucy was trying her best not to wake you until your foot popped out of the covers." Larry flopped onto the bed with me. "Coffee's ready. I came in to check on you but forgot I'd have company."

I raised up on one arm; when I found his face, I kissed him. "Coffee sounds awesome." I smirked as I tossed my nightgown to the floor, and Larry said, "Okay, naked Maggie. Coffee can wait."

He pulled me into his arms and kissed me while he rubbed my back. When I pulled off his shirt and tugged at his pants, he repeated, "Coffee can wait."

After his shower, Larry dressed then I rolled out of bed and put on a pair of sweatpants and a T-shirt while Larry popped the first pan of cinnamon rolls into the oven.

When I joined him in the kitchen, he handed me my coffee before he removed the pan. "Do I put the second pan into the oven?"

"Might as well; the oven's hot."

I inhaled the mingled aromas of sugar, cinnamon, and baked pastry. "We do good work. Smells wonderful."

"We need a little quality control around here. I'll cut one in half, so we can make sure they taste as good as they smell."

After the second pan went in, Larry carried our cinnamon roll as we headed out to the porch. We rocked, munched on our halves of pastry, and sipped our coffee; Palace Guard stayed near us on the porch while Lucy wandered, and Spike followed her.

"What's our plan after the brunch?" Larry asked.

"I think that's it for the day. Timer went off."

"Thanks. I knew you'd hear it."

After he went inside and removed the last pan of cinnamon rolls, he rejoined me on the porch. "I want to stop by the hardware store and get a couple of large pots to plant flowers, and you can select the flowers. I want you to visualize flowers around you when you're on the porch."

A tear slipped down my cheek, and I snuffled. "You are so sweet."

"It's my job," Larry said in a quiet voice. "I'll do whatever I can to make you happy."

"You do that every day." I smiled. "I'm ready for more coffee in my sippy cup then I'll shower and dress. What time is it?"

"It's ten. No rush. I'll have your fancy clothes ready for you when you get out of your shower."

Larry's phone buzzed a text. "It's Jennifer. She wants to know if I need her to come here next week. What do you think?"

"I think I need to adjust and not be coddled."

"I can't say that."

"Fix it then." I flipped my hair.

When Palace Guard poked me, Larry snickered. "Thanks, Palace Guard."

After Larry replied, I asked, "So, what did you say?"

He cleared his throat and read his text aloud: "GL is ornery. Needs to be independent."

"I am not ornery." I crossed my arms and stuck out my lip.

"Are too."

Larry's phone buzzed a text, and he said, "Jennifer replied, 'Got that right.'"

While Larry snickered, I polished off my coffee then rose to go inside. "Well played, Mr. Sexy Pants."

After I showered, I wrapped my towel around me and opened the bathroom door.

Larry accompanied me to the bedroom. "Your fancy clothes are on the bed."

"Tell me about them," I said as I picked up the pants. "These feel like my black slacks."

"Your slacks are navy."

"They're comfortable." I picked up the shirt. "It feels silky. Does it have buttons?"

"No buttons. Just pull it over your head."

I found the label, so I wouldn't put it on backwards. "What color is it?"

"It's traditional blue, and you look sharp. Jennifer's note said you could wear the navy blue and white checked eyepatch."

"Won't that be over-matched?"

Larry snorted.

"What?" I asked.

"You're the Gray Lady—you wore all gray from head to toe. Your slacks and blouse are coordinated, not matched."

I snorted. "You've never accused me of being coordinated before. Will my boots go with my slacks and coordinated top?"

"Your red boots go with everything. We can leave when you're ready; I wrapped up the cinnamon rolls while you showered."

"Isn't it too early to leave? Aren't we supposed to be fashionably late?"

"I'm ready. You're the Gray Lady. You don't need to worry about being early or late."

I giggled. "When I went to the art show at Mrs. Martin's house, there was a crowd of people there. Paul Vargas told me they were all assassins, and I relaxed."

"Sometimes you worry me. Let's go."

When Larry drove down the long driveway, I remembered the majestic, old pecan trees that lined both sides of the driveway,

He whistled. "This place is unbelievable. Darren must have a landscaper because it is very well kept."

When he parked in front of the old mansion, he said, "The front of the home appears to be undergoing renovations. What was it like when you were here?"

"The bases of the columns had dry rot, the gutters sagged, and the paint had grayed and was flaking. Why did Darren let it go when he could have kept it up?"

"His mother was in a senior center, and he was there to oversee her care when he wasn't working. He certainly would not have had the time to manage any repairs and may not have even seen how much the house had deteriorated."

I nodded. "He must have been planning for her to move back home because I know how particular he is about Mrs. Martin, and it didn't take him long to find someone to care for her during the day."

"You're probably right because these renovations have been in process for a while and aren't just cosmetic—they're being done right."

After Larry helped me up the steps, I remembered the wide veranda as we continued to the door. When I turned to talk to Larry, I blinked. *I can see Larry. He's not just a blurry blob.* I blinked again. *He's a blurry Larry.*

Larry knocked, and Darren opened the door. "Ms. Gray Lady, it's so nice to see you. You too, Mr. Larry. Welcome to our home. Ms. Gray Lady, Mama blackmailed me as only she can. I'm sure you understand. She told me several months ago before she became ill, that if I'd renovate her home, she could live much more comfortably at home than in a tiny room."

I giggled. "She's the best."

"Everyone's on the back patio," Darren said.

I paused. *Everyone?*

Larry wrapped my hand around his arm and patted it as he whispered, "The assassins await."

I snickered and squeezed his arm.

As Darren walked us through the foyer to the patio, I noticed the previous musty odor that had pervaded the old house was replaced by a sweet, floral fragrance.

"Roses?" I asked.

"Yes," Darren said. "Mama loved fresh flowers in her home. She supported the local florists and always kept a large vase of roses or other seasonal flowers in the foyer. I felt it was important to revive her tradition. She'll be excited that you noticed."

When we stepped onto the back patio, Larry said, "Darren, your patio reminds me of a charming, old world piazza, except I can see your mother's flair with the bright tablecloths on the round tables and small vases with flowers—wildflowers, right? I'll bet the tiki torches and strings of fairy lights give the patio an artsy atmosphere in the evening."

"You're right," Darren said. "When I learned that Mama could come home, the patio became my first priority because she always loved to entertain. We won't ever have the grand cocktail parties that she held in the past, but we're planning to host fund-raising events for local charities. Mama is particularly interested in supporting the arts."

After Darren directed us to a table, Larry held a chair for me while I sat.

"Ah, here's coffee," Darren said. "Would you like coffee now? We also have mimosas."

"Coffee sounds good," Larry said, and I nodded. "Only a half cup for me, please."

"I put your cup in front of you near your right hand, sweetie."

When I touched the cup, I lifted it with both hands and sipped carefully.

Wonder if I could have my mimosa in a sippy cup. Palace Guard poked my back.

"Mr. Larry, if you have a little time, and Ms. Gray Lady doesn't mind, I'd like for you to look at our security system," Darren said. "I think I need to upgrade it, but I'm over my head when it comes to electronics."

"Okay with you, sweetie?" Larry asked.

"I'll be fine. I love being outdoors."

After they left, Palace Guard tapped my arm with our good-guy signal.

A man approached my table. "Ms. Gray Lady, I'm Owen. You may have seen me around the senior center before the fire. May I join you for a few minutes?"

I smiled. *I've been wanting to talk to you, Owen, old man.*

"Please sit; I'd enjoy your company."

He pulled out a chair and sat across from me. "I wanted to tell you how much you were appreciated at the senior center. You were a breath of fresh air."

"Thank you. I'm glad you sat with me because I was interested in how Faith and Eric became acquainted and was completely confused by what I've heard. Weren't you a member of Faith's church group? I thought someone from the church group would know."

Owen chuckled. "I've been a member of the church group for years. I'm not surprised you've heard conflicting stories. The two major disadvantages of the senior center are that not everyone remembers the same version of gossip, and the center is a hotbed of talented storytellers. There are all kinds of versions, ranging from romantic, mystery, false news, to reality show. Which versions have you heard?"

I giggled. "I think I've heard every version except the factual one."

"Ah, yes. You wouldn't have heard that one because it's not as exciting as the others. Eric Stephens came to the senior center to discuss business with Gracie Jane. I heard he was a financial advisor, but I seriously doubt it. I chatted with him once and found him woefully ignorant. Gracie Jane introduced him to Faith, and he began coming to the senior center regularly. Faith was a wonderful person, but not very money savvy. When I heard Eric had a meeting with Hugo Bustamante, I was very concerned. Hugo's an old friend of mine, so I called him and told him to be sure to run any advice he hears from Eric past his own lawyer."

"How did the whole romance thing between Faith and Eric get started?"

CHAPTER FOURTEEN

"Eric could turn on the charm when he wanted. The church group bought into Faith's romantic story, and embellished it, from what I hear, and were convinced it was true because they wanted it to be. They conveniently forgot how much anger Faith had inside of her lately."

"I didn't understand how Faith could be so angry at John Howard."

"I don't have any evidence, but I strongly suspect that Eric Stephens rekindled her bitterness to his own advantage because Faith genuinely seemed over her hurt until Eric showed up. Put that down as potentially false news."

"I heard she'd been angry at John since he first broke off with her."

"I can't explain that except people have faulty memories. Faith certainly never announced that she had gotten over John, but she wasn't one to hold her feelings inside, and I thought her bitterness was gone."

"I didn't know Faith very long, but that sounds more like her."

"People are very complex," Owen said.

"They are, aren't they? Speaking of complex, Edna Cross told me to be careful because someone was setting a trap for me. I asked her who told her about a trap, and she told me to ask Gracie Jane about you. Because of the way Edna weaves her stories, I guessed that she meant that I should ask you either about Gracie Jane or who set a trap for me."

Owen chuckled. "It's delightful the way you managed to follow an Edna Cross story. I'll tell you what I know along with what I surmise. A number of the residents claimed to have named Gracie Jane as a beneficiary in their wills, but I suspect the actual number of residents who followed through was a small percentage. There was quite the hoopla for a while, and very few wanted to be left out."

"Is there any way to know who actually did?"

"I would think Gracie Jane would, but I doubt if she'd be willing to share that information. I heard she was seriously injured by the fire at the senior center and is in the burn unit at an Atlanta hospital, but the details border between sketchy and unbelievable."

Wonder who the doctor was who called Darren?

"Who would have set a trap for me?"

"I didn't know about a trap for you. If any trap were set, I would think it would be for John Howard."

"Really? Why?"

Owen was silent, and I waited.

"I have no idea—it just popped into my head," he said. "This is pure conjecture on my part—ignoring the fact that Faith was angry at him, he was her oldest friend. If she was worried about something before her abrupt bitterness, she would have confided in him."

"I think my head exploded," I said.

"No kidding—mine too."

When Owen rose, I said, "Call me if you think of a different twist. Darren has my number."

"Will do. I'll give you my business card. It's a little pretentious of me to have a business card after being retired for ten years, but we all have our weaknesses, don't we? Feel free to call if there's anything I can do for you."

I held out my hand, and he placed a card in it as Palace Guard touched my arm. *Larry's coming toward us?*

Palace Guard patted my back.

"Thank you for the discussion, Ms. Gray Lady," Owen said. "It isn't often I have a chance to exercise my brain cells so thoroughly."

Owen strolled away, and I placed his card into my pocket before Larry reached my table. After Larry sat next to me, he asked, "How did you exercise his brain cells?"

"I'll tell you later," I said.

"I'll remind you," he chuckled. "Brunch is being served buffet. Do you want to walk through the line, or shall I bring you a plate?"

"I'd rather not try to maneuver a buffet line. Is that totally anti-social of me?"

"Not at all. Darren told me he and his mother will join us at our table. Did you want a mimosa?"

"I don't think so. I need to practice drinking out of a regular cup or glass. I took a sip of my coffee, but it was too scary."

"If I spy a cup with a lid and a straw, I'll bring you some water."

I nodded. *Another point for the awesome husband.*

"Why did Palace Guard nod?" Larry asked.

"He approves."

"There's something more," Larry grumbled as he strode away.

I smiled as the swish of a wheelchair headed toward me on the tiled floor. *Mrs. Martin.*

"Hello, Maggie Flanagan. Hello, Palace Guard. You are as gorgeous as ever, Flanagan girl. How are you feeling?"

"My normal anti-social. I am really enjoying being here. Larry told me about all the improvements that have been made to your home."

"Darren and I talked about finding someone to stay with me during the day before I became so confused. He had started the renovations then decided to continue even after I was so ill. He told me he knew I'd get better. After he realized I'd be home sooner rather than later, he shifted all the focus on the patio because he knew I'd want to have a party. It was a delightful surprise for me when I came home."

"He's a wonderful, kindhearted man," I said.

"He is," she sighed. "Too kindhearted sometimes. Did he tell you about Gracie Jane's doctor calling him?"

"He did. He seemed very surprised."

"Gracie Jane would never have listed him as next of kin. That is such baloney."

"Why would she say that?"

Mrs. Martin snorted. "I have no idea; either she didn't, or she's got an ulterior motive. I vote the latter."

"Unanimous," I said. "Did he ever follow up?"

"Yes, and the hospital had no record of a patient named Gracie Jane Haroldsen, or a Doctor Smith other than Abigail Smith, a gynecologist."

"This is all so bizarre."

"Has to be criminal activity. We just don't know what quite yet, do we?" Mrs. Martin lowered her voice. "The fairies say your eye is improving, but you are obviously setting your own trap, so we're keeping what we know quiet."

"That's interesting." I nodded and smiled.

She patted my hand. "You let me know how we can help, Maggie Flanagan, especially if it's unladylike or anything that my son or Agent Ewing would not approve."

I put my hand on my forehead in feigned shock, and we laughed.

"What do you think about Owen?" I asked.

"Good guy. The fairies like him. He listens to them but doesn't realize it."

"That makes sense to me. Ask Darren to give Owen my cell phone number."

"Will do. We need to close our conspiracy door because here comes our food."

Larry set my plate on the table before he sat in his chair then scooted closer to me.

"Half of a cheese omelet at nine o'clock, half of a cinnamon roll at twelve, strawberries and melon in bite-sized pieces at three o'clock, and cheesy grits in the middle with half of a slice of bacon on top of your grits. Your napkin and silverware are on the right side of your plate. For a special treat, Darren had the caterer pour mimosas for you and Mrs. Martin into lidded paper cups with straws."

"That's awesome, Darren."

"You made him blush, Maggie Flanagan. My grip isn't what it used to be, and I broke many a glass until Darren ordered a supply of lidded cups and straws. I prefer to think he did that to keep the bugs out of my drinks."

Larry chuckled, and I snickered.

"That's the best reason to have a lidded cup," I said as Larry handed me my mimosa.

I found my straw and sipped. "Mmm. This is good. I'm not sure if I've ever had a mimosa before."

"You've probably never had one like this," Mrs. Martin said. "It has freshly squeezed orange juice with a touch of juice from a blood orange. The sparkling wine is my favorite from Spain."

I took a bite of my omelet then a strawberry. "Is the fruit local?" I asked.

"Of course," Mrs. Martin said. "I'm a foodie, and by the way, your cinnamon rolls are heavenly."

"Thank you." My face warmed, and Mrs. Martin tittered.

I finished my omelet and fruit, and ate half of my bacon, grits, and cinnamon roll. I patted my mouth with my napkin and placed my hands in my lap.

"That's my signal, right? Mine?" Larry asked.

"Of course," I giggled.

After Larry cleaned my plate for me, he said, "We're going to have to leave because Maggie's stamina is still low."

"Of course," Mrs. Martin said. "You are making wonderful progress, Maggie Flanagan. Take care of her, Agent Ewing."

"Yes, ma'am." Larry helped me to my feet.

On the way home, I asked, "How was Darren's security system?"

"Weak. I gave him some pointers and advised him to have two safes installed: a small wall safe behind a picture for Mrs. Martin's faux jewelry, and a large one that bolts to the floor in one of the closets for her valuable jewelry. He'd like a secure, climate-controlled room for his valuable art, and I told him that wouldn't be hard with all the renovations he's doing. He trusts his general contractor, so he's going to talk to him about it. What did you learn?"

I told him what I'd learned from Owen and what Mrs. Martin said about Gracie Jane.

"She's still in custody. We'll look into her more closely, especially in relation to the wills and resident deaths."

"Good."

When we were home, I pulled out Owen's business card and placed it on my computer desk before I sat on the sofa and kicked off my boots. "I have something to tell you."

"Will it make me mad?"

I smirked and took off my sunglasses and gazed at blurry Larry. "You're blurry."

"I know—I'm a blurry blob." He sat next to me and stretched out his arm behind me on the sofa.

I peered at his blurry face. "Nope, you're my blurry honey, Larry."

"I'm blurry Larry?"

"Yes." I giggled as he hugged me and cooed into my hair as he snuggled me. "My sweet, strong, beautiful Maggie Ewing."

I relaxed in his arms while I imagined fairy songs that whirled around us.

Later, when Lucy sniffed my face and woke me, I was stretched out on the sofa with the afghan over me. I stretched before I sat up. When I squinted with my right eye to scan the room, I saw blurry Lucy and Spike but no blurry Larry or Palace Guard.

"Where did they go?"

Spike raised an arm with exaggeration and pointed to the backyard. I picked up my jo, put on my boots, and opened the door. When I realized that Palace Guard was training Larry in knife work, I eased the door closed and sat on the sofa while I called Glenn.

"I'm not going to ask if you're fine, Maggie. What do you have for me?"

I snickered. "You know me so well." I summarized what Owen told me about Faith, John, Eric, and Mr. Bustamante.

"We could have never come up with all of that," he said.

"I need to know if there is any connection between Gracie Jane Haroldsen and Eric Stephens. I have it on reliable gossip that Gracie Jane was never burned or sent to a burn unit after the fire at the senior center and that Eric Stephens is somehow involved with Gracie Jane."

"Didn't you give him your card? Aren't you worried?"

"I wish I could tell you I did it with a plan in place, but I did it because I was convinced he was a nice guy. I got a taste of that charm that Owen told me about. Eric thinks I trust him, and that may be to my advantage."

"Have I told you lately that you scare me, Maggie? You do realize that you were badly injured and that you may never see normally again? Did I just overstep my bounds?"

"Sure you did, so what's your point?"

Glenn snorted. "I see why Larry's always called you Crazy Lady. What do you need me to do?"

"Keep digging on the corporation. What other states besides Georgia could they have incorporated? Instead of looking for the corporation name, is it possible to look for Haroldsen or Stephens as the agent or whatever the state calls the main contact?"

"Paul's going to be mad at himself for not thinking of it. Can I claim it was my idea?"

I laughed. "Who's going to argue with Detective Coyle?"

"Mrs. Detective Coyle. Be safe, Maggie."

Glenn hung up, and I nodded.

I would have hung up on me too.

I tapped to the bedroom and changed clothes. *Maybe we can go to the hardware store this afternoon.*

I returned to the kitchen and found my sippy cup then filled it with sweet tea. I was too wound up to listen to any documents on my computer, and my sight was too partial for me to read, so I paced. Blurry Spike and my blurry dog went out back.

Fine; desert me, traitors.

I walked to the bedroom, gathered the dirty clothes, and carried them to the washer after I barreled into the doorjamb of the bedroom then the walls in the hall.

I dumped the clothes into the washer then rubbed my forehead. *Ouch. Should have thought that one out first.*

When Larry and Palace Guard came inside, I was sitting in front of my computer, but I hadn't turned it on yet because I was thinking about killers, flowers, hosting parties, fairy lights, and jewelry thieves.

"My shirt is soaked. Palace Guard has been giving me a workout with knife training, and I believe I've progressed to the official skill level of mildly awful." Blurry Larry guffawed as he smacked a high five with blurry Palace Guard.

I grinned. "Take a shower, stinky man, then let's go to the hardware store. I want to see if I can pick out flowers by smell, but I want to search in the perennials."

After Larry showered and dressed, he said, "Let's go."

All five of us piled into his truck. "I sure hope this hardware store knows the rule for dogs who sit for treats."

"I stuck a treat in my pocket just in case," Larry said.

Lucy thumped the back seat with her enthusiastic tail wag.

When we entered through the outdoor garden section, Larry asked, "Would you and Palace Guard be okay if I look at a grass catcher for our lawnmower?"

"We'll be fine. I'll wander the aisles. You know Lucy and Spike will go with you because of your irresistible pocket, right?"

Larry chuckled. "We won't be long."

The bees hummed while they made their pollen rounds, and I peered at the long row of potted flowers. "I still don't see colors, which is kind of sad, but I can certainly hone in on the most fragrant flowers."

While I stood in front of a section of particularly fragrant, blurry flowers, Palace Guard gripped my arm with an urgent warning. *Bad guy.*

I tapped my jo as Palace Guard guided me to exit from the garden center to the main store then to the nearby women's restroom at the store's entrance. After the two of us crowded into a stall, I whispered, "Now what?"

Palace Guard left, and I waited. *I guess I'll just stand here.*

When the restroom door opened, I held my breath until a woman said, "Oh good. Let's use the larger stall."

"Hurry, mommy," a child said.

After they left, I leaned against the stall door. *This is definitely boring, but I appreciate the clean restroom.*

Three more women came into the restroom, and two of them had children in tow.

When Palace Guard returned, he guided me to the door. As I stepped out of the restroom, Larry said, "I found the grass catcher. Are you ready to pick out flowers?"

He put his arm around me and whispered, "Palace Guard let me know something was wrong and led me here. What's up?"

"He signaled bad guy and led me to the women's restroom. I knew he'd gone to find you."

"Who was it?" Larry asked.

"I don't know. I didn't see him, but the good news is that he might still be lurking around, so if Palace Guard sees him again, he can alert you."

Larry pushed his cart, and I hung onto his elbow as we continued to the garden center.

After I led Larry to the aisle with the flowers I liked, I pointed to a group of plants. "These are interesting."

"The sign says yarrow, and it's supposed to be a favorite of butterflies and hummingbirds."

"Let's plant yarrow; my vision goal is to see butterflies and hummingbirds."

Larry set three pots into his cart. "Are you sure? I don't want you to get discouraged."

"It's my stretch goal," I said. "My real goal is to see my nonblurry honey."

Before we checked out, Larry stopped at the seed packet rack. "We can plant some flower seeds too." After he read the backs of packets, he handed me three of them. "I have cornflower, cosmos, and marigold; all attract bees and butterflies. Shall we get these?"

"Yes. I'll hang onto them."

After we checked out and were in the truck, I said, "It's good to know there is a bad guy."

"I suppose," Larry said, "but I hate that he's stalking you. I'm sorry I didn't see him."

"He must have seen you first, but more good news—you would recognize him."

"I'm not sure my best strategy would be to arrest everyone I recognize," Larry said.

"Job security?" I snickered.

Larry snorted. "Funny, but not funny."

After we were home, Larry said, "Let's have some iced tea before we plant."

"You're so subtle, but you're right—I could use a break. Let's sit on the porch and plan where we'll put the flowers."

While we rocked and sipped sweet tea, I asked, "Does it bother you that we may be planting flowers that we'll never see?"

"Not really. Isn't there an old saying, it isn't the destination, it's the journey?"

"You are so smart." I smiled. *Attributed to Ralph Waldo Emerson, but I'm smart enough to keep my mouth shut. Sometimes.*

I didn't have to see Palace Guard's face to know he rolled his eyes.

Larry chuckled as Spike danced his jig. "Thanks, Spike."

Later that evening as we were getting ready for bed, Larry said, "We have a big week ahead, and it's all going to be crammed into three days. I sure hope you don't get worn out."

I snickered. "Mother always wore me out every time she walked into a room. I'm beginning to understand that she might have felt the same way. I'll be fine. I'm actually looking forward to seeing everyone."

After we were in bed, Larry snuggled me and mumbled as he fell asleep. "Call me if Palace Guard sees a bad guy again."

"Oh, sure," I said after I was certain that he was asleep.

My favorite morning aroma woke me, and I dressed quickly then grabbed my jo. As I hurried into the kitchen, I asked, "Did I sleep too long? Why didn't you wake me up? Will you be late for work? What time is it?"

"Slow down, Crazy Lady. Your coffee's on the table."

I sat on my chair, and after I found the cup of coffee in a ceramic mug, I said, "This isn't my sippy cup."

"Nope. No time like the present for you to practice drinking from a big girl mug; and there's no better motivation for my sweetie than the first cup of coffee in the morning."

"Meanie," I said as I lifted the cup with my right hand holding the mug handle and my left hand clutching the cup. I sipped my coffee and didn't pour it down my chin and onto my shirt.

"Well done, sweetheart. Your egg and cinnamon roll will be right up."

I took another sip of coffee and held onto my mug. "Today, a real coffee cup; tomorrow, the folks."

"One step leads to another, doesn't it? Do me a favor—text or call Heather and ask her about a clock or watch that can speak the time for you. I'm sure one must exist."

"Good thought. It does drive me crazy that I don't know what time it is. At least I can see enough light to know if it's day or night, but I don't have any cues for time."

After breakfast, Larry showered, dressed, and gave me a quick husband smooch before he dashed out the door.

I picked up my phone. "Send a text to Heather: Need a watch that can speak the time."

I stuck my phone into my pocket before I carried my partial cup of coffee to the back porch. While Lucy wandered the yard, I sipped my coffee and pretended I could see flowers.

When my phone rang, Heather said, "Hi, Gray Lady. We should have thought about a watch for you ages ago. I found one that is affordable and does exactly what we want, but it's ugly as all get out. I'll keep looking. If I can't find anything else, you'll have a nice, clunky watch. Gotta go."

After she hung up, I said, "Heather's on it, but we knew she would be, didn't we?" I held up my hand, and Spike gave me a high-five for Heather.

I rocked, listened to the birds, and named the ones that I recognized. *Cardinal, titmouse, blue jay, crow, hawk, and chickadee.* I smiled. *More than I thought.*

I squinted but couldn't see any. *We need a bird feeder and a bird bath in the backyard.*

When my eye teared, I went inside, put on my sleep mask, and put my feet up as I relaxed on the sofa. I was startled awake when my phone rang.

"Sweetie, I wanted you to hear it from me. Mr. Bustamante's sister went through the letters that she found in Faith's bedroom then turned them over to the police in Dothan, Alabama. The letters were from John Howard; he threatened Faith in the three most recent ones and is in custody at the Columbus Police Department. I have to tell you that I'm relieved beyond belief. Gotta go."

I held the phone close to my face, so I could glare at Larry until I realized I still wore my sleep mask.

I sighed. *Might as well rest my eye.* I left it on and called Glenn.

"You okay, Maggie?"

"No. The Columbus police took John Howard into custody. Faith's aunt from Alabama found some letters to Faith from John Howard in Faith's bedroom and turned them over to the police because the three latest letters threatened Faith. John Howard is in custody at the Columbus police department."

"That's a huge shock," Glenn said. "What do you think? Is it possible the so-called threats are being taken out of context? Is Faith's aunt prone to being dramatic?"

"Maybe, but I don't think so. I met her, and she seemed very level-headed to me."

"I continue digging, right?"

"Absolutely."

"I'll get back to you as soon as we have something."

After Glenn hung up, I leaned back on the sofa but couldn't relax. I took off my sleep mask.

"Palace Guard, can I ask you something?"

He knelt next to me so that we were face to face, except his was blurry.

"Was the bad guy you saw yesterday John Howard?"

The side-to-side movement of his blurry head was slow and exaggerated. "Definite no. That's what I thought, thank you."

I paced. "I hate that I'm stuck at home. I need to go somewhere and do something. I need to go for a walk."

I put on my sunglasses and grabbed my jo. Palace Guard was at the front door.

"Good, you're coming too."

I reached for the door, but he was in my way. I reached around him and pulled, but he leaned against the door.

I fumed and threw down my jo before I stomped to the bedroom. After I hit my shoulder on the door jamb and stumbled over the threshold, I slammed the door.

I slid down to my knees and banged my fists on the floor as I screamed, "Not fair! It's not fair!"

Palace Guard sat next to me on the floor and handed me tissues as I screamed and sobbed.

When my screams turned to sighs, and my tears dried up, I hiccupped, and blurry Palace Guard grinned. I tried to scold him, but my hiccups interrupted me, and I giggled and hiccupped.

"This is not—" I hiccupped and took in a big breath and held it. After I exhaled, I quickly continued, "—funny."

Maybe it is. I giggled then hiccupped again.

When I was sure the hiccups were gone, I said, "I am absolutely furious that I won't ever have normal vision." I inhaled and then exhaled slowly. "But I need to channel my rage and use it to stop the killer that gave the orders to incapacitate and murder. I need to stop focusing on what I can't do. Kate said that plans were my job; I need to get to work."

After Palace Guard helped me to my feet, he guided me to my jo as my phone rang.

"Gray Lady, this is Alba, Hugo's sister. I can't tell you how much I appreciate what you did for Hugo. He told me that you offered to stay with him until I arrived. He wanted me to call you to let you know that we made it here just fine. I have a spare bedroom that has its own bathroom on the main floor. He's settling in."

"I really appreciate your call. Faith was a close friend, and I learned a lot from her."

"She was a smart girl. It's so tragic." Alba cleared her throat. "I found some letters on the top of Faith's closet. She had tied them together with a ribbon. I thought that was sweet and was certain that the letters were important to her. I packed them then after Hugo was settled, I read them. They were from John Howard, and some of the letters were threatening, so I called the police. My brother and my son ganged up on me and told me I should have called you. After Butch pointed out some significant differences in the letters, Hugo asked him to make copies of the letters before the police arrived. Butch will email them to you."

After I told her my email address, she repeated it back to me, and continued, "I realized it was a mistake when I overlooked Faith's ribbon around the letters. Who does that to threatening letters?"

"Good point. I look forward to getting the letters. I have software on my computer that will read them to me."

"When I pointed out that John signed all the letters, Butch noticed that the early letters from John Howard were handwritten, but the last three letters were typed and threatening. I pointed out that John signed all of them, and Hugo said you'd find someone to verify the signatures. Gray Lady, Hugo said that you would find Faith's killer. I had my doubts and told Hugo that you're a tiny girl with a severe disability, and he laughed. Butch said I just described the killer's downfall—underestimating the delicate, blind Gray Lady."

I laughed, and Alba laughed with me.

"Tell Butch I appreciate the vote of confidence, and thanks for sending me the letters."

After we hung up, I hurried to my computer but forgot my jo and fell over a chair. *At least it was the soft chair.* Palace Guard handed me my jo, and I continued to my desk with more caution.

When the email arrived, I loaded the letters then listened. I began with the oldest date, which was five years ago; the letters were filled with praises of her skills and accomplishments with tinges of regret. After I listened to the fifth letter, I realized there had been one letter a year, and each one was dated February fourteenth. *Oh my goodness. These are love letters with a hope for forgiveness.* A tear ran down my cheek. *No wonder Faith wrapped them with a ribbon.*

The tone of the last three letters was completely different—angry and accusing with increasingly escalating threats, and none of them had a February fourteenth date. *Like they were written by another person.*

I tapped to the back door with my jo, and Lucy trotted to join me. We strolled the perimeter of the yard then I realized I was alone. I snickered. *My dog abandoned me for a belly rub.*

When I returned to the porch to rock, Palace Guard patted my hand. "Two different people wrote those letters. I'm surprised Alba missed that. I can't imagine the police would hold John for very long."

CHAPTER FIFTEEN

After lunch, Glenn called. "Are you busy?"

I snickered. "I'm sitting at my desk and staring at my computer screen with my sleep mask on, so I suppose I'm technically not terribly busy."

Glenn chuckled. "I've got news. Your idea to search for the business paid off. It's registered in Nevada, one of the states that doesn't require the names of the owners; instead, the business is registered in the name of a lawyer—ready?"

"Good lead in. Go."

"The lawyer is J.G. Stephens."

"Oh. I don't suppose J.G. Stephens is like Eric's brother or something."

"Nope."

"I give up—must be somebody or you wouldn't be dragging out the news Coyle-style."

Glenn guffawed. *I didn't know I was that funny.*

When he settled down, he said, "Janelle Grace Stephens."

"Gracie Jane?" I asked.

"Bingo," he said. "Janelle Grace Haroldsen and Eric Stephens were married fifteen years ago in New York while she was in her last year of law school."

"Wow. How on earth did you find that out?"

"It was all Paul. He told me it was easier to trace backward than forward sometimes."

"Things are definitely, almost falling into place," I said.

"My thought too. Gracie Jane posted bail. Paul's trying to find her."

"Is she missing?"

"Not officially, but Paul's suspicious. What do you have for me?"

"Mr. Bustamante wanted me to have copies of Faith's letters. His sister, Alba, called me at his request and told me that the last three letters were typed, and all the earlier letters were handwritten. Her son sent me copies by email. I'll forward them to you."

"Anything interesting?"

"You can judge."

"Getting me back? Never mind, of course you are."

I tried to hang up first, but he beat me. After I forwarded the email. I waited.

When my phone rang, I waited three rings then answered.

"I read through them pretty fast, but my first impression when I hit the typewritten letters was that we have two completely different authors," Glenn said.

"That's exactly what I thought."

"I didn't see any differences in the signatures, but Paul will send them to an expert. Paul didn't find a conviction for Philip Stephens for forgery yet, but he's still digging."

"Maybe Philip was too skilled and too cautious to be caught, and Eric learned from his father but pursued his own brand of criminal livelihood. Does Eric have a criminal record? Do we know why he left his last job?" I smacked my forehead. "I just remembered that Faith told me that her boyfriend Eric worked in Charleston, South Carolina."

"You may have told me about Charleston, but I don't think any of us thought it was very important at the time. I'll let Paul know. We didn't find a criminal record for Eric, but Paul can look deeper into his employment history. I'll call you tomorrow."

After he hung up, I said, "Send a text to Darren: I'd like to talk to your mama. Please call."

"Reply from Darren: "Come for coffee and dessert. Seven o'clock?"

"Automatic reply: Thank you," my phone said.

Not sure I like the automatic reply feature. I might have to ask Heather how to turn that off.

"Palace Guard, Larry and I are going to the Martins for dessert this evening. Do I wear fancy clothes?"

Blurry Palace Guard headed to the bedroom, and I followed him. When I opened the closet door, he pointed to my fancy blouses.

"Fancy shirt?" I asked, and he nodded then pointed to my jeans.

"Fancy shirt and jeans," I said, and Palace Guard patted my shoulder.

"Thanks."

I picked up my phone. "Send a text to Larry: Invited to Martins for dessert this evening."

"Larry replied, Okay."

My phone rang, and I snickered. *My phone has expanded my social life..*

"Ms. Gray Lady, this is Owen. I thought of something that might help. Hugo told me that Faith received more than one letter from John that made her very angry, so she confronted him, and he, of course, denied writing them. Evidently the letters were signed, and John told her to have someone verify the signature. Hugo thinks she either did or meant to before she was murdered, but he didn't know. More importantly, when you asked me who would set a trap for you, I am sure it's the person who sent the letters that made Faith angry. I would recommend asking John Howard for help."

"What if John wrote the letters?"

"I don't think he did, and I don't think you do, either, but if he did, you'll be ready for his trap."

The same thing Edna Cross said.

"How am I going to be ready?"

"Gray Lady style, of course."

Owen hung up before I said, "Dang it, Owen."

I called the jewelry shop and left a message on voice mail. "Hi, John. It's the Gray Lady. I have some questions for you about my jewelry. Call me when you're available."

After I hung up, two blurry, imaginary men stood in front of me; Spike had his arms crossed, and Palace Guard stood behind him. My computer desk was surrounded by a cloud of disapproval.

"Cut it out—it's all part of my plan to be ready for a trap. Now, leave me alone. I need to work out some of the details."

Ten minutes later, Larry's truck rolled into the driveway, and I met him at the door and hugged him. He kissed my forehead. "I picked up a roasted chicken and potato salad at the grocery store We'll have leftovers for Wednesday unless we want to make chicken salad for tomorrow."

Larry changed clothes while I set the table. As we ate, Larry asked, "How was your day?"

I told him about Faith's letters and Gracie Jane.

"I can see why Glenn and Paul are in such demand. Moe told me that the Coyle Detective Agency was really taking off, and Ella's trying to recruit him. Can you imagine Moe reporting to Ella?" Larry chuckled.

Why is that funny?

"John Howard wasn't detained after questioning," he continued. "I don't have any details, but I'll bet Paul isn't the only one working on verifying those signatures."

After Larry wrapped up our leftover chicken, we took Lucy for her evening stroll around the block. When we returned, we climbed into the truck.

"Every time the mansion comes into sight, I expect to see ladies with hoop skirts and parasols parading the grounds," Larry said.

I snickered. "At least one of them would be a pickpocket, and the gracious hostess would be a jewel thief."

"I'm talking fiction," Larry snorted, "Not the real life of Maggie Ewing."

Darren met us at the door and smiled. "Ms. Gray Lady, Mama is in the parlor. She had the decorators scrambling."

He led us to the room to the right of the large foyer.

"Maggie Flanagan, come right on in," Mrs. Martin said.

"Mr. Larry and I will join you in a few minutes, Mama. I need his opinion."

Larry helped me to my chair before he left with Darren.

"You brought sweet Lucy and your men with you," Mrs. Martin said. "I always feel safe when they're around."

"I've been thinking about my sleight of hand lesson. If I wanted to reach for something with my right hand, it would need to be a smooth motion while I make an exaggerated motion with my left hand as a misdirection. Is that right?"

"Yes, that's exactly it."

"Sleight of hand would work only with sighted people, right?"

"Yes, that's correct. I like the way you think. How are you going to practice?"

"I haven't gotten quite that far in my plan."

"The fairies said your sight will become restored enough to see them," Mrs. Martin said.

"That's the most exciting news I've had in ages. Any time frame?"

"I haven't heard yet. So, how can I help you?"

"Who is the forgery expert that you mentioned?"

"Edna Cross. Didn't I tell you that? She's retired, but she still has the eye to spot a forgery, if that's what you're interested in."

"She never told me that. In fact, she told me that Philip Stephens was a talented artist and forger, and his expertise was signatures."

"That's right. He was a talented artist, but Edna taught him forgery. It was a lark for her, but a serious occupation for him. She never forgave him for what she called debasing the fine art of forgery for personal gain."

I giggled. "So, how did she use her forgery talents?"

"Personal gain." Mrs. Martin tittered. "Edna always claimed she only righted wrongs with her talent, but Philip Stephens was a thug who plundered the innocent."

"That sounds like Edna Cross to me. Would she be able to examine two signatures and tell me if one was a forgery?"

"Very easily. She's still in the hospital, in case you wanted to visit her. Owen visits her almost every morning. I'll ask Darren to check with Owen to see if he'd take you to see her too, if you like."

"It wouldn't be bad manners to ask for a ride?"

"Not at all. I'm remarkably subtle; he won't even realize why you need to see Edna."

"That would be ideal."

"What would be ideal?" Larry asked as he came into the parlor.

"I may go visit Edna Cross in the hospital tomorrow morning. She hasn't been released yet."

"How are you going to get there? You can't walk."

From the tone of his voice, I knew Larry was scowling.

Mrs. Martin coughed. "Owen and I discussed going to visit her tomorrow, and Maggie Flanagan can ride along with us if we do."

"After we enjoy our dessert, I'll check with Owen to see if his plans have changed, Mama."

Impressive how quick Darren is on the uptake.

"I'll put a low table in front of you, Ms. Gray Lady, so you won't have to juggle coffee and dessert. Do you care for regular or decaf?"

"Decaf for me," Larry said.

"I'll have decaf too," I added. *I'd rather have a mimosa with a sippy cup.*

"I can pour coffee, Darren, if you'd like to plate the cheesecake."

"Thanks, Mr. Larry. Mama and I drink decaf in the evenings. Cherry topping?" he asked.

"Yes, for both of us."

Extra for me.

Palace Guard patted my back.

While we ate dessert, I heard the soft, musical tinkling of a bell.

"A light breeze must have caught the wind chimes on the back patio. Did you hear that quiet ring?" Larry asked.

"I'm not sure, but maybe I did," Darren said.

"Ah. The breeze will be strong sooner than you think," Mrs Martin said.

Exciting news. Thanks, fairies.

"May rain tonight after all," Larry said.

"Thanks for checking the security system." Darren collected my empty plate. "More coffee?"

"Not for me, thank you," I said.

"I'm glad the installer set it up so that you can turn it on and off with your phone," Larry said.

"I wouldn't have thought of it. Thanks for mentioning it yesterday."

"Darren bought me a phone, Maggie Flanagan. He said he'd show me how to use it."

"I'll send you Mama's number after we have it all set up," Darren said.

"I hate to cut the evening short, but it's been a full day for Maggie," Larry said.

"For me too," Mrs. Martin said.

"Thank you so much for dessert," I said. "The cheesecake was delicious."

Mrs. Martin tittered. "Darren loved my cheesecake so much when he was growing up, that he insisted that I teach him how to make it after he and the doctor revoked my kitchen privileges."

"You made the cheesecake?" Larry asked. "What a wonderful talent, Darren."

"Thank you, Mr. Larry. Mama was a good teacher."

Lucy clicked over to Mrs. Martin. "You're a sweet girl, Lucy. Thank you for visiting me."

On our way home, Larry said, "I was really impressed that Darren made the cheesecake. I need a specialty."

"We can go through Jennifer's recipes. You might find something there."

"Good idea."

After we were home, we accompanied Lucy on her final evening stroll around the backyard. As we headed back to the house, the wind increased, and by the time we were inside, rain pelted the windows.

"That was good timing," Larry said. "Ready to call it a night?"

"Yes."

As I listened to Larry's soft, rhythmic breathing, I thought about jewel thieves, master forgers, homemade cheesecake, and fairies.

* * *

"I might try to get off a little early this afternoon," Larry said on his way out the door. "Let me know what I can pick up."

I waved as he pulled out of the driveway; after I closed the door, my phone buzzed a text and said, "You have a text from Darren: Nine o'clock okay?"

"Send reply: Yes."

I printed the letters and placed them into a folder. I pouted because I didn't know what time it was until I remembered that when Heather helped me set up my phone to recognize my voice, she said there were other apps too.

I held my phone close to my right eye. *I can kind of make out the purpose of some of these blobby dots.* I tapped on one, and the blurry spinning download began.

I tapped on the new dot. *Here goes nothing.*

"What time is it?"

"The time is eight fourteen o'clock," said the stilted prerecorded voice.

"What's the expected high temperature today?" I asked.

"The high temperature for today's date was one hundred four degrees in nineteen twenty-three."

"Are you nuts?"

"Please repeat the question."

Forget it.

I fiddled with my phone until I was sure I'd uninstalled the time and temperature app.

"What time is it?" I asked and was pleased with no response.

I'll get by until Heather can find me a decent app or I can read the time for myself. The fairies said I'd see them sooner than I think anyway.

When Owen parked in the driveway, Lucy yipped.

"Sorry, girl. You aren't going this time." I stuck my small purse into my backpack before I opened the door.

"Good morning, Ms. Gray Lady. I'm glad you could join us to visit Edna. They moved her onto the medical floor yesterday afternoon."

When he opened the passenger's door, I asked, "Where's Mrs. Martin?"

"I'm allowing Owen to be my chauffeur. You may be my navigator," Mrs. Martin said from the back seat.

I giggled along with her.

On our way to the hospital, Owen's car splashed through puddles on the road.

"Did we get much rain last night?" I asked.

"Quite a bit, but the roads will be dry before lunch," Owen said.

I nodded. *I don't think it's appropriate for me to share the contents of these letters.*

"Mrs. Martin, would you mind going through these papers for me and picking out the signature pages?"

After I handed the folder to Mrs. Martin, she flipped through the letters.

"Here are the signature pages."

After I shuffled them and put them into the folder, she said, "And here is everything else."

I stuck the rest into my backpack.

When we reached the hospital, Owen parked at the entrance to the visitor drop-off. "I'll pull out Mrs. Martin's wheelchair from the trunk then the two of you can go to the second floor. Edna's room is two-fourteen. I'll meet you there after I park."

Palace Guard pushed Mrs. Martin's wheelchair while I held on and pretended I was pushing it. After we were on the elevator, Mrs. Martin pushed the second button.

"There are times where being invisible is a real asset," she said. "No one notices someone in a wheelchair; must be the same for someone with a cane, or in your case, a mountain walking stick. Thank you, Palace Guard, for pushing my wheelchair."

As we strolled down the hall, I said, "Stop a second."

I moved in front of Mrs. Martin. When I turned to face her, my left hand slipped on my jo, and as I grabbed for it and jerked it close to me I reached into my jeans picket with a smooth motion and pulled out my spoon and pointed it at her.

"Bang," she giggled. "That was excellent, Maggie Flanagan. I wondered what you were up to but when your stick almost fell, and you grabbed it, I was watching your stick. I didn't even see where your spoon came from." I heard a flutter, and Mrs. Martin said, "the fairies are very pleased."

When we reached her room, Edna said, "Oh my goodness, what a great surprise to see the two of you. This is exciting. Did Darren drive you here?"

"Owen did; he's parking and will be up here soon," I said.

"Come sit by me. Tell me all the gossip."

Palace Guard pushed Mrs. Martin's wheelchair close to Edna as I sat in the visitor's chair next to her bed. Palace Guard eased the door closed.

"I need your artist's eye, Edna, to look at something for me."

"Whatever I can do to help you out, Gray Lady."

"I think there might be a forged signature on these papers. The forensic experts are looking at them, but I hear they are stumped. I think they're being too technical. I think it would take an artist to see any differences."

I handed her the papers with the signatures, and she flipped through them once then handed me the sheets one at a time. "Authentic, authentic, fake, fake, authentic…"

After she was finished, I put the ones she called authentic into my backpack and folded the ones she called fake and slipped them into the folder.

"How are you doing?" I asked.

"I don't have the oxygen anymore. I discovered the hospital charges for air. Can you believe that? There's nothing wrong with the free air. I asked the doctor why they just can't use that, and she didn't have a good answer. I wonder if she's not as smart as I thought she was because she laughed so hard she got the hiccups. Isn't there a disease that people laugh uncontrollably? It isn't contagious, is it?"

"Sometimes laughing is contagious," I said.

"Isn't that the truth, even inappropriate laughing." Edna snickered. "I laughed at Gracie Jane, and it definitely wasn't appropriate, but she didn't catch me. She let all those old folks claim they designated her as a beneficiary in their wills, but do you know how many did? Three, and their families contested the wills when they died and won. Gracie Jane was mad."

"You mean she didn't get any of the will money she'd planned on?"

"She was like a boy I knew when I was a kid who got mad at a bear that chased him, so he set fire to the woods to teach it a lesson. I asked her if she was going to burn her law diploma, and she said that wasn't a bad idea right before she set the fire to the records in her office. When the fire reached the ceiling and tried to burn through to the sky, I quit spying on her and hurried to my room. Always respect fire."

"Did she have her law degree on her wall?"

"And her bachelor's certificate too, for a while, until someone asked her who did her forgery. It was actually pretty good."

"Was her law degree legit?"

"From what I understand, it was. Gracie Jane banned me from her office because I wasn't a volunteer. She was downright persnickety sometimes."

That's why Gracie Jane told me Edna Cross made things up.

"If Gracie Jane didn't want to be found, do you know where she'd go?" I asked.

"Probably to her sister's house. That's where I'd go except I don't have a sister. Do you have a sister, Gray Lady?"

"I do. She's my big sister."

"I think I'd want to be the big sister. What about you, Rebecca? Do you have a sister?"

"No, but I had a sweet sister-in-law, so maybe that counts."

"I'm pretty sure that counts," Edna said.

Owen came into the room. "Hello, Edna. You having a good day?"

"Thank you, I am. Are you the chauffeur for my delightful friends?"

"Yes, and I brought you something."

"Flowers? Those are beautiful. Thank you," Edna said. "The last time I had flowers was…I can't remember when." She chuckled.

I rose from the chair and motioned for Owen to sit next to Edna.

"I might need some fresh air," Mrs. Martin said. "We'll see you again. Be sure to stay in touch with Owen."

"Thanks for your help, Edna. I really appreciate it," I said.

While Mrs. Martin and I rode down in the elevator, I asked, "What do you think?"

"I think you're amazing. It will be interesting to see whether Edna picked out the forgeries, but she certainly surprised me with all the information she shared about Gracie Jane."

"How much of it was true?"

"Most of it was except the story about the bear," Mrs. Martin said as Palace Guard pushed her wheelchair from the elevator through the lobby and to the outside.

While we stood at the exit, I handed Mrs. Martin the folded pages.

"Typed letters or handwritten?"

"All typed." She handed them back to me. "You might be interested to know that she flipped through the pages with only the signatures showing, so she wasn't prejudiced by typed or handwritten."

"How did she find the fakes so quickly?"

"I'm certainly not an expert like Edna, but I do know that there's a certain hesitancy in creating each forgery that can't be duplicated in the next. Your authentic signatures wouldn't have had any hesitancy."

"Ah ha. Thank you."

When Owen joined us, he said, "I talked to Edna's nurse. They're moving her to hospice after lunch because she's declining faster than they expected."

Palace Guard caught me as I lost my balance. *Not Edna Cross. She's too young.*

Mrs. Martin gasped. "She's so young."

"I agree," Owen said. "She's a fighter. They didn't expect her to last this long, but the smoke inhalation was more than her body could take. She had some serious medical problems to start with, and now her systems are shutting down."

Mrs. Martin reached for my hand. "It's good we came to see her. She wanted to tell you what she knew because you'd know what to do. Are you going to be okay?"

"I guess I don't have a choice. What about you?"

"I'm an old woman, Maggie Flanagan, and I've known a lot of people, but I've never known anyone else quite like Edna Cross."

I nodded. "She is a loveable, delightful, naïve liar."

Mrs. Martin chuckled. "You're right. One of a kind. So, what do you have on your agenda for the rest of the day?"

"Larry and I are meeting our parents at a campground this evening for dinner. The complication is that I kind of said we'd provide the food. I think I may spend the rest of the day cooking."

"Sweet, impulsive Maggie Flanagan. You are so much like your great-grandmother. I can help with that. Tell Larry to come by my house on his way home. My personal chef has been chomping at the bit to provide a nice dinner for six, is it?"

"Yes, but you don't have to—"

"Don't be silly. You've been my dearest friend for four generations, if you believe in fairies or imaginary men. Of course, I have to help you out of a predicament that you created yourself."

I laughed. "You win."

"As she should," Owen said.

I spoke to my phone. "Send a text to Larry: Stop by Mrs. Martin's to pick up tonight's dinner."

"Larry replied: Okay."

"That phone voice is hard for me to understand. What was his reply?" Mrs. Martin asked.

"He said okay."

Mrs. Martin and I laughed so hard that I got the hiccups, and we laughed even harder.

After we settled down, Owen said, "I have no idea what was so funny."

"We know," Mrs. Martin said.

When Owen parked in my driveway, he circled his car and opened my door.

"Thank you, Mrs. Martin, for all your help, and especially with tonight's dinner."

"I was delighted to help. Thank you for going with us to see Edna."

Owen hovered while I tapped to the front door. "Thanks again, Owen, for chauffeuring us."

"I'm glad Darren called me; I was happy to spend a little time with my old friend Edna too."

After Palace Guard and I were inside, I said, "I need to call Glenn and to rest."

I sat on the sofa and kicked off my boots. Lucy jumped up next to me, and I stroked her neck before I leaned back. As tears flowed down my cheek, Lucy lay her head on my leg to comfort me. While I relaxed with Lucy, my phone rang.

"Hi Maggie, I've got you on speaker phone because Paul said I summarize too much. He talked to one of Eric Stephens' coworkers in Atlanta," Glenn said. "The coworker told him that Eric left abruptly, and no one was sorry to see him go. Paul called the company to request a reference for Eric, but the manager politely declined. Paul didn't find any history of Eric Stephens in South Carolina."

I told Glenn and Paul what Edna said about Gracie Jane's sister, bachelor's degree, the wills, and the fire.

"Mrs. Martin told me that Edna was an artist and a forger. I gave Edna the last pages with the signatures of all the letters and told her one was a forgery. She picked out all three of the typed letters and told me they were forged. I realize she's not a forensic expert, but Mrs. Martin told me that Edna kept the letters covered while she compared the signatures."

Glenn said, "I'll check to see if the fire marshal's report has been filed."

"I'll find our next piece of the puzzle, Gracie Jane's sister," Paul said.

"What do you have going on?" Glenn asked.

"Larry and I are meeting Mother, Sarge, and his parents at a nearby campground this evening, and we're having dinner with them at the campground."

"That explains why Jennifer invited the four of them to dinner here tomorrow night. She needs a second-hand report." Glenn chuckled.

"Ella and I are going to be there too," Paul said. "Any conversation topics you need for me to divert?"

I giggled. "I'll let you know after tonight."

CHAPTER SIXTEEN

After we hung up, I fixed my lunch plate with six crackers and one slice of spicy pepper cheese cut into six equal pieces. I stacked the cheese slices to be sure they were all equal before I covered each cracker with a piece of cheese. I filled my sippy cup with water because I didn't trust myself to lift the heavy, full gallon of tea and pour it into a glass without making a big mess. I cleared my plate and grabbed my sunglasses to go out back with Lucy when my phone rang again.

"Hey, Gray Lady," Heather said. "I'm on a stakeout and bored to tears. Catch me up on where we are with anything, and tell me to quit my boring job and be your sister."

I giggled then told her the latest on the signatures and the news about Gracie Jane and her sister.

"What about you?" I asked.

"Todd's still cute. Gossip is that the explosions were not related to the fire. Oops. On the move. Gotta go."

After Heather hung up, I wondered what she wore when she was on stakeout. *I'll have to ask her next time. I might need to go on a stakeout after I can see.*

I said, "Send Glenn a text: Cause of explosions known? Caused by fire?"

"Glenn replied: On it."

I went to the back door, and Lucy followed me.

While Lucy investigated her now-familiar yard, Spike followed her while I stood at the back fence with Palace Guard alongside me.

"I just realized that when Mr. Bustamante left town, Eric Stephens needed to find somewhere else to stay. Did he stay in Columbus? Who would know?"

John Howard would know. Why hasn't he returned my call?

Spike and Lucy headed to the door, and I joined them. *I need a nap before we go to the campground.*

After I curled up on the sofa, the afghan drifted down on me. "Thanks," I mumbled.

Lucy woke me with a nudge, and I sat up and stretched as Larry's truck pulled into the driveway. He rushed into the house after I stood with the help of my jo.

"Hi, sweetie. We have a magnificent campground dinner. Mrs. Martin's chef packed it into two insulated boxes with ice packs. Are you ready or do you want me to pick out a shirt for you?"

"Thanks. I'll bet my shirt is wrinkled from my nap. Go ahead and change then pick out a shirt for me."

As I brushed my hair, I considered a ponytail but changed my mind. I tapped my way to the bedroom.

"Your shirt is on the bed. It has buttons down the front."

"I'll be fine." When I put on the shirt, I buttoned the bottom button then buttoned up from that one.

"That was slick. How did you know to do that?"

"Librarians read everything, and spies remember everything."

"You're not a spy, sweetie."

I flipped my hair. "That's why I remember what I need to remember. Are you ready to go?"

On our way to the campground, I asked, "What do agents remember?"

"Agents remember when to change the subject. Guess what's for dinner."

"Fried chicken."

"You are right." Larry whistled as he drove to the campground.

"What else?" I asked as he turned at the entrance.

"I have a list. I was stalling until I could stop and read it to you."

He pulled to the side of the dirt road after he passed the campground office. "The list says southern fried chicken, pickled green beans, spicy chili jam, cracked wheat crackers, cheese, potato salad, basil dinner rolls and rum-laced apricot-cranberry tarts."

Now I understand why he was whistling on the way here.

As he continued toward the parents' sites, I said, "Wow. We have one fancy picnic."

"We're here."

While Larry pulled in to park, I asked, "Are they parked next to each other? Do I wear my sunglasses after dark?"

Larry chuckled. "Yes, and yes, if you want to."

Larry opened the door for Lucy, but before he made it around the truck to open my door, Sarge opened it. "Maggie," he boomed. "You are as beautiful as ever. Isn't she, Izzy?"

"Margaret, you look lovely. Do you need any help? I love your stick. Is that your seeing eye cane? Big D told me not to overwhelm you. He can help you out."

Sarge took my hand and put it on his arm. After I climbed out of the truck, he gave me a big Sarge hug. When he released me, I said, "Heather found me a staff that I can use as a cane to make sure I don't fall over anything or for balance."

"We have the chairs arranged for us to sit. I think I'm supposed to let you hold onto my elbow so I can guide you. Is that right?"

"That's perfect, Mother."

"Need some help?" Sarge asked Larry.

"We have two large boxes of food and two gallons of sweet tea," Larry said.

Before I sat, Larry's dad, Sean, pulled me into a Ewing hug. "It's so good to see you."

He smells like Larry.

Lauren, Larry's mom, was next in line for a hug. "I'm glad to see that you're doing so well, Maggie. Sean wouldn't let me cook anything for this evening. I can throw a cake into the oven in two shakes if you'd like dessert."

I smiled. "A good friend, Mrs. Martin, has been spoiling us with meals. Her personal chef made our dinner for tonight."

As I sat, Mother said, "I knew a Mrs. Martin when I was growing up."

"She's the same Mrs. Martin, Mother. She told me you used to visit her when you were a girl. She's in a wheelchair, but her mind is as sharp as anyone else's."

"What about the fairies?" Mother asked. "Does she still tell stories about her fairies? You know, that's where I got all my fairy stories."

"The fairies are still with her. Mrs. Martin wondered if you'd remember them."

"Who could forget fairies?" Lauren asked. "Sounds wonderful to me. You'll have to tell me some of the stories sometime, Isolde."

"I have wonderful memories of the fairies. Mrs. Martin was Grandmother Margarite's friend, and when we visited Mrs. Martin, I'd sit under her huge dining table while the fairies signed their fairy stories and songs for me. I thought they did that to be quiet, but later I realized how bad my hearing was and how much the fairies annoyed Mother. She didn't approve of them at all."

"Who could disapprove of fairies?" Lauren asked. "We'll have to talk more, but I need to set up the food buffet style on the picnic table."

"I'll help," Mother said.

I was completely wrong about Mother. She's not embarrassed by the fairies at all.

Sean sat in the chair that Mother vacated and placed his hand on my arm. "Maggie, you look great. Is there anything we can do to help?"

"I can't think of anything. I've been looking forward to seeing you all."

"Sarge told me you'd adapt like a champ. We think you're awesome."

I felt my face warm, and Sean patted my hand then rose when Lauren said, "Sean, would you grab some napkins and glasses?"

Larry kissed my cheek as he sat next to me. "Too much?" he whispered.

I shook my head. "Not at all, but I'm glad I took a nap. It's very exciting. What's Lucy doing?"

Larry continued in a low voice. "She's leaning against Sarge while he rubs her face. If I told the guys at the Harperville department how Sarge cuddles Lucy, they'd give me a breathalyzer test."

I snickered as I remembered how gruff Sarge sounded when I first met him.

"Food's all set up, everyone. We have beer, wine, and sweet tea. This is a serve yourself joint," Lauren said.

Larry rose, "I'll fix you a plate, sweetie. What do you want to drink?"

"Sweet tea."

Sarge sat next to me while Larry answered questions about the food and served our plates.

"Maggie, now that I've retired, I don't hear quite as much as I used to, but Detective Ross called to tell me that the Columbus police department got a tp that Gracie Jane Haroldsen was staying at her sister's place. The GBI arrested her late this afternoon at a cabin in the mountains near the Tennessee line."

Wow. They work fast.

"Tip came from you, didn't it?" he asked. I wished I could see his face because I was sure his eyes twinkled.

"Now, why would you think that?" I asked.

Sarge's booming laugh made me giggle.

"Oh, you know. Cop intuition," he said.

"I was keeping your bride company," Sarge said as he rose.

"What was that all about?" Larry asked.

"Gracie Jane was arrested," I said.

"No surprise. Dad put a small table in front of you, and your plate is on the table. Your chicken's at nine o'clock, potato salad's in the middle, and pickled green beans are at three o'clock. You have a small plate above your plate of food at one o'clock with three crackers and cheese and your roll. Your lidded cup with sweet tea is above your plate at eleven o'clock. Napkin on your left; fork on your right."

"Thanks."

"You're quite welcome. By the way, Heather told me about a tip. Well done, sweetie."

While we ate, Mother asked, "Where is Mrs. Martin? I'd love to see her before we return in the morning. Do you think that would be okay?"

"I'm sure she'd love to see you, Mother. She moved back to her mansion after she was released from the hospital. They kept her a few days because of her age, but she's doing very well. Larry can give Sarge Darren's phone number."

"I'm a little older than Darren," Mother said, "but I remember he was an excellent artist. Did he pursue art as a career?"

"He's made good use of it. He's extremely knowledgeable and sells and appraises art. He also volunteers with the local art museum."

"That's so nice to hear," Mother said.

"Do you suppose I could accompany you, Isolde, when you visit Mrs. Martin. I'd love to meet her. Or would that be inappropriate, Maggie?" Lauren asked.

I swallowed my bite of potato salad before I answered. *I'm not sure I'm the one to ask about inappropriate.* "I don't know what her schedule's like tomorrow, but I know Mrs. Martin loves to entertain."

"I'll send Darren a quick text," Larry said.

"Seconds, anyone?" Lauren asked.

"Don't mind if I do," Sean said.

"I've eaten all I can, Larry," I said.

"Saved me from getting up from my chair. Thanks."

"You know that's pretty smart," Sarge said. "Keeps your second portion size to about half, but you still get another taste of everything."

"I'll serve you half portions, if you like, Big D," Mother said.

"Oh, no. It's good for Larry. I'll taper back after we get home, and I step on the scale," Sarge chuckled.

"I'm right there with you, Sarge," Lauren said.

"Want to go for a walk, Lucy?" Sean asked.

"Here's her leash, Dad," Larry said. "She carries it."

Lauren chuckled. "She is so smart. I'll go along with you, and we can have dessert when we get back."

When they returned, Sean said, "We didn't go that far, but I think Lucy enjoyed it. I'm not sure if she turned back because she was getting tired or if she didn't want to wear out the old people."

"Speak for yourself. Lucy and I could have gone a couple more miles."

"I heard back from Darren," Larry said. "Mrs. Martin would like to invite you two for lunch tomorrow at noon."

"That would be wonderful," Mother said.

"Yes, we accept. Now, how are we going to get there?" Lauren asked.

"I've got some old pals at the Columbus police department that I'd like to have lunch with, but I didn't want to slow down anybody else. I could drop you off," Sarge said.

"Would you like to take me to lunch, Sean?" I asked. "I have a favorite café downtown that you might enjoy."

"Sounds great to me."

"I'll have my sandwich at work," Larry grumbled.

Sean laughed. "That's the sad lot of the working man."

"I put on a pot of coffee if anyone wants a cup with dessert," Lauren said.

After dessert, Larry packaged up the leftovers, and at his mother's insistence, loaded the box into his truck.

"Food's all packed up. We should probably go now," Larry said.

I rose from my chair. "It was great to see everyone."

I underwent a round of hugs, but Mother surprised me when she hugged me. "I'm so proud of you, Margaret."

On the way home, Larry asked, "Are you completely worn out?"

"Yes, but in a good way. I was excited that they were coming to visit, but I enjoyed this evening more than I expected."

"It really was a good idea to meet them at the campground; it was a relaxed visit for everyone. It took a lot of pressure off them because I know Mom would have worried that they were wearing you out, and I'm sure your mother would have too."

"What's Lucy doing?" I asked.

"She's asleep on Spike's lap."

Larry parked then helped me out of the truck before he unloaded the box and unlocked the door. After he put the leftovers into the refrigerator, he asked, "Are you ready for bed?"

"Not really. I'm tired, but I'm too wired to go to sleep. How about a beer?"

"We can sit outside while Lucy wanders or until the bugs chase us in."

Larry carried out our beer, and we relaxed in our chairs.

"This is the life," he said. "Now, what's the real reason you invited Dad to go to lunch?"

I choked on my beer.

"Warn me next time before you bring out the hot interrogation lights, would you?"

"Are you using my personal diversion technique on me?"

"I must be tired for it to be so obvious. Maybe I want to see Marissa or maybe I thought it would be a nice gesture," I said.

"Right. So, why?"

"I'd like to talk to John Howard. I think he might know where Eric Stephens is."

"Why would he? I wouldn't think he'd care where Eric Stephens was, as long as Eric's not around here."

"Have you ever heard the old saying: 'Keep your friends close, and your enemies closer'?"

"I must be tired—that makes sense."

I yawned. "I think I'm ready to go inside." I handed him my beer bottle. "I'm too full to finish it."

"I hate to do it, but I'm going to pour mine out too. That was a feast, wasn't it?"

* * *

When I woke, Larry had showered and was getting dressed in his uniform.

"Good morning, sweetie. Coffee's on."

I swung my feet to the floor and grabbed my jo. "On my way."

After breakfast, I showered and dressed. "What are my colors today?"

"Pink," Larry said.

"Really? Do I look weird?"

He hugged me. "Yes."

When I opened my mouth to scold him, he kissed me.

After a long, passionate kiss, I said, "You were sneaky."

"Yep. Your hair needs to be brushed. Shall I?"

"It's the least you can do."

As he brushed my hair he said, "I think I can do a single braid. I think it's kind of like making a lanyard, except it's with three strands instead of four. Should be easier."

After he finished the braid, he said, "Looks pretty good. Ready?"

When he parked, I said, "I'm nervous."

"I know, so am I."

Larry wrapped his arm around my shoulder as we strolled to the doctor's office together.

"Is my eyepatch pink too?"

"Yes."

"Good. I'm undercover."

"Palace Guard and I rolled our eyes. Just letting you know."

I snickered. "I'm glad you understand."

After a short wait, the nurse took us into an exam room, and the doctor breezed in as the nurse left.

"We've got a lot of tests to run today. Your eyes have had enough time to heal to give us an idea of what to expect for your progress. Ready?"

Larry squeezed my hand. "We're ready," I replied.

"Let's start with our usual eye check. Here's your paddle. Take off your sunglasses and eyepatch—love the pink, by the way—and cover your right eye."

I covered my right eye. "Nothing."

"No change, correct?" she asked.

"Yes."

I covered my left eye with the paddle, and she dimmed the lights and projected letters on the wall.

"Can you read any of the letters?"

I squinted as I tried to focus then sighed. "No."

After she returned the lights to normal, she typed notes on her tablet then asked. "Can you see me?"

"Yes, you're fuzzy. I can see more of the shape of your head and body, but the edges are blurry."

"That's great. We still don't know how much sight you'll have, but you're healing nicely."

After an hour of tests, the doctor said, "Your right eye is progressing beautifully. We need to do a little surgery on your left eye to clean up some of that dead tissue, but before you get mad and walk out on me, it's outpatient. I don't see any signs of infection in either eye, which is good. Keep wearing your sunglasses and your eyepatch, and keep applying your drops. Have you had tears from your right eye? Have any streamed down your face?"

"Yes, they have. Is that okay?"

"That's excellent news. Your eye is moist; I was hoping you'd made tears. The most exciting news is you have enough tears for them to overflow and run down your face. Major bonus. Hold up your hand." The doctor smacked a high five, and I laughed.

"If your eye feels dry, you can put in a few drops of artificial tears. We'll send you home with a small bottle and schedule the surgery for Friday morning."

On the way to the truck, I said, "Ugh."

"I know." Larry stopped and hugged me. "I wish I could make it better. I wish the fairies could make it better, and Palace Guard agrees. I'm glad you're having lunch with Dad. He's a good listener and won't feel like he has to fix anything."

"Is it okay if I mope all the way home?" I asked.

"You're entitled. Okay if I mope along with you?"

"I'd love the company. I wonder if the fairies have a song about moping."

"If they do, I'll make a point to listen to it," Larry said.

After we were home, Larry asked, "Are you going to be okay if I go to work? I can call in if you like."

"I'll be fine. Please go to work and catch bad guys."

"Okay. Please stay home and shoot to kill."

I laughed. "That's a change."

He sighed. "I really wish I could be alongside you like the old days. I don't know why we can't be normal newlyweds and fight over money and who stole the covers like other people."

"You're a wonderful man, Agent Kevin Larry Ewing, and I love you to pieces."

"I love you so much. Be safe." He hugged me then left.

I sat on the sofa and picked up my phone. "Call Jennifer."

When she answered, I said, "I'm okay. I called to talk to you."

"Do I need to grab my keys and Ella and head your way?"

"No," I snickered. "I just haven't had a chance to talk to you." I told her what the doctor said.

"How are you feeling?" she asked.

"I was mopey all the way home, but now that I've had time to think about it, I'm encouraged that I'll be able to see okay with my right eye. I wanted to thank you for the clothes and my eye- patches. I wore the pink eyepatch today. It just seemed appropriate for the Gray Lady to be in disguise."

Jennifer giggled. "That's my Maggie. Glenn and Paul are out of the office right now. I got a call just a few minutes ago that the explosions at the senior center and the fire in the office are not directly related. The second explosion was in the kitchen. It may have been the gas stove and was probably caused by the first explosion. The first explosion, however, was at the exit and was deliberate. I don't have any more information, but I know Glenn and Paul will jump all over it."

"I'm pretty sure Gracie Jane set the office fire. I don't know if it was on impulse or not, but unless she set off the explosion, how could anyone else know that she would light off papers in her office that resulted in an out-of-control fire? Although, I just had a thought. She was burned; just not as badly as was initially reported. What's the best way to cause an explosion to follow up an impulsive fire and could that be how she was burned?"

"More questions for Glenn and Paul—I'm taking notes. That sounds like the key to me. I just can't imagine the key to what. The first explosion was set for someone who would use the exit to escape the fire, right? I have no follow up for that, by the way."

I snickered. "It's our job to have theories."

"What else can I do for you, sweet girl?"

"You've done more than I could have imagined. I love knowing that you anticipate what I need when I don't even know it."

"I'm all teary. Take care, Maggie."

After Jennifer hung up, I smiled. "I should have told Jennifer that teary is good."

I put a spoon in my pocket then practiced my sleight of hand with my jo and my spoon. When I had it down, I practiced with my jo and my holstered pistol until I heard a car pull into the driveway.

"Sean?" I asked, and Palace Guard patted my shoulder. I opened the door, and Sean said, "You heard me coming? How did you know it was me?"

"I'll tell you sometime if you want to know," I said as I locked the front door.

"Why would I not?"

"It depends on how far you can stretch your imagination."

"Ah. So, tell me the real reason you invited me to take you to lunch."

"I need to see John Howard, and I'm hoping he's at his shop. If he isn't, we'll have a nice lunch, and I'll get to see my friend Marissa."

"Maggie, how do you make so many friends in a new town in such a short time?"

"I don't know. What's your theory?"

"Part of it is your reputation as the Gray Lady. Even my old friends were impressed when they learned my daughter-in-law is the Gray Lady. I may be retired, but I still am a police detective. How can I help?"

"I'm hoping John Howard can help me find Eric Stephens, who has suddenly dropped off the radar. Another point is that we've assumed that Gracie Jane and Eric were acting together. What if we find something that could drive a wedge of doubt between them? Which one would roll over and sacrifice the other?"

"I've got the rest of the morning and the entire afternoon to solve that puzzle, right?" Sean chuckled.

I snickered. "Take your time. No pressure."

As we neared downtown, Sean asked, "Where do I park?"

"Wherever you can find a spot. It's busy around here at lunchtime. I hope Marissa isn't too busy to chat. She's awesome."

"Who's Marissa?" Sean asked.

"She's the chef at the café where we'll have lunch."

Sean chuckled. "Do you know everyone in town?"

"Maybe." I snickered.

After Sean parked, he said, "We're two blocks away. Is that okay?"

"That's great."

I held onto Sean's arm as we strolled to the café. "Are you enjoying your retirement?"

He told me about his reluctance to retire and how much he enjoyed travelling in the RV. "Looking back, I laugh at myself for all my fears. Maggie, we're approaching the jewelry shop. Do we want to stop there first?"

"Yes."

"Lights are on in the shop," Sean said. "Ready to go in?"

Palace Guard pulled me back.

"Maybe you could go in to see who is there first. I'll wait here."

"Step to the left five or six steps. You're blocking the door to the dry cleaners."

Palace Guard guided me away from the doorway.

"That's better. Maybe I can find a nice necklace for Lauren," he chuckled.

He went inside while I exercised my patience to do nothing. *This is boring. Why couldn't I go in?*

Palace Guard patted my shoulder, and I sighed. *How long could it take to scope out a shop and not buy a necklace?*

Palace Guard tugged on my arm, and I walked away from the jewelry shop until Palace Guard indicated a turn to face another shop. With his guidance, I stepped up then reached for the door as he pulled it open.

When we went inside the shop, I inhaled a sweet, vanilla fragrance as a woman said, "Hello, Gray Lady. How can I help you?" Her voice had the soft drawl of a long-time Georgia resident.

I have absolutely no idea.

Palace Guard patted my neck. *Scarf?*

He patted my shoulder.

"Do you have a scarf that would go with my shirt?" I giggled. "I'll have to trust your taste."

"I think I might. Were you thinking silky or cotton?"

"I was thinking soft cotton."

"I have a pink and red scarf. It's much prettier than it sounds and would be perfect for you. I've had it a while because it's so unique. Shall we try it on?"

"Sounds interesting."

She placed the scarf around my neck.

"I love it on you."

I patted the scarf. "I love how soft it is. I've never had a scarf before."

"You can certainly return it if you change your mind. Were you on your way to the café for lunch?"

"Yes, I am."

"Ask Marissa. If she doesn't like it, bring it right back. I trust her judgement."

Perfect. "Let's ring it up." I smiled.

I made my way to the counter with Palace Guard's guidance and pulled out my phone. "I'll pay with my phone. Where do I tap?"

After the transaction completed, she said, "Here's your receipt."

I held out my hand, and she placed it on my palm.

"I'll open the door for you. Thank you so much for stopping. I'm tickled pink that I could help you." She giggled, and I smiled at her joke.

When I stepped onto the sidewalk, Sean joined me.

"I saw you in the dress shop. How did you know to go inside? Never mind, you'll tell me later, right? When I went into the jeweler's, there was a large, middle-aged man with brown hair behind the counter. I assumed he was John Howard."

I nodded.

"There was a second large, middle-aged man with dark hair in the shop, and the two of them were arguing when I walked in. After the customer slammed his fist on the glass, John said, 'Eric, get out.'

"He said, 'Eric'?" I froze.

CHAPTER SEVENTEEN

"Are you okay?" Sean stopped and took my elbow.

Thanks, Palace Guard. Good call.

"Just surprised. What else?"

As we resumed our walk, Sean said, "When Eric stormed out of the shop and turned toward the dry cleaners, I hurried to the door to see if he was going to confront you. You weren't in sight as he took off down the sidewalk. I watched him climb into his car and pull away."

As we headed to the café, Sean continued, "John apologized to me and asked how he could help me. We chatted, and I mentioned that you were my daughter-in-law. It just seemed right. He'll join us for lunch."

"Wow. You are awesome," I said. "I've been wanting to talk to John Howard."

"Good. So, that scarf you bought is definitely a Maggie scarf. How did you pick it out?"

"I didn't. The woman in the shop did. She told me to get Marissa's opinion and return it if Marissa doesn't like it."

When Sean opened the café door, Rafael greeted us. "Maggie, it is so good to see you. John said you were on your way. I'll show you to your table. You must be the father-in-law, Sean. Welcome to the Sano Café."

As Sean helped me sit at our table, John said, "Maggie, I'm sorry I missed hearing your message before today. I'm glad you and Sean chased me down."

"Sweet tea and today's special, everyone?" Rafael asked. "Maggie, you'll like your special, and Marissa will be right out."

When Marissa opened the door from the kitchen, I inhaled the aroma of cilantro, cumin, and garlic as Marissa hurried to our table then hugged me. "Maggie, I was worried about you. Silly me."

I snickered. "I was glad that Larry's dad could bring me here, so I could see you. You're supposed to fashion-critique my new scarf. What do you think?"

"I think it's a Maggie scarf."

"Can't get any better than that," Rafael said.

"I have to get back to the kitchen." Marissa gave me an extra squeeze before she rushed away.

Rafael brought our tea. "Maggie, your cup has a lid. I set it on your left above your placemat."

As I sipped my tea, John said, "After the police released me from questioning, I went to Dothan to see Mr. Bustamante. I wanted to be sure he was comfortable and that there were no bad feelings between us. I had a long talk with his sister, Alba, and her son showed me the typewritten letters she had found. I can certainly see why Alba immediately turned them over to the police. Mr. Bustamante told me you had copies of the letters; you know those last three are forgeries, right?"

"Yes. They're pretty good, but an expert confirmed they're forgeries."

Our server brought our food, and Rafael leaned close to me. "Your plate has four compartments, and the one at nine o'clock has salsa for a dip. Marissa made you pork empanadas, which are at six o'clock, and she cut your green chili, cheese, and chicken roll-up into pinwheels. They are at three o'clock. You have sweet plantains and a few tortilla chips at noon. Marissa said to tell you that we love you, chica."

After he straightened up, he said, "You gentlemen have empanadas, pinto bean sopa, and chicken enchiladas with salsa verde. Enjoy."

After we ate, John asked, "So, what did you want to talk to me about—not actually jewelry, right?"

"You're right. I needed to ask you about Eric Stephens because I thought you'd know where he is. I guess I was right." I smiled.

"I know he's staying in town. Because he's such a freeloading sponge, I would guess he's found someone to take him in—probably one of the residents at the senior center, or maybe he's staying at

Gracie Jane's place. I heard she's in jail, so that might be the perfect place for a squatter."

"I'll bet you're right. So, what was the argument about?" I asked.

John exhaled. "I've never liked or trusted Eric Stephens. He had the gall to come into my shop and try to blackmail me. He said he had proof that I murdered Faith. I told him for two cents, I'd murder him. He laughed like it was a joke. He told me I had twenty-four hours to pull together two hundred thousand dollars in cash, or he'd take his proof to the police. When he slammed his fist on the glass, I told him to get out, and Sean walked in."

"Did he say what the proof was?" I asked.

"He said he had a recorded statement from someone who saw me hit Faith."

"Edna Cross saw you and Faith argue in the parking lot. She told me Faith was waving her arms at you, and when you reached to touch her, she blocked your arm."

"That's interesting. I wonder who else saw us. I think it would be easy to edit a recording, but I don't know how."

"It's easy to tell if a recording has been edited," Sean said. "I'm with you, John; I couldn't do it, but it'd be easy to find someone who could."

"So, do I ask him for a copy of the recording as proof?" John asked.

"After you told him you'd murder him for two cents?" Sean asked. "No. I suggest you don't initiate any contact with him. Give us a chance to check out a few things. You have a cell phone, John? Do you mind giving us your number?"

I sipped my tea so my jaw wouldn't drop open. *He said, 'us.' Twice.*

"Not at all," John said, and the two men exchanged cell numbers.

Marissa joined us at the table. "We have a small dessert for you, Gray Lady. It's a new dessert, and I'm testing it out on you three— coconut flan. Let me know what you think."

The server set a plate in front of me, and Marissa said, "Put Gray Lady's spoon on her right."

After I put the first bite in my mouth, I said, "Mmm," and Marissa tittered.

"This is amazing, Marissa," I said.

"Good. Come for dinner Friday night, and I'll have some for you."

"That would be wonderful."

After we finished our dessert, Sean said, "I've got the check, John. It'll go on the expense account. Let me know if Eric tries to contact you again."

John pushed back his chair. "Will do. Thanks a lot, both of you."

I rose from my chair, and Marissa hugged me before we left.

After John helped me into his car, he asked, "Don't you have surgery on Friday?"

"Outpatient. Expense account?"

"Sure. In case I can convince Lauren to move to Harperville, so I can beg Glenn Coyle for a job."

I laughed. "Your son would have a fit."

"That would only be a bonus, wouldn't it?" He chuckled as he pulled away from the curb. "What's our next step, Gray Lady?"

"I'll have to revise my plan a bit."

"So, you don't have one yet. Tell me what you were going to tell me later."

"I was a librarian—"

"Wait. Were you at the library where the auditor was murdered?"

"Yes."

"Not long after Kevin was hired by the Harperville Police Department, he told me about a cute librarian he met at the library. I had forgotten about that. He called her the Gray Lady and said she was the funniest librarian he'd ever met. That was you, right? After the explosion, he was impossible to be around until he heard you were well enough to get out of the hospital."

"Really?"

"Yep. I'll try not to interrupt anymore."

"So, you know about the explosion and that I was in the hospital. When I was in physical therapy, which is lovingly called physical torture by those of us in the know, I couldn't stand up on my own, no matter how hard I tried. I finally decided I needed help. When I looked next to me, a Buckingham Palace Guard stood tall with his back straight, and his eyes straight ahead, so I copied him. Day after day, he stood with me in physical therapy. I knew he was imaginary, but he made a difference."

"He's imaginary, and he stayed with you. Is he here with us now?"

"Of course."

"Of course," Sean repeated.

"When the therapist pushed my wheelchair to a raised deck with three steps and wooden railings on both sides of the stairs, I knew the only way I could get up those stairs was to be tough. I needed reinforcements, and I remembered Spike. When I was a kid, Spike was a retired police detective and a legend. The big kids said Spike was so tough, bad guys turned themselves in, but we all loved him because he spent time with us and even played sandlot ball with all us kids. When I glanced to my right, Spike was with me. He punched my arm and swept his hand toward the steps."

"Ladies first?" Sean asked.

I snickered. "That's right. I raised my foot, and when Spike stepped with me, I brought my other foot up, lifted my head, and exhaled. Spike raised his arms in victory, and I raised my arms in victory just like he did. Of course, I fell and was in trouble with the therapist. After the hospital, Palace Guard and Spike worked me hard to build up my strength and stamina, and Spike taught me how to fight. He's a cheater and fights dirty, and Lucy loves him."

"Lucy can see the imaginary men?"

"Yes. I have a theory that only dogs, kids, and people who never really grew up can see imaginary men."

"And they're still with you. What does Kevin think about all this?"

"He's fine with it."

"Wait—he's a kid at heart. He can see them too, can't he?"

"I think it was a matter of self-preservation. Spike can be a real stinker sometimes."

"You know, when you talk about the imaginary men, they sound real."

I giggled. "Real imaginary men. That's what one of my close friends calls them."

"Are Palace Guard and Spike training you now?"

"Palace Guard is helping me to be more proficient with my jo."

"That's good. Do we know what our plan is yet?"

"Yes. I need for you to put John Howard's phone number in my cell, and I need to visit Edna Cross at a hospice, but I don't know where."

I pulled out my phone. "Call Owen."

When Owen answered, I said, "Hi, Owen. It's Gray Lady. Are you with Edna Cross?"

"No, I just left. She—"

I waited, but he didn't continue. "What's the address of the hospice? I'd like to send her a card."

He told me the address then said, "She'd like to see you."

"Thank you so much for everything you've done for her."

After Owen hung up, Sean pulled over, and I repeated the address to him. "Owen told me she'd like to see me."

He entered the address into his phone navigator. "Okay, got it."

Ten minutes later, he said, "We're here. Do you want me to go in with you?"

"Yes. Palace Guard is excellent at guiding me, but I get fewer stares if I have a visible human along."

"Lucy's another option." Sean parked then came around to open my door.

"Hadn't thought of Lucy as a service animal, but you're right," I said as we strolled to the building.

After we signed in and found Edna's room, Sean said, "I'll be right here. Let me know if you need me."

Palace Guard helped me to Edna's side. When I held out my hand, she grabbed it and pulled me close.

"Gray Lady," she whispered. "How did you get here so fast?"

"Larry's dad drove me. Are you faking?" I whispered.

"Yes. Could you collapse in grief or something?"

I dropped down into the chair at her bedside and sobbed. "Oh, Edna."

"Why are you faking?" I slipped back into a whisper.

"Eric Stephens came to see me in the hospital. He made me repeat lies. 'John hit her. John knocked her down. John murdered her. I saw him.'"

"How did he make you?"

"He held a pillow over my face then let me breathe. Over and over again."

"No marks."

"Right."

"What can I do?" I asked.

"Stop Eric."

"If I do, will you be well and leave hospice?"

"Yes. More sobbing, please."

I sobbed. "Sweet, sweet Edna."

I whispered, "Does Owen know you're faking?"

"Yes. He helped me."

"Do you need anything?"

"Chocolate candy bar."

"Be right back."

Palace Guard guided me to the door.

"Sean, I need a small vase of flowers. I'll wait here."

"Okay. There's a flower stall in the front lobby."

"Good." I dropped my voice to a whisper. "And a chocolate candy bar. Don't let anyone see it."

"Gotcha. Be right back."

He's a good man, just like his son.

When Sean returned, he said, "Here is a small vase of flowers. Shall I carry it for you?"

"Thank you."

"I'll put the vase on the table over here." After he set down the vase, Sean strode to me, took my hand, and slipped me a candy bar. "I'll be right outside the door if you need me."

Palace Guard and I returned to Edna's side, and I took her hand and passed the candy bar to her. "I'm glad you don't have any pain."

"I'm so glad you came," she said in a weak, quivering voice. "You always bring me such joy. Thank you."

"I'll let you rest." I leaned over and kissed her forehead, and she giggled.

"Thanks. You're the best," she whispered.

After we were in the car, Sean asked, "Why did I sneak you a candy bar?"

"Edna wanted a treat but didn't want anybody to know. She's hiding out in hospice from Eric Stephens. He forced her to name John as Faith's killer by threatening to murder her. She's very resourceful."

"What? She's okay after all? I thought it was a dying wish or something. You attract the most interesting people," Sean said, and Palace Guard patted my back.

After we reached the house, Sean walked me to the door and waited while I unlocked it.

"We're invited to the Coyles' tonight for dinner, so we'll be leaving town as soon as I get back and hook up the car to the RV. Call me if you need me, and we'll turn around. Be safe, Maggie." He hugged me and waited until I was inside.

After he pulled out of the driveway, I put up my feet as I relaxed on the sofa. I must have dozed off because my phone woke me.

"Hi, sweetie. How was lunch?"

"It was amazing. Marissa made me empanadas and sweet plantains, and your dad enjoyed his lunch too. He dropped me off then said they'd be leaving town soon."

"That's great. I have good news. Your doctor's office called, and your surgery has been rescheduled from Friday to early tomorrow morning."

How is that good news?

"Oh. Any special reason?"

"They got an opening; I've already changed my day off from Friday to tomorrow. I'll see you after work."

After Larry hung up, I said, "My surgery's tomorrow morning, and Larry's excited." Palace Guard patted my hand, and Lucy jumped up on the sofa with me.

I leaned back. *I should call Glenn.*

My phone rang as I picked it up to make my call.

"I'm okay. Are you?" Glenn asked.

"I'm fine. I was just getting ready to call you. What's up?"

"It's not official, but Paul just heard that Gracie Jane cut a deal. She confessed that she set the fire in her office and claims to have accidently set off the explosion after she tried to move a propane bottle away from the exit. That's a stretch because the on-scene evidence showed it was moved to the door not away. She said she was afraid Eric put it there to cause an explosion to frighten her."

"She's scrambling, isn't she?"

"Sure is. Gracie Jane also said that Eric murdered Nancy, an aide at the senior center, because she discovered the forged prescriptions for dan shen. After Faith caught him stealing jewelry at the center, she reported the jewelry and the forged prescriptions to Gracie Jane, and Eric overheard the conversation, so he murdered Faith. Another stretch, as far as I'm concerned, especially since Gracie Jane wasn't Faith's supervisor. Gracie Jane claimed Eric forced her to have the residents designate her as the beneficiary of their wills so that he could take the money from her, and when she balked, he threatened to kill as many residents as possible with the dan shen and implicate her."

"What a crock," I said. "There are a million holes, but it's interesting that she folded before Eric. I think it was a strategic move on her part because she's the dominant one of the two."

"I agree. We'll see how this plays out. I expect the authorities will check her story before they pick up Eric. Meanwhile, Gracie Jane is no longer in custody. I suspect she'll become scarce again."

After he hung up, I rose from the sofa. "Now, I'm all energized. I need to practice my sleight of hand with my jo and pistol."

Palace Guard stopped me then made a slashing motion across my hand with his finger.

"My knife, of course. Why didn't I think of that? Would you help me find it and my ankle holster?"

Palace Guard led me to the master bedroom closet then handed me my holster with my knife in it.

"It was on the top shelf, wasn't it?" I snickered.

After I strapped my holster onto my left leg, we went outside. Lucy came out with us but went back inside.

"Thanks, Spike," I called out.

I sat on the porch while Palace Guard set up a target. When he came to get me, he guided me to the target that was in the middle of the yard then to a spot near the fence. I practiced dropping my jo, reaching for my knife, and pulling it out until Palace Guard signaled for me to throw.

"I suppose I have to do the full sequence," I grumbled, and Palace Guard patted my back.

I dropped my jo as I bent to reach into my boot. As I straightened up, I pulled out my knife and swung it up with an arc as my finger pointed when I released it. *Felt good.*

"How'd I do?" I asked.

Palace Guard guided me to a spot; when we stopped, I felt with my toe and found my knife. I pulled it out of the grass.

"Where's the target?"

He guided me to my left and forward to the target then patted my back as I reached out and touched the target. *Good thing Spike's not out here because I just let a target kill me.*

"So, I didn't throw straight. I threw off to the left. I must have turned my head to watch the knife, which is a little goofy. What did I expect to see?" I sighed. "I need to throw with a little more force and stand up completely, so I'm facing the target before I let go of the knife."

After we returned to my jo, I returned the knife to its holster. Palace Guard put his hand on my shoulder then touched my ear.

"You're right. That definitely would help. My target would make some type of noise, right?"

After Palace Guard returned, I said, "I'm ready."

When I heard the rock in front of me, I dropped my jo, bent, grabbed, stood up and threw my knife in almost a single motion. "Felt much better." Palace Guard smacked my right hand then guided me to the target. *I'd hit the edge of the target paper, but at least I hit it.*

"This is exciting. I didn't overthink it. Again?"

He led me to a different spot. "I don't know where the target is now."

Of course, that's the point.

I held my jo and listened. When I heard the pebble, I snatched up my knife and threw it almost before my jo hit the ground. *Please be in the target.*

Palace Guard guided me on my walk to the target; when I moved my hand across the paper target, I felt my knife.

"I hit the target! Where's the bulls eye?"

Palace Guard guided my right hand to the middle of the target.

"About two inches away? That's not bad, right?"

We practiced until I was drenched with sweat and breathing hard.

Palace Guard led me to the porch.

"You're right. I need to cool down and hydrate."

As I went inside, Lucy went out, and Spike punched my arm when he passed me.

"Thanks, Spike."

I filled a glass with water and sat on the sofa. "That really felt good. I just had to get over the hump of thinking that I had to see my target to hit it."

When I drained my glass, I said, "It's probably about time for Larry to come home. I need a shower."

After my shower, I towel-dried my hair then brushed it. "My hair still feels tangled. What do I do?" I grumbled as I dressed.

I returned to the kitchen and refilled my glass before I picked up my phone.

"Send a text to Heather: Brushed my hair but it's still tangled. What do I do?"

"Reply from Heather: Get me fired."

I giggled. "Reply to Heather: Ha, ha. On my list."

My phone rang. When I answered, Sean said, "Real quick. We're leaving for the Coyles' in five minutes. What can I say?"

"Anything you want, except not in front of Mother or Moe. Wait. Moe has another name, Oh, dear—I remember. His name is Les."

Sean guffawed. "I'm so sorry you told me that. Les is Moe. Got it."

When he hung up, he was still laughing.

Maybe he'll get it out of his system before he gets to the Coyles'.

Larry bounded into the house and pulled me off the sofa in a big hug. When I turned my face up for a kiss, he obliged.

"Would you like some tea, sweetie? You smell good."

"Tea sounds good." While he filled my lidded cup, I said, "I tried to brush my hair, but I think it's still tangled. I sent Heather a text, and she said I should get her fired."

Larry chuckled. "I expect she'll come up with something. She'll probably call you after she gets off work."

He flopped down on the sofa next to me. "How was lunch?"

"John Howard joined us for lunch."

I told him about his dad going into the jewelry shop, Eric, and John then what John told us at lunch.

"Eric really is a scumbag," Larry said. "I'll be right back to hear more. I'm going to change and start a load of laundry."

After he returned, Larry said, "Supper's going to be easy. I have a fondness for leftovers. So, did you and Dad do anything else? Did you get a nap in today?"

"I told your dad about Palace Guard and Spike. I think he's still processing."

Larry laughed. "That's Dad. He wouldn't immediately dismiss the idea of imaginary men. I suspect he may even ask Glenn about them."

"There's more," I said.

"Of course. Go ahead."

I told him about Owen and Edna.

"Edna is faking? That's awesome news. She's really something, isn't she? Any truth to what she said about Eric?"

"I'm guessing yes because of what John said, but I don't know."

"Ready for dinner? I'm starved," Larry said.

While we ate, Larry said, "We can take a walk, but I know you'd rather run. The guys at work told me we could use the track at the high school. We could check to see if anyone's there. If there is, we could always go to the park for a walk."

"That sounds awesome. I'd love to run."

"I thought you would. If I run on one side of you, and Palace Guard runs on the other, we could help you stay in the middle of the track."

"Perfect."

After we ate, Larry found my running shoes and shorts, and we changed.

When he handed me my ballcap, I grinned. "You're the best."

On the way to the high school, Larry said, "Palace Guard has his running gear on too. Lucy's excited. I think she knows we're all going for a run."

I said, "No bang bark, Spike."

Larry chuckled. "You busted him. He must have been planning on it because he's sad."

When Larry parked at the high school, I asked, "Is anybody on the track?"

"Only two people," Larry said. "We can work around them."

As we strolled to the track, Larry said, "Looks like they're leaving."

I bounced on my seat in my excitement. "Let's go."

When we reached the track, I asked, "Do I run with my jo?"

"Palace Guard says yes, and I agree," Larry said. "Palace Guard can set the pace because you're used to running along with him, right? I'll keep pace with the two of you."

"Go," I said.

Palace Guard and I took off together, just like old times, and Larry ran alongside me.

"We need to go faster," I said.

"Palace Guard said no. This is the pace to build you up."

When Palace Guard slowed for a cool-down lap, I asked, "How many?"

Larry said, "Five. This is number six. How are you doing?"

"Great."

When we stepped off the track and headed to the car, Lucy loped along next to me. I said, "My jo got heavy. You didn't have to run with a big ole stick."

Larry chuckled.

When we got home, Larry said, "I'm going to take a quick rinse off shower. What about you?"

"Sounds good. Will you brush the tangles out of my hair?"

I dressed after my quick shower and relaxed on the back porch. I listened to a crow call for back up and to Lucy as she prowled the backyard. When Larry joined me, I inhaled his man smell.

"I brought your brush out with me. Shall I work on those tangles?"

"Yes, please."

As he brushed, he asked, "What didn't you tell me about today?"

"What makes you so suspicious?"

"Being married to you. Now, what else?"

"It's just gossip—not from any official source."

"Go ahead."

I told him about Gracie Jane, her confession about setting the fire, maybe causing the explosion, claiming that Eric murdered Nancy and Faith, and being released from jail.

Larry quit brushing my hair and sat in his chair next to me. "What do you think? If you didn't have Palace Guard and Spike, I'd have to quit my job. Gracie Jane and Eric scare me."

"It's hard to sort out the truth, but I think Gracie Jane just tossed her husband to the court prosecutor."

He resumed brushing. "I think you're right. She must be the brains of the operation. No way would she do that if she was afraid of him."

"Maybe she should be," I said.

"Why?"

"I don't know. Just a feeling I have."

"You have no more tangles," Larry said. "You can't have anything to eat or drink after midnight. How about a beer now for old times' sake?"

I giggled. "Too bad we can't sit on a balcony and write notes."

"We can pretend. You can use your imagination, can't you?"

Larry laughed as he went inside for beer and was still chuckling when he returned. "Here's your beer, Gray Lady."

CHAPTER EIGHTEEN

We clinked our bottles then I took a big sip before I pretended to hold a pen and waved my hand to write something in the air.

"Did you just write me an imaginary note?" Larry chuckled. "What did it say?"

"You are an awesome partner."

"It did not," he growled.

"Fine. It said, surgery sucks."

"Right there with you, sweetie."

We rocked until we finished our beer.

"You missed your nap today, didn't you? Ready for bed?" he asked.

I yawned. "I suppose."

* * *

I woke as Larry rubbed my back. "Time to get up, sweetie."

"I decided to skip surgery," I mumbled.

"I'll bring you a large cup of coffee as a treat after your surgery."

When I sat up, he said, "I set out your sweatpants for you. What color shirt do you want?"

"Orange."

"I don't think you have an orange shirt," Larry said.

I pulled the covers over my head. "Tell Jennifer. I'll wait."

"Put on your sweatpants. They're gray, and your gray shirt is next to them."

"Gray is very appropriate."

"Yep. Get dressed and put on your slippers then I'll brush your hair before we leave."

While he brushed my hair, I said, "I'm not going to brush my teeth. I'm going to breathe gross morning breath all over the doc."

He snorted. "Whatever you want, sweetie."

After he finished, I use my jo to find my way to the bathroom to brush my teeth. "You're no fun."

"And don't you forget it," he said.

After he parked at the hospital, he opened my door. "You're really snippy in the morning when you don't get your coffee."

"And don't you forget it," I grumbled.

"Good one." He chuckled.

After I was checked into my room, a nurse handed me a small paper cup. "This is to help you relax."

"I'm relaxed," I said.

"Take it," Larry growled.

Larry stroked my cheek then kissed my forehead. "Sweetie, I brought you coffee."

"I can't have it until after the surgery," I mumbled.

"Surgery's over. Your doctor told me you are healing beautifully. They cleaned out the dead tissue, and she said there was no sign of infection. We can go home in about an hour if you feel up to it."

"Coffee?"

"Yes. It's cooled down so you can sip it through a straw."

"You're the best husband in the world."

"I know. I had a long talk with your doctor about my upcoming class. She said that there was no reason we couldn't go. She wants to continue to manage your care and has an old friend who is an ophthalmologist in Knoxville that we can see with regular appointments. He will track your progress for her. I asked her about a prosthetic eye, and she said that was a discussion for the future. She is very hopeful about your vision in your right eye."

"Have I told you that you're the best husband in the world?"

Larry laughed, and I giggled.

Love to hear my man laugh.

After we were home, I said, "You don't have to hover; you can go to work. I'll relax on the sofa, nap, and be a slug all day. Palace Guard, Spike, and Lucy will keep an eye on me."

"I don't know. There are a couple of things I need to catch up on. What do you think, Palace Guard?"

I leaned back on the sofa and stretched out. When I realized I hadn't heard a reply from Larry, I asked, "What did you two decide?"

"After you're steady on your feet, I'll go in. We set up your phone so that my cell is on speed dial. Palace Guard will call my phone if I need to come home."

"That's slick. When did you do that?"

"While you napped, sweetie." Larry chuckled.

I sat up and touched my left eye. "I have a bandage over my eye? Can I have a patch over it? I need to call a bunch of people."

"I'll get one for you, and I called Glenn and Darren; they notified your multitude of fans."

I found my jo and rose. "Did you make coffee?"

"Sure did. I have your lidded cup all set up."

I tapped my way to the back door and stepped outside. "Nice breeze."

When I returned to the kitchen, Larry said, "Your coffee is on the table at your place. Is your traditional blue eyepatch okay?"

"Blue's perfect." I put the eyepatch over my bandage then Larry adjusted it.

"Anything else I can do before I leave?" he asked.

"Kiss the wife."

Larry hugged me and gave me a sweet kiss. "I can be home in less than five minutes."

After he left, I carried my coffee outside and sipped while I rocked. A large truck rumbled down our street and set off the neighborhood dogs, and Lucy joined in as the truck rumbled away.

Normal, neighborhood noises. Nice.

"Good job, Lucy. You scared away that bad truck."

My phone rang, and I answered.

"Are you home, Maggie? Is Larry there?" Glenn asked.

"I'm sitting on the back porch and sipping lukewarm coffee through a straw. Larry went to his office, but I'm sure he'll be home early. What's up?"

"We just heard on the news that Gracie Jane was murdered last night. She was shot as she got out of her car at her sister's house."

"Really? Any arrest?"

"I don't think so. The broadcast news has linked her death to the senior center fire and explosion, so they have plenty of old news to regurgitate with no substance. The official sources are very tightlipped. Paul, Sean, and I are worried. We decided that Paul was the least likely to be missed from the office. He's headed your way."

"You know Larry would be here in less than five minutes. He set up my phone, so Palace Guard can call him."

"We don't care. When Sarge calls me, I can tell him that Paul's on his way; otherwise, he'd hit the road too. Have you heard from Heather?"

"No."

"Moe told me Heather called in sick this morning. Heather and Paul may be racing."

"I think I just rolled my eye."

Glenn chuckled. "Dang it, Maggie. This is no laughing matter."

I wasn't the one that laughed.

"You know, you might want to confirm that Heather is coming here and turn Paul around," I said.

"I'll think about it."

"You know I speak Coyle, right? You won't do any such thing."

"Just stay in your house. Keep all the doors and windows locked and rest."

"You can always decide calling off Paul is your idea."

"Now that's logical."

After Glenn hung up, a neighbor started up a lawnmower, and before long, the scent of freshly mowed grass filled the air. I listened to the neighborhood sounds and rocked until my phone rang.

When I answered, Heather said, "How are you?"

"I'm being a slug. Larry went to work, and I'm supposed to relax. I heard that you're sick."

"Yep. I heard about Gracie Jane and decided I'm sick of not being there to braid your hair. I'll be there in less than an hour. I need to talk to you and Larry, anyway."

"What about?"

"Bad connection." Heather hung up.

That's not fair. Intrigue is my specialty.

"I don't suppose I could go for a walk around the block," I said.

A large hand clamped down on my shoulder.

"Just kidding, Spike. Kind of."

The hand didn't move.

"Fine. No walk."

Spike patted my shoulder with all the finesse of a heavy-handed gorilla, as my phone rang again.

When I answered, a man said, "This is Eric Stephens, Gray Lady. I heard you had surgery this morning and called to see if there was anything I could do."

Are you kidding me?

"It's nice of you to check, but I can't think of a thing."

"Good. Was your husband able to get the day off? Is anyone staying with you?"

Where is this going?

"No, he's taken a lot of time off lately and had to go into the office. One of my friends offered to stay with me and will be here in the morning."

"That's good. You know Edna Cross is in hospice, right? Gracie Jane had a few things in the safe that belong to Edna, and she asked me to get them to you. I can wait until this evening when your husband's home. I still have a few more things at Mr. Bustamante's to pack then I'll be leaving town first thing in the morning."

You were kicked out of Mr. Bustamante's house.

"That's sweet of Gracie Jane. Thank you."

"I guess you're tired. I'll see you around seven this evening."

"I appreciate it. I'm weaker than I expected."

After Eric hung up, I said, "Palace Guard, let's talk through our plan. That was Eric Stephens, and I think he was checking to see if anyone was here with me. Do I let him in the front door, or do I wait for him to come around to the back?"

Palace Guard walked me to the side gate and opened it. "We leave the gate open, so he'll come around to the back?"

He patted me on the shoulder then guided me back to the steps.

"Here are the steps."

He guided me a few feet away from the steps.

"We moved away from the stairs at an angle. Am I closer to the gate at about the same distance that I was target practicing with my knife?"

He patted my shoulder.

When I heard a pebble, I snatched out my knife and threw it at the sound then drew my pistol and pointed it in the same direction.

After Palace Guard gave me the all-clear, I reholstered my pistol and held out my hand, and we smacked a high five.

"Your training is superb."

He guided me to the grass where my knife had landed. After I picked it up, I slipped it into the ankle holster. "Okay, we're ready. So, I can relax on the porch because you'll take me to my spot to hit the target when Eric arrives."

A car turned the corner and slowly passed our house then continued down the block until it turned left at the next street.

I exhaled. "I didn't even realize I was holding my breath." I rose to stomp my feet, wiggle my arms, and stretch my neck and shoulders. I feinted a left jab then a right cross. "Better. I had to shake off my case of nerves."

A car turned the corner and went slowly past our house then turned into a driveway down the street and crept back then stopped in front of the house. When the car door slammed, I asked, "Eric?"

Palace Guard patted my shoulder.

I knew you'd check.

There was a soft knock on the front door followed by a louder knock. After Eric tried the doorknob, he stepped off the front porch, and Palace Guard led me to my spot.

Eric strode toward the back gate then said, "There you are, Gray Lady. Sitting baby duck. Dead duck." He snorted, and a rock hit the grass. My jo clattered against the porch as I snatched up my knife and tossed it, and Eric screamed. *Next, pistol.* Palace Guard redirected my aim with a tap on the back of my arm, and I corrected before I pulled the trigger and fired. I maintained my stance with my gun pointed where I had shot.

"Don't move," I growled.

A car sped down the street before it pulled into our driveway. Sirens sounded in the distance.

"It's me, sweetie. Put down your gun." Larry yelled before he rounded the corner of the house then grabbed me before I could rise from setting my pistol on the ground.

"Your knife is in his chest, and your headshot is spot on. He has one pistol in his left hand, and there is another gun on the ground near him. There's a spent cartridge next to him, so he shot at least once."

"How did you get here so fast?" I mumbled into his chest.

"I got the call from Palace Guard five minutes ago."

"You called after you checked and saw it was Eric?"

Larry said, "Palace Guard nodded. Sounds like a smart plan to me."

"Not mine. Palace Guard's."

As cars with blaring sirens turned the corner, Larry said, "Let's get you inside. I need to meet the officers."

Larry helped me to the sofa. "They'll want a statement. It's okay not to answer anything that makes you uncomfortable."

After he went out the front door, Lucy jumped on the sofa and snuggled against me.

"Thanks, girl. I'm feeling a little shaky."

A few minutes later, Larry opened the back door. "Sweetie, a detective and one of my colleagues want to talk to you. Should I tell them to come back tomorrow? They know you had surgery this morning."

"Now's fine."

"Okay, come on in, but if she needs to stop, we'll pick up tomorrow."

Larry growls when he's being protective.

Larry sat next to me, and I knew Palace Guard and Spike were standing next to the two men to read their notes. *I'm glad Larry can see them. They'll alert him if anything takes a wrong turn.*

I told my audience of men about Eric's call.

"He knocked on the front door first. When he came around back, he said, 'There you are, Gray Lady. Sitting baby duck. Dead duck.'"

"His exact words?" One of the men asked.

"Yes, so I dropped my cane, and it hit the porch. I pulled my knife out of my boot and threw it. He screamed then I heard a click, so I followed up with my shot."

"What?" The other man asked. "Excuse me, Mrs. Ewing, but haven't you lost your sight?"

"My wife has done undercover work for the FBI in the past. She's highly skilled."

"Wow. No kidding."

"You're the Gray Lady, aren't you, Mrs. Ewing?" The first man asked.

"Yes, she is," Larry said.

"Excuse me, detective," a woman at the back door said. "I've found the two bullets the perp fired."

Two?

The three men trooped out of the house.

I'll bet Palace Guard and Spike went too.

After a long discussion on the back porch, the three men, and probably the imaginary men, returned.

"Sweetie, when you dropped the jo, did it make a lot of noise when it hit the porch?"

"It did. I was shocked because I didn't mean to throw it out of my way so forcefully."

"Mrs. Ewing, you must have startled him just as he pulled the trigger because one bullet is lodged in the side of the house near the roofline. The second bullet is lodged in the side of the top step."

Mrs. Martin's sleight of hand training paid off.

A man opened the door and said, "Agent Ewing, there's a woman here who claims she's a detective from Harperville and a friend of the family."

"Heather," I squealed.

Larry chuckled. "Definitely. She's one of my wife's closest friends."

"Told you." Heather breezed past the police officer and into the house before she flopped down on the sofa next to me. "Anybody get out of line, Gray Lady?"

I snickered, and she laughed.

Larry cleared his throat. "Gentlemen, we can go over your notes outside to see if you have any more questions, but I have a feeling tomorrow would be better for my wife."

After the men left, Heather said, "So, tell me what happened, and I'm so sorry I couldn't get here any faster."

I told Heather all the details, including my new training and how nervous I was.

"Maggie, you are a rock star. We can talk more after Larry clears your yard of all those stuffy cops. I dressed up to visit you and had to bully my way to the door, by the way. I wore my super short black leather skirt, my fire engine red crop top with the sequins, and my four-inch shiny red heels."

I laughed. "Heather, you're a cop, but you're definitely not stuffy."

"Let's braid your hair. It looks like you went to a gun fight." Heather cackled, and I giggled.

While Heather braided my hair, I picked up my cell.

"Send a text to Owen: Tell Edna I stopped Eric."

"Reply from Owen: woo hoo."

I laughed then described Owen to Heather.

She chuckled. "Now, I understand why his reply was so funny."

After she finished with my hair, Heather said, "Go lie down on your bed. I'll wake you when the riff-raff is gone."

I nodded. "Thanks. I'm exhausted."

* * *

I woke when Larry sat beside me on the bed.

"Sweetie, are you interested in eating?" he asked.

I raised up on one elbow. "What time is it? Heather was going to wake me when everybody left."

"We voted to let you sleep."

I grabbed my jo, and Larry put his arm around me as we walked to the kitchen.

"Hi, Gray Lady," Heather said. "Food will be on the table in just a sec. I made my famous fried chicken and potato salad."

"I've got your pills, and we can change your bandage later," Larry said.

As we ate, Larry said, "It's not clear whether Gracie Jane or Eric killed Nancy and Faith, but we're certain one of them did, and there's no doubt that Eric killed Gracie Jane. There's no good reason to spend more time and resources on the cases with such clear evidence that no one else was involved."

After Heather cleared our dishes, and Larry loaded the dishwasher, we adjourned to the back porch, and I pretended to see the sunset.

"I smell beer." I raised my lidded cup. "I have sweet tea. Am I being left out?"

"Yes, you are. We have beer, but you don't because of your medicine. Heather's staying with us until Sunday," Larry said.

"I have to go to work on Monday," she said. "So, this is what I wanted to talk to the two of you about. I'm turning in my resignation on Monday and giving them two weeks' notice. I'll be undercover, so I'm sure you can guess who hired me."

"I always wanted to be your understudy," I said. "Still do."

Heather snickered. "That's funny because that's what I wanted to talk to you about. I need for the four of you to train me before I leave Sunday evening. Maggie, I need your skills. I won't need any extra training with my pistol, but I need everything else."

"Nope. The world isn't ready for a Gray Lady clone," Larry said. "Ow. Spike thinks it's a good idea."

"So, how do we do this?" Heather asked.

"Larry and the men can train you on Saturday and Sunday," I said. "I have an idea on how you can train with a knife tomorrow. We'll put one of my sleep masks on you, so you'll have to rely on what you hear, not on what you see. Palace Guard and I can work with you on that. I'm sure we can think of some other things we can do tomorrow before you spend the rest of the weekend learning how to fight dirty."

I held up my plastic lidded cup, and Larry and Heather tapped it with their beer bottles before they clinked their bottles together.

"While we're celebrating," Larry said. "I got a call this afternoon that I'm confirmed for the next class that starts in two weeks. I work one week then I have the following week for us to pack and move."

"Watch out, Tennessee," Heather said. "The Gray Lady's coming your way."

ACKNOWLEDGEMENTS

Huge thanks to my husband for his awesome advice and for his patience when I tell him something funny that Maggie said.

Thanks to the fabulous cooks and bakers in my family. You are an inspiration for Maggie. Thanks to my editor who is an absolute genius and my daughter and daughters-in-law, the original Mom Force.

Thank you for reading. *You keep reading; I'll keep writing!*

What to read next?

SEE BEYOND THE FOG, BOOK 5
MAGGIE SLOAN THRILLER

A deranged serial killer targets the vulnerable Maggie. Her life depends on seeing what no one else does.

Maggie navigates through the clues behind twenty years of suspicious deaths at the hand of the legendary Ghost of Wicked Hollow. Even though she has tragically lost her eyesight, she sees beyond the fog that has shrouded a serial killer from discovery for years. The murderer targets her to die.

Subscribe: to the newsletter!

Look for the Subscribe button on www.judithabarrett.com

ABOUT THE AUTHOR

Judith A. Barrett is an award-winning author of mystery, crime, and survival science fiction novels with action, adventure, and a touch of supernatural to spark the reader's imagination. Her unusual main characters are brilliant, talented, and down-to-earth folks who solve difficult problems and stop killers. Her novels are based in small towns and rural areas in south Georgia and north Florida with sojourns to other southern US states.

Judith lives in rural Georgia on a small farm with her husband and two dogs. When she's not busy writing, Judith is still busy working on the farm, hiking with her husband and dogs, or watching the beautiful sunsets from her porch.

Website   www.judithabarrett.com

Subscribe to the eNewsletter via her website

Let's keep in touch!